HARBINGER

DIVISION ZERO BOOK 5

MATTHEW S. COX

DIVISION ZERO PRESS

Division Zero: Harbinger

Book 5 of the Division Zero series.

ISBN (eBook): 978-1-949174-88-5

ISBN (Paperback): 978-1-949174-89-2

CONTENTS

1. Shared Experience   1
2. Priority Ten   14
3. Dark Spirit   21
4. Squeezy   33
5. Turf War   42
6. The Legend   55
7. More Demons   65
8. The Opposite of Cool   71
9. A Crazy Explanation   82
10. Blood Pentagram   89
11. Subject to Interpretation   102
12. Spaceship Earth   106
13. Witchcraft   117
14. Near Death Experience   129
15. Beneath and Beyond   140
16. Grey Devils   150
17. Warped in the Headware   157
18. Victim Number Three   163
19. The Gloomy Shadow   175
20. Seriously Bad Vibes   183
21. For the Taking   188
22. Lost Puppy   200
23. Weaponized   205
24. An Awkward Position   210
25. Middle Ground   215
26. Bring the Fire   223
27. Paradise   242
28. Climbing Fish   249
29. The Big Guns   258
30. The Fundamental Fabric of the Universe   263
31. Caring   271

Acknowledgments   281
About the Author   283
Other books by Matthew S. Cox   285

SHARED EXPERIENCE

Hopeful the day would remain quiet, Kirsten gazed up at the endless parade of ad-bots streaming along like blood in veins of plastisteel and glass. Small ones spiraled around the traffic lane, angling to thrust their holographic ads into positions of maximum visibility, while the big ones lumbered in straight lines like reimagined dirigibles, forcing all who came near to bask in the unabashed glow of commercialism.

She spent a moment staring at a twenty-by-thirty foot image of a little girl hugging and talking to a synthetic puppy—one just like it could be hers for a mere ℂ18,999… in twelve easy monthly payments. Her thoughts drifted aimlessly since she didn't need to pay much attention to hovercar traffic flowing in multiple directions a hundred feet overhead. Her patrol craft hung on auto-stabilize at the fortieth story, rear-end tucked against a building. Its systems would warn her of anyone breaking traffic laws. Most people let the autodrive take over, which increased efficiency as well as safety.

Mostly, she thought about Evan smiling, laughing, or cheering whenever they defeated a monster in the Monwyn game, but now and then, she tried to figure out how to feel about Samuel Chang. With the impossible at hand—a man who didn't run screaming at the first mention of the word 'psionic'—she had gone into unfamiliar territory. Though, after Konstantin, she didn't want to rush anything despite having a fairly strong feeling Sam wouldn't turn out to be a maleficar.

I never want to encounter another abyssal in my life.

Kirsten forced those thoughts away and smiled at the memory of Evan hugging her before racing off to school this morning. The huge screen trying to sell artificial puppies displayed a close up view of it peeing while scrolling text espoused the virtues of physical activity your kids will enjoy walking their new friend.

"Does it shred the furniture, too?" asked Dorian.

She chuckled.

"No idea how Div 1 officers tolerate this." He yawned. "I'm dead and I can't recall ever being this bored before. Oh wait, I can... the last time I participated in this detail while alive."

She randomly swiped her finger over the console, brushing away dust. "I dunno. Better we're bored than someone's getting hurt somewhere."

He glanced over from the passenger seat, his eyebrows a flat line. "This is West City. There's a shooting every 7.2 seconds, assault every 3.8 seconds... and so on."

"Those stats are for the entire city. We're only responsible for an area up to a three-minute flight from our assigned point." She half-grinned at the miles-long strand of aerodynamic blurs aglow in the red smear of taillights. "Sitting here on patrol isn't exactly what I signed up for."

"You didn't sign up for any of it, really."

Her whimsical mood dropped as dead as her partner. "Yeah... but it's better than growing up as a wild thing under the city." She stared into the distance. The enormous face of the little girl cringed away from the puppy's licking tongue while giggling. Kirsten shifted her gaze away from the happy child she never was to another bot showing an enthusiastic man slurping up noodles.

"It's not quite as rough as the Badlands. Discarded aside, settlements exist down there full of fringers and off-gridders. They would have taken you in."

"Sure, if I hadn't been terrified of adults. I expected they'd all be like Mother and beat the shit out of me as soon as they saw my eyes glow, or a ghost did some random thing trying to get my attention. And the only adult I wound up talking to down there..." She squirmed at the memory.

The intangible presence of Dorian's hand offering a reassuring grip chilled her arm. "I'm sorry for making you think of that. I... get why you avoided people."

"I guess that guy did me a favor in a way. If I hadn't done something so stupid, I wouldn't have been scared enough to risk going to the surface for food to avoid him finding me again."

"K," said Dorian, his voice as serious as she'd ever heard it. "You did not 'do something stupid.' An adult took horrible advantage of you when you were a child. You were attacked. It might not have been violent, but it was without a doubt an attack. Nothing he did to you is your fault."

Kirsten faked a chuckle to avoid crying. "Now you sound like Dr. Loring."

"She's only saying that because it's true."

"I know… I know." After a sigh, Kirsten wiped the corners of her eyes. "The bastard never even told me to keep quiet or threatened me, but I was still terrified of him."

"He had nothing to be afraid of. Police won't go down there. He probably tracked you for a while and knew you didn't have parents in some settlement who'd have killed him for it."

Flashing green and blue caught her eye as an ad-bot displaying a trailer for an upcoming new Monwyn movie went by overhead. "Can we talk about something less depressing please?"

"217,000 some odd people were murdered in West City last year."

She blinked at him. "That's *less* depressing?"

"To me." He patted her arm again. "Not as depressing as hearing about the worst moment in the life of a woman I've come to regard as my kid sister."

"Dorian…" She squirmed again and fidgeted with her hands. "What that man did to me is nowhere near as bad as murder on that scale."

"Tragedy is relative. A big number on a report doesn't mean as much as one individual you care about. And… drop that nonsense about some people have it worse. It doesn't make what happened to you any less significant."

She bowed her head. "Thanks. Maybe someday I'll really believe it wasn't my fault. I could've run away, could've said no…"

"In the state you were in back then, if you had been able to run away from the promise of real food… you would have."

Kirsten sighed.

"Anyway, you'd think they'd have sent something your way by now." He poked at the console. "The entire point of this 'shared experience' training is for Division 0 officers to get some field experience."

She patted the black PSI armor covering her thigh. "It's not exactly fair. Div 1 can't deal with our stuff, so they don't have to run our cases."

"You're not having Div 2 inquests dropped on your head. You're playing beat cop for the day."

"I know. Watch commander's probably giving me an easy ride. You saw the way he looked at me. Shortest one in the room. Probably thinks I'm a fifteen-year-old Admin cadet."

"With lieutenant bars?" He raised an eyebrow. "Besides, you're the only astral on the West Coast. They know you."

"I hardly think I'm the *only* Astral Sensitive on the west coast. Others haven't been located. Probably because they think they're insane. There's at least one in East City, that girl Hannah or something."

"The only one old enough anyway." He grinned. "She's thirteen."

Kirsten sighed.

"As opposed to *looking* like thirteen."

She laughed.

The holographic image of a twenty-something man with brown skin and black hair appeared in the middle of the console, shoulders of a plain blue jumpsuit framing the bottom of the portrait. "Unit 1815-014, please respond to active dispatch 0117. Additional units are being notified, but you are the closest. Patrol Officer Gage hit his panic button, and neither he nor his partner are responding to comms."

"Copy!" Kirsten flicked on the bar lights, flooding the area outside with rapid camera-flashes of blue, then accelerated into a climb up past the flow of traffic.

Hovercars partially scattered out of the lane. About ten drivers probably experienced near heart attacks at the sight of a police vehicle coming out of nowhere behind them with its lights on. Once she shot past them and leveled off a hundred feet over the civilian lane, the traffic stream beneath her collected back into an orderly flow. A faint siren noise played from the console, indicating her emergency transponder broadcast a warning tone to any hovercar within a quarter mile. The siren's volume varied to simulate distance and direction, even though the other cars' audio systems created it.

Two high-rises east from where she'd been lurking, she swung around a tower of glittering black glass, weaving up and down to dodge a veritable maze of walkways spanning the street between buildings.

A blinking red pin on the Navcon indicated a point 1.83 miles from her current location, a trip that barely took twelve seconds. She dove toward the flashing lights of a Division 1 patrol craft on the ground, flying nearly straight down at the blue-and-white vehicle.

"Wait!" shouted Dorian. "You don't know what you're running into."

Kirsten decided not to make a sarcastic remark to her ghostly partner about recklessly charging into a situation, something he'd done—once. She slowed the car and swiped at the windscreen, zooming in on the ground below.

Two Division 1 officers stood on the street corner, their sidearms leveled off at each other's helmets. A young boy around Evan's age with short, black hair and the well-worn clothes of a street urchin stood a few paces away, staring at the cops. Alarmingly, he didn't appear frightened.

He looked angry.

Kirsten blinked. "Okay, that's weird. You wanna go turn those guns off?"

Dorian nodded and glided down out of the patrol craft.

"Dispatch, this is unit 1815-014. I'm onsite at event 0117."

"Copy, 1815," said a voice from the console.

She rotated the car level at ten stories off the street, continuing to descend. The whirr of the ground wheels extending vibrated the frame. A barely-noticeable light orb floated around the two patrol officers since the electronic windscreen didn't do a good job of rendering ghosts.

The instant the car's weight settled onto its tires, Kirsten shoved the door open and stepped out, her view going from two cops and a glowing spot to two cops plus Dorian. Lights, and the ammo display, on the weapons had gone dark, giving her a tentative sense of security.

"Trouble agreeing on where to go for lunch?" asked Kirsten.

Both men twitched, their silver-visored helmets making it impossible to see facial expressions. They grunted and kept pointing their weapons at each other. She waited only a second before checking their surface thoughts—both men had succumbed to the effect of a psionic suggestion, compelling them to hold their weapons on each other and shoot if either tried to leave. Their most recent memory showed that boy ordering them to do it.

Kirsten redirected her attention on the kid, but couldn't bring herself to draw her E-90 on him. "Hi there. I need you to stop using your abilities on these officers."

"Okay," said the boy. "As soon as you guys find who killed my brother, Juan Miguel. *Point your gun* at them."

The incoming mental command washed over Kirsten's brain with a sensation similar to walking into raw egg in zero-gravity. She smirked, brushing it aside. "No. *Get on the ground.* And keep *still.*"

He emitted a small grunt, his string bean body shaking from his effort to resist her, and collapsed to the sidewalk like a gradually malfunctioning doll. Frustrated, he went past angry to crying.

Kirsten approached the officers, faint white light flashed in the eyes of her reflection on their mirrored visors. "*Ignore* the boy's command."

Both men let their arms drop limp at their sides.

"Son of a bitch," muttered the taller one, Gage. "Damn kid's lucky he's so small."

Officer Kepler slouched. "That was some psionic shit, wasn't it?"

"Yeah," said Kirsten in a flat tone, bracing for derision. "I got him." She poked a finger at the silver bud in her left ear. "Dispatch, this is Wren, 1815-OI4. Event neutralized."

"Copy that, 1815. Do you require additional resources on site?" asked a voice in her ear.

"Negative, Dispatch. Suspect is one psionic juvenile. I'm assuming jurisdiction."

"Copy. Transferring from active dispatch event to Inquest and tagging you."

"Thanks," she muttered.

"Oh crap..." Kepler saluted her. "Sorry, lieutenant... didn't notice the rank."

She returned the salute. "You don't need to salute me in the middle of an active situation."

"No weapons on the kid." Dorian stood up from a crouch beside the boy.

"Let me go!" shouted the kid.

"Not so fun, is it, brat?" Kepler started to point his weapon at the boy, but noticed the dark screen on the back end. He banged it on his armored leg a few times. "Crap. What the hell?"

Kirsten stepped around them and headed over to where the child lay on the sidewalk. "You're welcome."

"That's my line." Dorian smiled.

"Damn psionic weirdness. Now you guys can turn guns off with your minds?" Kepler swapped magazines. His gun lit up with a chirp, and he holstered it.

"A mag battery can be recharged. They can't put your brains back in." Kirsten pulled the psi inhibitor out of its belt case, flicked her wrist to make it snap open into a ring, and secured the thin metal headband in place on the boy.

"Bet these two would *love* hearing about ghosts." Dorian grinned.

"Exactly why I'm not bothering," whispered Kirsten.

"Hey, look." Kepler walked over. "I don't hate you guys. Just creeps me out being defenseless against anything a psio might wanna do to me."

She smirked up at him. "Welcome to being a woman."

He stared at her in stunned silence, fists clenching.

Kirsten raised an eyebrow. "Guess you're not big on subtlety. I wasn't calling you weak. We live with that feeling *constantly*. Starts right around the time we hit puberty and grown men start checking out our asses. If I wasn't psionic, I'd be on edge being in arms' reach of a guy your size I didn't know no matter how nice he was."

Dorian clasped his hands behind his back and grinned. "She still kind of is."

Neither cop reacted.

"Am not," muttered Kirsten, trying not to smile. "Well, unless they've got vibro claws."

"Oh." Kepler relaxed. "Right. Yeah. I get it. Sorry. Little fucked up from that kid making me hold my gun on Gage for the past twenty minutes."

"Damn!" Gage punched a vendomat on the corner next to a PubTran terminal.

"Took your money and didn't spit out the donut?" asked Dorian, not that either man noticed.

Kirsten bit her lip to avoid snickering as she secured the boy's hands behind him in plastic ties… his slender wrists would slip straight out of the metal binders. She lost a moment holding his hand, examining his grime-encrusted nails.

Gage snarled and slugged the giant boxy machine again.

"Feel better?" asked Kepler.

She patted the boy down, finding nothing in his pockets but a candy bar, two small toy cars, and several empty wrappers. "That thing take his credits?"

"Nah. Blowing off steam. Suspect is too damn small to tune up." Gage finally swapped magazines, bringing his sidearm back to life, and paced around.

Two more Division 1 cars swooped in to land.

"Just shoot me," muttered the boy.

She froze, nearly choking on the sudden lump in her throat.

Four additional officers rushed over, but upon seeing the situation diffused, put their weapons away and gathered in a cluster. When Kirsten hauled the kid up to his feet, the other patrol officers stared in shocked silence at the threat to two officers turning out to be a kid so small.

"Be right back." She ushered the boy over to her patrol craft and put him in the back seat. "What's your name?"

"Like you care." He looked away. "I'm just another piece of street meat to you."

"No, you're not." Kirsten patted him on the head. "Maybe to those two, but not me."

He whirled to stare at her. "*Let...*" His eyes scrunched closed in a pained expression. "Ngh! Ow!"

"The device around your head is a psionic inhibitor. Don't try to use any of your abilities, okay? It won't harm you, but it hurts. And yes, I know... they suck."

Sensing vulnerability, he attempted the non-psionic power of 'large sad eyes.'

"Why did you make those two officers do that?"

"'Cause. My brother was killed and they don't care. One even laughed."

"Those two?"

"Naw. The cops who took Juan Miguel's body off the street." He resumed crying. "He was my only family. Was just me an' him, and now he's gone."

Kirsten put a hand on his shoulder and squeezed. "Hey. I know exactly how you feel. I used to be on the street as a kid, with no one. I'll be back in a little while. Need a minute with those two."

He didn't react.

She turned on the radio for background noise so she didn't leave a kid wearing a psi inhibitor sitting in silence. Total quiet pushed the devices from annoying to torturous. He ignored her second attempt to offer a comforting smile. She closed the patrol craft door and headed back over to the group of six officers.

"Lieutenant," said Gage by way of greeting.

"I haven't gotten much out of him yet, but I don't have the feeling he intended to kill anyone. He wanted to try and force someone to investigate his brother's murder."

Kepler set his hands on his hips. "You're not gonna cut him loose? They always let the psionic ones get away with shit if they sign up."

She looked away and down. True, Division 0 often let criminal activity slide in psionic matters provided no one suffered permanent injury or death… though the whole thing would've been recorded by both of them as well as their patrol craft, available for viewing across the National Police Force. Plus, the kid messed with cops.

"No. Even though he's young, we don't look the other way when someone screws with cops. Sends the wrong message and we don't want to invite open season on us." Kirsten rubbed at her forehead before resuming eye contact with the cops. "The kid will be charged, though whether it's assaulting an officer or attempted murder, it's a bit early to say. I think he's scared, alone, and desperate and just wanted someone to pay attention to his brother's case."

They nodded. Kepler's aggressive posture notched back a tick.

"So… that it? We done here?" asked Gage. "Oh, and thanks again for the assist."

"You're welcome. Just a few questions. How did you guys encounter the kid?"

Gage gestured at their patrol craft parked by the curb. "We were sitting there having lunch and he walked up to us. Asked us to find whoever killed his brother. Took his info, found an inquest in the system already. Little bastard didn't like being told the detectives are working on it."

"Yeah." Kepler nodded. "He told us to get out of the car, and we couldn't stop ourselves. Next thing I know, we've got our duty weapons pointed at each other and the kid's demanding the police find the killer. Sounded like he planned to keep us like that the whole time."

"Damn, you psionics are really scary sometimes." Gage grinned. "We didn't even call it in as 'weird shit' yet you showed up."

Kirsten chuckled, shaking her head. "Simple luck. Shared experience training. I spent most of the morning drooling on myself watching traffic lanes."

"Must be good to be an LT." Kepler laughed. "Basically a day off for you."

"Honestly?" Kirsten held her arms out and let them drop. "Look at me. Command probably thought I'd get hurt doing anything else. Took a panic button for anything to come through."

"Damn." Gage sighed. "That had to be boring. Thanks, again… and sorry for that psionic crap I said."

"I appreciate that." She eyed the nearby storefronts. "So, the kid walks up to you, orders you out of the car, then makes you point your weapons at each other. That it? Any involvement with other citizens or property around here?"

"Nope, just made us look like idiots." Gage glowered at the ground.

Kirsten raised her left arm, accessing the holo-panel projected by her forearm guard. "All right. Consider the scene closed. I'll be adding everything to the inquest. If it goes before a judge, you two will need to show up, but I have a feeling due to his age and having no surviving family, it won't. He'll most likely be remanded to the secure dormitory until eighteen, and an eight-year sentence is more than normal adult cons do for punching us in the head. The problem with some psionic abilities is like giving a little boy a gun. Power, but little ability to understand when and how to use it. If it were up to me, I'd give him help, not a cell. But... because he attacked police, it's going through the proper channels. Maybe you guys could think of him as a scared kid who thought he had no other options. They'll be more inclined to help him if you let your captain know it's just a scared kid. Of course, if the shrinks and telepaths confirm he's actually dangerous, he'll be dealt with accordingly."

Gage and Kepler exchanged a glance, their expressions conflicted.

"I need to get back. Can't leave a detainee alone with an inhibitor on too long."

All the Division 1 officers nodded and muttered in a mixture of agreement and annoyance. Not so much at the boy but at how cons tended to never quite serve much time for things short of murder before they wound up on the street again. The group broke apart, heading back to their respective vehicles.

She hurried to her patrol craft and hopped in. Already, the interior had taken on the musty foulness of perpetually damp clothes. A decade ago, she would've smelled the same or worse—if she'd had actual clothes. A poncho made out of a plastic tarp with an electrical cord for a belt didn't hold much in the way of stink. The boy squirming around in the back seat talking to himself hadn't yet outgrown the clothes he'd been wearing when he wound up homeless. Kirsten's nightgown hadn't lasted long after she ran away. It had already been old and a little small. Mother didn't waste money buying things for a 'devil child.'

"Sorry for leaving you alone that long."

Dorian materialized in the passenger seat. "You had music on and it took less than six minutes. He's fine. He's also provisionally guilty of a felony. If either of those officers had slipped the command, one or both could be dead."

"I know," whispered Kirsten. "And not really. Class 4 handguns wouldn't have penetrated their helmets. Probably would've knocked them out, but…"

"I didn't say anything. Do you hear the voices too?" The boy paused a second. "Please make the voices stop."

"They're coming from the inhibitor." Kirsten de-registered from active status on the Division 1 patrol grid and set the car to drive itself to the Police Administrative Center, then turned in the seat to look at him as they rose into the air. "As soon as we're at the PAC, I'll remove it, okay? So, you're Rafael?"

"You're forgetting something." Dorian glanced over at her with a somber, resigned expression.

The boy froze. "Are you reading my mind?"

"No. You gave your information to the other officers when you asked them to find the person who killed your brother. It's in the file."

Rafael hung his head. "Oh."

Kirsten sighed at Dorian. "Rafael, I have to inform you that you're presently under arrest for use of psionic abilities in the commission of a crime. You are in the custody of Division 0." She paused. "I know you're what, nine?"

"Ten and a half."

"Attempted murder of an officer of the National Police Force. Unlawful psionic restraint. Kidnapping. Reckless endangerment…" Dorian picked a bit of lint from his uniform. The same bit of lint that always reappeared in the exact same spot. "Suppose he's a bit small to blather on about the full list of charges. The advocate will go over it with him—if you file them all."

A weak smile almost slid out from under her guilt. "There's some other stuff we usually explain, but you're too young to be legally responsible to understand it. I want you to know that what you did was dangerous and wrong, and you are in a bit of trouble. However, no one is going to harm you. You're lost and hurting, but you don't need to be afraid. Division 0 isn't like other types of police. There aren't so many of us. If you trust us, we can help you, okay?"

He nodded, still staring into his lap.

"I don't think you really wanted to hurt those officers."

"No. I wanted them to do their job. They're supposed to find killers. Juan Miguel died, but because he ran with the Scorpionz, the cops don't care." He bounced in time with 'they don't care.'

Kirsten closed her eyes. *Ten-year-olds should be upset about bedtime or too much homework, not on their way to detention...* She hated having to arrest a child, but she hated the situation he'd landed in more. Still, he had used his abilities both against the police and in a way that could've killed someone. *The secure dorms aren't as bad as prison.*

"I really wish you would have come to us. Division 0 I mean."

"They don't care about gang stuff either." Rafael kicked his shoe at the floor.

The psi inhibitor made surface thought skimming difficult. Random whispering voices and sensory input blurred the contents of his mind, but Kirsten got enough of a peek to understand he didn't at all care what happened to him.

"Tell me about Juan Miguel. What was he like?"

"What for? He's dead."

"So is my partner, but he's still here." Kirsten nodded toward Dorian. "I'm an astral sensitive. Maybe I can find him. You told the officers he's older than you and protected you? Good chance he might still be out there somewhere, unable to move on because he's worried about you."

Rafael looked up, eyes wide. "Really?"

"Yes. Dorian? Little help here?"

He leaned into the back seat, his head shifting shimmery-translucent for a few seconds, casting pale whitish light around the car.

"Whoa," whispered Rafael. "He's not a hologram... I *felt* him. Even with this thing on my head."

"How old was Juan Miguel?"

"Eighteen. Our parents died a couple years ago. The cops didn't care about them either 'cause of gang stuff. They weren't even in a gang, but where we lived, cops think everyone's bad." He tugged at his arms, but wound up wiping his nose on his knee. "Juan died like two weeks ago, and when I brought the cops to him, they laughed... made jokes about cleaning up the city and stuff, one even said a scorpion got stepped on. They said a detective would show up, but no one did. I just want someone to find out who killed my brother."

He succumbed to crying.

Kirsten re-swallowed the lump in her throat. *Maybe I am too soft for this job. Or it's because he's not much older than Evan.* "Rafael, listen to me. I'm an investigator, too. I don't usually work cases that aren't related to spirits or non-psionic crimes... but I promise you I'll do everything I can to find who killed Juan Miguel."

The car steered itself around in a gentle descent toward the road in front of the PAC.

"You're just—" He stared into her eyes. "Okay, maybe you're not lying."

She couldn't reach to pat him on the knee from the front seat—arms too short, car too big—so she put on her most reassuring smile. "It's not up to me to detain you or not. Too many cameras caught it, and you attacked police officers. But don't be scared. You're psionic and a child, so you're headed for the secure dorms, not jail. If you've been living on the street, it's an improvement. And I'm serious. I will do whatever I can to find who killed your brother. Even if I have to ask the dead for help."

He almost smiled.

2

PRIORITY TEN

K irsten lay draped over her desk, feeling like she'd just fed a live bunny rabbit to a trash disintegrator.

She'd brought Rafael in for intake processing, but couldn't bring herself to keep walking away when he'd started yell-begging her to stay with him. He'd even wanted her to stay with him while he showered. At least with her there, they didn't leave the inhibitor on him. Between her greater rank in Suggestion and an Admin telepath confirming the boy had no intent to use his abilities to attempt an escape, they mostly treated him like any other kid brought in… except for the pink detainee jumpsuit.

Juvenile inmates in the secure dorms lived fairly well for prisoners. The major differences between it and the standard dormitory mostly consisted of locked doors and a regimented schedule with varying degrees of access to things like video games depending on behavior. His hope that she would find his brother's killer eliminated any urge to lash out at the police, so the telepath, Rafael's legal advocate, and the secure dorm staff all expected he'd be no trouble at all.

Still, guilt clawed at her over the thought that a boy Evan's age—well, older than him by a few months—would be sleeping in a locked room for the foreseeable future. Of course, she couldn't really protest the situation. He *had* misused his powers against police. The true source of her guilt came from holding his future so directly in her hands. If he thought she gave up on finding her brother, or if she failed, he could easily go from basically a kid in a bad situation to an active problem—or just give up on life.

Evan's going to be ten in about five months. Next April. Crap. And there's some holiday in two months, isn't there? I need to get him some presents or something.

A heavy sigh slid out of Kirsten's throat. She'd grown up not knowing that one day, late in December, parents gave their kids stuff. Sometimes, adults even gave each other things. Her first experience with it had been around fifteen when Nicole gave her a little ragdoll when they shared a dorm room.

She leaned back in her chair, half wanting to cry at the memory as if she watched some movie about an abused girl other than herself. But, she'd been so confused at why Nicole gave it to her, the entire dorm went nuts. Everyone there gave her something that day. None of it had been grand or expensive, but she didn't care. That gesture had been the first crack in the door that finally allowed her to let the outside world in. She *still* had all the tiny ragdolls, figurines, and plushies in a box at home. Fifteen years of Wintermas all at once.

"Wren, you okay?" asked Morelli.

The shock of *him* initiating conversation with her stalled the emotions in her head to surprise. "Uhh, yeah. Just had to bring a kid in on felony assault. Being back in the dorm area set my thoughts wandering."

"You were SD?" Morelli drifted closer, one eyebrow cocked.

"No, normal dorms. I didn't break the law at all. When cops found me, they thought I was a normal kid until I mentioned ghosts. The psychiatrist didn't believe me so I figured I'd prove it and turned on Darksight. He freaked out when my eyes started glowing. Called Division 0 and here I am."

Morelli folded his arms. "Damn. Sorry you had it so rough."

"It's okay. I'm not jealous of anyone whose parents love them despite psionics."

"Man, the universe has some whacked out sense of irony, doesn't it?" He shook his head.

She blinked. "How so?"

"You're like the nicest girl in the whole city and you can Mind Blast." Morelli chuckled. "Though, that's a lot better than some psycho having it."

"I dunno. Maybe the universe does have a sense of humor." She sighed. "A twisted one."

"Of course it does," muttered Dorian. "Have you looked at Morelli?"

She snickered.

"Well, as long as you're okay." Morelli smiled. "You were giving off some odd emotions."

"Since when are you an empath?" She raised both eyebrows.

"Not sure when it started. Grade one. Just came up on the screening three days ago. Maybe it's from hanging around all your spooky things." He chuckled on his way back to his desk across the room.

"If exposure to spirits gave psionic powers, I'd have them all." She tucked closer to her desk and swiped at the holo-panels to unlock the workstation. "And no, I don't want to know what being sat on by a one-ton demonic flea would do."

"Besides hurt?" asked Dorian.

She raised her arm, pointing at the ceiling. "Yes. That sucked."

The file record for Juan Miguel Esparza contained a few mugshots of a young man with a strong resemblance to Rafael. He had evidently been a known member of a street gang, the Jade Scorpionz.

Upon seeing that, Kirsten groaned and rubbed her temples. "Why do people do that?"

"I'm sorry," said Dorian from behind. "Your question was not vague enough."

She gestured at the intangible screen. "Scorpions with a z. Are the damn *street gangs* using marketing logic now? I mean like Kwik Kleen? Why do people feel the need to mangle words like that. It's *so* frustrating."

"Well, it's not their fault you spent all that time in school learning the correct way to put letters in order." Dorian laughed.

"Right?" She rolled her eyes. "I got half the schooling those people did and I feel like a freakin' fid by comparison."

"Fid?" asked Dorian.

"Yeah, when someone's real smart, they put fid after their name."

He looked up from whatever indistinct object he 'read.' "I have not the first clue what you're talking about."

"Grr. Hang on." She pulled up a GlobeNet interface, hunted a little, and pulled up a record for a psychologist. "Here."

Dorian floated through his desk to stand beside her. "That's PhD. You say the letters individually."

"Oh. Well." She crossed her arms and glowered at the screen, cheeks warming. "I didn't even really finish high school, you know. Only had four years' worth of full time school *after* I got to the dorms. The only 'learning' Mother allowed me was out of her stupid mythology book. And at least one of those years was remedial. They tried to compress first to eighth grade into one year."

He set his hand on her shoulder, the chill of contact spreading down her arm. "I wasn't making fun of you. And, you did pass the test for a diploma, didn't you?"

"Barely," she muttered. "They wanted me out there so bad they curved me. I had to keep my grades up or they would've taken me off active duty —not that *I* would've minded. So, yeah, I technically have a grade twelve diploma, but…"

"Yet you excel in some areas. I remember you schooling that detective on forensics during the Motte case. That's reasonably impressive physics for someone who barely passed."

"They taught me what I 'needed to know.' How to pronounce PhD, not so much." She glanced back at the screen. "Cause of death: gang-related violence. Inquest priority ten. Yeah… that means no one's ever going to investigate it."

"That's not true."

She smirked. "Of course it is. P10 is the lowest priority. Those cases only get looked at when there's absolutely nothing else to do, and that *never* happens."

"Not what I meant." He poked her in the ear, causing a spike of frost to cross her brain.

"Gah!" she jumped.

"You're going to investigate it." He winked.

Kirsten clamped a hand over her right ear, playfully scowling at him. "You're almost as bad as Theodore. Only he didn't ice-finger me in the *ear*."

Dorian gawked.

"Broken mirror?" She grumbled. "My old apartment."

"Oh, right."

She spent a little over a half hour reading up on the brother's background. Rafael had a point. At a priority ten, the detectives from Division 2 would never get around to touching the case. Even if by some miracle all P1 through P9 cases wound up cleared, the system had over two million P10 inquests in an 'unassigned' state, some going back over thirty years. Almost all of them involved gang-on-gang violence, though a heartbreaking number of cases related to the deaths of young prostitutes like Rush and Stardance. At least they'd found justice. Nina hadn't left much of The Russian. Then again, a pissed-off and emotional Division 9 operative in a doll body became a force of nature.

Rush had already transcended at that point, but Stardance—who'd led the way right to her killer—stood there watching with her as the Harbingers dragged the guy away. Kirsten cringed, hoping that man never escaped the abyss. The Wharf Stalker had been bad, but The Russian coming back as an Abyssal would be an entirely new level of suck.

Kirsten stared over the floating holo-panel at Captain Eze's office. *No one ever told me I* can't *pluck an inquest from the Div 2 backlog... but I should probably run it by him first just in case. Don't see why anyone would care. Not like they're going to work it.*

She swiped a finger at her terminal to lock it and walked down the aisle between six empty desks. Her squad room held seven tactical officers as overflow despite technically belonging to I-Ops. But, Investigative Operations for Division 0 didn't exactly have a lot of people. She'd been put in this room as a sixteen-year-old agent, sneaking into a space mostly full of tactical officers. Though, a little over a year later, Jen Kurosawa and Alan Montez, two other I-Ops investigators, joined her in here. They still outranked her as first lieutenants, but the gap didn't feel quite as big now that she'd been promoted to second lieutenant.

Upon reaching Captain Eze's office, she leaned over and peered between the slats of the blinds in the giant window. He sat behind his desk, absorbed in whatever his terminal screen showed. She knocked softly and stuck her head in.

"Captain?"

"Wren?" He looked up, his expression a mixture of warmth and concern. "You seem troubled. What's on your mind?"

She stepped into the office and approached the desk, eyeing the small African masks lined up along the near edge. It bothered her feeling so anxious about her request, but a kid's future not only depended on him saying yes, but her ability to follow through.

"You're not going to ask for a car on your birthday are you?"

Kirsten laughed, all her tension bursting like a popped balloon. "No, sir. I wanted to ask if I could poach a P10 case from Div 2."

"Are you that bored?" He leaned back, smiling. "Best not make a habit of that or some half-bird colonel will decide we all should be doing that."

She sat in one of the chairs facing his desk, smiling. That problem, she'd already solved. "It's directly related to one of my cases, though the substance of the P10 inquest doesn't look like anything we'd normally bother with."

"I'm listening." He steepled his fingers, his expression saying he'd already agreed to it but wanted to hear her logic.

"The juvenile I brought in earlier lost his older brother a few weeks ago to gang homicide. It got P10-ed. Kid didn't think anyone cared, so he tried to hold a couple of Div 1 guys hostage thinking he could force an investigator to work the other case."

Captain Eze massaged the bridge of his nose, muttering to himself.

"Yeah. I wish he didn't do that, but I can't help but feel bad for him. As soon as I promised to find the killer, he completely changed. Even Velez signed off on him being compliant. I'm worried if I can't find whoever murdered his brother or if he thinks I've given up on him, he might go from a scared, lonely kid to a serious problem."

"That's a bit of a leap figuring he'll instantly go bad." He chuckled. "Depends on how long it takes him to give up. He might still turn out okay, then go vigilante after he's eighteen."

Kirsten glanced off to the side. *If he's too dangerous, they'd make him forget he ever had a brother.* "You're right. He's still a child who thinks of the cops as some kind of magical force that can just go out and find the killer right away. I don't know why I expected such a bad outcome."

"Children are resilient. Some can go through hell and grow into adults who always try to find the good in everyone."

She smoothed her hands down the clingy black fabric over her thighs. "Evan's doing really well. Sometimes it's almost like he's completely forgotten about the first nine years of his life." She paused, shifted her eyes to meet his, and managed a weak smile. "Oh. You weren't talking about him."

"Indeed. I understand why you feel the need to help him out, and as long as you don't prioritize it over any active Division 0 investigations you own, by all means, proceed."

Kirsten nodded. "Thank you, sir."

"Of course." He smiled. "And yes, I am aware you're presently not on the hook for anything."

"If they want me to start helping out with other investigations, I don't mind."

"Perhaps when you are no longer the only astral sensitive in the entire city. For now, Command wants you available on short notice… especially after what happened on the Moon. Don't worry about so much idle time. You are in no danger of being reassigned."

"I just feel guilty sitting around while everyone else is so backed up."

"Consider it compensation for being the only one in the division who's obligated to get slapped around by ten-foot-tall demons... or whatever that thing was."

She shuddered. "All right."

"Now"—Captain Eze pointed at her, smiling broadly—"you should probably go keep that promise you made."

"Yes, sir." She stood, smiled, and hurried back to her desk.

3

DARK SPIRIT

P age after page of data scrolled across the five holo-panels above Kirsten's desk, the faces and records of people ranging in age from mid-teens into their thirties. She'd combined the handful of Juan Miguel's 'known associates' with a system search by PID. Any NetMini that spent more than an hour in close proximity to his, or that stayed close to him for at least ten minutes multiple times per week— factoring out areas that coincided with maglevs, PubTran bus routes, or any public transportation.

The end result created a list of seventy-two people she considered likely sources of information. Fifty-three of them also belonged to the Jade Scorpionz gang, though thirteen showed up as having been murdered in one shot three months ago. A black shield icon at the corner of the tag for the inquest into that *execution* caught her eye.

According to that file, one clique within the gang had the misfortune of being gunned down by the Syndicate. Citycam video showed a plain black hovercar landing by an alley full of young men and a handful of women. Three men in suits got out and proceeded to shoot them one at a time except for the youngest woman who looked to be in her later teens. Her, they dragged into the car.

The Division 0 link in the file indicated the killing was related to a presently-rogue tactical officer by the name of Aaron Pryce. Investigators had located the remains of roughly a dozen Syndicate members in an abandoned retail property not far from that site, the majority of them liquefied by high-speed impact with the walls. According to the record, they believed Pryce did it with Telekinesis.

"Someone's been hitting the SynVod way too hard. Telekinesis doesn't have that much power," muttered Kirsten.

Investigators also located Andrea Cortez, the abducted girl, when she attempted to pass herself off as a fourteen-year-old and request placement with an adoptive family. Turned out, the girl was sixteen and she'd witnessed Pryce go on a rampage. Her current status showed as having been sent to an adoptive family on a colony world, Frontier-8.

"Poor kid. She must've been on some wild shit."

"What's that?" Dorian walked up behind her.

"This kid. She claims to have seen a telekinetic throw people into the wall with so much force they exploded like tomatoes."

Dorian cringed. "I've heard some rumors. It might actually be true. You read the thing about that little girl they've got set up out in the Badlands, right?"

"Yeah. So weird. Accelerated Healing working on *other* people? Why are they keeping her way out there? That's like exactly what shady corporations do. Is she some kind of top secret project?" Kirsten's heart almost jumped into her throat.

He shook his head. "No, she prefers it out there from what I overheard."

"Ugh. Okay, so the Syndicate may have something against this gang the brother used to be in."

Dorian pointed at the screen, managing to get the contents to scroll.

"Hey, you're getting better at that." She grinned.

"I've had some practice with terminals. That idiot two desks away from Sam." He laughed. "He's given up on the crystals, by the way. He's moved on to trying pagan symbols. I'm half tempted to leave him alone as long as they're up." He tapped the panel. "Here. Look, they just land and start shooting... and the girl said she was bait for some manner of trap."

"Yeah. So you're saying the Syndicate just pounced on the first gang they stumbled across in that area looking for a random teen girl to kidnap?"

He shrugged. "It's a theory. Only way to know for sure would be to go there and hope one of their ghosts is still around."

All five panels flashed black with red *incoming dispatch* scrolling across them.

"Figures." Kirsten bit back a sigh and touched the screen. "Wren. Go ahead."

A too-blonde woman appeared, one of the sub-sentient dolls at the National Police Force inter-division command center. "Lieutenant Wren, Division 1 is requesting your presence on suspicion of an unexplained paranormal event. There is a surviving victim and officers are on site now."

"Understood. Send the pin to my pat-vee. I'm on the way."

The young woman nodded. "I'll inform the officers you are en route."

She locked the terminal and jogged off down the hall. *Always twenty minutes before end of shift. Always.* The bud in her left ear chirped in response to a finger tap.

"Assad, Nila," said Kirsten, initiating a call to Dorian's former partner, a woman who she'd come to consider a close friend.

Beep. Beep. Beep.

"K. What's up?" asked Nila's voice in her ear.

She hurried down the overly white hallway to the elevator. "Just had a dispatch come in. No way am I going to wrap that up and get back in time to pick Evan up from school. Would you mind?"

"Ahh. The usual timing, huh?"

"Yep." Kirsten mashed her finger into the button for the ground floor motor pool deck.

"No problem."

"Thanks. You're the best!"

The soft pulsing lights along the elevator walls scrolled from floor to ceiling for the few seconds it took her to go down. On the way out of the elevator, she muttered, "Hey Suri?"

Her NetMini chirped. "Hi!"

"Please send a text to Evan and let him know I had a dispatch come in last minute." She dodged around two Admin cadets and ran through a door into the parking area. "Nila will pick him up and I'll be back as soon as I can."

"Okay," replied her device's AI in a cheerful tone.

Kirsten raced over to her patrol craft and hopped in, finding Dorian already in the passenger seat.

"You're getting faster."

"Thanks." She shoved forward on the left stick, accelerating out of the parking space into a left turn, then zoomed down the lane full of other hovercars and vans to the exit.

"For?"

"Powering the car up and not making a lame joke about winning 'the race.'"

He smiled. "It was only funny once, and... it bothered you."

"That wasn't bother. Just frustration."

An active dispatch plus going code three caused the gate to open automatically so she didn't have to wait for Samir—or whoever else staffed the booth—to open it for her. The instant the patrol craft cleared the ramp, she shifted to hover mode and went near vertical in a climb.

"You don't need to drive like someone is going to drop dead if you're a half second late. This is a normal I-Ops call. Investigate the crime scene after the bullets have stopped flying."

She leveled off at 600 feet, swung the car around toward the nav pin, and accelerated up to 325 mph. "I'm aware of that, but if there *is* a ghost, I don't want it wandering off before we get there."

Nine-ish minutes later, the destination neared. She slowed and began a fairly tame descent.

"Amazing," said Dorian.

"What?"

"We didn't collide with a single ad-bot. It's almost like someone remembered they're supposed to avoid an emergency vehicle."

She laughed. "For a moment there, I thought you were taking a shot at my driving."

"I would, but forty-four miles in a straight line ten stories above the traffic lane isn't exactly nerve-wracking. Though, I'm sure if a sushi boat went by, there would've been sashimi on the windscreen."

"You're a funny guy." She smirked to herself, picturing the hover-vans made up to look like ancient Japanese fishing boats. "And now I want sushi."

He snickered.

The fluttering red-blue glow of Division 1 patrol craft's light bars came into view up ahead. Multiple patrol craft clustered in an open square area surrounded on three sides by a four-story building covered with hundreds of doors, some manner of motel about three blocks deep into a grey zone.

"I'm guessing this isn't a five-star resort," said Dorian.

"Ugh. I'm going to want to shower just from looking at this place." She grimaced at the bullet-marked walls, occasional broken windows, and vast amount of dark stains adorning the mostly pea-green walls. "Ick."

"Don't worry too much. There's so many bodily fluids on everything here, the viruses are too busy killing each other to notice you."

Kirsten almost gagged.

Bits of plastic trash skittered away as she set the patrol craft down alongside the three Division 1 cars. Six officers in blue armor milled around a ground-level doorway in the glare of the headlights.

"At least I don't have to deal with stairs." She shoved her door up and open, regretting doing so in seconds.

A blast of piss-and-puke scented air mixed with some unidentifiable industrial chemical slapped her across the cheek. Of course, she'd smelled worse. The dark purplish-black slime that collected here and there in the Beneath *still* made her throw up if she caught a whiff of it. That had been one advantage of only having plastic sheeting for clothes back then… whenever she fell in a puddle, she could ditch it and go forage another scrap of clean tarp. Well, clean*er*.

The brief memory from months ago of removing her underpants, throwing them, and having them stick to the wall made her shiver. *Ugh. My entire uniform stuck to me.* After that horror, this place didn't even register on the scale of foul.

She trotted over to the officers, four men and two women.

"Lieutenant." The woman on the left saluted her. "Sergeant Burke."

Kirsten returned the salute. "Sergeant. What's the situation? They said you think there's something paranormal going on here?"

"Yeah. A couple things don't quite add up, and there's some really weird shit on video." Sergeant Burke whistled. "So, we get a gold screamer for this address. My guys come in little more than two minutes later, and find the victim restrained naked to the bed."

"Okay…" Kirsten's eyebrows scrunched together involuntarily until she remembered 'gold screamer' translated to Div 1 slang for a civilian panic button with a gold protection plan. Basically, someone with money. "That doesn't sound too weird so far, unless she had no way to set off her alarm while tied down."

"Nah, it's a headware unit. Mental command. That's the thing. She could've set it off at any time during her abduction, but didn't activate it until *after* her attacker fled the scene."

Dorian glanced at the room. "Maybe it was consensual until the guy left her tied to the bed?"

"Consensual sex gone wrong?" asked Kirsten.

"The woman claims not to remember how she got here at all. One minute, she's home, the next, here." Sergeant Burke headed for the door. "C'mon. She's still in there waiting for you. Medics already checked her out and got all the samples a detective could ask for."

She shivered.

"Another thing that doesn't make a lot of sense—at least until I saw the weird part—is the earlier video. The vic stepped out of a PubTran car, already naked, and wandered around the courtyard here until the suspect grabbed her."

"Threatened somehow?" asked Kirsten. "She have kids or something who someone would hurt if she didn't do this?"

Burke raised her left arm and a small holo-panel opened above it. "That *would* make sense, but nothing about this makes sense. The victim, Mia Sanchez, is still here. She thinks something paranormal happened. Asked for a Zero. No criminal record, single, no kids. Age twenty-three, residence is in Sector 244, a fair ride away from here."

"That's not a cheap place to live," muttered Kirsten while following the sergeant inside to a room every bit as foul and dingy as she expected.

Her skin prickled with a charge of supernatural energy, primarily emanating from the bed. *Crap. This one's strong.* If not for the clingy uniform covering her to the wrists, all the hairs on the backs of her arms would've stood on end, not from fear, but from the intensity.

"This one is going to be... interesting." Dorian wandered past a small table with a chair by the window, then peered into the bathroom. "Seems the spirit kept itself in one place."

A woman with a rounded face and light brown skin sat on the foot end of the bed, wrapped in a grey police-issue blanket. Flashing pink glowed from a NanoLED tattoo on her left cheek in the shape of a heart. A few tiny blue lights winked in and out under her hair behind her left ear. Her expression gave off clear shock. She barely reacted to them approaching her. Every ten seconds, all five fingernails on the visible hand clutching the blanket to her chest changed color.

"Miss Sanchez?" asked Kirsten.

"You're a psionic." The woman moved only her head, turning it to look at her.

Kirsten nodded.

Humanity flooded into Mia's formerly lifeless expression, a slow fade from sub-sentient doll to actual person. "Oh, thank you! I can stop concentrating now."

"Concentrating?" Kirsten stepped closer, peering around the room.

"I'm pretty sure something possessed me, so I was shielding my mind."

Kirsten skimmed the woman's surface thoughts, but sensed no psionic ability whatsoever. Though, Mia did *believe* concentrating intently on the image of a closed fist against a black background would keep 'evil stuff' out of her.

Dorian approached the bed, holding his hands out, palms down. "I have the distinct impression anyone who attempts a psychometric reading from this bed is going to need therapy."

"That strong?" asked Kirsten with a raised eyebrow.

Mia glanced at her. "What?"

"Oh. I'm talking to someone else." She smiled.

"No..." Dorian grinned. "Merely from being in *this* place. The things that've happened on this bed would probably break the minds of hardened killers. Though, whatever spirit was here has a lot of power. Enough that I suspect anyone who sleeps in it will have *interesting* dreams."

"Someone else?" Mia shrank in on herself.

Kirsten tapped her forearm guard to start active recording. "Please, don't worry. My partner is a spirit. Please tell me everything you can remember."

"That's good." Mia again looked where she thought Dorian might be. "If it comes back, she can fight it."

"He," said Kirsten, suppressing a smile. "You're not in any danger now. I can see spirits, too."

"Yes. The one from the NewsNet. The Moon thing." Mia smiled. "I'm glad they sent you."

"Looks like someone has a fan club." Dorian chuckled.

"I was home." Mia looked down. "I'd just gotten offline from work and went to the kitchen to make myself something to eat. A hand grabbed my ass. I screamed and spun around, but nothing was there. So, I figured I'd imagined it. Sometimes, spending ten hours plugged into the net can cause phantom sensations. The same hardware that makes the GlobeNet feel real can do things when you're out."

"Yes, I'm aware of the phenomenon," said Kirsten.

"It felt like someone kept touching me everywhere, running a hand up inside my legs." Mia squirmed.

Kirsten did as well, unable to help but think of Konstantin. "The touch felt normal, not icy?"

Mia offered a weak nod. "But, still nothing was there. So I figured Yavne might've pranked me with a pervert soft."

"Yavne?" Kirsten added another line to her notes. "Who's that?"

"Eli Yavne. He's one of the IT people where I work. Likes to play games, but it's not usually like him to go sexual like that. He does goofy stuff. So, I'm pretty sure at that point my headware had a glitch. Invisible fingers started tweaking my nipples and, umm… going other places." Mia blushed. "But there's nothing in the room with me so, I figured it's all in my head. Made it damn hard to put food together, so I decided to go lie down and run a diagnostic on my headware."

Kirsten nodded.

"When I got to my bedroom, Blot—my cat—hissed at me and ran out. That's when I knew it had to be a wraith or something. I tried to call you guys, but it's like he knew what I was about to do. Everything went black."

"He saw you going for your NetMini?"

Mia tapped her head. "No. I've got an internal one. The instant I thought about making a call, this wave of cold hit me and I blacked out. Next thing I know, I'm in here tied to the bed and some guy I've never seen before is climbing off me. I was so freaked out I couldn't say anything until he left. Hit my panic button. I couldn't move, and I didn't scream."

"Smart move." Dorian shot a dark look at the doorway. "The critters who live out here would've come running, and not to help."

"The police told me I took a Pub car here, naked. I don't remember anything after blacking out at home." Mia reached up and wiped tears off her cheeks. "I'm kinda freaked out that I'm not freaking out more. Did he do something to me? I should be going crazy or something, right?"

Kirsten initiated a telepathic link. Phantom hands caressed and squeezed her body, echoes of a memory in the other woman's head. Mia's intent to initiate a VidPhone call from a cybernetic implant preceded time skipping forward to her emerging naked from a PubTran car, struggling for control of her body as some outside force made her walk toward the building. She screamed in her head, alternatively ordering and begging whatever it was to let her go. It compelled her to wander back and forth by the rooms, approaching groups of dosers who all clapped and whistled at her exhibitionism, cheering her on. Neko-modders, people who added cat ears, tails, claws, and such, often walked around nude all the time, so the sight of Mia streaking surprised them only due to her lack of extra body parts.

Sharing that memory made Kirsten erupt in blush.

Mia, as well, shivered with embarrassment inside, though the entity controlling her appeared to savor the feeling of vulnerability. It kept her walking around for a while until a filthy man in his later thirties came out of nowhere and grabbed her from behind, knife at her throat. She struggled in the halfhearted way a bad actress filming an assault scene in a cheesy holovid might, not making any real effort to get away. All the while, the real Mia trapped inside the prison of her own flesh shrieked and screamed, feverishly trying to invoke the panic button in her headware.

He selected a door apparently at random and kicked it in. Mia screamed in her head while the entity continued to pretend-struggle. The man tore cord from the window blinds and tied her spread-eagle to the bed. Once she could no longer move, the entity struggled harder, savoring the sensation of confinement as well as Mia's genuine terror.

Mia stared at the grimy, cracked ceiling, unable to do anything but shriek inside her thoughts as the man climbed on top of her. Kirsten skipped ahead in the memory, having no desire to relive the entire scene. She jumped to the point where the man climbed off her and staggered out the door.

Coldness washed over Mia's body, left there spread eagle for whoever else might find her next. The entity made her squirm and struggle for a little while before, evidently sated, it released its control. Mia fought the cords holding her down, but couldn't move, or even sit up. The storm of emotions raging in the woman's head almost forced Kirsten to break the connection. She'd endured a similar mix of fear, guilt, and shame from her encounter with the man who gave her food so long ago. She forced herself not to think about how horribly wrong that *could* have gone.

Mia had no idea where she was or how she'd gotten there, but assumed the area to be bad based on the horrid condition of the room. She focused on a thought pattern totally alien to Kirsten—invoking a cybernetic implant—that set off a panic button inside her head, then lay back and waited, hoping with every ounce of her being that the next person to walk in the still-open door would be a cop. None of it seemed real to Mia laying there helpless in a dive motel room. Another feeling Kirsten knew all too well. It had taken her two days after she traded herself for beef stew before she believed she hadn't dreamed it.

Kirsten released the telepathic connection and stood there for a few seconds letting her brain acclimate to the present.

"Done?" asked Mia.

"Yes."

"Why am I so calm? That really happened to me, didn't it?"

"It did. You're in shock still. A MedVan should be on its way here for you already. I just need to do one little thing and then I can clear you to leave the scene."

"What's that?" Mia wiped her face with the blanket.

"I'd like to try and get a sense of the paranormal entity involved. That works best with physical contact, but I only need to hold your hand."

"Okay." Mia offered her left hand, the only part of her other than her face not covered by grey fabric.

Kirsten clasped it, focused on her astral sense. The spectral 'fingerprint' of an entity flooded her mind, none she had encountered before. Every ghost had a certain mix of feelings they triggered whenever she 'read' their presence. In this case, she felt somewhat like a deer hung up to be cleaned, with a hunter standing behind her, knife at her stomach. Coldness mixed with an electric tingle on her tongue, and an almost overwhelming mania.

She abruptly let go of Mia's hand, shuddering.

"Is that bad?"

Kirsten swallowed. "Not for you. This one's going to be a mess. Doubt I'll be able to convince him to stop."

"You arrest ghosts?"

"No. If I can't convince them to stop doing whatever, I… either umm, dispel them or they go to the bad place."

Mia nodded.

Kirsten glanced up at Sergeant Burke. "I've done all I can here for now. Can someone help her get home? Unless she wants to go to a med center."

"They had medics see me already. I'm… actually, I'd like to go to my parents' place. Can someone drop me there?" asked Mia.

Burke waved another officer over. "Bill, mind giving her a ride? Need a few more minutes with the LT."

"Sure." Officer Parks—Bill—eyed Mia's toes sticking out from the blanket. "It's pretty foul out there, ma'am. You don't want to go outside barefoot."

Mia fidgeted. "I don't really want to be in *here* barefoot either. The rug is sticky."

Kirsten shivered.

Officer Parks moved as if to pick the woman up. When Mia nodded, he scooped her into his arms and carried her outside.

"Okay, the real reason we called you is here." Sergeant Burke extended her left arm, showing the holo-panel. "Check this out."

The eight-by-twelve inch screen displayed video of the motel exterior via Citycam. Burke tapped her finger to the middle, starting playback. A few seconds later, the door to this room opened, revealing the man Kirsten saw from Mia's memory. He adjusted his belt on the way out, paused on the sidewalk in front of the door long enough to take a hit from an inhaler, then wobbled off.

"That's the guy," said Kirsten.

"Yeah, we know. Already picked him up. You'd have thought we were ghosts the way he looked at us." Sergeant Burke laughed. "No one ever expects us to show up in a grey zone. Umm, the guy's culpable right? He wasn't compelled or anything?"

Kirsten shook her head. "No, that guy deserves everything you can charge him with. The spirit didn't make *him* do anything."

"Okay. Here's the interesting part." Burke resumed the video.

About a minute after the living man left, a blurry male form glided out from the door as if walking away, vanishing into nothingness a short distance into the parking lot.

"Is that legit? Not like some hacker messing with us?"

"Based on what I saw in her memories and the feeling I'm picking up in the room, yeah. I'm convinced a malign spirit possessed her and purposefully put her in a situation at high risk for assault of a sexual nature."

"Yeah, this motel is notorious for that." Sergeant Burke shook her head. "And damn. What a sick bastard. Even executing these sons of bitches ain't enough to protect people?"

"Oh, it usually is." Dorian folded his arms. "Some of them just don't get the message the first time and need a second death."

Kirsten glanced sideways at him. "It's pretty rare that a criminal executed for their crimes turns into a dangerous spirit. Ghosts are weak at first and easily overtaken by... certain other entities who are, for lack of a better metaphor, like the trash collectors of the spirit world. Even if they aren't dark enough to attract that kind of attention, it often takes decades for them to build up enough power to affect the living in any way, much less do something like this. If I had to guess, I'd say this one's more than a century old."

Sergeant Burke shuddered. "That's so messed up. Like, I've got two black belts, some minor augs, and I still don't wanna be alone in this part of town. How the hell do you fight off something like this?"

"Are you asking me personally or about women in general?"

Burke laughed. "Well, I figure you got some tricks most of us don't. Meant that rhetorically. Is there anything us norms can do?"

"Well, Miss Sanchez had some cybernetic implants, but I don't think its enough to make her more vulnerable to psionic or spiritual influence. Usually, the intent to resist a ghost trying to take over your body is enough. It's incredibly difficult for them, and they almost always need the person to allow them in the door at first. Once they're in, getting rid of them is a little trickier, but this one's got enough power to kick that door down, so to speak."

"Shit."

Kirsten set her hands on her hips, frowning at the empty room. "I gotta find him fast. This son of a bitch is going to ruin lives."

"I'm sure he already has." Dorian glared at the door.

4

SQUEEZY

F ortunately, the scene didn't take up as much time as Kirsten feared it would.

She'd spent about half an hour sniffing around for any spectral trace of where the entity went, as did Dorian, but found nothing she could use to follow. The video capture of the blurry spectral form outside the motel room offered a reasonably detailed hint of a face. After sharpening it as much as possible, she started a search in the system.

Evan had already eaten dinner at Nila's, so Kirsten 'semmed a grilled chicken sandwich, munching on it while helping him with some homework. The third-grade math wasn't too bad, though the history homework baffled her. It didn't seem right that nine-year-olds had to learn about the Synthetic Revolt that ultimately led to the AI Sentience Act and a ban on companies manufacturing fully-sentient synthetics or dolls.

He seemed to understand she'd never learned any of that stuff, so their session turned into something akin to a pair of kids working together on an assignment that they both struggled with. His introductory robotics and electronics coursework might as well have been written in upside-down Russian, though he didn't seem to have difficulty with it. Kirsten thought back to the basic forensics training she'd received and wondered if the boy could calculate the angle of a distant shooter or estimate the power of a rifle based on damage pattern. That had seemed so impossibly difficult at first, but had become almost as easy as speaking. She sat there quietly watching him fill out diagrams, selecting the best component to use for a given role.

Who would I be if I'd grown up like a normal person?

Once he finished the last of his work, they migrated to the living room to watch episode seventy-nine of *Monwyn the Liberator.* The titular wizard had helped most of the Wild Elves escape physical captivity in the Shadow King's realm at that point, and the story involved their continued fight to remain free, warring with the armies of darkness.

Evan snuggled into her side, his attention absorbed entirely by the 150-inch holographic portal into another world. His bony little shoulder at her side made her think of Rafael, probably alone in a small, plain room behind a locked door. She'd never been stuck in the secure dorms, nor had she so much as visited them on a tour. At twelve, when she'd first been found by Division 0, no one had even mentioned them to her. Of course, once her talent screen came back positive for Mind Blast and Suggestion, she got 'the talk.' Most people considered Astrals harmless, but a 'severely abused' child with both of *those* abilities wound up on a watch list.

She wondered if that's where her expectation that Rafael may 'go bad, hard' if she let him down came from. Some staff at the dorms had watched her like a ticking bomb. Up until they told her she possessed those powers, she hadn't known. She never used either of them in the dorms, but if she'd known about Suggestion back home... Mother would've gone away. Kirsten would've commanded her to leave and never come back. Maybe she could've been happy with Dad. How such a passive, nice man wound up with a monster of a woman like that, she would never understand.

Though, he wouldn't have stayed around the ghosts either. It hadn't been Mother he avoided by going on business trips all the time. Perhaps he might've tolerated the supernatural oddities for her sake without the awful woman's influence. It's possible he feared that woman's reaction to the ghosts more than the ghosts themselves. Also, without Mother punishing her for using her abilities, she would've talked to the spirits, removing their need to throw things around the house. Dad might not have even known any of them had been there except for her—at the time —glowing eyes. Back then, she had to activate the ability to see spirits.

She'd kept it on so constantly while living in the Beneath, it had evolved into what Division 0 referred to as a 'passive ability,' always on, and her eyes no longer glowed simply from seeing ghosts.

If she'd known she had Suggestion, that man in the Beneath would've simply given her the ration. As soon as she understood what he wanted in exchange for food, she would've made him give it to her and not felt the least bit guilty over it. She wouldn't have had to trade herself for a decent meal.

"Ngh," grunted Evan. "Need air."

She relaxed her hug.

"Pause," said Evan.

The video froze.

He looked up at her, his eyes mostly hidden behind his dense light-brown hair. It had been an orb when she found him, but touched his shoulders now. Evan preferred his hair longish, so she saw no reason to force him to cut it.

"You're getting squeezy. What made you sad?"

Rafael and Mia bothered her the most, one for her doubts she'd be good enough to solve a seemingly random gang murder, the other for all the bad memories it dredged up—and worrying she'd not be able to track the spirit down before it attacked someone else. Of course, she couldn't tell her son about a rapist spirit. Theodore was a pervert, but he didn't act out of malice or intent to harm. No, this spirit made him look downright puritanical.

"Bad case. Boy about your age lost his older brother and the police weren't investigating it fast enough, so he took a pair of officers hostage."

Evan blinked. "That's kinda stupid. And dangerous."

"Yes. He's desperate and alone. Didn't think he had another choice."

"Oh." Evan looked down at his feet, swiping his toes at the carpet. "If you wanna let him move in with us, that's cool. It would be nice to have a brother."

Kirsten choked up. Only picturing Dorian cracking a joke about her having hundreds of kids by the time she's an old woman kept her from crying. "I don't think that's possible. He got himself in a lot of trouble with the law. They're not going to let him out of the dorms for a while."

"Oh. That's sad they put kids in jail."

"It's not really 'jail.' Those rooms are kinda close to the one you stayed in, only no video games and they lock the door."

"Ack! No video games?" Evan feigned horror. "That's cruel and unusual."

"Well, they need to make sure he understands that actions have consequences."

Evan cringed. "Yeah. Even good ones. They should've just given him cit points."

She tickled his side, making him giggle. "Are you going to run off and do something like that again without at least asking first?"

"No." He laughed, grabbing at her hand. "I promise... unless like someone's about to get hurt and I can stop it. Ghosts can wait for me to get permission."

"Be careful, okay?" She ruffled his hair. "The dorms are safe, so there shouldn't be any reason for you to jump into a dangerous situation to protect anyone."

Evan twisted his head around again, peering up at her with an 'are you crazy?' expression. "Mom... there's a few hundred psionic kids there. The wrong kid takes a spitball to the face, half the classroom is going to be on fire."

She started to laugh, but wound up staring at him.

"I'm joking. No one's that strong. And they keep telling us not to mess with each other because we're all outsiders. But still, everyone's a little afraid of new kids unless they have wimp powers like Astral Sense."

"Hah." She raspberried him.

Evan smiled and snuggled into her side again. "It's okay if you wanna get squeezy. Just let me breathe."

"Okay. Sorry." She rested her arm around him. "I love you too damn much, and seeing a boy your age in such a bad situation got me sad and worried."

"Don't." He grinned. "I have wimp powers. I can't break the law."

She snickered.

"Well... I guess I could snoop around astrally and see stuff I shouldn't, but... that's wrong."

A momentary horrifying thought—teenage Evan spying on girls from the Astral Realm—came and went. She didn't think he'd ever do such a thing. Then again, did the mothers of any criminal ever expect their 'sweet little boy' would grow up to become a killer, rapist, thief, or whatever? *How do people go from innocent kids to evil adults? Were they born dark or did it come from something outside while they grew up?*

The weight of responsibility crushed her into the sofa. Choices she made now would have such a huge effect on the man this boy could become. She squeezed Evan, making him gurgle.

"Are you okay, Mom?"

"Yeah. Just happy you're safe."

"Me too." He hugged her back. "Feel better?"

She still worried quite a bit, but her mood *had* improved. "Yeah."

"Play!" Evan thrust a finger into the air.

The rush of magical fireballs and galloping horses filled the air. For a little while, Kirsten tried to stop thinking about anything beyond having a wonderful moment with the boy she had come to love as a son.

Chimes leaked past the Monwyn soundtrack.

"Pause," said Evan. "Someone rang the doorbell."

"Terminal, door view."

A holo-projector in the ceiling created a floating window in front of her with a view into the hallway, showing Samuel Chang.

"Hi, Sam!" yelled Evan.

Kirsten jumped up and ran to the door. She could've told the house terminal to open it, but that felt too dismissive. How she'd gone from sleeping in piles of centuries-forgotten trash to having an apartment with a 150-inch holo panel and a remote-viewing doorbell, she couldn't even fathom. Part of her still felt like she trespassed somewhere she didn't belong, but this place didn't even come close to the awkwardness she'd felt while mingling with Konstantin's crowd.

She poked the dark silver panel on the wall, opening the door.

"Hey…" Sam stepped into an embrace, kissing her on the lips.

Losing herself in the moment, she pressed close to him. Knowing she didn't have to carry everything on her own made the load easier to bear. Not that Sam could do anything about a dangerous ghost but offer emotional support; however, having him there to talk with helped beyond measure.

"Hey to you, too." She leaned back from the hug, feeling recharged. "C'mon. Don't wanna keep Ev waiting too long. Bed time marches onward."

Sam nodded, following her to the sofa. Evan flopped between them rather than stay on her right, a gesture Kirsten took as a show of acceptance. She tried to let herself believe this reality, that after so long, she might've at last found a man who had no problem with her being psionic *and* seemed like a nice guy. That Evan trusted him meant a lot. Not only for his being her son, but his clairvoyance had a way of feeling a person out. He'd never been the least bit afraid of Theodore, which made sense once she realized despite the ghost's pervy exterior, he had a reasonably good heart—metaphorically speaking.

Nicole had run through numerous boyfriends, mostly because she had no tolerance for bullshit and wasn't above using telepathy on them.

For the remainder of the Monwyn episode, Kirsten paid attention to the screen to keep herself from wandering down frightening or sad thought paths. Plus, Evan loved Monwyn so much she couldn't let herself fall behind on the lore. Sometimes studying the fictional world felt like work, but she loved discussing it with him, watching him get so into it, and knowing she helped him be that happy. Completely worth the effort.

Once the episode ended, Evan hugged them both and ran off down the hall to get ready for bed. She'd let him stay up a little late to finish, but only about fifteen minutes. It pained her to think her frame of reference for an 8 p.m. bedtime came from Mother, but the time seemed appropriate for a nine-year-old. She'd probably extend it by an hour when he hit twelve, and push it out to 10 p.m. when he hit fourteen or so.

Sam scooted closer. "Bad case?"

"Is it that obvious?"

"You haven't said much all night."

"Yeah. Two bad cases. Though, one's just tragic. One's *bad.*" She leaned against him and explained both Rafael and the ghost.

He cringed. "I might be able to help out with the gang killings if the Citycams caught anything. The boy will understand your other inquest has to come first since you're the only one who could possibly do anything about it. If I strike gold and find the brother's killing on video, I could send it over to Div 2 and let them deal with it. It might be a P10, but if there's zero work beyond going to pick the suspect up, they'll do it."

"Sam... There's more." She looked up at him, but closed her mouth as Evan emerged from the hall in his pajamas.

The boy ran over and again hugged them one after the next. "Night, Mom. Night, Sam."

"Night little man." Sam pressed a fist to Evan's shoulder and gave a light push.

"Night, hon." Kirsten kissed him on the cheek.

Evan wandered off to his room. A moment later, the lights went out.

"Not sure where to start, but the longer I wait, the harder it gets. I don't want to ruin what we have."

He brushed a hand over her hair. "I don't think you could, but now I'm almost worried."

"The case is hard for me. More than most."

Sam took her hand in both of his. "If you were a victim of some kind of assault, I won't hold that against you at all. You don't have to worry I'm going to flip out."

"I spent so long thinking I'd done something wrong." Kirsten paused to gather the courage, then continued in a half-whisper. "Two days before the police found me, I was going down the ladder to look for food. This man I'd never seen before met me at the bottom. He seemed friendly. At that age, I was terribly afraid of adults. I wanted to run away, but he kinda blocked me from going anywhere but right back up. He didn't hit me or grab or anything, so I stood there. He had a tin of beef stew. Military rations. Said I could have it if I did something fun with him."

"Damn." He squeezed her hand. "I think I know where this is going. That wasn't your fault, Kirsten. You were, what, twelve?"

"Yeah." She stared at his hands engulfing hers. "At the time, I didn't know anything about anything. I suppose he'd been as gentle as could be given what he did to me. And yes, I know now that stew ration may as well have been a knife at my throat. Mother didn't feed me well, and if I didn't have ghosts helping me find things to eat down there, I wouldn't have made it. Anyone looking at me would clearly know I'd been half starved. How could I say no to real food? I didn't even know what sex was or that I was way too young for it."

"I'm so glad the police found you when they did."

She sent a sad smile into her lap. "I hid in my little cubby for a whole day. When the hunger got too much, I couldn't make myself go back down out of the plate. I thought he'd be there at the bottom of the ladder again... so I risked going up. I had a friend, a boy younger than me. He said the food up top was better. One day, he went up and never came back. I thought he'd been killed or hurt or something. Probably, the police found him and put him into the adoption program, but back then, I assumed the worst had happened. I didn't even know police existed. I crawled up a pipe I could barely fit in, rummaged some trash boxes for food and... I'd been so damn scared of that man, I couldn't bring myself to go back down into the plate... so I slept right there in the alley."

Sam pulled her into his lap and held her.

"Thanks." She rested her head on his shoulder. "I know it could've been worse. He could've grabbed me and done whatever he wanted. But that woman today... maybe I shouldn't have looked into her head. The man with me wasn't violent at all, and other than taking advantage of me starving, didn't force me to do anything. But, the way that woman felt... same. As soon as he started, I wanted to change my mind and tell him to stop. But he let me eat the ration first. I thought it would be stealing if I tried to run away..."

Sam leaned his head against hers. "You're the strongest woman I know. To survive your mother, to survive being alone in the Beneath for two years at that age... heck, you took on *two* literal demons. It's okay to hurt. It's okay to feel the way you do, and I'm right here to help you deal with it."

Kirsten teetered on the verge of tears for a few minutes, but they never quite flowed, pulled back by the relief that Sam wouldn't regard her as dirty or shameful. "Thank you, Sam. I'm still getting used to having someone I can talk about things with."

"Yeah." He let off a wistful sigh. "I fully expected to grow old alone."

"You did not." She poked him in the side.

He raised a hand. "Swear. Basement-dwelling techies aren't exactly in high demand."

"Sam, you're beautiful in more ways than simple appearance." She picked at her nails. "Dorian always told me I was silly for it, but my biggest fear was being alone, too. Evan fixed that, but I can't exactly talk about some things with him."

"You need to start listening to yourself more often." He kissed her atop the head. "You have a beautiful soul, Kirsten Wren."

She looked up into his eyes.

"And the outside matches the inside."

A powerful upwelling of emotions—joy, relief, and love—brought her to tears. She didn't bother trying to act like she had the first clue how to handle the moment, and telling Sam she had no idea how to function in a relationship sounded too pitiful. Just being with him in silence soothed her far more than the SynVod ever had.

"Sorry for being a mess tonight."

"I'd worry more if you ran into a situation like that and it didn't affect you at all."

She winced. "Ugh. I hope I never turn into one of *those* cops. They laughed at that boy's dead brother. Made jokes about a 'squished scorpion' or another dead ganger. And… I'm not going to dwell on that right now. Right now, I want to be right here, with you."

"Your wish is my command."

Kirsten looked up, kissed him, then smiled.

"Too cheesy?"

"A little, but cute. I don't mind. After today, I need cute."

5

TURF WAR

Faces and record sheets passed by in a seemingly endless march the next morning.

The indistinct still-image of the ghost she'd lifted from the Citycam system appeared to be a white male late thirties to early forties with short hair. His face blurred too much to make a positive identification easy, nor did the imprecise suggestion of dark clothing offer any clues to his true age.

Most spirits appeared as they had at the moment of death, a potentially unfortunate quality of the afterlife that could prove awkward in cases of bathtub suicides, sex crime victims, or ghosts like the people Konstantin murdered as sacrifices.

She tapped her finger at her mouth, thinking. *This one's old. He's probably figured out how to change his appearance... but he wouldn't care to when he didn't think anyone could see him.* The search she'd started the previous night still ran, though over 207,000 results had already appeared in a record set that continued to grow by the minute. Even restricting hits to men with a history of sex crimes, going back to the start of the post-Corporate-War recordkeeping time made for a huge search.

Somewhere, a CPU cluster wept quietly to itself waiting for the pain to stop.

"I hate this," muttered Kirsten.

"What's that?" Dorian walked around his desk to stand beside her, arms folded, gazing at the screen.

"That there's so many damn records here it's basically useless. I've got no way to stop this bastard. All I can do is sit here waiting for another victim and hope something happens differently that gives me more information." She grabbed her hair in frustration, but held back the scream. "Ghosts suck. No offense."

He laughed. "I know what you mean. We can be sneaky. It took thousands of years for the living to acknowledge we existed... and only a minority even do now."

"Right. And some of them think it's all the work of a made up devil." She clenched her fists, relaxed, then edited the search parameters to exclude anyone who murdered their victims.

"Don't think he's a killer?"

Kirsten leaned back in her chair, staring at the screens, her arms limp across her lap. "Not really. I mean, I can't say I've read the minds of many rapists before, but there's something odd about this."

"Other than a spirit possessing a woman, making her travel a quarter of the way across West City to a particular dive motel, and engineering her assault?" Dorian pursed his lips. "This is not the work of a sound mind."

She gestured at the army of holo-panels hanging over her desk. "It would take more than a lifetime to check every one of the records coming up."

He patted her on the shoulder. "You're young yet. Plenty of time."

"Argh." She sighed. "I need more information to even start looking. Maybe you have a point about that motel being significant... but I didn't feel anything out of the ordinary except for in that room. And the energy came from his being there. If this ghost spent a lot of time at the place, I would've sensed his residue all over."

Dorian burst into laughter.

Kirsten blushed. "You know what I meant. Residual energy, dammit."

"What you meant and what a dirty mind would hear are different things." He composed himself and rubbed his chin. "Probably not a good idea for you go out there alone. I could check around, see if I can find anything."

She shook her head. "I don't think that location had any special meaning to the ghost. If it had been somewhere he frequented while alive, he'd have haunted it for years. Most likely, he knew of its reputation as a hotspot for sexual assault."

"So…"

"So, I'm going to go check the motel again." Kirsten locked the terminal and stood.

"But that's exactly the wrong place for a young woman to go alone."

She smiled. "I'm not alone. You're with me. Also, I have Suggestion and I'm not afraid to use it—for self-defense."

KIRSTEN SET THE PATROL CRAFT DOWN IN A SQUARE PARKING LOT surrounded by cheap motel.

Four stories of balcony walkways dripped with dosers, prostitutes, and fringers loitering around hundreds of battered red doors. So many bodies lined each level, she could barely see the walls.

"Wow."

"Told you." Dorian raised an eyebrow. "This crowd took off or stayed in their rooms when Div 1 rolled in with three cars. If you go walking around here, there's a good chance you'll be making some ghosts today."

She gestured at the windscreen. "No, I mean, they're actually awake at before nine in the morning. That's shocking."

Dorian blinked, hesitated a few seconds, then looked around again. "Now that you mention it, yeah, that is kinda strange. Maybe they're still awake from last night. Still, not smart to get out of the car here."

"This ghost is powerful enough that I don't need to go into every room to get a read. If I so much as pass the door I should feel something. Though… I'm not too interested in trying to walk along those balconies."

"Considering you'd be naked by the time you reached the first corner, that's probably best."

She smirked at him. "What's that supposed to mean?"

"Highly aggressive pickpocketing."

"My uniform?"

"The people have skills." He winked.

"Okay. New plan." She lifted into the air again and set the car to auto-hover at 800 feet.

After settling in her seat, Kirsten closed her eyes and concentrated on astrally projecting herself out of her body. It took her a few seconds to set frustration aside and find enough calm to perceive the separation between her spirit and flesh. At a mental nudge, she floated free as a vaguely nude energy form of amber light. A thin silver cord emerged from between her eyes, connected back to the same spot on her living body.

"Ahh. Good plan." Dorian smiled, offering a hand. "Shall we?"

She accepted. "Let's."

They dove together down through the bottom of the car, flying to the motel eight stories below. She leveled off at the parking lot and drifted over to the room where the attack happened. Four twentysomething men in varying degrees of dress from nothing at all to the regalia of the 'Deth Express' gang lay passed out among a ridiculous amount of synthbeer canisters and pizza boxes. The table by the window held an assortment of chems: derms, autoinjectors, ampules, and even pills.

Her attention went straight to the bed, engulfed in a miasma of black energy that somewhat resembled fire. Both men draped over it sideways appeared to be experiencing fitful sleep. The naked guy face-down on the floor in the pile of silver canisters slept soundly, as did the dude in his underpants on the sofa with half a pizza over his face.

"Wow... retro." Dorian poked a finger at one pill, making it wobble. "Solids."

Having little interest or curiosity in the chems, Kirsten glided over to the bed. Being astral gave her a slightly different perspective, allowing her to see the energy she could only feel otherwise. She held a glowing amber hand out toward the black 'flames.' They radiated neither heat nor cold, rather, a palpable sense of malice. It gave her the sense of a spectral stain of sorts, a phantasmal footprint in reality more than anything the ghost may have done intentionally.

"This guy is so twisted, his presence here affected reality."

Dorian walked over, frowning. "The bed soaked up the energy he gave off during the attack. Think it's like food?"

"No, he didn't derive energy from this."

"I meant that more in the sense of experiencing food. We're both operating under the assumption that this spirit had been a criminal in life. That's not necessarily true. The man could have developed such an intense craving for sex he could no longer obtain, it drove him to do this? Like possessing a person at a restaurant to remember how it felt to eat."

Kirsten floated around the bed, not wanting to cross over it, and briefly stuck her head into the wall to check out the next room—empty. She pulled back and rotated to face Dorian. "If a ghost simply missed having sex, he'd randomly jump into someone already doing it. This guy targeted Mia at home and brought her 200 miles away to this place."

"True." He set his fists against his hips. "Maybe because she's well off? Bring the princess to the slums? Extra trauma?"

"Could be. I wish I knew why he targeted her."

"You assume there's a reason other than wrong time, wrong place?"

She drifted around the other side of the room, but picked up no trace of paranormal energy there. "I hope that's not it. If so, finding this guy's going to be a chore."

"This one is going to be painful."

"Yeah. C'mon. Let's get out of here before someone starts taking shots at the pat-vee."

Kirsten flew from room to room, too fast to pay much attention to what the people inside them did, unless she picked up a trace of spiritual energy. Other than a handful of recently murdered gang thugs, the vicinity of the motel held nothing of paranormal interest.

She grasped the silver cord and shot back to her body in a second, jolting upright in the seat with a gasp. The disorientation of her surroundings changing so abruptly left her woozy, the world spinning. Fortunately, her astral form had no sense of smell, so whatever horrors lurked in the rooms—especially the one with the black stuff growing in the bathtub—had not stained her memory.

Dorian reappeared beside her. "That was a waste of time, though your thoroughness is an asset."

"Being thorough usually has a payoff." She swiped at the terminal screen, pulling up the results for her search on Rafael's brother's associates.

"Didn't Eze ask you not to let the P10 inquest steal time from your primary duties?"

She shrugged. "It's not like I *can* do anything else at the moment other than waiting for the next victim to show up. Might as well do something productive."

The file showed Juan Miguel Esparza spent most of his time in the company of another Jade Scorpionz member named Nestor Ortega, at least by how often their NetMinis occupied the same location. Kirsten plugged the address into the Navcon and swung the patrol craft around to point in that direction.

"You're frustrated and planning to cheat with telepathy, aren't you?"

"Yep." Kirsten narrowed her eyes. "There will be much cheating."

NESTOR ORTEGA'S ADDRESS LED TO A WORN-DOWN LOOKING CENTURY tower four blocks away from a grey zone.

Despite being nineteen, the man had the look of someone in their later twenties with a thick neck and muscular shoulders. The expression on his most recent booking photo surprised her: he grinned. Granted, he'd been picked up for discharging a firearm in public without due cause, a minor offense on par with a traffic citation—provided it didn't occur in a sector full of high-end businesses or wealthy citizens. There, they'd call it 'public endangerment.'

Kirsten dove out of the traffic lane at the fiftieth story, chasing the Navcon pin that the computer drew in over the world outside as a giant literal pushpin stuck in the side of a 102-story building. The structure lacked roof parking for hovercars, though it did at least have a small flat spot marked for emergency vehicles only. While she couldn't call her presence here responding to an emergency situation, she still visited in an official capacity, so didn't feel too guilty about parking there. Fire suppression units didn't need to land to do their thing, and she left plenty of room for a MedVan to set down beside her patrol craft.

The roof access door led to an elevator smelling of lubricant fluid and sweat. She rode it to the thirty-seventh floor and proceeded to apartment 379. A woman in her later forties answered, surprisingly short—only eye level to Kirsten. Two toddler boys crawled around on the floor behind her, and a thin tween girl sat on the sofa watching something on a holo-screen. Thick, warm air laden with the scent of Mexican food, child, and a hint of fruity 'kid perfume' rolled out from the open door.

"Hi. I'm looking for Nestor Ortega. Just need to talk to him for a sec."

The woman frowned. "What did he do this time?"

Kirsten peeked at the woman's thoughts. Nestor's mother reacted much the way she imagined most parents would to their kid 'misbehaving at school,' likely since Nestor hadn't been arrested (yet) for anything worse than shoplifting, vandalism, randomly shooting inanimate objects, and of course, gang fights. But Div 1 only arrested people for gang fighting as a means to stop the violence of the moment. Most wound up released within a day or two, unless they attacked the police.

"I'm not here about anything he may or may not have done, Mrs. Ortega. A friend of his was recently killed. I'm investigating that... wanted to talk to Nestor about what he knows of it."

"Oh." Mrs. Ortega's posture relaxed. "He's probably downstairs either in the lobby, the courtyard, or out behind the building with his friends. I think he'll be surprised anyone's bothering. They don't usually put much effort into crimes around here."

"We're overwhelmed," said Kirsten with a bit of a sigh.

"And the law works better for people with money." Dorian wandered past the wall into the apartment.

Both toddler boys looked up at him, turning their heads to follow as he went by. The maybe-eleven-year-old girl on the sofa showed no reaction. Curious, Kirsten surface-skimmed the boys. They saw a light ball go by... perhaps a product of them being so little. But, neither had any trace of psionic ability.

"At least you're honest about the police here." Mrs. Ortega shook her head. "Juan Miguel was almost like a brother to Nestor. How's his little brother, Rafael, doing?"

Kirsten's heart sank. "He's... well, he's off the street."

Mrs. Ortega's eyebrows went up. "Oh, no. He was always such a nice boy."

"They always say that," called Dorian from deeper in the apartment.

"He's not hurt. But he's in a bit of trouble." Kirsten tried to stay positive. "Still, he's safe."

"Oh, that's good." Mrs. Ortega put a hand over her heart, smiling. "Rafael's a nice, quiet boy. Some other boys from the building were giving my daughter Julie some trouble. I don't know what Rafael said to them, but they haven't come near her since."

The girl on the couch laughed. "He told them to go away and leave me alone... and if they wanted to grab a butt, grab each other's butts." She laughed again. "Julio grabbed Eddie's ass, and they like got into this big fight."

"That was... nice of him." Kirsten fought hard to keep a straight face.

Dorian reappeared and walked out into the hall. "Nestor's not in there. Wonder if his gang buddies know he still lives with his mom."

"Thank you, Mrs. Ortega. I'll see if he's downstairs."

The woman nodded. "All right."

A few steps away from the door, Kirsten snickered at the 'lives with his mom' remark.

"I suppose that's a fairly tame thing to do with Suggestion, but the boy is young." Dorian whistled innocently. "What do you suppose that hotel man you told to go eff himself would've done if you didn't stop him?"

Kirsten shivered. "One: that was an accident. I didn't mean it to be a command. Two: I don't want to know."

She stepped into the elevator and rode it to the lobby. The instant the doors opened, a weak eerie feeling prickled at her senses. Kirsten peered out at a mostly empty room, save for a crude doll receptionist—a torso and arms on a post—which had seen better days. Five dosers lay here and there, propped up against the walls, all high enough to be staring into the eighth dimension. None paid any attention to her as she crossed the lobby to a hallway that led past several utility rooms to the alley behind the building.

Seven people loitered around, sitting on dumpsters, old boxes, or the railing by the basement access of the building across the street. All wore some manner of green, from logo jackets with the Jade Scorpionz symbol to green belts or earrings.

Nestor Ortega turned out to be quite a bit shorter than she expected from his photo, barely a half inch taller than her, though his arms looked thicker than her thighs. At the sight of her emerging from the building, he smiled and waved.

The others glanced at her with varying degrees of 'hey what's up' or indifference.

Kirsten walked over to them. "Nestor, right?"

He nodded. "Yeah. Hey girl."

A few of the Scorpionz regarded her with confusion.

"Yo, that a real uniform?" asked a twentyish teal-haired woman sitting on the railing. Her large cyan eyes brimmed with interest as she studied the lines of Kirsten's body.

"Sure is." The young man beside her in a Jade Scorpionz hoodie raised his head enough to reveal striking amber irises. "The cops have psionics, too. She's one of 'em."

A thin guy and a busty teen girl on the far right stiffened, radiating nervousness at the mention of psionics.

"They why you bailed on that other group you ran with?" asked the girl with teal hair.

"Nah. Dude running it was legit psycho." He stuffed his hands in the front pocket of his hoodie. "Couldn't shake the feeling a shitstorm was coming."

Kirsten glanced at him. Division 0 protocol required trying to talk psionics into joining, though she suspected he'd already been given the sales pitch. "We talk to you already?"

He nodded.

"So, what brings you out here?" Nestor stepped closer, offering a handshake.

"This guy seems oddly friendly," said Dorian. "Unusual for a street gang. They're not often happy to see the police. But... he probably knows Zero won't bust their balls."

Kirsten accepted the handshake, reading nothing from the guy's surface thoughts to indicate hostility. "I'm looking into Juan Miguel's death. Trying to collect information that might help me figure out who killed him."

Nestor's smile evaporated to an expression of grimness. "You for real?"

"Yeah."

The other Scorpionz murmured in surprise.

"Yo," said the teal-haired girl. "You involved 'cause Juan was psionic?"

"Dude couldn't have been psionic." The busty teen rolled her eyes. "He never saw it coming."

Nestor shot her a dire glare.

"Not cool, Val." The amber-eyed man sighed. "We don't all see the future. And no, I don't either."

Kirsten cleared her throat to get their attention. "I hadn't known Juan was psionic, but it makes sense given his brother is."

"What happened to the little guy?" asked Nestor. "Haven't seen him in a while."

"He's why I'm on this case. Rafael's safe, but he got into a little trouble attempting to force a couple cops to find the killer."

The Scorpionz all cringed at once.

"He seems like a good kid. I'm sure he'll be fine. But, I also promised him I'd find who killed his brother."

Nestor shook his head rapidly. "Don't you go believin' any of that bullshit about this bein' some kinda turf war. Juan Miguel vanished for like a week. Then his body turned up here. Alex"—he nodded to indicate the guy with amber eyes—"said he felt real fucked up around the spot."

"You think Juan Miguel may have been abducted?" asked Kirsten.

"Something like that, yeah. He wouldn't have gone off and left Rafael alone like that. Not unless he got arrested or some shit." Nestor paced about, muttering to himself. "Just dunno why anyone would've taken him out. Juan Miguel didn't have no static with no one."

Dorian tilted his head. "Does that mean he had static with someone, or...?"

"Do you have any idea who would've done it?" asked Kirsten.

"Had to be some random shit. Maybe some dumbass who sees a dude wearin' colors but don't know shit about us so he thinks he's bein' a vigilante or somethin'."

Kirsten held her left arm up to access the terminal and opened the record for Juan Miguel's case. "They found him not too far from here."

"Yeah." Nestor pointed down the alley. "Right over there."

"Mind showing me the spot? Maybe he's lingering around."

Alex looked up again. "Lingering around? What, like a ghost?"

Kirsten nodded.

"You see one around here? Kinda getting that same weird feeling I did around his body, but not as strong." Alex scanned the area, but didn't appear to see Dorian.

"Yes, but not Juan Miguel." Kirsten started walking down the alley.

Nestor pushed away from the wall he'd been leaning on and hurried to catch up. "Pretty sure someone dumped him there, covered him up, too. No one around here heard anything happen."

The medical examiner's report indicated the cause of death as a stab wound, so silence didn't necessarily prove he'd been killed elsewhere. Kirsten closed the terminal and followed the Scorpionz down two blocks and over one. A sense of eeriness grew stronger as they neared the spot. Alex, who'd decided to tag along at the rear, fidgeted and kept looking over his shoulder. He reminded her of a little boy afraid to go into the basement alone. When they rounded the last corner and Nestor pointed at a spot of ground, the intensity of the dark energy in the air took on a familiar tone.

Abyssal.

Kirsten looked back at him. *I feel it, too.*

Demasiado extraño, replied Alex via telepathy.

She sighed out her nose. *Not weird... evil. I've felt this before. Something from the abyss was here.*

His cheeks faded from light brown to Marsborn white.

"Here." Nestor kicked at a battered dumpster. "Juan Miguel was on the ground beside this, covered in trash."

Kirsten looked around at the alley. Though it had been saturated in dark energy—enough to put even the non-psionics around her on edge— no paranormal entities other than Dorian appeared anywhere she could see. She squinted up at a couple of Citycam pods on poles, then at the ground where the body had been.

"No idea what happened, but it was fubar." Nestor spat to the side.

The energy shifted to a sense of being watched.

She pivoted toward the impression of sentience, but whatever entity checked her out remained too bashful to show itself. Kirsten concentrated on wanting to see the entity in an effort to overwhelm a spirit trying to hide from her, but it didn't help. It had to be behind a wall or in a patch of darkness, like any ordinary person trying to remain unseen.

She accessed her armband terminal again placing a vid call to Samuel Chang. In a moment, his face appeared. "Hey. Can you do me a favor and check the Citycams around me for sixteen days ago. A murder victim was found where I'm standing now."

"Sure thing. Give me a few minutes." Sam smiled at her then looked off to the side at another screen.

"There's something here, isn't there?" asked Val. "Feels so messed up. Like someone's staring at me and they wanna do something bad."

Again, Kirsten turned, looking at every shadow. "Some spirits don't like the living hanging around places they've claimed. This feels like how they scare people away. Radiant fear. I don't see anything."

"Bad energy in this place," said Alex.

"Maybe you can find it. Your ass is awakened, right?" Val poked him.

Kirsten raised both eyebrows. "What?"

"Naw." Alex sighed. "Used to be in a gang that called themselves that. Just an ordinary psionic."

Nestor laughed. "Ordinary and psionic…"

"But your eyes," said the busty teen. "Don't that mean you're like über or something?"

"Some of them have weird eyes, yeah. I had mine modded to throw people off." Alex smiled. "But the dude runnin' that show? He's all kinds of fucked up. Don't trust it."

"If you have any information about him, you should really go talk to some of my associates." Kirsten walked around the alley, reaching out her paranormal feelers. "That group is a serious threat to psionics as a whole."

"I don't know much more than not wanting to associate with 'em." Alex shrugged. "Never saw the dude in person. He kept some of us split up in smaller groups out there looking for more members. Had a main compound, but I didn't go there. He says everyone is free to leave if they disagree with his vision, but rumor said he abducted some kid against her will 'cause she had some crazy powerful ability. Little, too. Like ten or so."

The other Scorpionz grumbled.

"Got something for you," said Sam.

Kirsten raised her arm again. "Wow. Really?"

"Yep." Sam smiled. "The killers didn't appear too concerned with who saw what. Here's the video feed."

Another window opened on the floating panel, containing a view of this alley from one of the nearby pole cameras. Ten seconds after playback started, a beat-up black van decorated with a red pentagram on the side pulled to a stop. Five men in black jackets bearing the red pentagram logo of the Diablos gang hopped out, opened the back doors, and dragged the nude corpse of Juan Miguel Esparza out. They unceremoniously tossed him against the wall, threw as much trash as they could grab on top of him, then got back into the van and drove off.

Nestor, close enough to watch the video, erupted in a storm of Spanish obscenities.

"That does look like gang violence." Dorian gestured at the image. "But… Diablos don't usually kill people they abduct."

Kirsten shuddered. She'd only gone through the 'basic' training on gangs since her position with Division 0 didn't normally involve much contact with them. Still, the Diablos stood out in her memory. Not only did their fixation on mythology tweak that same nerve that Mother did, but she also remembered the instructor describing how they abducted random people off the street, tortured them for days, weeks, or even months until they shattered mentally… then released them alive.

It didn't surprise her that Division 1 more or less shot Diablos on sight. Of course, Diablos frequently fired on cops first.

"I'll try to see if I can get some faces from the video." Sam looked off screen again while typing. "But, don't hold your breath. These guys aren't usually in the system."

"Thanks, Sam." Kirsten let her arm fall to her side, the screen turning itself off. *No wonder Div 2 let this one sit. Diablos…*

"Damn." Nestor shook his head. "Didn't think those crazy bastards gave a shit about revenge."

"Revenge? Did Juan Miguel have a prior issue with them?" asked Kirsten.

"Not personally. Couple of those freaks came by here like a month ago. Figure they had a probie with 'em and he needed a kill or two to get in. So they saw us and started shooting. We got lucky. No one bit it."

"What about them?"

He chuckled at her. "See all them holes in the van? Dunno if we sent any of them to their little devil man, but there had ta be blood. Guess they did come back to get revenge after all. Still doesn't feel right."

Kirsten surveyed the darker parts of the alley around them, certain something still watched. "Yeah. There's more going on here than a pissing contest."

"You still gonna get the fuckers who did this, right?" Nestor rested a hand on her shoulder, staring into her eyes.

"Dude," said the busty teen. "There's like shitloads of Diablos. She'll never find the one who stabbed him."

Alex smirked. "Normal cops couldn't. Bet she will." He stared at her.

"Dude!" She jumped back. "Knock that shit off, you know it freaks me out."

"Tara..." Nestor cackled. "Why do you think he does it?"

"I don't wanna like get brain cancer or shit." Tara scowled. She gasped, stared at Alex, and yelled, "I *do* have a brain, you asshole."

He grinned.

Kirsten looked around at the Scorpionz. "I'm guessing none of you know these particular Diablos or where they hang out?"

"Wish I did, but nah." Nestor folded his arms. "'Course, you find 'em and want a couple extra guns, give me a call."

"Thanks, but bringing civilians along on a raid is outside the regs." She attempted a trick handshake, which made them all laugh. "But I appreciate the offer. And yeah, I will find the guy. I promised Rafael."

In a moment of solemn quiet, the Scorpionz all bowed their heads.

"It's strange that his ghost isn't here," said Dorian.

Kirsten gave him the side eye, but didn't say what she thought until after she got back to the elevator leading to the roof where she'd parked. As soon as the doors closed, she faced him. "I'm really not liking where this is going. Abyssal energy, dead to a knife wound, no sign of a ghost..."

"You're thinking what I'm thinking?"

"Yeah." She hung her head. "Another damn demon."

6

THE LEGEND

E van daydreamed about a Monwyn quest he wanted to run later while pushing a cleaning rag around a desk.

He'd been doing tons of after-school work to burn off citizenship points for the past few weeks. Plenty of cleaning, some dusting, sorting crap in the Archives, nothing particularly exciting, dangerous, or difficult. This classroom had huge desks, meant for older teens, so he had to climb up to stand on the seat to reach the surface.

Shawn Fields and Walter Jordan, two other boys from his third grade class, joined him today along with an older girl who he figured for a sixth-grader. She had a sullen quiet air about her, grinding her cleaning rag into the wall as if to punish it for her situation. Her attitude made him want to talk to her as much as it scared him away. He wanted to ask what put her in such a bad mood.

Walter and Shawn had been in and out of citizenship point time over the past few weeks. As usual, they both had on the same baggy grey pants and plain lighter grey tops given to kids who lived in the dorms. Neither had gotten as many points Evan pulled, but Shawn, big for nine, got in trouble a lot and Walter always followed him. They'd started off picking on Evan for being a 'wimpy astral,' but wound up on friendly terms. Shawn's father had slapped him around a lot as well, though at least his parents had never locked him in his bedroom.

Concern won out over fear, so Evan cleaned desks in a path that brought him closer to the girl, watching her swipe a dusting wand at the wall. She wore a purple pleated mini-dress over tight black leggings that reminded him of Mom's uniform pants. Her high sneakers had a cartoon rabbit on the sides holding up a middle finger over the word Netßunny.

"Hey, what's up?"

The girl ignored him.

"*Hola! Cómo estás?*" asked Evan.

"We're not supposed to talk," muttered the girl, most of her light brown face concealed under a black bob. "And I'm not Spanish."

"They just don't want us getting loud and sounding like we're having fun. Besides, Mr. Short isn't even in here watching us." Evan spritzed cleaning solution on a desk and wiped it around in an expanding circle. "Sorry you're sad."

"Don't mind him," called Shawn from the other side of the room. "Little Man's like half empath."

The girl twisted to peer at Shawn, then at him. He froze, never having seen such a vibrant shade of emerald in anyone's eyes before.

"I'm not sad. I'm pissed off," said the girl.

"Cit points aren't that bad." He grunted, scrubbing at a stubborn dark spot. "Just boring. I'm Evan. What's your name?"

"I'm mad at getting caught." She swiped a duster at the wall, then moved a few steps to the right to start on a shelf of boxes. "Maela."

"Cool." Evan smiled.

Shawn paused his mopping to grin at her. "What are you in for?"

"What about you guys?" Maela kept dusting.

"Talking back to a teacher." Shawn shrugged and resumed mopping. "Only got forty points. We called this other girl dumb."

"We weren't trying to be mean." Walter snickered. "Hayley isn't smart."

"You're new, right?" Evan smiled over at her. Standing on the seat, he wound up a little taller than her. "Never saw you before in the cafeteria."

Maela jabbed the duster at the shelf like a sword. "Yeah. Just got here."

"Wow. Cit points your first week? That's epic." Shawn raised a fist in salute.

"It's not bad here." Evan hopped down from the desk and moved to the next one.

Maela flopped in place and hung her head, seeming out of breath.

Walter looked up from air-dusting a desk terminal. "You okay?"

"Yeah. Just a bit tired. Still not used to it here."

"It isn't *that* bad." Shawn shot her an odd look. "How's dusting make you tired?"

Maela stretched. "Existing makes me tired. I'm from Mars. Everything's so heavy here. They said I'll adjust in a couple of months."

"No way," said Walter with a big grin. "You're messing with us. People from Mars are as white as this wall. Even paler than Little Man."

Evan swiveled to look at him. "You're the same size as me."

"You're skinny." Walter flexed his—not too impressive—bicep. "We may be the same height, but you're still smaller."

Maela sighed. "Not everyone from Mars has the bleach job."

"Bleach job?" asked Shawn. "I thought it's 'cause they all live in tunnels like moles or something."

She shook her head. "No. It was some political thing university students did generations ago. Genetic modification."

"So, what'd you do to get points?" Shawn leaned the mop on a desk and walked over.

"Have you been missing class?" She peered up at him.

"No..."

Evan laughed. "Shawn's in third with us. He's just huge."

Maela gawked. "You're nine?"

"He is. His dad's a mutant from the Badlands." Walter wobbled around, miming a troll.

Shawn flipped him off.

"Didn't feel like doing homework, so I just changed records to make it look like I finished it all." Maela shrugged. "Stupid Mrs. Grey caught me. It's not fair the teacher's psionic, too."

All three boys laughed.

"Well, this *is* the dorm for psionic kids." Shawn threw an arm around Evan. "Wren here holds the record for the most cit points ever awarded in one shot in the history of the school. Five hundred."

"Holy shit." Maela blinked.

The boys all chuckled at her language.

"I'm almost finished with them." Evan couldn't wait to be free from the stink of cleaning solution. The smell had even started to invade his dreams. "Only have like eighty left."

Maela whistled. "They only gave me thirty."

"Little Man is a legend." Walter wandered over to play-punch Evan in the shoulder. "No one will ever get that many that fast again."

"I took points from—" He froze, feeling watched. A moment's

concentration activated Astral Seeing, and the wall behind Maela lit up from the pale white glow in his eyes. He turned in place, looking around, but the room appeared devoid of ghosts despite feeling like one had joined them.

"What the hell?" Maela cringed back, pressing herself into the wall. "Your eyes are on fire."

"He's doing the ghost thing again." Shawn eyed the back corner of the room. "Feels creepy in here now."

"Ghost thing?" asked Maela, her voice quivering.

"I'm an astral. I can see and talk to ghosts. They show up sometimes asking for help. Mostly, they just want me to tell people stuff before they go away. Feels like there's one around, but I don't see them."

Walter opened a panel on the next desk terminal and shot it with the air blast to knock dust out of the components. "You let somethin' loose again?"

"No." Evan shook his head. "Might be a ghost wandering around, already went through the wall before I turned my eyes on."

"Still creepy in here." Maela relaxed and resumed dusting the shelves. "Just thought it felt weird because this hallway is empty. Places like this are scary when there's no one around."

Evan smiled to himself at the worried expression on Shawn's face. Despite his size, he frightened pretty easily—especially from supernatural things. "Two more desks."

"Last terminal," said Walter.

Maela puffed air at the shelf. "I'm done. This is stupid anyway. Why are they making you mop? There's bots for that."

"It's just some chores to do." Shawn smeared dirty water around the floor in a back-and-forth pattern. "The bots are gonna come out and clean it again as soon as we leave. We're not here to clean anything, just to kill time doing something un-fun."

"Bots don't wipe desks or dust shelves." Evan moved to the next desk.

A shadow moving near the back of the room made him spin. He caught a hint of face and shoulder sinking into the wall. The sudden motion startled a yelp out of Maela. Her unexpected yell made Shawn jump.

"Dude, not cool." Shawn frowned. "Talk about ghosts then scream like that."

"I didn't scream," said Maela with a superior tone. "I was simply startled and—"

"Screamed," deadpanned Walter.

"*No.*" Maela sighed. "It's like a yelp or something. I'd show you what a real scream is, but we'll get in trouble for making noise."

"Whatever." Shawn laughed.

"Just… don't talk about ghosts and jump like that." She pointed at Evan. "And those glowing eyes are creepy."

"Sorry." He continued looking at the wall. "I saw someone peering in at us."

"Ghost?" Walter's expression lit up with eagerness. "Cool. Who is it?"

"I dunno. Just saw like half a face."

"Eww!" Maela cringed.

"No… not like 'cut off' half a face, like part of a face sticking out from the wall." Evan sprayed the second-to-last desk down and wiped fast, not liking the mood radiating from the spirit. "I don't think he's a nice ghost."

Everyone hurried the last of their chores, except Maela who considered herself done already.

Once he finished the desks, Evan jogged over to the wall terminal by the door and paged Mr. Short, a teacher from the Admin group who supervised the afternoon's citizenship point crew—from across the building and three floors down.

The holographic head of a twenty-something man in the ubiquitous clingy black uniform appeared in front of the panel, wearing a senshelmet with the eye-blocker shield lifted up to expose his face. "Hey, kid. What's up?"

"Hi Mr. Short," said Evan. "We're done in here. Ready for you to check it out."

"Oh, cool." The hologram head stretched up, pivoted around, then shrank back with a smile. "Looks good. C'mon back down here so you can do the thumbprint thing."

"Okay. We'll be right there." Evan smiled and hung up.

"Aren't you supposed to salute him or some bogus thing like that?" asked Maela.

Evan turned away from the console. "Nope. I'm not a cadet and he's not an officer."

"Besides, only the buttheads make little kids salute them." Walter rolled his eyes.

"Okay, cool. So we're done? I kinda wanna get outta here." Maela edged toward the door, giving the back of the room a wary stare.

"Yeah, me too," said Shawn in an uncharacteristically timid voice.

Evan and Shawn locked eyes for a second, another mutual note of agreement that the secret of Shawn having a teddy bear would not leave Evan's lips. Since he didn't fear the spirit anywhere near as much as the other kids, he let them all go out into the hall first, keeping watch on the corner. Whoever it was, they didn't show themselves.

He feels mean. I should tell Mom about him later.

Shawn led the way past a bunch of empty classrooms and labs used by the high school kids to the elevator at the far end of the corridor. White plastisteel with all the warmth of a hospital surrounded them, making the eeriness of emptiness stronger. The continuous paranormal energy intensified the sense of dread flooding the area. By the time they reached the plain white door marked 'Level 04,' Shawn, Walter, and Maela all clung to each other, not quite trembling.

"You see anything?" whispered Walter. "*Something* is definitely here."

Evan twisted around to look down the hall. "Nope. He's hiding."

"He who?" asked Maela.

"I dunno. A ghost. Maybe he's mad for being a ghost." Evan faced the hall and cupped his hands around his mouth. "Hey, I can see and talk to you. If you need help, let me know." His voice echoed a few times to silence.

The other three kids stood in the corner by the elevator, watching in rapt silence.

"Nope." Evan poked the elevator button. "That means he probably wants to mess with us."

"Can they hurt us?" asked Shawn.

"Old ones can, but this one isn't that old."

Maela eyed the corridor. "How do you know that?"

"I can feel it. Old ones give off more power. This guy is too new to do anything to us. He's just being a creepy butthead." Evan folded his arms. "He thinks he's scary."

Ping.

The other three all jumped.

Evan grinned, but held back the laugh.

They filed into the elevator. Shawn hit the button for the ground floor. The doors closed again. In seconds, light pulses slid up the four corners of the cube-shaped chamber, a visual indicator of going down. The numeric display at the top of the panel ticked from four, to three, to two, to one, then negative one, negative two, negative three.

"You hit the wrong button," said Walter. "We want the first floor, not the basement."

"There's no basement." Maela looked up at the ceiling. "We're down inside the plate."

"We're not allowed here." Evan poked the button for the ground floor.

"No shit." Shawn also hit the button. "And I didn't hit the wrong one."

"You had to have." Walter flailed his arms. "Why else would we be down here?"

The elevator reached the negative fifth floor.

"Dude!" shouted Shawn. "It's totally going the wrong way."

"Stop hitting the wrong button," snapped Maela.

Shawn whirled on her. "I'm not! These floors are restricted. It shouldn't even let us go here."

"I think the ghost did it." Evan stared down at his Monwyn the Magnificent T-shirt, the mage in a dramatic pose with fire streaming from his outstretched hand.

"Hey…" Walter nudged Maela. "You're a techno, right? *Make* the thing take us up."

"O-okay." She reached out and pressed her hand on the panel, her nails flaked with mostly-worn-off black polish.

"That's really cool the way they can plug into machines just by touching them." Shawn nodded.

"Dude, quiet," whispered Evan. "Let her concentrate."

The elevator hung in silence for a moment, save for soft breathing.

Sparks erupted from the panel with a loud buzzing crackle. Maela jumped back, screaming and waving her hand. Sudden acceleration threw all four kids to the floor as the elevator shot upward. Evan landed sprawled on top of Shawn. He pushed himself up to look at the counter. It stopped at -1.

"Better than neg five," whispered Shawn.

Another burst of sparks flew from the console.

Evan leapt up and hammered the 'door open' button, but it didn't work. The spectral fingers of a black glove appeared, then sank back into the metal.

The lights went out.

Everyone screamed as they plummeted for a few seconds, then jerked to a stop, again crashing into a tangled pile of limbs. Someone's sneaker hit Evan in the side of the head.

Maela emitted a loud *oof,* then yelled, "Get off meeeeeeeee!"

The elevator dropped again, turning her demand into another scream.

Near weightlessness came to a harsh end with a loud metallic *boom* and the elevator cab tilting slightly to the left. Evan crashed down on top of someone else, though he couldn't tell who. His elbow hit something soft, and a wheezing gasp flooded his right ear.

Silence.

Evan waited two breaths before asking, "Anyone hurt?"

"Umm. Ouch, but I don't think serious," said Maela.

"I'm good." Shawn grunted. "Sorry. Can't see anything. Not like I tried to land on top of you."

"Ow," whispered Walter. "My balls."

Evan activated Darksight; his surroundings appeared in a wavering sepia-toned blur. He glanced down at his elbow in Walter's crotch, and moved it. "Oops. Sorry."

Skinny Maela looked like a gummy bear run over by a truck, splayed out on the floor with Shawn crawling off her. A little blood ran down her chin from her lip.

"Crap, you broke the elevator," said Shawn, in as un-accusing a tone as possible for such a statement.

Maela sat up, gazing around blind in the dark. She appeared frightened and on the verge of erupting in tears. "Sorry."

Everyone jumped at another *bzzt* and flash of sparks from the control panel.

"She didn't mess up. The ghost did it." Evan looked down at where his hands touched the floor, and concentrated on Blockade. As soon as he sensed the power take effect, the lights came back on.

A male voice outside the elevator growled.

Shawn grabbed the handrail on the side and pulled himself up before offering a hand to Maela. Walter curled up on his side, cradling his groin.

Evan stood, scowling at the door. "I made it so ghosts can't come in here."

"Is it broken?" Shawn pointed at the floor display showing 'ER.'

"Yeah it's fried." Maela held on to the railing to keep from sliding. "We're tilted. This elevator isn't going back up ever again."

Walter and Shawn fell quiet.

Another spark sizzled out of the control panel. The doors snapped open with a loud metal scrape, revealing a man dressed in a long black coat over an armored vest, also black. Shawn and Maela both yelled in surprise at the doors moving, but didn't react to the man.

Evan clenched his hands into fists, worried at seeing a ghost ignore a Blockade. They shouldn't be able to open doors... but he realized the spirit had only tweaked a circuit, not actually touched the door. Still, he did *not* like this ghost, and missed his mother. "What do you want?"

The man scowled, stepping into the elevator and grabbing him around the throat. His strangulation grip squeezed with less force than a dress shirt collar.

"Whoa. It just got creepy in here again." Shawn backed against the innermost wall.

"Ghost's here, trying to choke me," said Evan in a calm voice. "He hasn't been a ghost very long."

Snarling, the spirit abandoned his attempt to choke him to death, took a step back, and exploded into a mangled mass of smashed limbs with a crushed head and dangling eyeballs.

Evan cringed. "Eww. Are you trying to scare us or something?"

He collected himself back to a relatively normal appearance, and glowered, pointing. "That bitch did this to me, and she's going to regret it."

"I can help you. Just tell me who you need to send a message to and I'll make sure they get it."

"Damn, kid. You're as dense as your mother."

Evan blinked. "My *mom* killed you?"

"Now he gets it." The man grumbled. "Damn elevator didn't work."

"That's because you broke it." Evan tapped his foot.

The other three kids stared in silence. The feathery tickle of surface reads poked at his brain. He let them all in so they could see the guy, too —via his thoughts.

"It was *supposed* to break through the bottom and fall fifty meters so you went splat like I did."

Evan nodded toward the others. "Why do you want to hurt them?"

"Collateral damage. Nothing personal." Again, he tried strangling him, but couldn't manage much of a solid grip.

"At least let them go back up." Evan poked at the control panel, to no effect.

"Bit late for that, kid." The man gave up trying to choke him and pointed. "Sit tight. I'll be back with some friends."

He stormed off to the left, revealing a narrow metal-walled passage with a grating mesh floor, pipes everywhere, and numerous signs warning of 'restricted area' and 'hardhat required.'

Evan narrowed his eyes at the departing spirit.

"Hey, Little Man," whispered Shawn. "What did he mean by getting friends?"

"Umm. I dunno. Maybe he's going to look for an older ghost who can affect the living. Or, he's gonna lure monsters to us."

"There's no monsters down here. That's all made up." Walter rolled onto his back, wheezing. "Damn that hurt. I think my nuts are smashed."

Shawn emitted a nervous laugh. "What?"

"Someone ran me over like a truck," said Maela. "And I think those are my teeth marks on your forehead."

"Umm." Shawn rubbed his forehead. "You're bleeding."

"Bit my lip. No big deal." She tugged Evan back from the door. "Stay calm. We just need to sit here and wait."

"Wait? What for?" asked Walter.

"For someone to notice the elevator crashed and send help."

Shawn wagged his eyebrows. "Or for monsters to find us."

7

MORE DEMONS

Kirsten fell heavily into her chair at the squad room, glaring at her terminal.

Fortunately, the case had gone from worst case scenario—anyone could've done it—to merely an awful one: four unidentified Diablos. But, they'd only dropped off the body. The killer could've been someone else entirely. She planned to find them and hopefully prolong the inevitable shootout enough to pluck the identity of the actual killer from their thoughts. Of course, even finding those four particular Diablos would be a task.

"Someone dumping a body has to know who killed the guy, right?" she whispered mostly to herself.

"If we were investigating the Syndicate, I'd say not necessarily. But these clowns? Probably." Dorian sat on the side of her desk, arms folded. "More than likely, one of those four did it."

She reached forward and opened the medical examiner's report on Juan Miguel Esparza. The remains had already been cremated and sent off to a mass grave, standard procedure for anyone with no family to claim the ashes. Whether or not it was true, she pictured a giant chamber with a single mound of ashes in the middle, the commingled remnants of thousands of people too poor to matter to 'society.' The 'mass grave' might consist of a storage room filled with small boxes of individual ash, but after her run in with Senator Winchester, it seemed unlikely the government would spend the money.

She sighed at herself.

"What now?"

"Disposed of the remains already. Can't check out the body."

"That sigh was too introspective for that." Dorian teased her with a half-smile.

Kirsten glanced sideways at him. "Just annoyed at the mass grave thing. You know, in all the years I've been seeing spirits, I've never run into one who had been upset about 'improper burial.'"

"Of course not. What defines a burial as improper? Mostly mythology. Dumping a body on the side of the road or in an alley is considered bad, but throwing one overboard at sea or blowing them out an airlock in space is somehow proper?"

"I don't really know why people decided this crap. Just that no ghost I've ever run into has been lingering because they weren't buried on sanctified ground or no one muttered the funny words over the grave."

"But you *have* encountered sanctified ground."

Kirsten crossed her arms on the desk and set her forehead down on them. "I can't explain that."

"It bothers you that it appeared to exist?"

"If an engine falls off an intercoastal shuttle and lands on some tribal out in the Badlands, his friends will think some magical sky man decided he should die. Random objects from the clouds don't prove a conscious action from a nonexistent higher power. The interior of a so-called church destroying an abyssal doesn't necessarily prove the existence of a higher power either."

"So, Father Villera had garden variety incendiary linoleum installed?"

She couldn't help herself and laughed. "No... I mean, maybe those Seraphim saw him and liked him and decided to help out. Yeah, there are two opposing forces on the other side, but that doesn't mean there's like a king or whatever. It doesn't make any sense. Why wouldn't something like that make itself known? Especially if it demands worship?"

"I can't answer that. Haven't stuck my head through that door yet. Sometimes I think there may be something out there akin to a creative force, but it's so vast and incomprehensible to us, communication is impossible. Like a human looking at an anthill."

"What the heck is an anthill?" She lifted her head off her arms.

"All that time you spent in the Beneath as a kid and you don't know what an anthill is?"

"Oh... you mean those little dirt piles with the ants crawling on them?"

"Yeah. The ants probably didn't have much awareness of you standing there looking at them. You couldn't talk to them."

She chuckled. "Nor do I particularly care if they gather in an expensive building once a week. Any ant that claims I want them to do something is lying for personal gain."

Dorian snickered.

With a sigh, she leaned her chin on her hand and re-read the file. The autopsy report indicated Juan Miguel died to a single stab wound in the heart approximately twenty-four days ago. Bruising and cuts consistent with metal binders were found on his wrists, along with several bruises around the left eye socket, broken ribs, and some missing teeth. The medical examiner's opinion stated that she believed the decedent suffered a beating that likely rendered him unconscious prior to receiving the fatal wound.

"Hmm. They found him a little more than two weeks ago. He'd been missing for two weeks before his body turned up, so the Diablos didn't keep him around long after killing him. And... if this *was* some kind of revenge issue, they'd have just shot him where he stood."

"I agree." Dorian hopped off the desk and proceeded to pace around. "Perhaps we should open ourselves to the idea that the Diablos we saw disposing of the body were not, in fact, actual Diablos."

Kirsten grabbed her head in both hands. "What are you saying now?"

"Maybe Juan Miguel had gotten involved in something over his head and someone wanted him disposed of. What better way to make an investigation go nowhere than to cast blame on a gang so notoriously psychotic that almost everything involving them goes straight to Division 6 when it's not simply thrown into the 'oh, fuck that' basket."

She pulled at her hair for a second before flopping back, feeling overwhelmed. "Exactly what could a kid like Juan Miguel get involved with that anyone would go to this length to get rid of him? Hell, he ran with a street gang, even one as... tame as the Scorpionz. They could've just shot him and it probably would've sat in P10 hell forever. In order for anyone to have checked the Citycam feed to see the Diablos dumping him, an investigator would've had to actually *take* the case."

"That only rules out anyone who would understand the inner

workings of Division 2. The public at large doesn't know murdered gang members tend to be ignored."

"Argh! Investigating a case is supposed to narrow it down, not make it seem harder."

"Now you understand why most Division 2 detectives wind up either drunk or in mental health care." He chuckled.

She side-eyed him again. "That drunk detective thing is a stupid cliché."

"Just like cops and donuts." He grinned. "Doesn't mean no cop ever eats a donut."

Again, Kirsten read over the file. Stab wound to the heart. Handcuff marks on the body. Abyssal-tainted energy at the murder site. It all felt far too familiar.

Emitting a continuous mutter of "no more demons," she bent forward and banged her head on the desk over and over, though not hard enough to hurt—much.

"Most cops use booze for that," said Morelli.

"See?" Dorian gestured at him. "Now please stop that before you hurt yourself."

"What happened to Konstantin's mask?" Kirsten sat up, swiped her hands at the screens to move the search aside, and opened the screen to start a new one.

"In the Archives."

"Still?"

Dorian walked to his desk and stuck his hand into the terminal. When it turned on, Morelli jumped with a yelp. Kurosawa and Montez startled at him almost falling out of his chair.

"Jeez, Tom," muttered Kurosawa, hand on her chest. "Marsh's ghost has been in this room for years and you *still* haven't gotten used to it?"

"I'm a he, thank you very much," muttered Dorian.

"I think she meant 'it' in terms of the situation of your being here," said Kirsten.

Montez snickered.

"Yeah." Kurosawa looked toward the empty desk. "That's what I meant."

Kirsten keyed in a search for any murder victims cataloged during the past three months with similar injuries to Juan Miguel. The system came back with sixteen matches. She skimmed over each one, eliminating cases where the victim had been stabbed multiple times, found dead in their home, died over 300 miles away, or had been linked to a suspect taken into custody prior to Juan Miguel's death.

That left four additional victims, all of whom had been found within the past two weeks.

The first, nineteen-year-old Lin Tran, didn't show any obvious gang affiliation by his clothing in the file image, which came from his PID record. Cobalt blue hair didn't strike her as having any significance in that regard either, though she did spend a few minutes checking other databases to see if it matched up with any street gang's 'dress code.' It didn't. He'd been found in similar circumstances to Juan Miguel. A naked corpse hidden in an alley under trash, dead to a single stab wound. He didn't have facial bruising or any signs of damage from restraints, though his toxicology screen came back positive for a large dose of Sandman. She found no criminal record of any kind on him, though he also had little footprint in the system. Probably a fringer, living with as minimum a digital trail as possible.

Victim three came up as a John Doe, an average-looking young man who could've been anywhere from eighteen to twenty. Identification would be impossible as the corpse had already been cremated, he'd been found naked, and didn't exist at all in the system. Like the others, he'd suffered a solitary stab wound to the heart. John Doe had broken four fingers on his right hand and suffered two pages of documented bruises and broken bones.

"Ouch. He didn't go down without a fight," said Dorian. "He might still be hanging around as a ghost."

The fourth victim, Diego Rojas, smirked at her from a booking image taken only eight days before his death. His record showed him as a member of the Angels, a mostly-Latin gang primarily involved in the manufacture and traffic of low-to-mid grade street chems. Aside from the drug trade, their war with the Fei Len (another gang) brought them to the notice of the police more than anything else. Rojas, as with the others, had also been found naked and stabbed once in the heart. His body turned up inside a dumpster that had been welded shut. Of the lot, he'd been placed as the oldest time of death, preceding Juan Miguel by three days.

The last hit in the search, another John Doe, brought up a morgue image of a ghastly chalk-white face shaved bald. Two black letters, a D and a B in an angular script reminiscent of Greek lettering, marked his cheeks under each eye. The medical examiner noted the tattoo's significance as the decedent belonging to the Dead Boyz gang.

Kirsten groaned.

"What?" asked Dorian.

"Again with the z thing." She gestured at the screen. "What the hell is the point of that?"

Dorian shrugged. "I suppose it's cool or intimidating."

"To who?"

He chuckled.

"What z thing?" asked Morelli.

"Gangs are as bad as over-marketed products." Kirsten thrust her arm into the holo-panel. "Scorpionz with a z. Dead Boyz with a z. Seriously, why do they do that?"

Morelli, Kurosawa, and Montez all shrugged.

"Well…" Dorian patted her on the shoulder. "That looks like a pattern to me. Want the good news or the bad news first?"

She grimaced. "Good news."

"You've got more information to follow up on now."

"That's the *good* news?" She glanced up at him. "More work? What's the bad news?"

He flicked a finger at her terminal, scrolling among the victims. "Five people all killed within a few days of each other under ritualistic overtones? There's probably another demon out there."

"Ugh." She flopped forward, her head striking the desk with a hollow, metallic *thud.* "Why does it have to be demons?"

8

THE OPPOSITE OF COOL

W alter grabbed the handrail and pulled himself to his feet, gasping in pain.

"Sorry man," muttered Evan, frowning at the 'no signal' message on his NetMini. He stuffed the useless thing back into his pocket, hoping Mom would notice he'd gone offline.

The boy groaned, still unable to stand fully upright. "It's okay. Not like you meant to. The lights were out."

"So, umm…" Shawn leaned out of the elevator, peering into the hallway. "Should we sit here and wait or do you really think that ghost is going to bring someone back to hurt us?"

"There's no monsters, dude." Walter shook his head.

Maela rubbed the back of her head where it had hit the floor.

Shawn spun to face everyone. "I know that. I mean like people. Crazy people live down here. Heard they're like cannibals sometimes, too."

"Or mutants." Walter nodded. "Stuff the military tested and went wrong, so they set them loose down here."

"No such thing," said Evan.

"Yeah." Walter let go of the railing, wobbling on his legs like a newborn foal. "Badlands has dog people. The corporations made them during the war. Remember history class?"

"Cat ones too." Evan grinned. "But, they can't get inside the wall."

Maela paced, wiping at blood on her lip. "Great. I'm stranded babysitting a pack of nine-year-olds."

Shawn, almost as tall as her, gave her an up-and-down look. "You're not in charge of us."

"I'm the oldest." Maela held her chin high. "That means I'm in charge by default."

"I'm stronger than you."

Walter patted him on the arm with the back of his hand. "Dude. We're not pirates. Ev said there's a ghost who wants to hurt him and is probably going to bring bad stuff here. We should hide. Besides." He pointed up. "This elevator is fried. It'll take them weeks to fix it."

"Someone will notice it broke and send someone to check on it. There should be a hatch. Maybe we can climb up a ladder inside the shaft." Maela stared at the ceiling for a little while before sighing. "Grr. I don't see a hatch. Still, they'll find us. We should wait here." She scooted into the back corner, arms folded, gazing off to the side and down.

"Still got some blood on your chin." Walter pointed.

Maela wiped it on her sleeve.

"Is there anything out there?" asked Shawn.

Evan peered into the dark plastisteel passage that looked like the guts of a long-abandoned starship. "Nope. Mom says there's lots of ghosts down here, but they're mostly nice."

Shawn grabbed his shoulder. "Stop talking about ghosts, 'kay?"

"Sorry. It's not scary. She was our age and lived down here for like two years, and all she had was wimpy Astral Sense." Evan stuck out his tongue. "Walter's got Telekinesis and we're all telepathic, right?"

Everyone nodded.

"And you're a Kinetic." Evan poked Shawn in the arm. "You can make yourself as strong as a grown up."

"Yeah but not for long and I get tired fast."

"That's why his dad threw him out," said Walter. "Shawn kicked his ass."

The look on the big kid's face gave off both pride and shame.

"Sounds like you wanna go exploring or something." Walter walked around in a circle, breathing funny.

"Are you okay?" asked Maela.

"I dunno. Feels like I took a Fusion Elbow to the nuts."

Evan grimaced. "You kinda did. But by accident."

"What the crap is a fusion elbow?" Maela blinked.

"Gee-ball move." Shawn pantomimed leaping into the air to drop an elbow strike on someone lying on the ground.

"Someone kicked me in the face," said Shawn.

"That might've been me." Maela offered a sheepish look. "But you crushed me flat."

"Guys." Evan pointed out the door. "The ghost might have been trying to scare us, or maybe he really is going to bring someone or something back here that'll hurt us."

Maela put her hand on the panel and concentrated again. "No! The connection's dead. I think the crash cut a wire or something. I can't call for help."

Shawn climbed up out of the elevator to the floor outside, which crossed the doorway about waist-height to him at a sharp angle. "The elevator is jammed. Look how far it tilted. C'mon. Little Man's right. I don't wanna sit here and wait for some crazy person to find us when we're trapped in a box."

"But they're gonna come looking for us and we won't be here." Maela stomped. "Mr. Short is already wondering where we are."

"Sure he is." Shawn rolled his eyes. "He's playing a game and has no idea how much time is passing."

Maela bit her lip in doubt.

Walter looked up. "If anyone noticed us fall, someone would've been shouting into the elevator shaft already."

"Okay. Fine." Maela looked at Evan. "What do you think we should do?"

"My mom was down here a long time and she was okay, and she went all the way to the real ground. We shouldn't do that. Just move away from the elevator and find a hiding place so if someone bad does come looking for us, they won't find us. There's hatches to the surface, too, but they're locked with codes. You might be able to open one."

"Okay." Maela climbed out of the elevator. "Don't touch anything."

Evan grinned, spun on his heel, and marched down the corridor to a submarine style door with a wheel in the middle. He grabbed and turned, but it wouldn't budge. Shawn and Maela walked up behind him, Walter limping along at the rear. Shawn grasped the wheel, stared at it intently for a few seconds, then turned it to the left.

"Wow. Nice." Evan grinned.

Shawn slouched. "I guess."

"You don't like being strong?" asked Maela.

The 'world's biggest nine-year-old' stepped past the door, shaking his head. "It's not that... I almost killed my dad."

"Oh." She looked down.

"He was hitting my mother and wouldn't stop, so I got mad and punched him. Broke his jaw. Almost broke his neck." Anger swirled around Shawn, though he also seemed close to tears. "They were both scared of me after that. Gave me away to the cops."

"Parents suck," muttered Maela. "Mine kicked me out, too."

"My other mom is a junkie. She had a boyfriend who hit me all the time. I used to go astral so I didn't have to feel him hitting me." Evan stuffed his hands in his pockets and trudged forward past the door into another hallway going left to right. At the silence, he glanced back to find Shawn and Maela peering expectantly at Walter.

"Umm, mine died. I don't remember anything about it really. Happened a long time ago. One of them did something and the company they worked for sent assassins. The killer left me alone 'cause I was only like three. Cops sent me to the dorms when they saw me making toys float or something. I don't remember any of it, or my parents. Feels like I've always been at the dorm."

Eyes closed, Evan forced all thoughts of Mick or his bad mom out of his head, focusing on his real mom, Monwyn stuff, and even Sam. He didn't want to say anything about that though, since the others might become sad.

"Look for something that opens." Shawn pointed at the ceiling, full of old pipes, support struts, and wire bundles. Large swaths of plastisteel had been stained green from decades of dripping chemicals.

"Which way?" asked Maela. "Everything looks the same."

"Umm." Evan kept glancing back and forth.

Shawn poked him in the back. "Ev's a precog. Which way?"

"I'm not that much of a precog. Sometimes I just feel scared when something's going to hurt my mom."

"The junkie?" asked Maela.

"No, real mom, not the one who had me as a baby." Neither direction gave off any more or less sense of good idea, so he randomly chose left. "Let's go this way."

They followed his lead, eight sneakers clanking on metal grating. The noise echoed for what felt like miles into a maze of passageways. Here and there, flashing yellow lights on the ceiling jutted out from boxes with 'dangerous voltage' warnings. Other cabinets appeared to hold data conduits full of shimmering blue fiber bundles.

Except for things labeled as dangerous, they pulled and tugged on any rectangular panel that resembled a door or hatch cover, looking for a hiding place. Evan kept his eyes high more than on the walls, hoping to spot one of the ladders Mom described that would lead to the surface. She'd said they had code-locked hatches, but that didn't bother him. The worst they'd do is summon the police for tampering, and that would be even better than Maela opening them. Having the police pull them out of the plate beat wandering the city alone.

A pipe about as big around as his forearm leaked a spray of water up ahead, creating a small area full of rain. Evan grinned and ran through it, the others following. The passage eventually ended at another T junction. To the right, several more leaky water pipes made the corridor look like a car wash. Left appeared dry, but a soft electronic buzz came from that direction.

Evan glanced back and forth, this time sensing a mild pull to the right. "We should go that way."

"Oh, man. Really? It's soaked." Shawn took a step toward the left.

"I don't want to get drenched. Let's go left," said Maela.

"Guys, if a precog says go right, you go right." Walter took two steps toward the wet passage.

Maela whined. "How bad is it? Is someone gonna die?"

Evan again looked to the left and thought about going that way. A quiver of nervousness simmered along the underside of his stomach, but nowhere near as bad as any of the times his mother wound up in danger. "Umm. I don't think so, but something bad's probably going to happen."

"Okay, no death, I say we stay dry." Maela hurried off to the left.

Shawn followed with Walter behind him, no longer limping. Still nervous, Evan dragged his feet, trailing behind the other three. They kept checking panels, exposing valves or circuitry, but finding no place big enough for them to crawl into.

The floor collapsed with a jangling screech of failing metal, calving into a ramp dangling on gradually bending pipes.

Shawn, near the bottom end of the falling section, dropped straight. Walter spilled forward onto his chest and slid face-first down the incline, stopping with his shoes a few inches away from the break. Maela, near the front end of the collapse, jumped forward. She landed half on solid ground at the forward side of the hole, armpit deep in the floor. Only her fingers laced in the metal grid kept her from falling.

She showed the boys what a 'real' scream sounded like.

Evan, still on stable ground, jumped forward, grabbing Walter's ankles while hooking his leg around a vertical pipe by the wall. Shawn wound up dangling off the end of the metal slab, his legs waving out in midair above a long drop. Several feet separated him from Walter's hands.

"Ahh!" screamed Shawn. "Shit! It's gonna break!"

Walter glanced back at Evan for a split second, then thrust an arm toward Shawn, who, seconds later, let out a yowl.

"Hey," shouted Shawn. "Not the best time for a TK wedgie."

Grunting, Walter made a series of faces. Shawn's clothing compressed in response to invisible telekinetic force.

The dangling section of floor creaked and slipped another few inches. Maela pulled herself up on the other side, clawing at the grating while her sneakers mostly slipped on it.

Shawn slid up toward them as if pulled by a magnet. He, too, stuck his fingers in the grating, pulling himself along until he grabbed hold of Walter. Seconds after he climbed over the boy to unbroken floor, the slab broke away and fell, leaving Walter suspended upside down by Evan's grip on his legs, which started to fail.

"Shawn, help," rasped Evan. "My fingers are slipping."

Walter flailed, trying to bend backward and grab onto something, but couldn't fold himself in half.

"Hang on, Walt!" Shawn scrambled around and grabbed the boy's right leg.

Evan shifted his grip, clamping both hands on Walter's left ankle. Together, they hauled him up—though Shawn did most of the lifting. Walt hugged them together, shaking like a terrified chihuahua.

"I'm sorry." Maela, twenty feet away on the other side of the hole, bowed her head. "We should've listened to Evan."

"What the hell, man?" Shawn grabbed a fistful of Evan's shirt and pulled him close. "You said no one was gonna die."

Evan shrugged. "No one did."

Shawn blinked.

"It's not like watching a movie. If you were gonna fall and die, I probably would've freaked out like I did in class."

"Wouldn't that mean you love Shawn like you love your mom?" Walter grinned.

Shawn released Evan's shirt and grabbed Walter's.

"Okay, I probably wouldn't have freaked out that bad. But I would've *demanded* we go the other way."

"Whoa," whispered Maela. "It's a bottomless pit."

The boys all looked.

She stood close to the break, peering down, her chin-length black hair fluttering. A weak, but steady breeze invaded the space courtesy of the new hole, carrying a stink of chemicals mixed with something like sour raspberries and dead fish.

Evan crawled close enough to peek as well, staring down at the collapsing roofs of houses abandoned for centuries. A few light sources, places where color filled in over the sepia-toned world of Darksight moved around. "It's not bottomless, just dark."

"You can see?" asked Maela.

"Yeah. Astrals can see in the dark." Walter patted him on the shoulder. "Like the one useful thing they can do."

Evan shook his head, rolling his eyes to himself.

Maela telepathically 'knocked.' He smiled, nodding. She linked to his surface thoughts, whistling in awe at the images in his mind. "Why is everything that weird brown color, and like shifting around?"

"It's the way the astral realm looks. Mom said we're not really seeing in the dark, but looking into the astral place. She said the astral world is like a reflection of the real world. Usually, it matches, but some stuff like trashcans or cars don't show up unless they've been sitting there for a long time."

"That's kinda creepy." She shivered. "Okay, but now what do we do?"

"Well, the three of us are over here and you're over there. We should go back and get wet," said Shawn. "Can you make it to us?"

Maela examined the walls, studying the pipes. "I think so."

"Whoa." Walter stared at his hands. "I never lifted something as heavy as a person with telekinesis before."

"You were scared." Evan grinned. "That made you stronger for a bit."

"Guys, get ready to grab me if something else breaks." Maela climbed up on the wall pipes, tugged a bit to check their strength, then shimmied sideways out over the breach in the floor.

Shawn leaned over the hole and spit. He and Walter chuckled.

Evan grabbed them and pulled them back. "We need to get away from this. That ghost might try to scare someone into falling."

Maela whined. "Why did you say that now? You couldn't wait for me to get all the way across. Oh, no. You had to say something creepy and scary when I'm hanging off 200-year-old water pipes over a fifty-meter drop."

"Sorry," muttered Evan.

She rushed the last few feet, and kept going a bit past the start of the hole before climbing down. Evan led the way back toward the rainy passage, picking up to a run to get past the six spraying leaks before rounding a corner at the end into yet another section full of pipes and component cabinets.

"We are going to get so damn lost." Shawn slung water off his arms.

Evan kept going. "No turning back."

"What are we even looking for again?" asked Maela.

"Any way to go up," said Evan.

"Dude, we're at the bottom of the plate. The ladders to the surface are near the top." Shawn hurried after him.

"We still need to go up then." Evan shrugged. "Just means we gotta climb more ladders."

Two passages later, red lettering haphazardly smeared on the walls spelled out, 'beware of mutants.'

"Is that paint or blood?" Walter leaned closer to the words, sniffing.

"Umm. We should probably go another way." Maela backed up a step.

"It's all made up." Evan shook his head. "Mom said all those stories are to scare people away so they don't go down here. She never saw a mutant."

"Why?" Maela brushed at her sleeves, flinging water.

"I dunno. She didn't say." Evan shrugged.

"Probably because there's lots of important stuff to break down here." Shawn pointed at the pipes and electronics cabinets. "They put all the wires and stuff down here in the plates. Like the power, and the GlobeNet, and all the sewers and water. If someone bad came down here, they could break the whole city."

A short distance later, the same red lettering adorned the wall with, 'trez passor will be eated.'

"What does that mean?" asked Walter, squinting at it.

"It means someone didn't go to school." Maela's voice quivered too much to match her blasé expression. "Seriously, it means we need to get out of here, now."

"Hey, what's that?" Walter pointed at blinking green lights up ahead.

A round section of wall swelled into the passage. A split double-door

THE OPPOSITE OF COOL | 79

that looked an awful lot like a capsule-shaped elevator from a space ship sat at the middle of the curve.

"That's a way up," cheered Shawn. He dashed past Evan and ran over to it, pressing a button on the wall.

It buzzed.

"Invalid access," said an electronic male voice.

Maela stepped up on the hatch. "Oh, we'll see about that."

She cracked her knuckles and rested both hands on the panel. The small display screen went from showing the word 'denied' to a scramble of random characters, then shifting colors. A moment later, the doors parted, sliding into the wall on either side. The cylindrical chamber behind them appeared reasonably clean, and a whole lot like an elevator. Maela put her arms around Evan and Walter, ushering them inside.

"Hah. Stuff your access." She held her nose in the air.

"Huh, that's weird," said Shawn. "The thing only has one button."

"Obviously, duh…" Walter faked a shocked expression. "We're already at the bottom. It can only go up."

"Right." Shawn pushed it, but the same buzz and 'invalid access' voice happened.

"Ooh! I hate these things." Maela put her hand on the panel.

"Wait." Evan looked around. "This might not be a good idea."

"Are you getting a precog feeling or just being a scared little kid?" asked Maela.

"I'm not sure how to tell the difference when it's this weak." He grinned. "But Mom never said anything about there being elevators down here. She used ladders."

Walter elbowed him playfully. "She also isn't a techno, right? And she was our age when she came down here. So… she wouldn't have been able to get this door open to see the elevator."

"I guess." Evan sighed.

Maela turned her attention back to the panel and closed her eyes.

The ghost in the black coat materialized out of the wall, grabbing her from behind. Neither her mini dress nor her body reacted to his touch, his hands sinking wrist deep into her sides. Before Evan could even shout, a spike of malevolent energy filled the air.

"Eeeeee!" Maela shrieked.

Flames leapt out of the panel, along with sparks. The elevator plummeted, leaving the ghost behind. Walter screamed, swooning to his knees with both hands protectively covering his groin. They plummeted fast, but not free-fall fast. Gravity increased slightly as the capsule slowed itself before coming to a stop. The doors snapped open with a pneumatic *whoosh* that threw a weak cyclone around the chamber.

Evan gawked at a street paved with black stuff, lined on both sides by the crumbling remains of high-rises and cars so old they'd collapsed into metal chunks and dingy plastic panels. "Umm. Guys... we went all the way down."

Maela whimpered.

"Mae?" Evan whirled.

She lay on her side, curled up and shivering. Evan dropped to kneel beside her, and without even thinking about being embarrassed, reached down her shirt to put a hand over her heart. Her skin had become as cold as snow, but only in a small area.

"W-what are you d-doing?" A little blush reddened her cheeks.

"The ghost tried to grab your heart. It's cold."

"N-no s-shit." She couldn't seem to stop her teeth from chattering.

Evan pulled his hand out and started rubbing her back, trying to build up warmth.

Shawn stared at the burning panel. "Guys, that was the opposite of cool."

"N-no." Maela shook her head. "That was fuckin' *cold*."

Evan gasped.

"Aww, watch the bad language around the little boy," said Shawn in a patronizing tone.

Growling, Maela pushed herself up to sit. "You're *all* little boys." She eyed Shawn. "Okay, maybe you're not that little. But you're still nine."

"It's okay." Evan smiled. "Sometimes, stuff happens that's so bad you gotta swear. Just not in front of Mom."

"Hey, check this out." Walter pulled open a small locker. "There's like lights in here. We're already down here, might as well look for another way up."

"Are you"—Maela lowered her voice from shout to whisper—"nuts? Go *out* there?"

"Mom said there's lots of ghosts in the Beneath. They're mostly nice. One of them will help us." Evan leaned out to look around. "I don't see any."

Maela futilely poked the console. "It's dead."

"No one is going to find us here." Shawn handed her a large flashlight with a yellow battery case. "We can't just stand here."

Walter handed Evan a light, but hesitated. "Umm."

Evan laughed.

"Little Man's eyes make enough light for us to see." Shawn laughed.

"Not really." Maela fussed with her flashlight until it turned on. "Wow. They actually work. Ugh. This is such a bad idea. We're going to get kidnapped and cooked."

"Oh come on." Walter groaned. "There are crazy people down here, not like goblins."

"Shade goblins do eat kids, but not the marsh goblins." Evan stepped out of the elevator. "But, this isn't the Monwyn world, so there aren't any goblins down here."

"So your plan is what?" asked Maela. "Find a ghost and ask for help?"

"Yeah, basically." Evan shrugged. "Anyone got a better idea?"

9

A CRAZY EXPLANATION

A beep from the console drew Kirsten's attention to a flashing panel.

She scrolled back to the first search she started. A record had popped up from six years ago, only a few months before Division 0 activated her. The case involved a woman who had been recorded via Citycam stripping, then chaining herself to a railing at the edge of a black zone. A man nearby saw her from his laundromat and called the police.

Division 6 had rolled in before the locals did much more than take pictures and paw at her. They handed it off to Division 1 once they transported her back to civilization. Her case got filed away as a mental issue despite the woman claiming a complete blackout between traveling home from work and coming to handcuffed to a post.

Kirsten copied the old inquest as a potential related link to her current case, sighed at the list of five murdered (potential) gang members, and stood. "Gotta stop that ghost first."

"If there *is* a demon involved with the other thing, that would squarely pull the inquest into your jurisdiction. It wouldn't be you poaching a P10 to be nice to a kid."

She locked her terminal and headed off toward the garage. "True. Still. I would prefer it isn't a demon."

"You and me both."

KIRSTEN SET THE PATROL CRAFT DOWN ON THE ROOF OF A RESIDENCE TOWER in Sector 6640, a middle-class district full of apartments. The parking area contained only two other hovercars.

"Wow. This can't be a new building…"

"Almost every tower in this area sublets the ground floors for stores or restaurants. Between delivery bots and having anything reasonably necessary within walking distance, no one really ever has to go far. And I'm sure most of them work by senshelmet."

"That's almost sad." She shoved the door open. "It's amazing they're not all huge."

Dorian laughed. "Well, pet hamsters need a wheel to run on. I'm sure they've all got treadmills or stationary bikes. And the more expensive buildings have fitness centers. Everything's all nice and self-contained."

"Okay, that's not *almost* sad. That *is* sad." She sighed. "Everyone just isolated like that? No wonder our society is so disconnected."

"You've played Monwyn. There's a hundred other games like that. People socialize in virtual worlds, making friends thousands of miles away." He stepped through the elevator doors before they opened.

Kirsten frowned, waiting for it to arrive. The dark burgundy panel slid open, revealing Dorian with a big grin inside a shiny metal elevator cube. "Still strikes me as sad not to go out and see people, do things for real, you know?"

"Everything is electricity going into the brain. Does it really matter if it's riding a nerve from the eyes and ears, or coming in by M3 jack?"

"Yeah. Being both a psionic and a ghost, you should know there's energy that wires can't carry. Humans have a connection to the Earth… though you wouldn't really know it anymore the way things are."

Dorian raised an eyebrow. "K, you've been playing that elf too much in Monwyn. What's next, you go running around Sanctuary Park wearing nothing but pointed ears?"

"Asara the Huntress does not run around naked." Kirsten huffed.

"You haven't seen *all* the movies… and there are mods for the games."

Kirsten gawked. "How do you know that?"

He laughed. "I don't. But… One: she's a female character in a popular media franchise. Two: young programmers are horny as hell."

"I hate that you're probably right. I just don't want Evan stumbling across anything like that."

"He's too small to even appreciate it now. Wait until he's like twelve."

The doors opened on the 66th floor, but she didn't get out. "Twelve? That's…"

"When I started trying to peek at certain content on the GlobeNet." He laughed. "Didn't have much luck back then, but I tried."

Kirsten shrank in on herself.

"Oh, shit. Sorry." He stared at the floor.

"No, no… it's okay. Not your fault I had a far from normal life. I don't even know what age is normal for a girl to start getting curious. I went straight from being totally focused on not starving to death to knowing way more than I wanted to about sex."

"I'd imagine it's probably around the same. Biological urges are biological urges. *Humans* are weird about females… nature isn't."

She managed to chuckle. "Yeah. I don't know what I'm going to do the first time I catch him… Yeah. Not thinking about that now."

Kirsten stopped midway down the hall and rang the bell of apartment 6608.

A little over a minute later, a tiny light winked on at the middle of the door about eye level—which put it a bit above Kirsten's. "Who is—oh, the police?" asked a woman's voice. "Sorry, one moment." The door slid to the left with a soft *pssh*. A dark-skinned woman in her late twenties of diminutive height adjusted her pink bathrobe before smiling at Kirsten. "Wow, you're kinda small for a cop. Not used to seeing them my size."

She'd heard that so often, it didn't even warrant an eye roll anymore. "Miss Parker?"

"Please." The woman offered a hand. "Call me Quinn… unless you're here to arrest me, but I can't imagine why."

"No." Kirsten shook her hand. "I'm Lieutenant Kirsten Wren with Division 0. I wanted to speak to you about an incident that happened six years ago that may be related to a case I'm presently investigating."

"Umm." Quinn fidgeted. "Wow. I figured everyone had forgotten about that. People thought I was crazy. I still don't really understand it at all."

"Can we talk for a bit?"

"Guess there's no harm in it. Other than being mortified, nothing really happened to me." She backed up enough for Kirsten to slip inside, then hit the button to close the door, slicing Dorian in half. His form stretched away from the door, everything past the 'cut' blurry and fog-like for a few seconds until he reintegrated.

Quinn strolled into the living room, a long braid interwoven of multiple smaller dreadlocks hung down past her butt. The apartment's thick pale-beige carpeting held the ghost of her footprints for several seconds.

"That is so annoying." Dorian scowled at the door. "They never wait for me."

Kirsten smiled back at him, then put on 'serious face' before Quinn caught her. "What do you remember of that night?"

"I was on the way home from the office. Had one of those irritating high-confidential meetings the managers didn't want online. One minute, I'm sitting in a PubTran car, the next thing I know, my clothes are all gone and I'm hugging a metal post in a dangerous part of town."

Kirsten opened her armband terminal screen and typed notes as fast as she could.

"Oh, wow… old school. I didn't think anyone actually used the virtual keyboards anymore. Well, except for kids. Are you like a cadet or something?"

"No, I'm over eighteen," said Kirsten, still typing. "I'm psionic. Cybernetic implants freak me out."

"Ahh. Yeah, I read something about that." Quinn gestured at an archway to the kitchen. "You want some coffee or tea or something else to drink?"

"Thanks, I'm okay. Is the blackout the strangest thing you experienced?"

"No. After I woke up, I couldn't move or scream. It was as if my body had a mind of its own. Not sure screaming would've really been a good idea there, though. Eventually, a bunch of punks came out of the alleys and surrounded me, but a whole shitload of cops showed up before any of them did worse than grope. The moment the police arrived, I got this real strong sense of being pissed off, but it faded."

Kirsten looked around the apartment. A sleek black net deck sat on a small table in front of the couch, a slim line of cobalt blue light glowing across the front. The NinTek logo also lit up with the same shade of blue.

"Anything?" asked Dorian.

"No… This place is giving off about as much paranormal energy as three-day-old OmniSoy leftovers."

"Wow that much?" Dorian raised both eyebrows.

She shot a smirk at him before turning back to Quinn. "Has anything else unusual happened to you since?"

"Unusual like that? No. Plenty of weird luck, but nothing even close to that feeling. Do you think I'm nuts too?"

"Felt like you were possessed?"

"That's a good way to put it, yeah."

Kirsten shook her head. "No. I don't think you're nuts. I believe you were likely the victim of a ghost attack."

"Oh." Quinn slouched with relief. "That's awesome."

"Awesome?" Kirsten blinked in surprise.

"A reasonable explanation that doesn't involve me being insane. I've spent the past six years worrying if I'm schizophrenic. Been to a few doctors, none of them found any sign of a problem."

Dorian laughed. "Most people wouldn't call 'you were possessed by a ghost' a reasonable explanation."

"I think you're the first person I've ever met who accepted the idea of a ghost without flinching." She rested her hands on her hips and scanned the room again. "Unfortunately, it happened too long ago for me to get any kind of read. And, he didn't show up here."

"Pretty sure the apartment I grew up in had a ghost or two in it. Stuff like that's all over a city this old… and violent. People who *don't* believe in ghosts are just afraid of how weird reality can get." Quinn smiled. "It hasn't come back. Never happened to me again."

Kirsten asked a few usual questions trying to determine if the woman might've potentially been in the same location as the more recent victim, or anything that might give away a 'home' location for the ghost, but drew a blank. Quinn Parker and Mia Sanchez's paths never came within a hundred miles of each other.

"That's all I can think of for now. Sorry for bothering you, and I appreciate you taking the time to talk about an experience like that."

"Oh, no problem at all. You just made my month."—Quinn pointed at herself—"This girl is *not* psycho." The woman walked her to the door. "Drive safe and stuff. So glad I don't need to risk that anymore."

"Thanks. Have a nice day." Kirsten nodded farewell and headed down the hallway.

"Both victims so far have been in their younger twenties at the time of the attack and on the short side," said Dorian.

She glanced at him. "If you're trying to freak me out, it's not working. I'm aware I'm also in my young twenties and on the short side… but neither of those victims had any defense against spirits. If that bastard thinks he's going to possess me when I finally find him, he's in for a rude surprise. Actually, I kind of hope he comes after me. That will only make my job easier."

"I don't think he'll target you out of the blue. You've got a certain energy to you that would scare him off."

"Really?" She looked over at him while hitting the elevator call button.

"It's gotten stronger ever since you beat the snot out of that giant flea. Any spirit more than a decade or two old would be able to tell there's something different about you. It might be enough to scare this one off."

Kirsten stepped into the elevator. "Ugh. I hope I don't have to chase this piece of shit around the city for years."

"You and me both. Though, I'm sure I can slow him down enough for you to catch up."

"This one's old, Dorian. Don't do anything reckless. I'd rather run around in circles than lose you."

He clasped his hands in front of himself, bowing his head with a faint chuckle. "I sincerely doubt he will hit anywhere near as hard as that damn giant flea."

Kirsten shifted her gaze toward him without turning her head. "Are you not saying the name on purpose or did you forget it."

"On purpose."

"Okay. That's probably a good idea." She stared at her reflection in the silver doors for a few seconds. "Can demons just pop out of the abyss if you speak their name?"

"No idea. You could ask that expert at the National Archives. Oh, wait… he wound up being absorbed into a giant demon that you threw back down into the Abyss. Oops."

"Oops indeed." Kirsten squeezed her fists, furious all over again at Konstantin for influencing her mind.

The doors opened with a *ping*, letting in a strong, chilly wind. Kirsten's hair clip gave out and snapped off three steps onto the roof. She stood there for a few seconds trying to channel calm thoughts, eyes closed as her hair whipped around at her face.

"This is turning into not my day real fast."

Dorian's hand pat spread a chill over her shoulder. "That's a trivial annoyance. A day can get *way* worse than a broken hair clip."

"Don't jinx me." She hurried after the runaway clip, scooped it up, and held it up to examine it. "It only popped off. Not broken."

He grinned. "See? It's a good day."

Kirsten trudged over to the patrol craft, got in, and put her hair back up. "I'll call it a good day when I do more than waste time chasing empty leads."

"Patience, young cricket."

"Isn't it grasshopper?" She swiped at the console to bring the drive system online.

"I think so. Wanted to change it up a bit." He winked. "Wake me up when we get there."

With that, Dorian melted into the seat.

"I'm so jealous. Wherever we go, you're home."

Dorian's faint chuckle came out of the sound system.

BLOOD PENTAGRAM

I f desire had any ability to affect the real world, Kirsten's need to stop the ghost would've caused it to appear in the back seat.

Alas, with no idea where to go and nothing in the Division 0 database identifying any matching victims, she found herself staring blankly at the Navcon for a few minutes. Once she accepted she *couldn't* do more than wait for another victim or sighting, she brought up the inquest record for Juan Miguel Esparza's death and keyed in the address for the second victim, Lin Tran.

He'd been found two sectors north of a black zone, again at the edge where the grey surrounding it mixed with normal civilization. She sighed at the screen, wondering why the government decided to disavow the 'black zones' and simply erase them from the navigation system instead of sending the military in to clear them out.

Captain Eze likened them to self-contained prisons, being that the conditions inside these areas amounted to incarceration. The government didn't think it worth it in terms of cost—both lives and credits—to invade one prison only to relocate whatever inhabitants survived to another.

After setting the car to auto-drive, she leaned on the center console and re-read the file on 'victim two.'

Lin Tran had been found naked, a single stab wound to the heart. This reminded her too much of Konstantin's victims, suggesting someone else ran around the city summoning (or trying to summon) an abyssal.

"This feels too damn familiar. What's the connection between rituals and nudity?"

Dorian shrugged. "You're asking the wrong person there, K. The only thing I can think of would be to conceal forensic evidence that might've been on the victims' clothing. However, if we *are* dealing with Diablos, they're neither smart enough to consider that, nor would they care. Most of them aren't even in the system, and they'd think of the police going after them as a fun day playing bullet tag."

"Some of those archives have paintings of 'witches' dancing naked around fires and so on. Is there something mystical there or is it like the same reason all those ancient statues were always nude?"

"I read somewhere that some ritualists think they collect magical energy wherever their skin is touched by the natural world. But, it could be simple artistic license. Why?"

She paged down the autopsy report. "Just trying to figure out if this is a real ritual murder or if someone's trying to stage it based on what they see in movies."

"You never did ask Konnie why he stripped his victims. Then again, he did keep them in restraints for an extended time. It may have been a matter of hygiene, not so much anything arcane."

She scowled. "These victims didn't show any signs of long-term confinement."

"Diablos often keep people they abduct for weeks or months, torturing them with repeated beatings and sexual assaults."

Bile danced in the back of her throat. "Is there a reason we haven't rolled in there and wiped them out?"

"I'm sure there is, and it probably starts with a c and ends with 'redits.' Though, they are subject to summary execution almost every time they make contact with police, so there's that."

Sighing, Kirsten shook her head. "Always money. And they just shoot everyone in a Diablos jacket?"

"Not right away. Usually, they wait for the gang to shoot first—which if it's a real Diablo, doesn't take long."

"Right. Well, none of these people showed any signs of long-term confinement. They were likely grabbed off the street and killed within a few hours."

A chime announcing she'd come within a quarter mile of the programmed destination drew her attention back to the windscreen. She took over flight control and steered the patrol craft into a canyon of formerly-silver high rise buildings. Grime and scorch marks had painted the towers on the left side nearly black, while the opposite side of the street had merely dulled to 'no longer shiny.' Various holographic signs flashed in pastel colors from ad-bots or window signs at street level, stores occupying the ground floors of cheap apartments.

The low, mechanical drone of the extending ground wheels filled the silence for a few seconds as she flew in to land beside an open-faced restaurant. A handful of people sat on stools behind a cloth curtain covered in giant Chinese characters, only their legs visible. English appeared in small white letters, courtesy of the electronic windows, reading 'Johnny's Express Noodles.'

She shoved the gull wing door open and got up, emerging into a cloud of steam laced with the fragrance of shrimp and salt. *Hmm. Never did get around to having lunch.* The place right by the alley she needed to check out smelled okay and looked reasonably clean—at least to her. Two years scavenging food from trash bins tended to make almost any restaurant feel clean.

Her armband terminal showed a map of the area, leading her past the noodle counter to the alley running along its left side. A colony of plastiboard cartons repurposed into tiny houses stood in and among a milieu of metal dumpsters arranged under a network of fat pipes that ferried garbage down from the apartments overhead. She figured that made the buildings at least 120 years old, since anything built more recently would've had in-unit *de*-assemblers that broke trash down into a contiguous mass of grey slime. Initially, they'd made it beige, but it looked too much like OmniSoy and there had been some unfortunate mix-ups. Of course, cheaper places sometimes did still use disposal chutes instead of de-assemblers for cost reasons.

An unsettling supernatural presence lurked at the edge of her awareness, not as strong as where Juan Miguel had been found, but noticeable. Here, she couldn't say with certainty that it carried the taint of the Abyss, but it came close. Whatever spirit had been here was *dark*.

The locals eyed her from their nests, a sea of suspicious eyes lurking in the gloomy spaces among the dumpsters and cartons. Kirsten did her best to look directly at them with her best 'don't mind me, I'm not here to cause trouble' expression. Truth be told, she felt more kinship with these people than with any of the crowd Konstantin associated with. Especially that stuck-up bitch in that sex club. Kirsten's telekinesis barely ranked as grade one. She struggled to move objects like keys around—but had enough power to tip over a wine glass.

No surprise, none of the vagrants appeared younger than their twenties. The police scooped up vagrant children as soon as they saw them, sending the little ones off to colony adoptions and giving the over-fourteen crowd the option of a boarding program on Earth that ended with their joining the military. *Take great care of them young and they love the government.*

Her file didn't show the exact location Lin Tran had been found, though the crime scene images allowed her to approximate a spot about twenty feet deep into the alley. People emerged from their hiding spots behind her, not quite closing her in. All appeared Asian or mixed with Asian, and their expressions gave off curiosity at why the police would be here.

A woman not much taller than her watched from beside a black plastiboard carton with blue NinTek Corporation logos. Her skinny body vanished in a too-large jacket bearing a crude green scorpion logo above the words 'Jade Scorpionz.'

Somewhere back a few decades, a media channel—Real World Entertainment—started a reality show focusing on gang warfare, giving money and prizes to street gangs that 'won' battles or gained territory. For a while, they'd essentially turned both East and West City into a giant sandbox video game. Ever since, gangs from the large and organized to the ones with ten members all adopted cutesy names and logos like sports teams. It galled Kirsten that the government hadn't shut that show down, but at least it had lost its shock value and sank to what some called a 'ratings footnote.'

To this day, the black camera orbs with the neon green RWE 'lightning' logo were the only bots that could go in and out of black zones without ending up shot to pieces.

Kirsten approached the woman in the Scorpionz jacket. "Hey. Did you know Lin Tran?"

The woman breathed into her hands, trying to warm them. "Who?"

"Your buddy who they found dead here."

"I don't know any man dead here."

She peered into the woman's thoughts: mostly worry Kirsten would confiscate her new jacket. This woman *had* seen Lin Tran's corpse, even watching Diablos dump him here… and ran over to scavenge his jacket. In her memory, the man had been fully dressed when they dropped him off, but the locals had stripped him clean—even his bloody shirt and underwear.

"Right," muttered Kirsten, turning away. "Thanks."

One by one, she checked a few other people's surface thoughts. A handful witnessed the Diablo van. Some participated in the looting. She spotted Lin's pants on one guy, his bloodstained shirt on another, shoes on a third. None of them knew the names of the Diablos, nor did they much care to.

Kirsten located the exact spot where the body had been dropped. There, she crouched and pressed a hand to the plastisteel ground, trying to open herself up for any latent energies. Lacking any clairvoyant talent, she had no ability to search for visions. A scrap of spiritual energy remained, but weak, no stronger than if Dorian had become angry and punched a wall to blow off steam.

She headed back to the street and ducked under the long tapestry that gave people eating noodles a little privacy from pedestrian traffic. A heavyset bald guy with a thin mustache and a stained apron approached with a big grin.

"Hey, welcome to Johnny's."

"Thanks." She sat on one of the stools, eyeing the holographic menus above him. "Can I get a shrimp-seaweed bowl?"

He nodded. "Couple minutes. Somethin' bad goin' on around here?"

"Nothing recent. Just following up on an older case."

"Ahh, yeah. Poor kid." The cook looked down, shaking his head.

"Kid?" asked Kirsten, worried.

"Oh, well. To me." He flashed a wan smile while scooping ingredients into a bowl. "You're talkin' about Lin, right? Kid was only nineteen."

"Yeah. Did you know him?"

The cook offered a one-shoulder shrug, set the bowl down, and threw a handful of shrimp into a wok with some seasonings. Two small robotic arms came to life and kept the food moving as it cooked. "He stopped by here now and then. Lived three buildings over. Seemed nice enough."

"He have any family around?"

"Not sure. If he did, he didn't talk much about them."

Kirsten nodded, reading over the file again. Division 1 had made contact with his parents already and she doubted they expected any killer would ever be found. She didn't envy those officers the job of talking to bereaved relatives, and also saw no reason to upset the family further by trying to talk to them herself. Even if Lin Tran had some particular issue that caused him to be targeted, she already knew the Diablos did it, and had little expectation his parents would know the name or names of the gang members involved.

She paid for the soup, thanked the cook, and took her take-out meal back to the patrol craft. A few of the fringers from the alley hovered at the edge, watching her. Only one radiated hostility, a fiftyish man with an explosion of wild white hair and beard that made him look like an electrocuted dandelion with eyes.

His surface thoughts contained biblical sounding nonsense. One of Reverend Harris' anti-psionic morons, or at least someone who agreed with them. He'd evidently recognized the black uniform. She frowned at him, but since the man wasn't fanatically stupid enough to attack a police officer, she ignored him and got into the car with her late lunch.

The street counter ramen tasted amazing... the sort of meal her ten-year-old self could only have daydreamed about. She savored every bite, giving a mental middle-finger to all of Konstantin's high society crowd, picturing them gasping and hand waving at someone eating food from an area like this.

"That must be good," said Dorian.

"Yeah. I think the shrimp are vat grown."

"Wow." He glanced out the passenger side 'window.' "Never would've known that from looking at the place."

She smirked. "You're a cop."

"So?"

"You should know the restaurants with the best food often look like hell. And this place doesn't look *that* bad."

"Exactly why I expected OmniSoy shrimp. This noodle counter is too clean." He grinned.

THE NEXT VICTIM, A JOHN DOE, HAD BEEN DISCOVERED THREE SECTORS west and one south from where Lin Tran turned up.

Kirsten landed the patrol craft in an area abutting the remains of a small park/playground much smaller than Sanctuary Park. This one didn't take up an entire sector, merely half a block. Old play equipment sat largely abandoned and covered in an array of graffiti. If any children lived in the residence towers near this spot, their parents kept them indoors. Probably for the best.

The thought that school hours ended not long ago made her think of Evan, who would most likely be doing some manner of chore around the Division 0 school to work off his citizenship points. Kirsten sighed at the old playground, thinking back to the only time she'd ever been punished with points as a kid in that school. It happened the second week she'd been there, from an asshole instructor who didn't like her being quiet and afraid to talk to adults. The woman had threatened her with a hundred points if she didn't answer some question in class. For at least her first six months at the dorm, she couldn't bring herself to speak over a whisper, and with the attention of the entire class—and an angry adult woman—focused on her, she couldn't speak at all.

Fortunately, the school administrator intervened. Kirsten had been spared the points but wound up required to attend extra therapy sessions to deal with her selective mutism. She smirked. She hadn't considered herself mute, even selectively… merely terrified of grown women. With ghosts, other kids, or non-aggressive men, she could talk just fine.

Kirsten shoved the door open and got out.

A slim girl appeared out of nowhere seated on one of the swings. She looked to be in her early teens, but wore clothing from fifty years ago, back when glowing lines in fabric had been a fad. The young woman gave off energy like a spirit, but not as strong as the eerie presence in the alley across the street from the park. As soon as Kirsten locked eyes with her, the girl jumped in shock—much the way normal people reacted to seeing ghosts.

Kirsten looked back and forth from the spirit to the alley, then decided to go talk to the girl first, her throat nearly closing up with sorrow at the sight of a girl around thirteen who'd died. Dorian followed, looking around at the area.

"Hi," said the girl.

"Hey," rasped Kirsten.

She smiled at Dorian. "Wow. I didn't know they have police on this side."

"I'm an exception." He nodded in greeting. "Most of us don't stick around too long."

She looked at Kirsten again. "Oh, don't be sad. I wasn't this young when I died. At least not when I died physically."

"What?" Confusion grabbed Kirsten's building sadness in a headlock and pulled it out of the way of her voice. She cleared her throat. "Died physically?"

The girl smiled. "My mom died when I was fourteen. Dad didn't cope well, and I wound up taking care of him and my siblings. My childhood died. Making myself look like this reminds me of being happy. I survived to sixty-three, but I'm not sure I ever truly smiled again."

"Sorry." Kirsten let out a sigh. *I should know better. Kid spirits don't linger. Either demons or... situations like this.* "Is there anything I can help you with...?"

"Mila. Thanks, but I'm not stuck here for revenge or guilt or anything like that. Just chasing my own personal heaven. That's all any of us can really do, right? Focus on the best parts of our life and try to make them into some version of paradise."

"Sitting on a swing set?" asked Dorian. "I don't mean to criticize your choice of haunt, but this area is... a bit bleak."

"It's all right." Mila smiled. "This place is different from how it looked years ago, but I still see it as I remember. I'm trying to remind myself how it felt to be happy and not have to worry about anything."

A tiny bit of jealousy rose up, but died in seconds. Kirsten had never had such a time in her life. Well, perhaps her life had been normal before she reached six years of age and her powers manifested, but she couldn't remember anything from that long ago. Plenty of people had wonderful childhoods, and her lack of one shouldn't make her resent them. If anything, it cemented her resolve to give Evan that kind of life. Some might consider her an indulgent parent, but the boy didn't seem the type to be spoiled or ungrateful. He deserved whatever happiness she could give him.

"Is it working?" asked Kirsten with a sad smile.

"A bit. Kinda lonely though. Maybe I'll move on eventually. I used to play here before the area became bad. It's so weird to meet someone who can see me."

"There aren't many astrals." Kirsten gestured at the alley. "Did you notice anything strange happen in that alley over there?"

Mila stopped swinging. "Yes. I'm not sure how long ago it happened... time is somewhat fuzzy to me. But, I remember seeing some men pull a dead man out of a van and drop him there. People came by and took his things. Then this burst of black fog blew out of him."

"Burst of black fog?" Kirsten's eyebrows went up. "Do you remember when that happened compared to when those guys dumped the body?"

"No... it felt like minutes to me, but it could've been days."

Dorian scratched at his chin. "If you're daydreaming of the past most of the time, that'll happen. Time gets blurry for us on this side. I do tend to lose track of when I'm not actively following my partner around."

"So you're not bored at night?" Kirsten blinked, then smiled at him. "That makes me feel better."

"Not usually, no. Feels like you leave for the day and come back in a few minutes. Gives me time to recharge."

Kirsten faced the alley. "So, those guys left the body here, people looted it, then at some later point, you observed a release of black vapor?"

Mila nodded.

"Did the body give off any strange feelings prior to that?" asked Kirsten.

"A little, but I didn't get too close. Dead people freak me out." Mila shivered.

Dorian chuckled.

"Oh, not ghosts." She laughed. "Just bodies. I know it sounds stupid since I'm dead, but, they still bug me."

"Thank you for the info." Kirsten turned back to smile at Mila. "If you ever think you need me to help you with anything, please let me know... like passing a message to the living."

"I appreciate that. Alas, my siblings are all gone and I never had kids," said Mila, no trace of regret in her voice. "At the moment, this place is everything I need."

"All right." Kirsten managed to smile at her despite her appearing to have died way too young. "I need to go work on a case."

Mila waved, and resumed swinging.

Kirsten headed out of the old park, crossing the street and going past the patrol craft into the alley. This sector had shorter, more spread out buildings rather than the usual high-rises that made her feel like a bug walking at the bottom of pile carpeting. The instant she passed the corner, a sense of spectral gloom intensified.

Cold wisps surrounded her legs as though she waded into a standing cloud of heavy air, thicker and more fluid than the rest of the atmosphere. All the windows visible from the alley appeared filled with black smoke. Up ahead, a half-block long section of alley had taken on the washed out sepia tone of the astral realm.

"There could be a rip here." Kirsten gestured at the shadowy windows. "Last time I saw that, we were pretty close to a gateway."

"Charles Prentice," whispered Dorian. "I mean, where he died."

Kirsten nodded once, continuing to advance. The abyssal energy tainting this area seemed much stronger than the other sites, almost aware. She stared into all the hiding places and black windows, increasingly certain that an entity of some kind—quite likely an abyssal—watched her.

"Oh, you know I'm here, don't you?" She stopped walking in the area of washed-out color, and turned about, studying every shadow. "Why don't you do us both a favor and just stay on your side of the line, huh?"

Nothing appeared, spoke, or made a noise... though she found the complete silence here stranger than any spirit.

Not even the whirr of a distant ad-bot reached her. Kirsten's heartbeat and breathing filled in where all of West City had ceased. A sense of something moving to her right made her swivel, though no apparitions manifested. She couldn't quite call it 'malice' per se, but an apparition made of dread incarnate and wrapped in fear stalked her... or at least observed her from a distance.

"Guess you're not in a talking mood then. Maybe you haven't crossed over yet, but if you do, I'm going to have to send you back. Can we maybe skip that whole runaround?"

Kirsten gazed up past the six-story buildings surrounding her at the relatively clear—albeit sepia-colored—sky. *Are those Seraphim watching me?* She pictured the two she'd seen, the counterparts of Harbingers... One, a woman with scintillating wings of white-blue energy ribbons, the other, a man with flaming, feathered wings. They sure looked a lot like Mother's mythological 'angels,' but that did make sense in a way. The Seraphim likely had shown themselves to people a long time ago, and, as they had done with Kirsten, probably didn't offer much of any explanations... so humans filled in the missing parts by guessing.

A blur of shadows raced by on the left. She spun, but not fast enough to see anything.

"Are you here or teasing me from the other side?"

Shaking, Kirsten reached out with a mental feeler, searching for the thin spot between realms. For no reason she could understand, the idea of locating a breach between the tangible and astral worlds frightened her. Projecting didn't bother her. She'd seen the Astral Realm plenty of times, but a hole in the fabric of the world offered the risk of being drawn across physically. Not knowing how a living body would react to the energies of that place worried her.

Now, more than ever before in her life, she couldn't let herself die. Not with Evan needing her.

Like a child venturing into a creepy basement, Kirsten edged deeper into the alley, drawn toward a side passage that gave off a somewhat more intense darkness than the rest of the area. She grasped the corner of a grungy thermacrete building in both hands and peered around into a narrow channel full of jutting component boxes and narrow pipes. A person *could* squeeze down there, but it would be far from comfortable. Only windblown trash stared back at her, despite her near certainty that *something* watched.

"Last chance to talk. I'm about to leave since you only seem to be toying with me. I don't think you've really crossed over yet." She eased away from the maintenance passage, eyeing her surroundings. After a moment of nothing appearing or speaking, she sighed. "Yeah… you're just playing with my head."

Grumbling, Kirsten returned to the patrol craft, flopped in the driver's seat, and pulled up the Navcon. The prior two plots stood out as forming a curved line… and when she added the location of the fourth victim, Diego Rojas—a member of the Angels gang—she blinked at the clear hint of a circle.

"Crap."

"What?" asked Dorian.

She added victim five, another John Doe who belonged to a gang called the Dead Boyz, then stared at the five dots on the Navcon screen surrounding a large black zone with Sector 4196 as its heart, one additional five-mile-square sector in each direction also blacked out, with a two-sector-deep layer of grey around it. In short, a horrible place.

"It's a damn pentacle." She pointed at the Navcon. "A five pointed star. Juan Miguel in Sector 4141, John Doe #1 in 4350, Lin Tran in 4354, John Doe #2 in 4147 and Diego Rojas in 3988. The bodies were discovered in five locations that outline a pentacle with a freakin' giant disavowed area at the center."

"Wouldn't that be a pentagram?" Dorian glanced at her.

"Why, because it's being used for something dark?"

Dorian gestured at the screen. "No, because two points are on the north end, the single point to the south. That's an inversion of the elemental star. I have no idea if it actually matters, but the practitioners of dark occultism reverse it on purpose."

"Fair point but…" Kirsten folded her arms. "These are Diablos. Do you really think they've managed to figure out legit occultism?"

"Did you or did you not feel something in that alley?"

She shivered, not from the energy, rather the idea that people as psychotic as Diablos might have unlocked genuine... something. Her brain refused to call it magic. "Well, it might just be theatrics. The Diablos could have simply dumped the bodies in a five-pointed-star arrangement to draw their symbol on the map."

"Possible. Though, an entity of some kind was lurking in that alley." Dorian floated up in his seat, sticking his head out through the roof. "It's still there, but it's not showing itself."

"Any idea what it is?"

"Feels like a weak abyssal. Perhaps the same critter that threw the Oblivion guy out the window—or tried to." He sank back into the car.

Kirsten scrunched her eyebrows together. "Oblivion guy?"

"Adrienne's apartment? Possessed that big dude who shit his pants. If I remember correctly, his rear end was perilously close to your face at the time."

"Ugh. Stop. Yeah, okay, I remember." She shuddered. "That thing has been running around for a while yet, laying low. I'm fairly sure Konstantin summoned it as a trial run for Char—the big flea."

Dorian chuckled. "Now I've got you refusing to say the name. Don't tell me you've become superstitious."

"No sense tempting fate. But, the one from Adrienne's has been around for a while. The Diablos wouldn't have summoned it... at least not with these five murders."

"Maybe they haven't summoned anything at all, but whatever they attempted to do attracted it."

Kirsten flipped screens and read over the case notes. "The Diablos are believed to reside in Sector 4196. This could just be their version of putting the heads of their enemies on posts as a warning. They've drawn a pentagram around their home base with corpses."

"So, perfectly normal stuff for a Diablo to do on a weekend." Dorian cocked his head at her.

She grabbed the control sticks. "Might as well check the other two spots."

"Hoping to find something in particular?"

"At this point, finding anything new would be an improvement. Am I *expecting* to? Not really. But I have to be thorough." She pulled the patrol craft into the air, oriented it toward the next Navcon dot, and accelerated.

"Right."

A moment passed filled with only the soft thrum of the car's electronics.

"Dorian?"

He glanced over.

"How do I tell if I've stepped over the thin line between being thorough and wasting time?"

"That's a good question. If humanity ever figures it out, let me know."

Kirsten sighed, and accelerated. "If I'm going to waste time, I might as well waste as little as possible."

11

SUBJECT TO INTERPRETATION

Diego Rojas had been dumped in a vacant lot near the sector border, partially buried in a mound of wires and hoses.

Kirsten landed the patrol craft right in the lot since it had enough space. Trash, plastic hoses, and small fragments of whatever building used to stand there skittered away from the ionic downblast of the engines. She watched the thin blue sparks dance around on the plastisteel ground for a few seconds, then stared off to the south at the increasingly intact buildings moving away from the grey zone toward Sector 4040 a few hundred meters north of her.

As with everyone the Diablos had killed—at least in relation to this apparent ritual—the victim had been left near the separation between civilization and grey. Disavowed sectors or 'black zones' had a tendency to spread decay outward as those with money or a sense of self-preservation left the areas around them, allowing in the desperate poor and even more gangs.

She didn't know what caused the creeping blight to stop, but every grey zone eventually had an edge... or at least slowed down its expansion enough to feel like a border had formed. Maybe the kids who went off for colony adoptions had the right idea. Earth, at least in the United Coalition Front, did seem to be woefully overcrowded and bleak. AIs and dolls had taken over almost every job here that didn't require advanced education or a 'human touch.' No one quite accepted artificial people running a day care center, for example.

This, of course, created vast amounts of idle youth with no hope of escaping life on the streets—at least not without leaving the planet. Fortunately, OmniSoy provided such a cheap source of food that the population of fringers didn't starve. Between Cyberburger's charity (mostly motivated for good PR), government assistance, and dumpster-diving, anyone on the street that thought to look for it could find something to eat. Southern West City had more fringers due to the warmer climate.

Diego Rojas had been part of the Angels gang, named for the area they considered their territory. Centuries ago, it had been called Los Angeles… or rather the ground seventy-five meters below the city surface had been called that. Whatever remained of LA sat beneath the city plates, out of sight.

Kirsten exited the patrol craft and looked over the roof at a mound of electrical junk, trash, and hoses. The area held a charge of dark supernatural energy, but more in a residual way. Unlike the last site, nothing here made her feel as if something watched her. She let off a belabored sigh and walked over to crouch by the spot where she assumed the body had been concealed.

"This area is…" Dorian whistled. "Pretty rough for a grey zone. They're going to black this one out in a few years, I bet."

"Am I picking up on a ritual, or is this place tainted because of all the awful stuff that happens here?" She traced her fingers over a length of ridged black hose. "Diego Rojas, are you still around somewhere?"

Eyes closed, she beaconed into the Astral Realm, calling out to his spirit.

"Oh, shit," muttered Dorian, breaking her concentration a moment later.

Her thoughts returned to the physical world and the crunch of footsteps approaching from behind. Kirsten leapt to her feet, spinning with a hand on her E-90. A group of mostly men drew close, all wearing the dirty torn-up clothes of street-dwelling fringers. None displayed gang logos, though more than half had obvious cybernetics, including the man her attention focused on.

A startlingly tall guy with a scarecrow thin frame stood at the middle of the pack, his already imposing stature made more threatening by a pair of metal arms, each as long as her legs. Shaggy dark green hair half covered a long, narrow face studded with patches of beard growing around scars.

"That's close enough," said Kirsten when they reached about ten feet away.

The tall man took another step, stopping two paces from her, his stomach at her eye level. He leaned forward into a looming, buzzard-like posture. "We don't allow cops here. But..." The man straightened to his full height. "You's pretty, so maybe we make an exception if you're nice enough."

Kirsten leaned back, not terribly interested in the man's surface thoughts picturing her 'entertaining' his entire crew. "How about 'no.'"

"Go on and reach for that pop gun," said Tall Man. "Your body will still be warm enough for a good while."

She narrowed her eyes. "*Go fuck yourself.*"

Tall Man blinked once, tilted his head in contemplation, and walked off into an alley at a brisk pace. His associates all took a step back at Kirsten's eyes glowing in time with her Suggestion. Unease spread over them, and in seconds, they scattered like roaches into the shadows.

"Not an accident that time," said Kirsten.

Dorian walked up beside her, rubbing his chin. "Now, what do you suppose that man is going to do?"

"Don't know. Don't care." She scowled at the alley where the tall man went, then stormed back over to the patrol craft.

"Well, suggestions are often subject to interpretation." Dorian chuckled. "I find myself simultaneously curious and horrified at what might be going on over there."

A blue light flashed on the buildings in the alley with an accompanying electric sizzle and a male voice moaning.

"Okay. Forget curious. Make that simply horrified." Dorian shook his head.

"Oh, man, that's just *wrong*," yelled a woman from the alley.

Dorian chuckled.

She glanced at him with raised eyebrows. "I wasn't trying to be funny."

"No, I'm not amused at that... mess going on over there. More that outside of Division 5, most cops are terrified of augs. You didn't even flinch when that cretin loomed over you."

Kirsten shrugged. "Do I look like most cops?"

"True." Dorian opened his mouth to say something more, but pointed at her. "Incoming."

She whirled around, pulling her E-90, but relaxed at the sight of a man in normal, modern clothing hurrying toward them with an expression of urgency on his face. He looked like he belonged in a middle-management position at a corporate office. Other than the cluster of bullet holes in the middle of his chest, he didn't stand out much: light brown skin, dark hair, clean shaven.

"Please help!" The man ran right past her and grabbed Dorian's arm. "They're going to kill my daughter!"

"What?" yelled Kirsten. "Who's going to kill your daughter? Where?"

The ghost swiveled to stare at her in shock. "You can see me?"

"Yes."

"But you're alive." He reached for her arm, but his fingers passed through without contact.

"Last time I checked... Usually if living people are about to kill someone, another ghost isn't going to help much. Look, I'll explain later. Who's going to kill your kid?"

He hurried off to the right—away from the alley where the fringers went—"the same bastards who shot me. Please, hurry!"

She started after him, but stopped, glancing back and forth between the spirit and the patrol craft. A strong feeling of worry about Evan hit her out of nowhere, making her want to race back to the PAC to find him. She'd never tested as having the least bit of clairvoyance, so she figured the sudden spike of clinginess toward him came from hearing about another child in danger. "Is it far? Should I drive?"

"No... just over there." The ghost pointed at a building across the street and down about a third of a block.

"I'll float the car out of reach of idiots." Dorian headed for the patrol craft. "Keep going. I'll catch up."

Kirsten pulled her E-90 and sprinted after the distancing spirit.

12

SPACESHIP EARTH

E van frowned at his face reflected in the blank, black screen of his
NetMini.

Still no signal. He clutched the device tight to his chest,
concentrating for a moment on wanting his mother to help him. The
teacher who conducted the clairvoyance workshops had been going over
an ability they called 'Summoning' last week. With it, a clairvoyant could
project their psionic power into the world, focused on someone they
knew. When done right, that person would experience a strong desire to
either go to or make contact with the psionic. The stronger the personal
connection, the more likely the ability would work.

Alternatively, a clairvoyant holding an object a total stranger
considered dear could trigger a desire within that person to travel to the
location of said object. The kids in the workshop all tried to 'summon'
each other using stuff they'd brought in. This girl, Gia, who held Evan's
favorite Monwyn action figure managed to give him something of an
urge to walk across the room. But, that could've just been him not really
trusting she wouldn't break it.

However, if emotional connection meant anything, his mother would
be trying to call his NetMini right now, not getting an answer, and
proceeding to rip the city apart to find him.

Unless she thought they made him shut it down while working off cit
points. It hadn't gotten late enough for him to *definitely* be away from

school. They only let him stay two hours after last class for punishment, even if he wanted to do more to get rid of points faster.

"Dude…" Shawn stepped out of the elevator, shining the large flashlight around. "This is kinda cool. Like landing on another planet or something."

"Copy, bridge," said Walter. "This is Lieutenant Jordan. Me and…" He glanced at Maela. "What's your last name?"

She folded her arms. "Why?"

"'Cause military people always call each other by their last names."

"We're not…" Maela sighed. "Fine… it's Pon."

Evan grinned. "That's a cool name."

"It's a little weird." Shawn shrugged. "But she *is* from Mars."

Maela frowned.

"I mean weird unusual, not weird bad." Shawn pointed his light at a 400-year-old dead car. "Whoa. I've spotted some kind of alien shuttle craft. Looks like it crashed here."

"Commander Pon, what do you think it is?" asked Walter.

Shawn glanced at him. "Why's she a commander?"

"Because she's older than us." Walter put his 'starship guy' voice back on. "Bridge, Lieutenant Fields has located a derelict shuttle, unidentified type."

"Got anything on long range scans, Wren?" asked Walter.

"Guys," whispered Maela. "This isn't a game. We're really in trouble. He doesn't really have scanners."

"Of course he does." Shawn pointed the flashlight at her face. "Wren can see in the dark with astral stuff. Look at his thoughts. It's like daytime to him and we're stuck with these things."

Evan surveyed the street full of decaying houses. As far as he looked in any direction, a metal sky stretched overhead. Giant columns like the one containing the capsule elevator stood in a regular grid pattern, the twenty-foot-wide shafts holding the entire city above them off the ground. He remembered from history class that the first elevated city plate happened in the year 2112, and they stopped building more by 2184. No one had lived down here—at least officially—for almost 300 years.

"Negative contact on the scan, Lieutenant," said Evan. "Abandoned houses—umm, alien dwellings in all directions."

Maela pinched the bridge of her nose, seeming annoyed. Her irritation faded fast, and she stepped out of the elevator with her head held high.

"We need to find a secure location to await a rescue shuttle. We can't allow the aliens to become aware of our invasion."

Shawn grinned. "Copy that, commander. Wren, you got point."

"What about the ladder?" Evan pointed at the outside of the column. A bare ladder led fifty meters up to the underside of the city plate, and a small hatch.

Flashlights clustered on it, sliding up at different speeds to the top.

"Umm, no." Maela shook her head. "We're going to fall and die."

"My mom climbed up and down those ladders a lot when she was a kid."

Maela shivered. "Your mother got super lucky. Look, the metal's all covered in like grease and stuff. What if we lose our grip and fall?"

"I'm with her." Walter threw an arm around Maela. "The ladder is too dangerous."

Shawn shrugged. "I'd try it, but only Mae can open the hatch and she doesn't wanna go up there... so, Wren, lead on."

No direction seemed more appealing than any other, so Evan followed the path of the old paving. A physical sign on the corner read 'E Cortez St.' It felt a bit weird to be walking out in the middle of the road, but he didn't think any cars would drive here ever again. On the left, an ancient car with lights on the roof sat parked in the driveway of a ruined house. Lettering on the door read 'City of West Covina Police.'

"The aliens must have been researching humans. They use our writing." Evan pointed at the car.

Three flashlight beams converged on the reflective lettering.

"We haven't gone too far away from the PAC." Evan pointed up. "Umm, I mean the ship. We should look for a hiding spot fairly close so we can find the rescue team."

"Wow, you know that's old as hell." Shawn headed over to the car. "It's a police car and it can't even fly."

Walter crossed the lawn to the front door, which had fallen off a long time ago. "This dwelling might make a good hiding place."

When no one voiced serious protest, he went inside. The others followed, Evan the most hesitant. They explored the house for a while, dropping the starship crew game as their fascination with ancient things proved too distracting. Finding what appeared to be a video game system in the living room connected to a giant, physical display screen baffled them the most.

"Where are the helmets?" asked Shawn. "How did they play games without them?"

Maela pointed at the rectangular thing on the wall. "I think that's a tee-vee. It displayed pictures kinda like a holo-panel, only it's solid."

"Ugh." Walter scrunched up his face as if he'd stepped in dog poo. "Really, a screen? How could anyone play a game when they can only see a little bit in a box? Stuff could sneak up behind you *so* easy."

"And there's no smells or feeling anything." Walter whistled. "So primitive."

Evan shrugged. "Yeah, I dunno. That had to suck."

"Oh, it wasn't that bad," said an old man voice behind him.

"Gah!" Evan screamed and jumped.

Shawn froze statue still. Walter shrieked and dropped his flashlight. Maela emitted a short, high-pitched scream and cringed back, her left leg raised defensively.

A white-haired older man in a pale blue sweater-shirt with 'LA Dodgers' on it stood in the archway between the living room and the hall deeper into the house. He seemed like a friendly, grandfatherly sort of person, and fought hard not to smile at the kids' reaction of fright.

"Don't *do* that!" yelled Maela. "You scared the crap out of me."

"Yeah, man." Shawn turned his hand to point the flashlight at Evan. "Not cool. This place is creepy enough already."

Walter meeped.

"Hi." Evan waved at the ghost. "My friends can't see you, but I can. I'm Evan. That's Shawn, Walter, and Maela. She's from Mars."

"Mars, huh?" asked the old man. "I thought I heard something about them sending people up there. Nice to meet you, Evan. You can call me Jeff."

"Shouldn't it be mister something?" asked Evan. "I'm just a kid."

"Nah. Too late for that nonsense." Jeff stuck his hand into the wall.

"Whoa…" Shawn pointed the flashlight almost at the ghost. "Who are you talking to, Wren?"

"There's a spirit here. But don't be scared. He seems nice." Evan smiled. "His name is Jeff."

Maela shivered. "Is that why it feels weird in here?"

"Yes." Evan nodded. "Any psionic can feel it when a ghost's around."

"Aww, crap." Shawn swallowed. "I used to feel like this back home a lot. Does that mean there was a ghost in that apartment?"

Evan shrugged. "Probably." He looked back to Jeff. "Who is Lah and what did they dodge?"

"Pardon?" asked Jeff.

"Your shirt. It says Lah dodgers."

"Aha!" Jeff cackled with glee. "They used to be a baseball team."

"Baseball?" asked Evan, tilting his head. "What's that?"

Jeff blinked. "Oh, no. You don't know what baseball is?"

Evan shook his head. "I know about Gee-ball, but I'm not that into sports."

The other kids gradually resumed exploring the house.

"You should tell them not to go into the back rooms." Jeff pointed. "The floors in there are weak and they'll fall through to the basement."

"Guys!" yelled Evan. "Stop."

Again, they all jumped, though only Walter shrieked this time.

"What now?" asked Shawn.

"Jeff said the floors in the back of the house are gonna break."

Maela backed up. "Okay, you three. Outside right now. We shouldn't go in any of these places. It's too dangerous."

"Aww," whined Shawn.

"She's right, man." Walter play-punched him on the shoulder. "I don't wanna break my legs."

"Yeah." Evan nodded. "C'mon."

Jeff followed them outside. "So what are you children doing down here? I thought people gave up on this town what with that new fancy mess in the sky."

"Another ghost is being a butthead." Evan looked around again, just in case, but didn't see the spirit in the long, black coat. "He made the elevator break. Do you know somewhere safe we can hide until people come looking for us?"

"Sure. There's a place not too far from here where you'll be safe. Much more so than out here." Jeff headed off, following the street.

Evan started after him, waving his arm at the others to follow. "He knows a good hiding spot."

Maela, Shawn, and Walter walked in single file behind him, occasionally moving their flashlights off the ground ahead of their feet to examine the surroundings. Evan had never adored being an astral as much as he did at that moment. Being trapped down here in total darkness except for the view of a flashlight would've been terrifying.

Astral Sense might be a 'wimp' power, but he wouldn't trade it for anything.

"Do you have any family you need me to send a message to?" asked Evan.

"Nah. They're all long gone by now." Jeff stuck his hands in his pockets. "Honestly, if you're right and baseball's gone... I don't have much reason to stick around."

Evan started to say something, but the old man's joking tone made him stop. "You're teasing me."

Jeff laughed. "Yep. I suppose I am."

"How'd he die?" asked Shawn.

"I'm not sure. Went to bed one night, sat up as a ghost. Probably a heart attack. Who knows?" Jeff shrugged.

Evan relayed.

"That's sad. I'm sorry," said Maela.

"Thank you, sweetie."

Evan looked at her. "Thank you, sweetie."

"Oh, Little Man's in love," said Shawn in a teasing tone.

"I'm just repeating what the ghost said." Evan looked away from all of them, cheeks burning.

Maela laughed.

"Has he been a ghost long?" Walter aimed his flashlight around the street, hunting for Jeff.

"A little bit, yeah." Jeff winked. "They hadn't built this monstrosity to block the sky yet."

"Do you remember the Corporate War?" asked Evan.

"The what? Oh... that nonsense to the east? No, that happened after I died."

"Are you messing with us?" Shawn squinted at him, then went wide-eyed in time with a surface thought read. "Whoa, no... there really is an old man there."

Of course, Maela and Walter also had to peek. Evan sighed, but let them in.

Jeff led them past crumbling houses and dead lawns. The withered remains of trees stood here and there, perhaps the only thing that made Evan regret being able to see in the dark. Creepy, abandoned buildings unnerved him already, but something about bare, dead trees added that little extra bit of fear that put him on edge.

"Hey, there's light up ahead." Shawn pointed.

It took Evan a moment to figure out what they'd seen, since to him, light didn't stand out as much. Rather than a distant glowing spot in the dark that drew the eye in an instant, it took the form of areas appearing in normal color rather than the monochromatic sepia of the Astral Realm. The scent of wet soil and boiling vegetables lingered in the air, trading places every other breath with the constant sour-raspberry-fishy-chemical nastiness.

Jeff kept walking, leading the children toward a barrier of scrap wood, aluminum siding, car hoods/trunks, and doors that formed a wall across the street. Two men and a woman stood under an awning made from an orange tarpaulin stretched between poles, like guards from a Monwyn video game at the town gate. Rather than armor, they wore clothes made of plastic sheets, canvas scraps, power cables, and bits of scavenged fabric. The man on the left had a long beard in addition to wild hair while the other man had evidently tried to shave… with a dull knife.

No sooner had the kids pointed their flashlights at the sentries, all three adults returned the favor. Evan raised his arm to block the glare blinding him.

"Here ya go." Jeff smiled. "I know they look kinda scary, but they won't hurt you."

"Children," whispered the man on the left.

Amid the rustling of plastic garments, the three adults approached. The woman and the man on the right both wore swords hanging from their power cable belts, while the man on the left carried a crossbow, though he didn't point it at them. Crossbow Man appeared to be the oldest, with streaks of grey in his shaggy brown hair.

"Spirit," said the woman—looking at Evan. "You have brought these strange children here?"

"I'm not a spirit, Jeff is." He pointed at the ghost. "I'm a boy."

"Your eyes have light." Crossbow Man gestured at him. "This is an omen."

"Come, little ones." The woman offered a hand. "You will be safe here."

Maela eyed the hand hovering in front of her. "We're not looking for a place to live, only somewhere to wait for help. We need to go back to the surface."

"Don't be foolish, girl," said the beardless man. "You're too small to run around out there. Monsters'll get ya. This your home now."

"Safe in 'ere. None monsters grab yas." The woman smiled, and offered Walter her hand.

Evan glanced up at Jeff. "You said this place would be safe?"

"It is." Jeff nodded. "These people won't hurt you. They're a little, umm, uneducated, but they will protect you from the other stuff down here."

"Umm…" Evan looked at the adults. "We only need to stay here until my mom finds us. We live on the surface and need to go back up."

"Aww, them's just little kid stories," said the woman. "All that's out there is space and vacuums."

Shawn pointed up. "That's a metal ceiling, and there's a big city out there."

The younger man shook his head. "Ain't nothin' but planets out there. An' outer spaces. They don't want no one to know it, but the Earth blowed up. We're all that's left, inside the lifeboat ship."

"Oh, wow." Maela whistled. "You guys… it's not a ship. We're still on Earth, *under* the city."

"Yeah." Shawn nodded. "This isn't a spaceship."

Crossbow Man grabbed at Maela, but she jumped back. "Someone told ya stories. Sad ya believe such nonsense. Is okay. We safe here. Nothin' will get ya here."

Evan skimmed the adults' surface thoughts. All three thought the kids made up stories about there being a city, genuinely believing themselves trapped in some kind of massive 'escape pod' ship that left Earth soon before it exploded. They intended to drag the kids inside as permanent members of the tribe. It didn't look *too* scary, except for the whole 'not letting them leave' part. His mother could come down here looking for them and never find him.

"They're gonna keep us forever," yelled Evan, before bolting into a run.

"Sorry. We can't stay here," said Maela, backing up.

"Go!" shouted Shawn.

Walter waved. "Uhh, bye."

Evan looked back at his friends running away from the adults. The woman chased after them, while the two men hurried back to the settlement, calling for someone to bring more light-throwers.

The clap of sneakers on pavement rushed up behind him, along with spots on the road where flashlight beams darkened the sepia brown to the physical world's blacktop. Evan hauled ass to the nearest corner, dashing around and sprinting down the sidewalk for two blocks before jumping a fallen wooden pole covered in wires. There, he paused to look back and wait for the others, who hadn't moved quite as fast due to having limited vision.

"Watch out for the pole," said Evan, past gasps of air.

Maela reached the fallen pole first and cleared it like a hurdle jumper. Shawn tripped over it but somehow fell into a somersault that bounced him back to his feet. He didn't stop, continuing to run past Evan and Maela. Walter leapt the post and also kept running.

"Ugh," rasped Maela.

Evan gave her a 'yeah, I know' look.

They turned at the same time and hurried after the boys.

Debris from a collapsed house blocked most of the road up ahead.

"Wait, there's junk in the way," yelled Evan. "Stop."

Shawn and Walter slowed enough for him to run past them and veer left.

"This way."

He dashed over a lot full of dry hay, likely a former lawn, scaled a fence, and cut through a backyard with a long-dried-out swimming pool. The wooden fence on the other side had collapsed already, making for a quick exit to the next street. Evan looked around for a hiding spot, saw nothing of interest, and kept going to the left.

A few minutes later, he randomly took a corner instead of going straight. Two houses down, a large van sat half up on the sidewalk, all the rubber of its tires missing. It looked like a nice place to hide, so Evan dashed straight for it. He stopped at the back end, turning to face his friends so they could see his glowing eyes. He stood there, holding the door open as they all ran up and climbed inside.

Once Walter got in, Evan followed, pulling the door shut behind him... or at least as shut as a bent door could get.

Everyone collapsed, wheezing.

"Holy crap we almost got kidnapped," whispered Maela, her legs shaking. "I hate Earth gravity. I can't run anymore."

Shawn flopped flat on his back in the middle of the mostly empty cargo van. "Whoa. Yeah."

Walter shut off his flashlight. "Guys, turn the lights off, or they'll find us."

"But it'll get dark," whispered Shawn.

"Yeah, and it's super easy for people to see flashlights when it's totally dark." Maela shut hers off. "Do it."

Shawn sat up and clicked his light off.

"Wow, Ev," said Walter. "Your eyes are glowing bright enough that we can see a little in here."

"Maybe you should stop seeing in the dark?" asked Maela. "They can see that."

Evan sat beside her. "Yeah… I guess."

"Crap, crap, crap." Shawn shivered. "Are there really monsters down here?"

"No." Maela rolled her eyes. "Those monsters are about as real as us being in a spaceship."

Walter kept picking his fingernail at the flashlight.

Maela trembled. "They're not gonna find us in here."

"That's good, right?" whispered Shawn.

"Not really." She poked Evan. "You're still glowing. And, I mean people from the school. No one is gonna find us down here. People are afraid to go to the Beneath. I've only been on this planet for two weeks and even I know that." She sniffled, her voice warped with the tone of imminent crying. "We're gonna die down here."

"Guys, relax." Evan looked around at them. "Calm down. We're going to be fine. I got an idea."

"What?" Walter sat up, wrapped his arms around his legs, and let out a long, slow breath.

"As long as it doesn't involve us dying down here, let's hear it." Shawn bumped him on the knee with a fist.

Evan scooted around to lay flat on his back and closed his eyes. "A lot of cops are afraid to come down here. But my mom isn't. I'm gonna go get her. It doesn't matter if we're hiding, I'll bring her right to us."

"Huh? How?" asked Maela.

"Astral Projection. I'm gonna jump outta my body and fly up to the city. Don't freak out, okay? I'm gonna look like I'm dead, but I'm not, just sleeping."

"Little Man," muttered Shawn. "You ain't gonna look like anything 'cause it's too damn dark to see."

"O-okay," said Maela, her voice shaking. "That's not a bad idea. How long is it gonna take?"

"Umm. I don't know. Only a couple seconds to get to the city, but I still gotta find Mom… and lead her back."

"Do it, Little Man," said Shawn. "Everyone, stay quiet."

Evan inhaled a deep breath, let it out slow, and did it again, trying to calm down. It didn't take much effort to feel out the separation between his energy body and his meat body. After over a year of using projection to get away from having to feel his birth mom's boyfriend hitting him, hiding in a van from well-meaning but dangerously stupid people didn't even rank as scary. He could find the 'necessary calm' to project with a drunken asshole throttling him. Best of all, his *real* mom had totally destroyed that guy right in front of him. Every time Evan thought about Mick's ghost exploding into scraps of ectoplasm, he smiled at the sense of safety that came with knowing he would *never* again see that guy.

Coolness washed over him as he sat up out of himself. Maela had her hand in front of her face, gawking at how dark it was to her in the van. With no one able to see him, Shawn stopped trying to appear brave and had the wide-eyed expression of a frightened nine-year-old.

Walter felt around until he found Evan's shoulder, then fist-bumped it. "C'mon, Little Man. You can do it."

"Be right back," said Evan, not that any of them could hear.

He floated the rest of the way out of his legs, his shimmery amber energy body making the whole inside of the van glow. Fortunately, only astrals or spirits could see this light, and he wouldn't give them away if the 'spaceship people' even bothered following them.

A mental nudge launched him straight up toward the city…

And Mom.

13

WITCHCRAFT

K irsten hurried down the street chasing the ghostly man to the building he'd pointed at.

It turned out to be a residence tower, abandoned for being far enough past the demarcation between grey and civilization. The instant she followed him in the door, her eyes watered from caustic smoky fumes. Though she didn't see anything burning, that smell could only come from a fire-in-progress. Of course, it might've only been some idiot burning stuff in a metal drum for heat. A few dosers lay passed out on the floor in the lobby, using plastic trash for blankets.

She coughed, hurrying to the far end of the lobby where the ghost had gone into a corridor marked 'management staff only.' Kirsten tapped the bud in her left ear.

"Ops, need Division 1 backup at my location."

"Copy that Lieutenant Wren, oh… crap what are you doing in the grey?" asked a young man. "Umm. Hang on. This is probably going to go to Div 6."

"Whatever."

The ghost darted past a few grey doors and phased through a closed red door at the end of the corridor. Kirsten skidded to a stop and raised her left forearm, about to transmit an override code, but realized the door didn't have any electronics in it. Also, it had been broken open already. She pulled it aside, releasing a blast of dark smoke that hit her in the face.

Coughing, she ducked and backed up, letting the black mass rise out of her way.

"Ops," she croaked. "Be advised. Possible fire in progress."

"May your unclean soul suffer the purification of fire," shouted a woman.

"Back to the devil with you!" roared a man.

Kirsten froze, eyebrows flattening to a line.

"Let me go!" shouted a child's voice before breaking into sobs of "Daddy!"

"Your daddy's gone, sweet pea," drawled another man. "He ain't gonna help you now."

The ghost paused halfway down the stairs, sending an anguished look back at Kirsten.

She held her breath and ran into the smoke, grabbing the metal railing at the switchback to swing around to the second set of steps. The air cleared the deeper she went, revealing a cinder block wall aglow with the shifting orange light of a large fire. Chain clanked against metal, and the low, murmured chants of several adult voices invoked prayer-like phrases. One even muttered in Latin.

E-90 up, Kirsten took the last six steps as quiet as she could, advanced another few feet to the end of a tiny corridor, and aimed around the corner.

The fire raged in the middle of a large basement room, between a pair of massive tanks that could've been industrial hot water heaters or boilers. A young girl with the same light brown complexion as the ghost struggled at the center of the flames, wrapped up in a thick chain that secured her to a crude cross made of steel I-beams. Wild dark brown hair framed a face smudged in dirt and full of terror. Flames rose part way up her chest. The child stared down at a burning pile of mashed furniture and debris stacked against her legs, her expression grim.

At the sight of a little girl Evan's age being burned at the stake, Kirsten nearly fainted... until she noticed the child hadn't suffered any injury, not even her hair had ignited. The same couldn't be said for her clothing. All that remained of whatever she'd been wearing existed as flakes of ash on the wind and a scrap of fabric on her shoulders covered in flame.

"Save this poor tainted one's soul, O Lord," wailed a woman in a frumpy purple dress.

"The fiend isn't burning." A man pointed at her. "Shoot it."

The woman shook her head. "No. The creature grows tired. It will eventually burn. Only the purification of fire will save its soul. If we destroy the shell with the crudeness of lead, the innocent this creature should have been will be lost for eternity."

Six adults—two women and four men—stood in an arc around the pyre, as close as they could get without catching fire. They all appeared roughly in their thirties, their clothing shabby but not fringer dirty. The woman in the purple dress and one man held e-readers, the rest chanted or spouted off 'scripture' from memory. A pudgy man with short black hair and darkish brown skin nursed a bloody nose.

Holy shit... She briefly thought back to Ashley Harris being so worried that her grandfather's 'flock' would burn her alive if they found out about her psionic abilities. *Wow... She wasn't saying that to be dramatic.*

The girl's futile struggle to free herself caused the burning scrap of fabric still clinging to her shoulders to fall into the pyre.

"No one will question it if you summary these bastards," said Dorian out of nowhere behind her. The darkness in his voice left her no doubt that had he not been a ghost, he'd have started shooting already.

Only seeing the child unhurt allowed her to maintain composure. If that girl had been burning alive, she had little doubt she'd have simply opened fire without a word. But... the girl, somehow, didn't appear in *immediate* danger. Executing these people still didn't feel right.

"I'd question it." She scowled, raised her E-90, and shouted, "Police! On the ground now. Do *not* make sudden movements or you will be shot."

All six adults rotated in slow, telegraphed motions and locked stares with her.

"Help!" screamed the girl, squirming. "It's getting too hot! I don't wanna die!"

"That's not a cop; it's one of *them*," shouted the woman with dirty-blonde hair, perhaps the oldest of the lot at nearly forty. She wagged her fist at Kirsten. "Surrender to the purification of righteous fire or suffer the damnation of eternity."

"On. The. Ground. Now!" shouted Kirsten.

Something in the pyre exploded with a *snap* and a shower of sparks that scattered over the dry concrete behind the zealots. The girl gasped in response and stopped struggling, taking on the visage of a meditating monk while focusing all her attention on the flames surrounding her.

"Demon spawn!" roared a thick-bodied man with a ginger beard, as he grabbed for the handgun on his hip.

Kirsten pivoted and fired. The dark azure laser from her E-90 bore into his chest, passing through him with little perceptible delay and hitting the wall in the distance. His body fell away from a stunned ghost clutching at its chest. The other five zealots drew handguns like a vigilante firing squad from an Old West holovid. Dorian rushed at them, reaching his arms out to either side, but three shots went off before tiny threads of light leapt from the weapons to his fingertips.

Flinching from a spray of pulverized cinder block dust in the face, Kirsten fired at the woman in the purple dress; the laser pierced the blue muzzle flare erupting from the zealot's gun before nailing her high in the chest—not a kill, but the woman went down.

The remaining four clicked useless triggers.

"You son of a bitch!" shouted the ghostly father while attempting to punch the spirit of Red Beard.

His fist and the man's face both burst into clouds of indistinct light for a second before coalescing back to normal.

Kirsten stepped out from the corner, wincing at a burning slice across the outside of her right thigh. "Get down, now!"

"Help me!" shouted the child. "It's starting to hurt! I can't move!"

"Concentrate on the flames. Don't look at me!" yelled Kirsten.

A man in a green shirt pulled a knife.

"Don't." Kirsten pointed the E-90 at him.

"I act in the name of the Lord thy God. Yea though I walk in the valley of the shadow of death, I fear no evil. He shall protect me from the likes of—"

"*Get down!*" shouted Kirsten, her eyes flaring bright in response to the Suggestion.

Green Shirt dove for the floor like someone had thrown a grenade at him.

"Foul witch," hissed the blonde woman, also pulling a knife.

"Pleeeeeease!" shouted the girl over the rattle of chain.

"*Sleep!*" said Kirsten at the woman, who dropped in place.

"Fiend!" shouted the man with the e-reader. He pulled a short sword from behind his back and ran at her at the same time the pudgy dark-skinned man charged.

"*Hug the floor!*" shouted Kirsten.

Spreading her Suggestion over two brains dimmed the effect. The heavyset guy staggered to a halt with a bewildered expression, but the other man zombie-walked closer, raising his blade. Fury at what they did to a child plus her innate loathing of people who cloaked their sadistic natures in false claims of virtue almost made her shoot the man in the face. An instant before she clicked the trigger, a sense of *not* wanting to lash out in anger and hate won out.

Kirsten lunged into the man's charge, spinning under his arm and managing a passable ju jitsu flip that left him flat on his back with his arm in her grip. Before the man could process he'd wound up on his back, she fired a laser blast into his shoulder. The wound cauterized in an instant; he screamed.

"Stay still."

A flash of white light in her eyes glowed upon his face. His expression glazed over. She released his dead arm and spun to point the E-90 at the pudgy guy, who continued staring at her like he couldn't even remember his own name.

"Just freakin' get on the damned floor already."

He complied, still mentally out of it.

"You should've just shot them." Dorian ran to the kid. "This girl's short on time."

Kirsten hurried over, stopping as close as she could get before the pyre became too painfully hot. The acrid fumes made her choke, though fortunately, they collected mostly at the high ceiling. Probably because the child wasn't tall enough to reach the horizontal bar of the cross, the zealots had wrapped her in thick tow chain, pinning her arms to her sides. The heavy gauge links squeezed tight around her neck and waist, also looped through multiple holes in the steel, trapping her against the I-beam. Due to the brightness of the fire, Kirsten couldn't see much of the girl below the stomach. She tentatively reached in toward her, but recoiled from the heat.

"Dorian, can you do anything about that fire?"

"Not really… I can make the kid feel colder, but it wouldn't stop actual burning."

Pain in Kirsten's leg grew. She briefly glanced at a grazing wound that had torn a rip in the side of her Division 0 blacks, exposing an inch of bloody skin. "Grr." She pulled a stimpak out of a belt case and stabbed it into her leg next to the wound.

The girl grunted, struggling to move and straining until the chain around her neck made her gag. "Please let me out of here! The woman in purple has keys. There's like six padlocks. I don't wanna die."

"Animals," muttered Kirsten. "Who could do something like this to a child?"

"It is a demon cloaked in the visage of innocence," said one of the men.

The girl's father and the dead zealot continued attempting to fistfight, but neither seemed capable of doing anything to the other beyond briefly dispersing their forms into fog.

"Do something," yelled the girl. "Please... If I don't burn, I'm gonna get poisoned. This stuff is full of chemicals."

"Foul demon," said the man. "The fires of hell will take you."

Kirsten twisted toward him, aiming her E-90 for half a second before shouting, "Will you *shut up!*"

He glared at her with a mixture of rage and fear, moving his jaw around, but saying nothing.

I can't get any closer to this kid... that steel is starting to glow red. Damn thing will melt soon. She blinked. *Melt!*

"Please help me!" The girl coughed as she squirmed side to side, barely able to move.

"Hold still." Kirsten stepped left and aimed for where the uppermost spot of chain looped around a hole in the steel, angling the laser so she couldn't hit the child.

"I can't do anything *but* hold still!" shouted the girl, sounding more terrified than angry.

Kirsten fired, the laser melting a quarter-inch slice of chain into a spray of molten metal. The loop around the girl's throat loosened. Kirsten fired at the next point where the chain passed through the beam, then the next, working her way downward. After the third, the girl wriggled an arm loose and pulled the links away from her throat. When Kirsten shot out the fifth loop, the child wriggled free of the unraveling chain, kicked out from the pile of burning junk, and hurried away from the flames. Upon reaching a safe distance, she slouched as if releasing a heavy burden, then fell to all fours, breathing hard. After a moment, she rolled around to sit on the floor and peeled the smoldering remains of sneaker soles from the bottoms of her feet.

Her skin bore compression marks where the chain had dug in, as well as welts from zip ties on her wrists and ankles—though no sign of any plastic remained. Kirsten instinctively went to scoop her up, but the child leaned back, raising her hands.

"Don't touch me!"

"Shh, it's okay, sweetie. I'm not going to hurt you."

"No. It's not that." She sniffled. "I'm so hot I'll burn you. I need to cool down."

"Oh." Kirsten exhaled in relief. "I had no idea pyrokinetics could do that… stand in fire and not burn."

The girl lifted her head, offering a sheepish stare. "Neither did I."

Her ghostly father walked over. "Please don't let her go over there behind the boiler. She didn't watch them shoot me, but she heard it. I don't want her to see that."

Kirsten nodded at him.

Twenty seconds later, the girl sprang upright, leapt into a hug, and burst into tears, muttering "They were gonna kill me" over and over. She remained hot to the touch, but not enough to hurt.

"Don't be deceived," said Green Shirt while struggling to overpower the psionic compulsion making him hug the floor. "She's trying to trick you."

Having a bawling child clinging to her pushed her over the line. Kirsten pointed the E-90 at him. "You go vertical, and you're going right back down… permanently. Murder of one man, attempted murder of a child, *and* attempted murder of a police officer. Any other cop would've commenced a summary execution on all six of you."

"Why didn't you shoot them?" sniveled the girl. "They killed my daddy."

"Because she's too damn nice for her own good," said Dorian, shaking his head. He sighed, then smiled. "But that's what makes her, her. Just be damn careful, huh? These crazy bastards will stab you the instant that compulsion wears off."

Kirsten glanced sideways at him, though the girl didn't react at all to his voice.

Growling, Green Shirt kept trying to push himself upright, but his body refused to obey. "I'd rather be in the kingdom of the Lord than in a world overrun with evil. Take this witchcraft off me, demon!"

Kirsten lowered the E-90. "You haven't seen a 'world overrun with evil' yet. But you're going to. Attempted murder of a police officer is an automatic asteroid mining prison sentence—when it isn't summary execution. You belong up there, surrounded by people every bit as fucked in the head as you are."

"You said a bad word," whispered the girl.

"Yeah… yeah, I did." Kirsten backed toward the way in, moving the kid away from her father's remains. "Can I put you down for a sec?"

"I'm scared." She squeezed tighter.

"Just a sec, I'll come right back and you can keep holding me."

"'Kay."

Kirsten set the girl down on her feet, then looked at the mute guy. "Take your *shirt off.*"

The man rolled around on the floor like a simple robot following a basic program. She kept her E-90 trained on the zealots in case one of them picked that moment to break the compulsion holding them on the floor. One by one, she navigated around them, searching them for weapons and kicking their handguns aside. She considered restraining one, but it didn't seem worth the bother since she only had one pair of binders on her belt. Suggestion would work just as well until her backup arrived.

She grabbed the shirt and backed up to where the child stood shivering. "Here."

The girl made a face at it, but need overpowered disgust and she pulled it on like a dress before once again clinging to Kirsten's side.

For the next several minutes, Kirsten relied on Suggestion to keep the surviving zealots down, silent, and stationary. She also used one stimpak to prevent the woman she'd shot from becoming the third new ghost of the day. Eventually, the ground rumbled with the arrival of a heavy vehicle outside.

"Lieutenant Wren?" asked a man in her earbud. "This is Sergeant Corwin with Division 6. Your signal's a bit fuzzy. Where are we going and what's the situation?"

"Six suspects, one in need of medical attention, one down." She guided them into the building and down to the basement over comms. As soon as the armored officers entered and secured the zealots in binders, Kirsten put her weapon away and carried the child upstairs to the former lobby.

Since the weather had become too cold to bring a kid wearing only a T-shirt outside, she summoned her patrol craft closer, and stood in the lobby waiting.

"What's your name, sweetie?"

"Willow Stephens," whispered the girl.

"I'm Kirsten."

"My daddy's dead. They shot him again and again." Willow lapsed into sobbing.

Kirsten picked the girl up and held her. The kid's hair had soaked up the stink of burning plastic. Her father's ghost sidled up beside them, attempting to rub his daughter's back.

The electric whirr of ion engines roared outside. Four orbs of cyan light glowed from the underside of the patrol craft at each corner as the car oriented itself to land beside a massive blue A3V, its six-wheels taller than an average man.

Division 6 officers dragged the zealots upstairs and hauled them out to the waiting transport. The first two started shouting at Kirsten upon seeing her, but the armored officers arranged a few close encounters between their heads and the wall. The remaining zealots settled for smoldering looks of hatred, except for the woman in the purple dress— she went out on a stretcher, still unconscious.

"Where do you want 'em?" asked Sergeant Corwin.

Kirsten turned toward his voice, finding herself eye-to-pectoral with a large set of dark blue armor. "None of the suspects are psionic. An ordinary person attempting to murder a psionic isn't technically our jurisdiction. This case can go through the normal channels. But... murder of one citizen, attempted murder on a minor child, attempted murder on me..." She peered at the father's ghost, who remained close to Willow, trying to brush a hand over her hair.

"Surprised you didn't just deal with it?" asked a big woman in Division 6 armor. "You Zeroes squeamish about that or are you a special case?"

"She's a special case," said Dorian, his voice coming mostly out of the Division 6 officers' helmet speakers.

Corwin glanced around. "Okay, that was weird."

"Not weird, Dorian... my partner. He's a ghost." Kirsten smiled.

"Riiight." Corwin rubbed his visor, armored fingertips squeaking. "So..."

"Lieutenant Wren, Division 0. Tag me in the inquest record and I'll crosslink my video feed." She tapped the rank insignia on her chest, which also contained a holo-recorder. "Should be plenty of evidence that they fired on me. Oh, get an image of my leg. Don't think Div 2 is going to come check out this crime scene."

"Not in the grey, they won't." He chuckled and took a picture of where a bullet had torn open her uniform.

"All their weapons are dead... can you explain how the power cells in six magazines all failed at the same time?" asked the female trooper.

"I could explain it, but would you want to believe my ghostly partner did that?"

"It's something to put in the report... seems anything goes with you guys." Corwin chuckled. "Okay. So these are all norms?"

"Yeah. Their only mystical power is hatred."

"Right." Sergeant Corwin nodded. "Got you in the system. All right. We'll send the paperwork over as soon as we can."

"Thanks for coming all the way out here."

"Anytime, Lieutenant." Corwin gave her a back pat that knocked her forward a step. "Crap. Sorry. Too damn used to people in armor."

"Ow…" Kirsten rolled her shoulder. "It's… okay. Anything that doesn't require a stimpak is no big deal."

She followed the Division 6 people out and headed over to the patrol craft, easing Willow into the back seat before taking a standard grey police-issue blanket from the trunk and hopping in. The girl wrapped herself in it, and resumed crying. Her father's ghost blurred into the car and appeared in the seat beside her.

"What's gonna happen to me, now? My mom is gone."

"Gone?" asked Kirsten.

"Martina, umm… left us." The ghost sighed. "I never told her I had gifts, and when Willow's power manifested, she didn't handle it well. When she found out I was psionic, too… she left that night. Didn't even take much of her stuff, she wanted out so bad."

Kirsten let out a slow, sad sigh. "All right. I'll need to get everything into the system on our side, meaning Division 0. What's your name, and what happened here?"

"Darren Stephens," said the ghost. "I was at work and got a call from Willow's NetMini, only that bitch in the purple dress was on the other end. They had my daughter and pretended to be dosers demanding a small ransom. When I got here, they brought me into a room where they had Willow, but they weren't dosers at all."

"I know… I've run into these idiots before." Kirsten scowled.

"Huh?" asked Willow, sniffling.

Kirsten's heart thudded in her chest. "Honey, your father is right here with us. I'm an astral sensitive."

"Daddy?" Willow looked around. "Why did they do that to us? What did we do?"

"Nothing." Kirsten squeezed her hand. "You didn't do anything wrong. Those people are insane."

"Tell her I'm sorry. I should've enrolled her at the school you people kept pestering me about. I… didn't really trust it. Those morons never would've been able to abduct her from a school run by the police."

Kirsten nodded. "It's all right. You're not the only one who distrusts the government."

"Anyone with a functioning capacity for critical thought should distrust the government." Dorian tapped himself on the head. "Always question authority. Sometimes they're right, but we shouldn't follow them purely because they're 'in charge.'"

"I'd rather that than put Willow through being an orphan." Darren sighed. "Don't bother trying to contact my ex-wife. She won't want anything to do with her."

"Understood. If you don't mind me asking, what happened next? How is it you wound up being shot?"

Willow collapsed into tears again.

Her father attempted—unsuccessfully—to hug her. "I tried to fight. I'm... umm. Well, was... I had Mind Blast. Read enough about it on the net to understand you guys are kinda shitty to people with it."

"Some of us are." Kirsten wagged her eyebrows. "Ask me how I know."

Darren blinked. "You?"

"Yeah, but not that strong, only a grade two." She smirked mentally at herself. *Though, after my Princess Xiana escape from Konstantin's mansion, I might rate a three now.*

"Those crazy fuckers knew what Mind Blast was, too. I let that bitch in the purple dress have it... and out came the guns. Don't see why people are so freaked out about that power, it just leaves someone loopy for a little while. It can't even kill anyone."

Kirsten cringed. "Not in a biological sense, but it can totally destroy someone's mind, leave them a vegetable. Or erase an entire personality. That's why people are afraid of it." She glanced down at her armband terminal. "So, they kidnapped Willow to lure you in, then planned to kill you both."

"Yes." Darren hung his head, breaking up into tears at his continued inability to touch his daughter's hand.

"What's going to happen to me?" Willow shivered. "I can't go home, can I?"

Kirsten lightly shook her head. "I'm afraid I can't let you go live alone, not at... ten?"

"I'm nine... birthday last month."

Kirsten struggled to keep her voice from cracking with emotion. "You'll be safe at the dorms with other kids like you... psionic. I grew up there, too."

Her eyes welled up again. "I don't wanna lose my Daddy."

"Tell her I'll stay with her," said Darren. "I can do that, right? Or am I going to be sent somewhere now that she's safe?"

Kirsten pulled the blanket-wrapped girl into her lap, holding her as she wept. "There is a place that spirits can go, but as far as I understand, it's a choice. You aren't forced to leave. If you want to, umm, 'haunt' her, you can. Dorian can help you out with ways to communicate."

"What about my cat?" asked Willow.

"Your cat can absolutely stay with you at the dorm." Kirsten smiled.

"Really?" The girl's mood brightened.

"Yep. And someone will take you back to your home so you can gather whatever things you want to keep."

Willow wiped her eyes. "Did you have a cat when you lived in the dorms?"

"No... I *was* the cat. Spent most of my time hiding under the bed at first."

"Really?" Willow grinned. "What were you scared of if you said it's nice there?"

"Adults. The grown-ups I'd been around had not been nice to me at all. It took me a while to understand I could trust the people at the dorms."

"Is my dad still here?"

"I'm right next to you, hon," said Darren.

Kirsten nodded, snugging the blanket around the girl. "Yes. He's sitting beside you. Now... we should really get out of this sector. Are you hurt? Did those people do anything to you?"

"Only kidnapped me and tried to burn me." Willow shivered. "And they ruined my favorite shirt." Tears started again. "Dad just gave it to me for my birthday."

"We'll get you a new one, okay?"

She looked down. "I'd rather have my father back."

Kirsten closed her eyes, trying to keep herself from crying as well. "I know exactly how you feel. I miss mine, too."

14

NEAR DEATH EXPERIENCE

Evan's astral body hurtled toward the plastisteel sky.

He cringed involuntarily at the moment of impact, though the lower surface of the city plate had no more solidity to him than a thick cobweb. The interior blurred by in the span of an eye blink, and he emerged in the middle of a large room full of people.

The glowing violet logo for Digital Creations Unlimited on the wall behind a reception desk suggested he'd found his way into a corporate lobby. Men and women in nice clothing walked by, some crashing into him—not that they noticed. Evan dodged the crowd and flew out the doors to the sidewalk, climbing higher to skim over the stream of pedestrians.

A few dogs barked, dragging their bewildered owners along in their effort to chase him.

Evan looked around at the cars, buildings, and traffic overhead, not recognizing the area. He peered straight up and ascended past the tops of the office towers. Hovering about 1,500 feet off the ground, he spun in place until locating the rather obvious Police Administrative Center in the distance.

"Wow… we walked far."

He leaned forward, arms at his sides, and flew toward the PAC, grinning with eagerness at the prospect of soon finding his mother and getting the heck out of the Beneath. She'd told him enough about it down there to make it sound like an astral sensitive didn't have much to worry about. Plenty of spirits roamed the abandoned under-city who were willing to look out for a lost kid. However, his friends had no ability to see ghosts, nor had they heard his mother describe living down there for two years.

Then again, she also said something really bad happened that made her run to the surface to get away, but wouldn't tell him exactly what. He figured someone crazy tried to kill her.

All the time he'd spent flying around out here with his mother in astral form allowed him to easily recognize the layout of the PAC complex and dive in the window nearest her squad room. He cruised down an immaculate white hallway, slaloming between people even though he didn't really have to. More than half of them paused to look around, sensing his energy but lacking any ability to see him.

Evan's heart sank when he found her desk empty. Only Captain Eze remained in his office, as usual, working on his terminal. He flew in anyway, hovering over the desk, and shouted, "Captain Ezzeh?"

The man didn't look up from the screen. "Hello, Sergeant Marsh... if that's you. If not, hello whoever you are."

"You can sense I'm here but can't see me." Evan sighed. "Where's Mom?"

Captain Eze didn't react.

Evan floated back to his mother's desk and waved at her terminal, but the screens ignored him. The wall clock announced the time as 6:08 p.m., so she must've gotten stuck on a case. She should've been off work by now. He didn't think she went home, since she wouldn't have left him at the school.

She could be out there looking for me already. If she tried to call me, it would've gone right to vidmail.

He raced out of the squad room, checking door after door on the way down the hall. More offices, a cube farm, and a shower area all showed no sign of his mother. He spotted Nicole in an autoshower and floated up to her. Of course, she couldn't see him and continued singing to herself while the machine covered her in soap foam.

Sighing, Evan glided into the wall and went up two floors to the combat simulation and training room. Sometimes, his mother went there to learn fighting stuff. He stuck his head out of the wall, peering around at the various cushioned beds and giant neural interface rigs for people without M3 implants. Still, no sign of Mom.

Gotta be an emergency.

A faint sense of danger rose up, the same sort of nagging worry he used to experience all the time when he projected to avoid Mick's beating. The man had usually been so drunk he kept on hitting him anyway despite his body appearing dead. If not for his Accelerated Healing ability, the man might well have killed him. At the time, he didn't really understand why he got better so fast, but the Division 0 techs had explained he could make his body repair itself thousands of times faster than normal. His mother always cried whenever someone implied having that power is the only reason he'd survived Asshole's beatings.

Evan smirked. *Walt or Shawn are probably messing with me.*

Disregarding the notion that someone tampered with his body, he glided back to the shower room and floated up to Nicole's tube.

"Hey!" He waved both hands. "Do you know where my mom went?"

A woman and three guys started looking around, no doubt reacting to the sense of paranormal energy in the air. They didn't look at him, and Nicole didn't react at all, lost to her singing. Evan stuck his finger into the plastic cylinder and wrote 'help' in the fog, but Nicole didn't notice it. Thinking of Theodore, he narrowed his eyes and reached an arm into the shower, attempting to tickle the woman's side.

Nicole screamed like someone poured ice down her back, and spun. "Which one of you assholes did that?"

Everyone else in the room looked at her with varying degrees of confusion. Nicole glared at them, probably checking surface thoughts. She relaxed, went from angry to confused, and rolled her eyes.

"Oh, one of Kirsten's ghosties is playing with me I bet. Is that you, Theodore? That's the one who messes with people in the shower, right?"

He poked his finger into the tube again to try writing in the fog, but the feeling that his meat body was in serious danger grew stronger than it had ever been. Worried, Evan grabbed the silver thread emerging from between his eyes and concentrated on the want to go back right away.

The world blurred into a smear of color along with a sensation of falling backward at high speed.

He landed hard on his back, as if he'd fallen a few stories and came down on a big padded mattress. Grit and wood bits crunched beneath him, poking into his skin. A breeze washing over his front told him all his clothes were missing. An awful smell somewhere between burnt meat and roadkill surrounded him.

Something had gone *really* wrong.

At a whiff of strong alcohol, Evan opened his eyes, staring up at an older man in a grungy olive-drab coat poised to pour the contents of a giant red can onto him. He locked stares with the man, who froze statue still, tears rolling down his cheeks.

Evan lifted his head, gazing down at his naked body laid upon a bed of kindling and ash inside a large black metal tub. Rough edges around the rim suggested it had once been a tank someone cut in half, big enough for a grown man to lay down in. He looked back to the old man and peeked at his thoughts. The elder wept over what he assumed to be a dead little boy, and prepared to pour ethanol over the body so they could cremate him. *Oh, crap. They think I'm dead!*

He sat up fast, waving his arms. "Stop! I'm not dead! Don't burn me!"

"Yeaaargh!" screamed the man. He staggered backward and collapsed, clutching his chest.

The big can hit the ground with a slosh, clear liquid gurgling out of it.

"Uh oh." Evan grabbed the rim of the metal tub and jumped out, rushing over to pull the huge can upright before too much of the flammable stuff splashed out of it.

The older man gawped at him, clutching his chest, then passed out.

"Ugh. This is nasty." Evan brushed at the white ash coating him while looking around at the fenced-in backyard of a decaying house. Tiny bits of wood stuck to his back, butt, and legs.

A handful of LED bricks hanging from a wire overhead illuminated the yard in wobbling light. Firewood had been stacked into a sizable pile near the fence opposite the rear wall of the former home. No grass remained alive, reducing the yard to a simple dirt lot littered with broken patio furniture. He'd climbed out of a large tank of quarter-inch-thick metal, blackened by frequent fire. It gave off a strong sense of residual energy due to its role with the dead, though no spirits lingered anywhere in sight. Beside the burn vessel stood a beat up picnic table. Smears in the dust coating it suggested where he'd been set on top of it. A plastic bag nearby appeared to hold all his stuff. He figured the old man didn't want to waste useful clothing by burning it along with a dead kid.

I'm not dead... and crap! Those people found us!

Evan bit his lip, trying not to panic. That feeling of someone messing with his body hadn't been his friends doing dumb stuff. It must've come from these people poking and prodding him to 'make sure' he was dead, or carrying him back to the settlement, or maybe the old man peeling him out of his clothes. Not until the guy prepared to cover him in alcohol and light him on fire did the 'alarm' really go off.

"Hank? You okay?" shouted a man inside the house.

Crap!

Evan darted to the table, grabbed the plastic bag containing his stuff, and sprinted for the fence. He climb-jumped over it mere seconds before several adults entered the yard, likely having heard the man scream. The suburban street behind the property looked deserted—and dark—but it made sense that the place where the primitive settlers burned bodies would be isolated from the rest of the town.

After activating Darksight, he streaked for a block and a half before running up a hilly front yard, brittle dead grass crackling under his feet. He jumped an ancient lawn mower and raced around the side of the house. No one had yelled at him, so he felt reasonably confident he'd escaped without being seen. About midway down the length of the house, he ducked behind an old central air machine and sat on the dirt, cringing at the layer of oily ash all over his body. Despite it being October, the Beneath remained warm enough that he didn't shiver despite wearing only a layer of ash. Or maybe adrenaline kept him warm.

"Eww. I'm covered in dead guy."

He stood again, brushing and swatting at himself for a few minutes until he got the last of the wood fragments, then pulled his clothes out of the bag and got dressed. The older guy who'd prepared him for cremation hadn't stolen anything… even his NetMini remained. He smirked at it.

"That guy wouldn't even know what this is."

Since the device still showed a 'no signal' error, he stuffed it in his pocket.

Mom's out on a call. She'll go back to the squad room. Or, she'll try to find me and freak out. "I can't just sit here… The others probably got captured."

Evan stood. "I gotta help them escape first."

He crept to the end of the wall and peered out. People swarmed around a house in the distance that appeared focused and in color as opposed to the wavering sepia-toned everything else. He figured it for the place he'd been taken for burning. No one looked in his direction at least, but they had to realize he hadn't died. It didn't seem likely they'd insist on burning him alive—people just didn't do that sort of thing to other people, especially little kids—so he didn't *fear* being caught as much as he considered it potentially annoying.

Of course, other than running the risk of being mistaken for dead again, he could always project and go searching for his mother even if captured. Jeff, the ghost, didn't think the settlers would hurt them. Any reasonable adult wouldn't let nine-year-olds run around a dangerous area alone. Then again, 'reasonable' adults also didn't think they rode on a giant spaceship after Earth had been destroyed.

He raced across the street, went down two blocks, and turned left, heading back in the general direction of where he woke up. As soon as he entered an area awash in color, he turned off Darksight. Glowing eyes would definitely give him away as odd. In the dim light, old cars, dead bushes, and trash cans offered convenient hiding places that allowed him to explore the settlement without drawing too much attention to himself. Not like the real world worked the same way as video games—the town didn't have a bunch of 'guards' who all somehow magically knew he'd done something wrong and would come after him on sight.

A few people spotted him, though other than curious stares at his clean (ish) modern clothing, they regarded him as just some kid running around playing. He moved from hiding spot to hiding spot, pausing after crawling under a centuries-old pickup truck to wait for an opening. The street ahead had too many people at the moment, and he feared someone would grab him.

No one here wore anything even remotely similar to his clothing. The few other kids he noticed didn't have much beyond scraps of material hanging like loincloths from belts of old electrical cords. Some of the adults wore similar garments, ponchos made from tarps, or togas that had probably once been bed sheets. A few settlers of varying ages wore nothing more than dirt. It reminded him of the way his doser of a birth mom would lay around the house all the time naked. When she hadn't been passed out, she'd been too lazy to do anything more than sit there inhaling chems—and she'd sold most of their clothes for extra credits to get high. She once tried to sell off some of Mick's stuff, and he'd slapped the hell out of her for it.

At the time his *real* mom found him, the entirety of his possessions consisted of the single pair of briefs he'd had on. Safely hidden on his belly under an old pickup truck, Evan lost a few minutes crying. Back then, barely eating, barely having clothes, freezing every night, living in the constant fear that Mick would hit him just a little too hard one time had been life. It hadn't seemed all that bad until his new mom showed him how it was *supposed* to be. If he didn't project that night and play with the dog in that cyberware shop, he never would've met his mom.

Fair chance he might not even still be alive.

Wanting to hug her, but being trapped down here made his tears worse, though he dared not make a sound for fear of being caught. These people would probably come over to check on a crying kid, see his modern clothes, and realize he didn't belong.

I gotta get us out of here.

He tried his best to put aside his need for his mother by telling himself over and over that these people, though primitive and ignorant, wouldn't hurt him. The worst they'd do is keep him here and not let him leave. But… that couldn't stop his astral form. First, though, he needed to find his friends.

When the street cleared of people, he crawled out from under the truck and ran to the next ancient vehicle, a smallish car. Its tires had rotted, making the space underneath too narrow for him to crawl in, so he hid behind it. Dull, repetitive clacking drew his attention to the right. He pushed off the car and crept up to a wooden fence. Brighter than average light glowed on the other side from two big LED lamps. Evan figured they had somehow tapped into a power line from the city overhead, mistaking it for the 'space ship.' The intermittent clacking continued, so he grabbed the top of the fence and pulled himself up enough to peek over.

Two pale boys a little older than him, one wearing a skirt of blue plastic tarp, the other nothing, engaged in a sword fight with wooden blades. Three other kids, a small boy, and two pale tween girls, all clad in wire belts with dangling scraps of plastic or metal for loincloths, watched intently from nearby while an adult man in a pink tarp toga with a frizzy tan beard scooted around the combatants like a referee during a fight in Gee-ball. Only, he didn't try to break it up, rather shouted tips and pointers. The girl with lighter hair also had a bloody nose, though she didn't appear bothered by it. She'd even drawn 'war paint' lines on her chest in her own blood.

The two boys swinging at each other circled, measuring their attacks and defenses. Neither appeared angry, more like students learning how to fight.

A dented hubcap on the ground nearby with some wires hanging off it suggested the boy with nothing on had lost his 'loincloth' to a low blow. Evan squirmed in discomfort at the idea of wearing a hubcap. He also had no interest in watching sword training.

He dropped down and ran onward.

Not long after the *clonk, clonk, clonk* of practice swords striking each other faded into the distance, Maela's shout of "You're not listening!" caught his ear.

Evan squeezed past a gap in another broken wooden fence three houses away from the combat school and stopped short, waving his arms for balance while teetering at the edge of a drained swimming pool he almost didn't notice in the dark. Falling eight feet into a dry concrete pit full of junk would *suck.* He skirted around it and headed for the gap between houses.

Walter yelled something he couldn't quite make out, but the sound led him one yard left to a lit window with bars. He couldn't tell if the current settlers had bolted a cage around the outside of the window or if it had been there from long ago... however, someone had turned a bedroom into a jail. Then again, *all* the ground-floor windows of the house had them, so maybe whoever lived here centuries ago wanted to keep people *out.*

He crept up to the window, which had no glass left, grasped the lowest horizontal bar, and pulled himself up, bracing his left foot on a central air unit, his right against a dead bush. His friends occupied a small room, its plain white door closed and probably locked. One small light bulb hung from an exposed wire near the middle of the ceiling, clearly added by unskilled hands more recently. Shawn reclined on a cot along the right side of the room while Maela paced around in the middle. Walter sat on the edge of another cot on the left, looking glum.

"Guys," said Evan. "What happened?"

"Shit!" Maela ran to the window. "They thought you were dead. They didn't believe us!"

"Yeah. They almost burned me."

Shawn got up and walked over. "What's all that white crap on your face?"

"Umm... ashes. Probably dead people. Why are you guys in jail?"

"Eww." Maela squirmed.

"We tried to get away," said Shawn. "Almost made it."

"They found us in the van." Walter tapped his sneakers together. "They don't want us running off alone, so they locked us in here until they figure out what family we join."

"This place is so backward." Maela grabbed her head in both hands. "Like some of them aren't even wearing clothes."

"Yeah." Shawn laughed. "They keep looking at us like we're from outer space because we're wearing 'alien uniforms.'"

Evan rolled his eyes. "Yeah… they really think the Earth blew up."

"Is your mom coming?" asked Shawn. "Did you find her?"

"Not yet. I think she's out on a call. I had to come back fast 'cause some guy was about to light me on fire." He looked at the bars, a 'cage' that had been bolted into the house from outside. "I'm gonna get you out of here."

"How?" Maela reached out and wiped her hand at his face. "Eww. I can't believe I'm touching dead person, but you're filthy. And the door is locked. You're not gonna be able to steal the key or convince them to let us go. You're just a kid, too. You'll wind up in here with us."

"So?" asked Evan. "Even if they catch me, I can still project and get Mom."

"They'll think you died again." Walter shook his head. "You should go hide somewhere they won't find you. That way you can fly around as long as it takes to find her."

"Why his mom?" Shawn raised his arms and let them flap against his side. "Find any cop."

"Only Mom can see me when I'm astral." Evan looked among his friends. "Any of you guys suggestive?"

Everyone shook their heads to the negative.

"How long do you have before you get forced to join families?" asked Evan.

"Umm, a day or two." Maela shrugged. "They said there's some law or something they gotta figure out first."

Shawn shook his head. "It doesn't matter. The worst thing that will happen is we get split up. We'll still all be in this settlement, so when the cops raid it, we're good."

"The worst that'll happen is we get stuck here forever and there's no technology in this place!" Maela flailed. "Do you know how much it sucks for me here? I can't do anything. I'm a *techno*kinetic and the most advanced machines here are levers."

Shawn poked her. "Calm down. It's not like they're gonna kill us or anything. They think we're orphans."

"Umm, Shawn… we technically *are* orphans." Walter set his hands on his hips. "Except Little Man out there… he got adopted."

Evan cringed a little, feeling bad for them, but mostly because he missed his mom.

"What about her?" asked Shawn.

"My parents aren't dead. They're assholes." Maela scowled. "Didn't want a psionic kid. Found out I was a technokinetic after I turned eight. At first, I was thrilled to have super powers, but when I showed my parents, they freaked out. I went from their daughter to this creature neither one of them wanted to touch." Tears ran down her face. "We lived in Arcadia City. My father lied and said we were going on a fun trip. He took me to Primus. We went down to like the ninth tier and he abandoned me there."

"Sorry." Shawn put a hand on her shoulder.

"Ninth what?" asked Walter.

"Tier." Maela 'drew' horizontal lines in the air. "It's an underground city. Each level is called a tier."

"He just left you there?" Evan reached past the bars to take her hand. "That's super evil. I'm gonna tell Mom and she's gonna make sure they get arrested."

"Thanks…" Maela squeezed his hand. "That's sweet of you. But it's Mars. The MDF has enough to worry about. They don't have time to arrest assholes for abandoning their kids."

"MDF?" Walter tilted his head.

"Mars Defense Force. The police." She sighed. "Don't you guys know anything about Mars?"

"No, not really." Walter shrugged.

"How'd you wind up coming to Earth?" asked Evan.

"I got arrested for stealing from a vendomat. The MDF sent me to Division 0 when they realized *how* I made the machine give me stuff. And, I only stole food and clothes, so they let me slide for being a kid." She grinned at Evan. "The guy who arrested me made the same face you did when I told him my dad abandoned me."

"Well, that's really sad and wrong." Evan frowned. "My old mom didn't want me either."

"Mars sounds kinda cool, do you miss it?" asked Shawn.

"Not really. It was scary being alone in the tunnels. If I didn't sleep in a vent too small for adults to fit in, I'd get kidnapped or robbed. And, Mars makes even this dump look clean. You guys call this place 'the Beneath,' but it's nothing compared to Primus. The tunnels where I used to live are like fourteen stories underground. We're not technically even underground here."

"You said nine stories before." Shawn raised the Eyebrow of Doubt.

"Tiers are bigger than stories, and there's like twenty meters of solid ground above everything as like a shield or something. They made those cities before Mars had air."

"Woah," whispered Walter.

Evan's right sneaker slipped down a few inches on the dead bush stalk. "Okay. I'm gonna go find a place to hide and try to find my mom again."

"Be careful." Maela looked around at the room. "We'll, uhh, wait right here."

"Umm, we can't leave. We're locked in," said Shawn.

She shot him side eye. "You *have* heard of sarcasm, right?"

"Oh. Duh."

Evan didn't need telepathy to sense the fear coming from his friends. They all probably wanted to be adopted, but *not* by crazy underground primitives. "Okay. Going. Be back as fast as I can."

He jumped down from the window, listened for a moment in case anyone might be coming, then ran out of the yard in search of a hiding place.

15

BENEATH AND BEYOND

C onsidering his best chance to avoid being caught involved going away from the settlement, Evan walked in a straight line until his surroundings became too black to see.

He activated Darksight and kept going, roaming back and forth across the street to peer into abandoned houses. A few had people in them, so he hurried away. The others looked too dangerous. Remembering Jeff's warning about falling through the floor, Evan gave up on houses and ran into an alley.

"Hey!" shouted a man from behind.

Evan whirled, staring at a thirtyish guy in a poncho of bright hazard orange with numerous holes. The guy pointed a battered katana at him, but whatever he'd been about to say stalled in his throat. His surface thoughts contained mostly fear at the sight of Evan's glowing white eyes and couldn't quite figure out if he'd found 'one of the aliens' or a monster from the deep dark who would kill him with 'laser eyes.'

"You there." Evan pointed up at the man. "I am the great mage Monwyn the Magnificent, and I demand the freedom of my friends. Your townspeople are holding them prisoner. Release them at once!"

"Bwaaaa!" yelled the man before running away in a panic, screaming about aliens.

For a few seconds, Evan felt quite impressive, but wound up sighing. That hadn't helped anything. In fact, the man would probably come back with more adults. He briefly considered just waiting for them and allowing himself to be taken prisoner, but on the chance they'd think he was a 'monster,' a mutant, or a legit alien, he decided to keep running.

His mother had told him about those Harris cultists who hated psionics for no real reason other than something she called a 'made up sky wizard.' She'd explained that humans don't like things or people who are different, often hating them and wanting to destroy whatever they couldn't understand.

Since he didn't want to be destroyed, he hauled ass.

Three streets down, he spotted a large, green dumpster as big as a truck trailer with white lettering on the side reading 'O'Malley Construction.' He climbed up onto the remains of a car beside it and peeked over the rim. The huge dumpster contained pieces of wood and slabs of white stuff he didn't recognize, but the debris came close enough to the top that he figured he'd be able to get back out. This metal box would hide him from view.

Evan threw a leg over and sat on the top to look around. Nothing moved as far as he could see, so he felt safe that he hadn't been followed here. He jumped down inside, the crunch of old wood and crumbling drywall beneath his sneakers. For added security, he wriggled in under some of the junk so anyone casually peering into the container might not see him right away.

Once settled in, he closed his eyes and concentrated on Astral Projection.

Being flat on his back reminded him of the burning pit enough to squirm and shiver.

Okay. If I feel worried again, I'm gonna grab the cord right away.

Once the tingle of astral energy washed over him, he sat up out of his body and glided past the dumpster wall to hover in the street. A growl came from the right. Evan spun, instinctively leaping back from a large blurry form rushing toward him.

The malevolent ghost in the long, black coat attempted to grab him in a bear hug. Evan dropped straight down, nearly sitting on the road. The ghost's arms closed on nothingness over his head. Before the man could recover his balance, Evan darted forward between his legs and flew down the street.

That tingle of his body being messed with came on again, but weak.

Evan stopped and whirled around. The ghost's rear end stuck out of the dumpster, but whatever he tried to do to didn't seem to work as he gave up and stormed around in a circle. Upon noticing Evan watching him from a distance, he pointed, flashed a dark smile, and ran off into the Beneath.

Uh oh. I better hurry.

He stared straight up and zoomed, crossing his arms over his face and closing his eyes when the city plate drew near. The squishy compress of going through a solid object happened, then a few smaller brushes with pipes or gratings, and another heavy mush as he pierced the top of the plate. Evan uncurled himself and climbed higher into the air. Hands shaking from worry that the ghost would lead something worse than a primitive settler to his body, he zoomed up high enough to spot the PAC. Once he found it, he rocketed toward it as fast as he could will himself to fly.

By the time he reached the building, he felt out of breath even though physical effort had no bearing on his speed in astral form. Evan zipped in a straight line, ignoring walls, bee-lining for his mother's squad room.

He burst out from the wall and hung in midair—in an empty, mostly dark, office.

"No..."

Heartbroken, he glided over to her desk and orbited it. Worse than her not being there, the PAC showed no obvious signs of alarm. If anyone had noticed the four of them missing, the place would be in a frenzy. He dove into the floor again, heading for the Admin area where Mr. Short should've been waiting for them to check in after cleaning the classroom.

He found the teacher—well, trainee teacher—still sitting at a desk with a senshelmet on, playing a video game.

Evan let out a heavy sigh. "He doesn't even know we're missing!"

Frustrated, he floated up high enough to kick the man in the head... his bare foot whiffing without contact.

"Gah. Ugh," said Mr. Short, leaning forward. "Weird brain freeze."

He settled back into his seat.

"You're derelicting your duty," yelled Evan, but the guy didn't react.

Shivering from worry, Evan spun in circles, dreading what could possibly happen to his defenseless body at any second. He probably should zip back to it and move somewhere else the ghost wouldn't see... but what if his mother returned to her office in the time it took him to re-hide and come back. No way would she ever go home with him missing. He wouldn't know where to search for her if he didn't get her at the office.

Desperate, he launched himself into the ceiling and flew back to the squad room.

He emerged out the wall at the back of the room the same moment his mother fell into her chair and let out a heavy, sad sigh. She bent over the desk, head on her arms, and sniffled.

"Mom!" shouted Evan, barely able to talk past the urge to cry from joy.

Kirsten jumped and spun around. The sight of his astral body appeared to confuse her, so he doubted she'd been crying over him going missing. "Ev... Sorry I'm late."

"Mom... Mom...!" He flew in for a hug—and sailed clean through her. He stopped himself and turned to face her.

A shimmer of amber light ran over her body. He zipped into her arms, clamped on, and burst into tears, overwhelmed with having his mother hold him.

"Hey, kiddo. I'm sorry. I'm here now. It's okay."

Evan sniffled and leaned back. "I'm not upset because you're working late. We're in trouble. Why were you crying?"

She squeezed his spongy astral form tight. "Bad case... people being cruel to a child your age. What do you mean you're in trouble? We who?"

"A ghost tried to kill me. He made the elevator go nuts and dumped us in the Beneath. My friends from school got kidnapped by settlers and locked in a room. I'm hiding in a dumpster near them, but that ghost saw me. I think he's going to make something bad find me."

Dorian materialized by his desk and hurried over. He looked at Evan, then Kirsten. "Stay here with your mother. I'll follow your thread down there and make sure nothing messes with you."

"Okay." Evan nodded.

Kirsten jumped to her feet, still clinging to his astral body.

"Meet you there." Dorian sank into the floor.

His mother took his hand and ran down the hall, towing him like a helium balloon. He could fly much faster than running, but it wouldn't do any good to bring his mother down there as an astral projection. She rushed to the elevator, rode it to the first level, and dashed down the hall to the motor pool.

"It's not *that* far. Only like a couple miles," said Evan.

"Something's threatening you... I'm not going to waste time running across the city." She hopped in, frantically mashing the console to bring the car online.

Evan settled in Dorian's usual seat as much as he could. "It would be faster if I flew outside the car and you followed me."

Kirsten grumbled. "I won't be able to see you with the electronic window."

"Don't freak, Mom. The people who have my friends aren't gonna hurt them. They're only like stupid primitive settlers."

"Oh… them. Spaceship Earth people?"

"Yeah. You met them?"

Kirsten made the tires squeak pulling out of the parking space, nearly fishtailing the heavy patrol craft as she turned down the lane between rows of various other hovercars and A3Vs. "Met? Not exactly. Spied on from a distance and stole food from, yes."

Evan laughed.

Once she drove outside and switched to flight mode, Evan pointed in the direction they needed to go. Finding his way back proved quite simple as he needed only to follow the silver thread connecting him to his body. He directed her in as straight a line as high-rise buildings allowed until reaching the point where the cord plunged straight down in the middle of a street.

"We're here!" he zipped down out of the car and hovered by the ground.

Passing cars paid him no mind, occasionally making his legs blur when they hit him.

His mother's patrol craft glided off to the side and landed in the nearest open space among parked cars. She hopped out and waved for him to come closer. He zipped over to her.

"It's right under us."

"I can't go straight through the ground." She pointed at an alley. "The nearest hatch is this way."

"Oh. Right. Duh." Evan smacked himself in the forehead.

She jogged around the corner of a building that looked like a bar with 'Tittie City' glowing in pink holographic letters in front of the otherwise blacked-out window.

"Don't go in there," called Kirsten from up ahead.

Evan shrugged and flew after her.

His mother hurried along for a minute or so before stopping at a squarish hatch plate in the middle of the alley. She crouched nearby, waved her left forearm at it, and an electronic chirp sounded. Kirsten grasped the handle at the center and pulled. With a blast of white fog and a loud *hiss*, the panel separated from the ground and rose on mechanical struts.

"Are you gonna get squeezy later?"

Kirsten, sitting on the road with her legs hanging, looked at him. "Yeah. Most likely."

"Good."

"Don't make me cry now." She smiled, despite her eyes being watery.

He followed her down the ladder. The hatch closed itself a few seconds later. Kirsten made her way down the narrow passage, and a switchback stairwell that spanned all eight levels within the plate. She checked her armband display every few seconds until the map led her to another hatch in the floor. It opened to a perilous ladder that went down the outside of one of the giant columns holding up the city.

"Mom," said Evan. "Why are you climbing the ladder? There's elevators inside the columns."

"I don't trust them. Everything down here is hundreds of years old. I don't want to wind up trapped in a capsule."

"Oh. It worked for us."

She stared at him. "What the heck were you doing in one of those elevators?"

"We thought it would go *up*." He stuffed his hands in pockets his astral body didn't have, and kicked at a nonexistent rock. "It didn't. The ghost made it break."

"Why is a ghost after you?"

"He's mad at you. Said he wanted to hurt me to make you sad. He's kinda weak though."

Kirsten glowered. "Dammit."

She dropped onto the rungs and made her way down the fifty-meter column to the ground. Once she reached the bottom, Evan glided off, following the silver cord. He couldn't wait to get back in his body and hug his mother for real.

Kirsten ran after him for several blocks until they rounded a corner and the dumpster came into view. Dorian and the ghost that had been harassing the kids spun around and around in the middle of a fistfight. From the look of it, Dorian had the advantage. Two living men in tattered grey ponchos ran off in the distance, still screaming.

"Who is that, Mom?" asked Evan, hanging next to her at eye level. "And Dorian's kicking his butt like a level twenty character hunting goblins."

Kirsten narrowed her eyes. "I'm not really sure. I don't recognize him... but goblins? Nah. He's not even that powerful."

"Heh." Evan grinned.

"Sniper," said Dorian with a grunt. "Henry Motte's house."

She called the Astral Lash and walked closer.

Evan shied away from the burning energy radiating from the glowing whip. At the moment, it could hurt him. He smacked himself in the forehead for being dumb and grabbed the cord. In an instant, he found himself flat on his back in the dumpster, once more in his body and unable to see a damn thing.

"I didn't kill anyone at Motte's house," said Kirsten

Dorian chuckled. "I got this guy. He was about to shoot you from down the street, so I gave him a little scare. He jumped straight off the building and fell forty stories. Bet that hurt. Shame that corporate assassins don't follow proper safety protocols for high-altitude work."

"Fuck you," roared the ghost.

A few meaty slaps and grunts followed.

After activating Darksight, Evan pushed the debris off himself and stood, but couldn't reach the top of the container. He climbed up to stand on a slab of material that looked like a piece of kitchen countertop, grabbed the upper edge of the dumpster, and pulled himself up to peer over the metal wall.

His mother hovered close to Dorian and the assassin ghost, arm cocked back for an attack with the lash, but she hesitated.

"Watch your language. There's a kid present." Dorian flipped the assassin over and grabbed him in a headlock. "This guy hasn't been a spirit that long."

Evan climbed over the container's wall and jumped down to the road. As much as he wanted to run right over to his mother and grab on, he circled away from the fighting ghosts to a safe spot behind her.

"Hold him... gonna call a friend to pick him up." Kirsten closed her eyes.

"Bitch!" roared the assassin.

He melted out of Dorian's grip and rushed at Kirsten.

"Mom!" shouted Evan.

She brought her arms up in a defensive maneuver, but the ghost ran straight through her—and plunged his hand into Evan's chest. Icy fingers clamped around his heart. Evan stared down at the wrist sticking out of him.

He's trying to make my heart stop.

Evan focused on the chill in his chest, commanding his heart to warm up and keep going. For the few seconds it took Kirsten to recover from the stun of having a ghost crash into her, he engaged in a battle with the spirit—accelerated healing fighting off a chilling touch.

Kirsten whirled around, screaming in rage. A flash of white energy went by, swatting the assassin ghost to the side. Evan gasped, clutched his chest, and fell to his knees. Pain stabbed him like a giant icicle, but he concentrated too much on keeping his heart moving to cry. Somewhere off to the side, Kirsten shouted a whole mess of bad words along with the ethereal whisper of the lash going back and forth.

Inky blackness rushed by from the left.

Evan stared at the ground in front of his knees, trying to rub warmth into his chest. It felt like if he stopped channeling his self-healing, he'd pass clear out. Dorian said something. The assassin ghost screamed in terror. A strong sense of dread, the same sort of darkness he'd felt when the abyssal appeared in their old apartment, built to a peak, but he didn't let it break his focus.

The next thing he knew, his body shook back and forth.

"Ev? Ev!" shouted Kirsten.

He looked up, nearly nose to nose with her. She knelt in front of him, paler than usual.

"I'm okay... just cold." His stomach growled. "And, I'm really hungry."

Kirsten fussed at him, pulling his shirt up to examine his chest. "Ack! What's all this grey dust?"

"Ashes." Evan coughed.

Not seeing any obvious injuries, she tugged his shirt back down and pulled him into a tight hug. He lost himself in crying for a little while—better to let it out now before his friends would see. After a minute or two, he sniffled back the rest of his tears. Those could wait until they got home.

"We have to get Shawn, Walter, and Maela out of there. The settlers have them locked in a room. They're gonna assign them families and never let them leave."

Kirsten squeezed him. "Okay. Show me where."

Evan took her by the hand and led her toward the settlement. "Are you going to ask them or do you want to sneak in and break them out? The window has bars, but the E-90 would melt them."

"And go through half their city. It might hit someone I can't see. Let's try talking. If they won't listen to reason, I'll just have to ask nicely."

He brought her in the back way, straight to the yard behind the house with the barred windows. Two men in plastic tarp robes—one with an old steel colander for a hat—and a woman holding an enormous sword had evidently spotted two pairs of glowing eyes approaching and came to investigate.

Evan couldn't help himself and giggled at the woman for wearing metal bowls for a bikini top along with grimy plastic sheeting as a skirt.

"The aliens have returned," whispered the man with the colander on his head.

"Every now and then," said Dorian, "life presents us with a situation wherein it is nearly impossible not to laugh at the absurdity of it."

"I'm here to collect three lost children who don't belong down here." Kirsten took a step forward. "Please release them so I can bring them back to their homes."

"They've come to finish what they started!" yelled the woman, raising her giant sword.

Kirsten sighed. "*Stop.*"

All three froze.

Maela, Shawn, and Walter appeared in the window, peering out between the bars.

"If you honestly think we're aliens that have the power to blow up the Earth, exactly what do you expect to do to me with swords?" Kirsten scratched her head. "Seriously?"

"We can't let you kill those children by taking them out into space for alien probes," said Colander Man.

Dorian whistled. "They really shouldn't drink the water down here."

"Mom, there's other kids living down here. If the water's bad, we should help them all get to the surface."

"He's being a smartass. But, I'll talk to Eze and see if we can do something about relocating them at some point." She pointed at the man without the colander. "*Release* the *children.*"

The man walked off to the front of the house.

"You two should *go home.*" Kirsten waved, shooing them.

Both other settlers wandered away without much sense of urgency in their stride. A moment later, Walter, Maela, and Shawn backed away from the window. They soon came running down the passage between the house and the adjacent one, gathering around Evan.

"It worked!" Shawn smiled at Kirsten. "Thanks for getting our asses out of there."

"They took our flashlights." Maela gestured at the Beneath. "It's too dark."

Kirsten appeared about to say something about him cursing, but didn't bother. She reached toward Maela. "Everyone hold hands and follow me."

The kids formed a chain. As much as he wanted to hang onto his mother, Evan put himself at the end so he could watch for anything coming up behind them. Hand-in-hand, they followed her back to the same column.

Much to Evan's surprise, none of his friends wanted to use the capsule elevator.

EVAN JUMPED OUT OF THE AUTOSHOWER TUBE, PULLED ON HIS PAJAMA pants, and ran out to the living room. He curled up beside his mother and finished explaining everything that happened, including waking up in a burn pit.

He'd been right.

She got squeezy.

16

GREY DEVILS

K irsten dragged herself into the squad room under protest.

She didn't object so much to entering the squad room, more being awake. The evil alarm clock had vented its infernal wrath upon her far too early. For the first time in her life, she messaged Captain Eze that she would be late, not caring at all if he said no. She managed only one more hour of sleep before she couldn't close her eyes again.

Evan had spent the night in her bed, though she couldn't tell if she comforted a frightened child or had *been* the frightened child clinging to her favorite bear. Perhaps reciprocity had occurred. She marveled at how easily he'd brushed off the whole 'getting lost in the Beneath' thing. Although, except for the ghost grabbing him by the heart, he really hadn't been in all that much danger. The worst part of the ordeal had been how those primitive people reminded him of that horrible woman biology called his mother.

She didn't even bother going to her desk and proceeded right to Eze's office, assuming he'd call her in to talk.

"Good morning." He smiled, his teeth perfect and blinding white. "So... what happened? Is this about the Stephens case?"

"Somewhat. Mostly Evan." She sank into the chair and explained about the kids winding up trapped in the Beneath. "I think someone should have a talk with Mr. Short. He should've been in the classroom supervising them while they worked on cit points, not three stories away in the Admin offices playing a damn video game while my son and his friends fell down an elevator shaft."

Captain Eze nodded. "I agree. So, this spirit... is it an ongoing problem?"

"No. He's... elsewhere now."

"The Harbingers claimed him," said Dorian before appearing beside her. His voice also emanated from a speaker in the desk terminal.

"That is... interesting." Captain Eze glanced at the computer. "I'm glad to hear the kids are well."

"Little freaked out, but I think they'll be okay." Kirsten smoothed her hands down her legs, itching at the new fabric of her replacement uniform pants.

"Regarding the Stephens case. I'm fully behind you on this one, though the Command Council has some concern regarding the appearance we may be executing the religious."

Kirsten held back the urge to roll her eyes. "Sir, look at my video feed from the event. First of all, only one of them died... and I fired *after* they shot at me. Second, those Harris cultists aren't 'religious.' They're insane. There's nothing at all spiritual about them."

"You didn't have to wait for them to shoot first, K." Dorian tried to squeeze her shoulder. "Not in that situation you walked into."

"And"—Kirsten held her arms out to each side—"release my video feed. Show the world these assholes trying to burn a damned nine-year-old child to death on a f—freakin' metal cross. If that kid wasn't a pyrokinetic..." She choked up.

Captain Eze stifled a chuckle. "Fortunate if a bit ironic."

"Not really. They apparently burn all psionics to death. When I brought Ashley Harris in, she told me she'd been terrified they'd do the same to her. At the time, I thought she might've been exaggerating but... I think she witnessed them do it once. And they murdered Willow's father basically right in front of her."

"She saw it?" Captain Eze raised both eyebrows.

"No. They had her tied up in another room while they dragged her father around behind a boiler and executed him. She didn't see the body, but once we got her settled in at the dorm, I spent two hours with her last night so she could talk to his ghost. I really don't understand why Command is so worried about *offending* these morons. They're an active danger to people."

Dorian folded his arms. "Guarantee they're going to keep this entire incident classified. No NewsNet bots caught any of it on camera, so no one needs to know about a Division 0 officer taking the life of an anti-psionic zealot, no matter how justified it was."

She sighed.

"Oh, something new is on your plate." Captain Eze swiped at a holo-panel over his desk. "Please tell me it isn't related to you investigating those dead gang members."

"Umm... I sure hope not. I'm not aware of anything new." She tensed up, expecting horrible news. "What's up?"

"It just came in, late last night. A fairly high-ranking member of an organized street gang known as the Grey Devils was found dead of unexplained causes."

"Probably an overdose of something experimental they don't know how to screen for," said Dorian.

Kirsten checked her armband terminal and, sure enough, a new inquest had popped up in her list of active cases. "Chems?"

"Doubtful. You'll understand why this one came to us when you see the body."

"Oh, boy." She leaned back in the chair and sighed. "This sounds bad."

THE INSTANT KIRSTEN STEPPED INTO THE STORAGE ROOM AT THE MORGUE, strong abyssal energy crashed over her.

Three walls each had sixteen body coolers in a four-by-four grid, bluish plastisteel squares with rounded corners aglow with status displays wherever a space held some poor unfortunate person. Only murder victims wound up in this wing, kept on ice for as long as it took to extract all possible data about their deaths.

The morgue attendant, a woman in her younger twenties with dark brown skin, long straight black hair, and a pleasant smile, crossed to the wall opposite the door. She reached up to the third door of the topmost row and pushed a glowing white square on the hatch.

A soft hiss broke the silence. The panel opened upward, a body tray sliding out into view then lowering to the level of a standard operating table. Lights around the edges of the clean, white platform projected the shadow of a man's form on the plastic covering him. The radiant energy coming from the body almost certainly came from an abyssal, though of an intensity she hadn't yet encountered: stronger than Seneschal and his team of returned mercenaries, but not as potent as Charazu.

This is either a really nasty abyssal or a minor demon.

Kirsten stood there in silence, somewhat dreading what she might see when the woman pulled back the covering. She looked across the body at the woman in a long white lab coat, Bhanu Anand according to the ID badge dangling from the breast pocket. A yellow line below the name identified her as a grad-student intern, still in university.

"The doctor was unable to explain the nature of the injuries," said Bhanu.

"How bad is it?"

Bhanu clasped her hands in front of herself. "It is unusual. I've never encountered anything like it before. And yes, I'm aware I'm only twenty-four and my career isn't exactly epic." She smiled. "I would call it 'odd,' not ghastly."

"What killed him?"

"I can answer you in terms of the literal reason he died, but we cannot explain how such an injury was inflicted. The deceased suffered five internal lacerations without damage to the epidermis or lining of the thoracic cavity. The heart and all its major blood vessels were completely divided in three slices. Both lungs suffered damage as well, though the laceration across the right lung had a more horizontal orientation." She raised her voice. "Terminal, activate."

A large holo-panel appeared in midair next to her. She poked at it for a moment until a scan image appeared of the body, showing four slashes in the center of the chest with another one offset on the left at a flatter angle.

"That looks like claws," said Kirsten. She held her hand up to the screen, mimicking a five-fingered clawing motion. "The thumb clipped the right lung."

"Wraith?" asked Dorian.

Bhanu raised an eyebrow. "Do claws typically cause damage commensurate with frostbite? Tissue to a depth of a quarter inch around each laceration showed signs of having been frozen and thawed."

"Depends on what kind of claws we're talking about. A wraith could, yes."

The tech's confidence faltered. She stared wide-eyed at Kirsten for a few seconds. "Er... now that you mention it, I do get a strange feeling around this body. Sometimes, when I'm alone in this place, it feels like I'm being watched. But... with this decedent, I'm getting that feeling even now, with you here."

Kirsten faced the platform and pulled the covering back. "There's some serious bad energy on this guy."

Jagged black marks on the dead man's pallid white skin appeared to match the scan image of the internal lacerations. Of course, the body's internal organs had already been removed during the autopsy and likely sat in gel canisters somewhere else as evidence. It didn't seem too likely a wraith would go to trial, but she didn't yet feel completely comfortable telling the morgue they could incinerate the remains.

Kirsten gingerly rested her hand on the man's shoulder. The dark taint of the presence clarified—definitely abyssal in nature. Bhanu's description of the lacerations being flash frozen reminded her of how it felt when Mariko's sword pierced her leg. Despite a historical association between 'demons' and fire, it seemed they rather favored cold. Then again, much like this woman's nascent career, Kirsten couldn't exactly claim to have 'seen it all' either.

"I don't think a wraith did this." She pulled the sheet back over the man's face and grumbled, "Demons again."

"Seriously?" asked Bhanu, leaning back.

"Keeping my fingers crossed it isn't an actual demon, but a dark ghost." Kirsten accessed her armband terminal and pulled up the inquest.

"That stuff is real? Are you teasing me?"

Dorian chuckled.

"There's something after the world you think of as real. I don't really believe there's any such thing as gods looking down on us, but I've seen entities of light and entities of darkness, and ghosts go in one direction or the other depending on what they did in life. The ones who are too dark for the silvery doorway but not so far gone they're drawn to the other place linger around as haunts. Someone once told me the concept of Purgatory isn't so much a separate plane as merely ghosts stuck here in the normal world trying to figure out which way to go."

"That's... interesting." Bhanu looked around at the other coolers. "Are there any ghosts in here?"

"Just my partner."

The woman blinked. "Your partner is a ghost?"

Dorian wandered about, smiling.

"He's not officially in the system as an active-duty officer anymore since he's dead, but... for all intents and purposes, yes. He is my partner.

People weren't exactly racing to pair up with the creepy astral sensitive. And honestly, unless they're an astral as well, they really wouldn't help all that much with what I deal with."

"What you're *supposed* to deal with." Dorian winked. "You seem to keep winding up in dangerous situations."

She sighed at him. "As long as this case doesn't end with me having to take on another creature so big I'm eye-level to its balls, I'll call it a win."

Dorian cringed.

"I'm not sure I want to know what that means." Bhanu offered a nervous smile.

"You'll be happier not to." Kirsten sighed and resumed reading over the notes.

The deceased went by the singular name Modeus. Division 1 had a record on him going back twelve years. They listed him as twenty-nine, but the corpse appeared ten years older, though that might've been an aftereffect of death by abyssal. He'd been the fourth in command of a large street gang, the Grey Devils, which operated primarily out of grey zones. A crosslink to the Division 1 notes on the gang showed a network of distribution channels for various street chems, protection schemes, prostitution, even contract killings or mercenary work.

"Wow… Except for their dealing in illegal stuff, this gang sounds as organized as a corporation." Kirsten whistled at the screen.

Dorian smiled. "If they paid taxes, they wouldn't be considered a gang."

"Cynical." She smirked. "It's not so much what they are selling, but the way they deal with competition. The Grey Devils are basically Syndicate Lite."

"The Syndicate wears nicer suits."

"Excuse me," said Bhanu. "Can I help with anything else here, or are you done with the deceased?"

Kirsten looked over the holo-panel at her. "I don't think I can get anything more from the body… and something tells me asking a clairvoyant to read him would not end well. So, yeah. Done with him for now. Thank you."

"All right." Bhanu pressed a button on the side of the table.

The slab rose back toward the ceiling, then slid into its cubby, which sealed.

Near the end of the explanation of the Grey Devils, a single line made Kirsten pause, staring at the screen.

Known to frequently clash with Diablos over territory.

"Oh... no way."

"What?" asked Bhanu and Dorian simultaneously.

"I thought their being into mysticism was just BS."

"Pardon?" Bhanu glanced back and forth from the cabinet to Kirsten. "Who?"

"Sorry. I was talking to Dorian. The Diablos, street gang. They're all wrapped up in rumors about mystical stuff."

Bhanu shivered. "Yes, I know. I've heard of them."

Dorian quirked an eyebrow. "You're not suggesting..."

"The other killings had a ritualistic nature. Diablos dumped those corpses. What if they really did manage to summon something, and they sent it after this guy like an assassin?"

"Might want to hold on to that theory until you have something more than speculation to back it up. Command will lose their minds over that." Dorian eyed the cooler holding Modeus. "Not that I doubt you. In fact, I think you're right."

"Yeah. I really need to—"

Dispatch broke in, via a young woman's voice in her left ear. "Lieutenant Wren, please acknowledge."

"I'm here. Go ahead."

"Your presence is requested in Sector 2928. Division 1 is on scene at a murder site and requesting assistance related to suspected paranormal activity."

Kirsten shook the tech's hand. "Thanks for the help. I need to go."

"All right. Good luck with your investigation."

"Keep a bed cool for the next guest." Dorian saluted Bhanu with two fingers.

Ugh. Kirsten wanted to protest his callous remark, but... worried he wouldn't be wrong.

17

WARPED IN THE HEADWARE

S ector 2928 consisted of middle class residence towers surrounded by several more sectors of middle class residence towers in all directions. The sameness of the buildings would've made finding a particular apartment daunting without electronic navigation aids... but everyone had NetMinis, even most fringers.

Kirsten followed the Navcon point and set down on the roof of a 102-story building beside two Division 1 patrol craft and an A3HV hover-van with Division 2 forensics team markings. A short elevator ride took her to the 84th floor. The doors parted to reveal an unsettling hallway with reddish-beige walls and burgundy carpet.

An odd mood in the air made her feel as though she'd stepped into a horror vid. Much like the outside, the sameness struck her as creepy. Red doors stood opposite each other in pairs all the way down the length of the corridor, past a four-way intersection at the likely center of the building. The eeriness faded after a few seconds once her brain adjusted to the paranormal energy saturating everything.

"Shit," muttered Kirsten. "The same thing that killed Modeus got someone else. I'm going to wind up chasing corpses for... too long. I shouldn't even be here now. It's going to kill someone else while I'm wasting time staring at a body that won't tell me anything I don't already know."

"At least go through the motions, even if you hurry. It's an official call."

Dorian stepped out of the elevator. "You can't just leave... not without an emergency dispatch."

"Right."

She fast-walked to the intersection, turned right, and approached apartment 8416. A woman in Division 1 armor sorta-blocked the door, but moved out of her way when she approached. Stronger dark energy inside the living room seeped from the walls.

"Lieutenant," said the cop, saluting.

"Officer Lockwood," replied Kirsten after glancing at the woman's nameplate. She returned the salute. "What's the situation?"

The woman gestured at the apartment, walking in beside her. "We received multiple calls of suspected electromagnetic terrorism. Apartments near this one, including above and below, all experienced a blowout of electronic devices at the same time. We calculated this as the epicenter, and the resident didn't call to complain, so, we figured he either deliberately set off an EMP device or accidentally set one off while constructing it."

Kirsten nodded. "Okay... but something like that wouldn't make you guys call us."

"This place feel funky to you?"

"Oh yeah." She looked around. A few wisps of smoke rose from the holo-bar in the living room, several devices in the kitchen appeared obviously burned. The walls brimmed with shadowy energy steeped in guilt, strong enough that the room seemed to be breathing in and out.

"*I* feel it too. And I ain't psionic at all. But, wait 'til you see the dead guy."

"Grey Devil?" asked Kirsten.

"Living in *this* area? Nah. Dead man was one Zack Rivera, age thirty-six. Bounty hunter. Probably lost two-hundred grand in energy weapons when all the electronics fried."

"Let me guess, this guy went after Diablos a lot."

Lockwood blinked. "Holy shit, you *are* psionic."

Kirsten went around the couch and crossed the living room to an area set up like a home office. A handful of forensics people and a Division 2 detective milled around doing little more than talking. They all glanced over at her. Most nodded in greeting. One crime scene tech looked away fast, going pale.

She ignored them and approached the sheet-covered body on the floor. Like Modeus, this man radiated abyssal energy, though the undertone of guilt caught her off guard. From what little she had seen of abyssals, she didn't think that particular emotion existed in their repertoire. She tugged the covering back enough to examine his face and chest.

Unsurprisingly, jagged black stains scored the body's chest, his skin not *quite* as pale as Modeus had been, but close. For a radius of about two feet from the heart, the body had blanched. Beyond that, he still had a medium brown complexion.

"Now, that's not something you see every day." Dorian whistled. "As if it drained the life right out of him."

"That's… strange." Kirsten crouched for a closer look. The black 'burn' marks on the chest appeared close enough to the ones on Modeus for her to feel sure the same entity had caused them.

"Yeah," said the detective, chuckling. "That's not the most fucked up thing I've ever heard of."

Kirsten re-covered the body, stood, and started down the hall toward the bedroom in search of spirits or any other energy traces, intending to ignore the cops swapping stories. She peered into the master bedroom at the end, finding only somewhat weaker energy. Officer Lockwood followed, presumably out of curiosity.

"This case from sixty years ago beats all," said the detective.

"You ain't *that* old." A woman laughed. "Come on, stop pulling our leg."

Kirsten stepped into the bathroom, which also had little paranormal energy. "I'm just going to check around real quick and get out of here. Whatever did this is long gone."

"Agreed," said Dorian, following her.

"Think so?" asked Lockwood. "Place feels all sorts of amped up."

"It's only residual energy. I'm ninety-nine percent sure the killer is a paranormal entity, probably sent here by the Diablos to get rid of this guy, and it's no longer here."

The detective snickered. "Nah, Morris. It wasn't my case. Heard about it during training after I made the promotion off street patrol. It came up during class one day, left everyone speechless."

Kirsten checked a hall closet just because. Still nothing useful, except a few sets of WEC Duster body armor—personal protection made to look like an Old West cowboy's coat and vest.

She smirked. *Little boys love dressing up and playing with guns.*

"So, this cyber-freak with a whole bunch of headware decides to become a serial rapist… only there's a twist," said the detective.

"Isn't there always?" asked Morris.

Kirsten shut the closet door and walked back down the hall into the office area that probably should've been a dining room.

"See, this guy would target women with M3 ports and enough cybernetic implants to suit his little fetish."

Ugh. Sick bastard. Kirsten headed for the kitchen, shaking her head.

"Dude was a serial rapist. He'd tie his victims down, then plug his M3 port into their M3 port so he could experience the rape from the victim's perspective. See what they see, feel what they feel, total head case."

The techs, Morris, and Officer Lockwood all whistled in disgusted awe.

"That guy had way too much circuitry in his skull," said Morris. "Totally snapped."

Kirsten stopped short. *Experience the rape from the victim's side?* Her thoughts leapt straight to her active case with the woman who'd been possessed and dragged to a motel in a grey zone. She turned back, staring at the detective. He looked to be in his early thirties with brown hair, though he had a little grey going on over the ears.

"Yeah. A real sick son of a bitch." The detective started to smile, impressed with his own story, but wound up going flat-faced when he noticed Kirsten watching him.

"Did they ever get him?" asked Morris, a woman in a forensic jumpsuit.

The detective continued looking at Kirsten for a few seconds before breaking eye contact and glancing at the techs around him. "Yeah... Didn't go to trial though. His last victim's father was in Division 5."

All the techs—and Officer Lockwood—whistled in a 'that's not good' way.

The detective went to drink from his empty hand. "Damn. Need coffee."

Kirsten walked over to the group. "Excuse me... Detective?"

"Smith."

She blinked. "Seriously?"

He sighed. "Yes. Seriously."

"Wow." Dorian snickered. "That's almost as bad as someone actually named John Doe."

"What was the inquest number on that case?" Kirsten held her left arm up, opening the holo-panel.

Detective Smith bit back a laugh. "It's a sixty-year-old case and what was left of the guy wouldn't have filled a sandwich bag."

"It's probably just folklore," said Lockwood. "You know how cops are. Tall tales to freak out the rooks. What kind of twisted son of a bitch would want to rape himself? That shit's way too sick to be real."

Kirsten shook her head. "It *is* real. And the guy's not done."

"Not done? He's a splat mark," said Smith, laughing.

"I investigate issues related to paranormal entities, predominantly ghosts. An extremely violent death can produce a haunt of exceptional power. I've got an active case that sounds an awful lot like that case you were talking about, enough that I need to ask you for that inquest number."

"Look, kid." Detective Smith rested his hands on her shoulders. "You're way too young to even read that file. Some of the stuff in there would turn your hair white."

"I'm not a kid, detective. And I'm sure some of the cases I've handled would leave you hiding under your bed sucking your thumb. Trust me, I can handle anything a mortal can do."

Dorian gave her a funny look, but said nothing.

"All right, fine. It's your psyche to shatter. Gimme a sec to look it up." Smith took out his NetMini and accessed his police login.

Kirsten glanced at Dorian.

"Some things the living can do to each other would affect you. Not going to put those thoughts in your head." He offered a protective smile.

Stuff with kids involved. She cringed internally, thinking back to Willow and how she might've reacted if the girl hadn't been pyrokinetic.

"Here it is. Inquest 23061122CC."

Kirsten snapped out of her depressive thoughts and keyed the number into her armband terminal. "You said sixty years. 2306? This is a 102-year-old case."

He shrugged. "I guessed. Been a couple years since I actually looked at it. The guy's long gone."

She typed the last few characters before looking up at him. "He's long dead. Not long *gone*. You're a detective. Check Inquest 24181018B2, read what happened, and you tell me what *you* think about the cases being related."

Smith one-finger typed at his NetMini. The screen glare on his face changed from bright to neon green. He read her notes, his cheeks gradually paling over the next few minutes. "Feh. You're messing with me."

"Serial rapist with cybernetics plugs into his victims to 'feel' it from their side? Unknown paranormal entity possesses at least two women that we know of and places them in situations to be assaulted, not releasing them until *after* the assault is finished? I'll ask you again, Detective Smith... for the sake of argument, consider ghosts to be real. What would that evidence tell you?"

He eyed his NetMini for a few seconds. "It tells me I'm going to be needing heavy doses of Sandman to ever sleep again."

Lockwood, Morris, and two other women on the forensics crew all shivered.

"I need to track this son of a bitch down and deal with him, but he's impossible to pinpoint. There's no pattern to the attacks. He appears to be choosing his victims absolutely at random. Most spirits have a 'home' of sorts that they don't stray far from, but this one doesn't. I have no idea where to start looking. This old case might just give me enough information to figure out where he, well for lack of a better word, sleeps." Kirsten sighed. "Thanks."

Detective Smith nodded, though still seemed quite freaked out.

"Please send Zack Rivera's remains in under Inquest 24181021AF." She backed toward the door. "There's not much more I can do here. The entity that did this is gone and I think it was likely ordered to go after this guy specifically. You might want to send a note over to the Gang Crimes Task Force that anyone high up on the Diablos' shit list might have a disturbing paranormal encounter."

"Right," said Smith. "About that coffee..."

18

VICTIM NUMBER THREE

At several points in her life, Kirsten had read things that made her squirm, made it difficult to sleep, or gave her nightmares.

Mostly, they'd been scary stories that Nicole dared her to read... and they had nothing on Inquest 23061122CC. The investigation began in 2036, two years before the suspect, Malden Walker, met a brutal —though quick—death. Pris Ramirez had been his forty-seventh, and last victim. By the time he attacked the twenty-year-old daughter of a Division 5 trooper, the entire city knew of his existence. Miss Ramirez had loaded a virus soft into her headware on the off chance she wound up being one of his victims.

That virus got into Walker's Neural Interface Unit when he linked to her, and while it didn't do anything to him that he noticed, it allowed the authorities to track him down. Ramirez never expected her father would boot in the door of the dive motel where Walker had been staying at the time and feed him three high-explosive rounds from an ABR20.

Kirsten winced at the site images. One showed Sergeant Tito Ramirez standing there like a triumphant hunter with the massive pump-shotgun-style rifle over his shoulder. Two smoking bits of leg and scraps of electronics clinging to a spatter of red on the walls appeared to be the extent of Walker's remains.

That gun is supposed to be used on borgs. Walker only had artificial eyes and some headware.

According to the inquest, Malden Walker targeted younger women between eighteen and twenty-five who had at least one cybernetic eye and an M2 port (it happened over a hundred years ago before the M3 had hit the consumer market). In all but the first three attacks, after he finished, Walker forced the victims to shower, then placed them nude, hogtied, gagged, and blindfolded into a PubTran car and sent it to the nearest Division 1 station. Some investigators' comments in the file theorize that he destroyed the victim's clothing to eliminate potential evidence, while others believed the PubTran ride was intended to inflict humiliation and mental trauma.

The first three victims, he'd left at the scene of the attack, trapped inside hotel autoshower tubes he'd sealed with duct tape.

In every case, the victims suffered only minor injuries: bruising from being grabbed and resisting, cuts and skin lesions caused by their struggling against restraints, and of course bruising and abrasion to the genital region. Kirsten (and the original Division 2 investigators) thought it unusual that Walker appeared to go out of his way to minimize injury. Victims reported that he mostly spoke in a sing-song whispery voice, called them 'delicate flowers,' and—most disturbing of all, while he'd connected his headware to his victims' headware, tapping into what they saw, heard, and felt, the women reported hearing his voice in their heads mimicking a woman or a child, screaming at himself to stop as if he were the victim. Most of the women stated that they thought he mocked their pleas, but the original investigators theorized Walker had likely suffered severe abuse as a boy and, for reasons they couldn't figure out, had some compulsion to continually relive it vicariously.

Kirsten stared at that line for a moment before leaning back from the holo-panel and rubbing her eyes.

"That bad?" asked Dorian.

She covered her eyes. "You read it."

A chilly presence manifested on her left. After a moment, Dorian whistled.

"The investigators think he didn't consider the women personally significant... Like, he didn't care who they were, he only needed a means to re-victimize himself over and over again." She shivered. "Why didn't the guy just go into some twisted VR sim? All the really sick bastards do that now. They can get away with anything in VR and not be shot for it. Did that not exist back then?"

Dorian muttered something in Arabic that sounded like curse words.

"It did. I can't say for sure since I wasn't around then, but from what I remember hearing, what we think of as the GlobeNet now was quite a bit more obvious as being in a video game with the M2 port. Pixilation, not-quite-right looking people, no sense of smell, that sort of thing. With the M3s these days, it's quite easy for a person to lose track of if they're in the real world or the virtual."

"So you're saying this guy just wanted more realism? I don't buy it. There had to be some component here of taking power over people he thought of as weak. Rape is more about power than an act of sex."

"Yes… only in this case, I think Walker was looking for power over himself. Maybe he somehow internalized blame for what happened to him as a child and thought he deserved more. Maybe he'd been so broken he wound up liking it?"

"Ugh." Kirsten rubbed her temples. "I didn't sign up to deal with anything this twisted."

Dorian smiled. "You didn't 'sign up' for any of it. They kind of just handed you an E-90 and sent you out there."

"Yeah… so, this file is helpful, but not as helpful as I thought. I couldn't find anything about his former residences, associates, or family beyond a younger brother who migrated off Earth in 2309. As far as I can tell, he hadn't done anything wrong, but his relationship to Walker caused him to become a target for angry citizens." She looked up at Dorian. "I really doubt this ghost is zooming off into space to sleep on another planet. No way his brother is even still alive at this point. He'd be a little over a hundred years old."

"Yeah. Fair bet he's gone."

"It's so weird this guy tried to avoid injuring his victims and even sent them straight to the police afterward." She tapped a finger on her desk, thinking.

Dorian shifted his jaw side to side in thought. "Perhaps death made him less nice. Leaving Mia Sanchez tied to a bed in a grey zone motel wasn't exactly healthy… She's damn lucky she had an implanted comm and didn't need her hands to call for help."

A momentary flash of lying naked on Konstantin's bed came and went. She remembered the way she'd wanted him at the time, and it nauseated her. Those thoughts and desires hadn't been hers at all. They'd come from the minor abyssal spirit in the bracelet. She'd been every bit as helpless as Mia Sanchez. If not for his NetMini ringing at that exact moment…

"What's wrong?" asked Dorian in a gentle tone.

"Just having bad thoughts."

"Him again?"

"Yeah."

Dorian leaned on her desk—or at least appeared to. "The man only did that because he believed it was the best way to control you. He had no real interest in you sexually, and certainly didn't want a relationship."

"I know... I know." She grabbed her cup and drained the last of the coffee in it.

"Lieutenant Wren?" asked a childish voice from the right.

Kirsten lowered the cup away from her eyes, revealing the overly serious face of a familiar eleven-year-old girl wearing Division 0 blacks—without the utility belt or laser pistol. Cadet Samantha Peña saluted her as soon as they made eye contact.

The sight of at least one psionic kid whose parents loved them brightened Kirsten's mood. She returned the salute. "Cadet?"

"Lieutenant, there's a woman here who claims a ghost attacked her. She wants to talk to someone. They sent me up here to get you."

Crap. Please be something stupid like Theodore. "All right." Kirsten locked her desk terminal.

Cadet Peña raised her left forearm and accessed a holographic screen.

"Aww. She's adorable," said Dorian. "Like a tiny version of you, only with actual color in her skin."

Since the girl looked down at her armband, Kirsten picked her eye with her middle finger.

Dorian snickered.

"Interview room C-8," said Cadet Peña, reading from her screen. She lowered her left arm and smiled.

"Thank you, Samantha."

The girl snapped to attention and nodded, then hurried off.

Kirsten sighed.

"She's into it," said Dorian. "The cadets that young aren't forced to salute anyone... well, some hard-ons get bent out of shape if they don't, but I can only think of two, and they're both majors and up."

"Oh, yeah. You're right. I've been spending too much time around your cynicism. And I never did the cadet thing. At her age, I was sleeping in a tiny chamber below the city with a dozen ghosts for 'parents.'"

"Surprised none of them told you to go to the surface."

"Wish they would have." Kirsten walked out to the hall, heading for the elevator. "But, they didn't know anything outside the world down there.

Most of them died long before West City existed. Some of them did try to convince me to go to settlements, but I was too afraid of adults."

"Speaking of… how's your father doing? Haven't seen him in a while." Dorian stepped into the elevator next to her.

"He's okay. Comes around now and then to check up on me. He's happy I'm with Sam."

"Are *you* happy you're with Sam?"

Kirsten grinned, daydreaming of snuggling with him on the couch. "Yeah."

A *ping* preceded the doors opening. Kirsten stepped out on the third floor and headed past a security checkpoint toward the interview area.

They'd put the woman in one of the 'nice' rooms, as opposed to suspect interrogation areas. Rather than a steel table with points to secure binders, Kirsten stepped into a pleasant space decorated in neutral colors with comfortable but not terribly expensive cushioned chairs. As soon as she saw the shivering red-haired woman crying into a wad of tissue, her heart sank.

At the *click* of Kirsten nudging the door closed, the woman looked up. "You're the ghost expert?"

"As much of one as we've got, yes." She lowered herself to sit catty-corner to the woman. "I'm Lieutenant Kirsten Wren, but please just call me Kirsten."

"Sienna West." She looked down at her lap. "They assured me you won't think I'm mental."

"If you're going to tell me that you believe a ghost assaulted you, I won't."

Dorian smiled. "She'll only think you're mental if you claim the Zombie Ballerinas make decent music."

Sienna didn't react to him, though Kirsten shot him a 'not now' side eye.

"Can I infer by your emotional state that you were the victim of a serious assault?"

"Yes." Sienna fidgeted at the tissue. "Sorry. I haven't slept."

Kirsten used the terminal on the table and opened a blank file. If, as she suspected, this woman met Malden Walker, she'd attach it to the inquest later. Otherwise, she'd save it as a new one. "Take your time and tell me as much as you feel comfortable with."

"All right. You're really not going to think I'm crazy?"

"Not at all. I've been seeing and speaking with ghosts since I was a child. The crazy ones are people who see evidence staring them in the face and ignore it because it conflicts with the cozy little world they like to believe they're in."

"Heh." Sienna managed a weak smile. "I took the maglev home from work. It's not all that unusual for me to feel stared at or followed, but last night, that feeling stayed with me after I got off the tram and walked from the platform to my building. I didn't see anyone obviously tailing me, so I brushed it off as needing a vacation."

Kirsten nodded.

"It felt like someone was next to me in the elevator and went with me right into my bedroom. When I changed out of my work clothes, it felt like a man grabbed me from behind and shoved me down on my Comforgel pad." She cringed and lost a moment crying into the tissue. Over the next few minutes, she described being held down and pawed by an invisible man. "I thought for sure I had some creepy son of a bitch with CamNano who turned himself invisible. I mean, I saw his handprints on my skin. I sliced around but... nothing."

"Sliced around?" asked Kirsten.

"I've got self-defense blades in my right hand."

"Ahh. Okay." Kirsten noted 'cybernetic claws' in the report.

"I tried to get up, but couldn't. One hand on my shoulder felt like it weighed as much as a damn PubTran bus. Then it got weird."

Dorian scratched at his eyebrow. "*Got* weird? Sounds already rather strange... at least for a normal person."

"What happened?" asked Kirsten.

"A cold breeze fell on me and my whole body went stiff. I couldn't move at all for a few minutes, just remember laying there bent over the Comforgel, with this dreadful fear that I was helpless to go anywhere, waiting for someone terrifying who would show up any minute and..." She choked up.

Kirsten squirmed. *Glimpse into Malden's early life? That had to come from him.* "I think I know what you're going to say, you don't have to."

"Thanks. Yeah. Nothing happened. After a few minutes, I got up, but it wasn't me. Something else was in control. My arms moved on their own. It made me take my bra off, and I just walked out of my apartment naked." Sienna's face turned crimson. "Those stupid damn cat-mod people..."

"You were attacked by Neko-chans?" asked Kirsten with a head tilt.

"No... I mean... they're always running around naked all the time, so people don't even think it's weird anymore. I must've passed hundreds of people and no one even asked me if I was okay." She scowled. "Plenty took pictures, though. I was screaming in my head to stop, to get out, leave me alone, go away, but whatever had me didn't."

Kirsten nodded.

"It made me walk for over an hour into a shitty area..."

Somehow, Kirsten kept a straight face while the woman described being forced to roam around until a pack of fringers decided to attack her. Two held her down for a third man, while four others watched. After the first one finished, the others got into an argument about who would go next. Their shouting attracted the attention of more fringers who surprisingly ran in to help her. As the fight started, the ghost let go of its control. She took advantage of the argument, slashed the hell out of the men holding her down, and ran.

Three of the guys who ran in to help found her curled up inside a plastiboard box, hiding a block or two away, and helped her get to a PubTran car.

"Not all fringers are bad," said Dorian.

"Most aren't," muttered Kirsten. "Malden seems to have a knack for finding the special ones."

"Look." Sienna lifted her head, making eye contact. "I know there's almost no chance in hell the police are going to raid a grey zone looking for a pack of filthy men I can't really even give a good description of. I blame that... entity more than those guys." She squirmed in her seat. "I mean, if you can find the bastards who raped me, please do... but I know how cops are."

"It's not a lack of concern, Miss West." Kirsten linked her notes to the inquest for Malden Walker. "Raiding a grey zone is a reasonably involved undertaking that requires planning. We would absolutely do it if we had enough information to identify a suspect in an assault like this. Are you certain you can't describe the men who attacked you?"

"My head was foggy from whatever that spirit did to me. All of them looked the same. Tattered clothes, wild beards, dark faces with eyes that seemed like they glowed yellow. Everything smelled like piss and stale cheese. I'm sure it made me see nightmares instead of reality. Those three men who found me hiding didn't look at all like that. One even gave me his coat. It stank like a public toilet, but it beat nothing."

"Do you remember what sector the spirit brought you to?"

"No. The walk felt like it took an hour, but it had to be longer. I didn't get home until nearly four in the morning. The normal police already interviewed me and did all their tests. If the man's DNA is in the system, they'll know who he is. But, fringers aren't usually in the system. They thought I was crazy when I told them I was possessed." She frowned. "They tested me for drugs when they gave me the shots to kill any diseases the bastard might've given me."

Kirsten tapped a finger on the table, thinking. "We could run the PubTran logs to see where that ride originated."

"The guys who helped me used their 'mini for it. It's not under my PID."

"Oh."

Sienna dabbed at her eyes. "I've been up all night doing research. You're the one who did something on the Moon, right? Destroyed some kind of big ghost? I know it all sounds like conspiracy stuff and no one's officially saying anything happened, but there are a lot of discussions about it."

"Well..." Kirsten bit her lip, unsure how much of what happened she could divulge to a civilian. Not that she thought it mattered, but she didn't want Captain Eze to get chewed out for her saying too much. "Yes. There was a supernatural entity that I confronted on the Moon. It's destroyed now."

Sienna's expression hardened. "I want you to destroy the one that did this to me."

"She sounds like Senator Winchester," said Dorian. "Only, I think *her* request is a lot more reasonable."

"It's quite possible it will end that way once I find him." Kirsten eyed the text on the screen in front of her. "But I have to find him first." *This one's going to be a nightmare to track down.*

"I understand." Sienna fidgeted at her coat. "Thank you for believing me."

"Of course."

She looked up. "Have there been many other victims?"

"I've become aware of two others."

"Only two?" Sienna blinked. "Not that I want him to attack more people, but... why me?"

"Do you have an M3 port or an artificial eye?" asked Kirsten.

"Who doesn't have an M3?" Sienna shrugged. "Eyes, no. They're still mine."

Dorian walked around to look at the woman from the other side. "As a ghost, I don't think he'd need the M3 anymore to satisfy his particular desires. But, he may still be targeting women who have them as it's deeply ingrained in his MO."

"Where do you work?" Kirsten hovered her hands over the keyboard.

"You don't have a port, do you?" Sienna chuckled. "You're actually typing."

"Many psionics skip cybernetic implants. I hear people say they mess with our 'aura' or whatever, but personally, the idea of putting metal under my skin just creeps me out."

Sienna nodded. "Yeah, that makes sense. I didn't really like it, but I got the port just because it's so damn convenient. After an incident in university, I added the blades. I'm employed by Peyton & Rausch as a stock trader."

"Impressive for twenty-five."

"Junior stock trader." Sienna lapsed into trembling. "Fuck. I don't know how to handle this. Bad enough I'm constantly afraid *living* guys are going to grab me. How am I supposed to protect myself from a ghost? I'm not even safe in my own home."

Before Kirsten could think of anything to say, the woman broke down sobbing. She took Sienna's hand and tried her best to be reassuring, using some of the same phrases Dr. Loring often said to her. Only, the psychologist had been trying to convince Kirsten the abuse she suffered at her mother's hands hadn't been her fault. She *still* hadn't told the doctor about the man who gave her food.

Sienna continued freaking out over the idea that this ghost could come back and victimize her again whenever it wanted to and neither she, nor the police, could do a damn thing about it. She sobbed rapid-fire questions about how to protect herself without waiting for any sort of answer for a little while, then fell silent.

"Miss West, this is an extremely rare situation. This ghost is one of a kind in the entire database of our awareness of such things. I know it probably doesn't sound very believable after what just happened to you, but the chances that you will ever again be attacked in that manner by a ghost are pretty much nil."

"What if he comes back?" Sienna blew her nose, still unable to stop her hands from shaking.

"From what I know of this spirit, he didn't target his victims with any sense of specificity to who they were. He chose women with certain attributes, about as impersonal as a crime of this nature can get."

"What do you mean by 'certain attributes?'"

"Younger twenties, NIU, interface port... I think he's extremely disturbed mentally." Kirsten cringed.

"Oh, just a little," said Dorian.

"So, there's nothing I can do to protect myself?" Sienna fished a new tissue out of her coat pocket and wiped at her eyes.

"Barring your being an astral sensitive, nothing I'm confident enough in even mentioning. The archives contain a few mentions of what I can only describe as 'magic' that supposedly can affect spirits. I've seen ghosts all my life and even I don't really believe that stuff works."

Sienna abruptly laughed. "If ghosts are real, wouldn't magic be, too?"

"It's more likely that 'magic' was merely people with psionic abilities before we understood what psionic abilities are."

"Explain Konstantin summoning abyssals. Or that ghost-eating gem." Dorian raised the Eyebrow of Checkmate.

Kirsten drew in a breath to lash out, but held it, grabbing fistfuls of air. "I... don't know. I *do* know that I will find this spirit and make sure he doesn't hurt anyone again."

"Thank you." Sienna bowed her head. "Really... thank you for listening to me and I hope you kill that son of a bitch before he attacks anyone else."

So do I. Kirsten's smile felt forced. She didn't trust herself to find him with the information she had. His mortal remains had been reduced to thin liquid spread over the walls of a...

She blinked. *The motel! His blood saturated the walls... and ceiling. If he has a home, it would be that room.*

Sienna sensed the increased confidence in her and sat up straighter. "Is there anything else I can help with?"

"A few bits of info..." Kirsten took down her address, the route she took back and forth to work, and anywhere she had been 'out and about' over the past month where the ghost might have spotted her as a potential target.

That done, Kirsten walked her out and helped her get a PubTran car home so she could try and sleep.

On the way back into the squad room, Captain Eze waved her over from his door, his expression grim.

Crap. This is going to be bad news.

She went past her desk and into his office. "Captain?"

"Wren..." He didn't even go back to his chair—another bad sign. "There have been three more deaths that fit the same pattern as Modeus and Zack Rivera, that bounty hunter. Same black lines on the chest. One is Santiago Herrera, the number two man in the Angels."

"They're not exactly angels," grumbled Kirsten. "They're not even particularly nice."

"As street gangs go, the Angels are on the tamer side… except for that territory stuff with the Fei Len. And their name is based on an old city name, not people with wings."

"They're affiliated with forced prostitution," said Kirsten.

Captain Eze raised his hands in surrender. "I'm not saying they're good people… just when compared to groups like the Diablos or the Dead Boyz, they aren't *as* psychotic."

"The Diablos aren't terribly intelligent. Maybe they're only doing it to start a gang war?" asked Dorian. "They're uninhibited nihilistic hedonists, heavy on the nihilism."

"Say that three times fast." Kirsten sighed.

"Pardon?" asked Captain Eze.

"Dorian thinks the Diablos may be attempting to start a gang war, then called them 'uninhibited nihilistic hedonists.'"

"Ahh. An apt description. And he's potentially right there. Modeus was a key player in the Grey Devils. Herrera basically ran the Angels. Both of those groups actively fight the Diablos." Captain Eze rubbed his chin. "Your inquest notes imply that the Diablos somehow managed to summon an abyssal. Is your feeling that they are using it as a paranormal assassin solid or speculation?"

"Speculation moving rapidly to certainty," said Kirsten. "It's too much of a coincidence for a bigwig with the Angels, a boss in the Grey Devils, and even a bounty hunter who made a name for himself specifically going into the black zones to rescue people from Diablos all to die of paranormal means so close together and so soon after…"

"So soon after what?" The captain finally walked around his desk and fell heavily into his chair. Two of his African mask statuettes along the desk's front edge fell over forward.

Kirsten moved over and stood them up again. "Remember that P10 inquest I asked you about taking?"

He nodded.

She explained finding five murdered people in a pentagram formation around a black zone with a major presence of Diablos. "It's looking more and more like they actually *did* summon something. Exactly what, I'm not sure yet."

"Herrera only turned up an hour ago. Maybe you can get something from the site?" Captain Eze laced his fingers, hands in his lap.

"I'll go check it out, but I'll be shocked if there's anything useful there."

He nodded. "Be careful."

She exchanged salutes, and hurried out.

THE GLOOMY SHADOW

Twenty-two minutes after leaving the PAC, Kirsten guided the patrol craft down from the hover lane toward a large mass of people in the street.

Sector 3317, roughly eighty miles south and twenty-five east from the 'pentacle' on the Navcon map, teetered on the edge of grey. Depending on the version of software update in any given system, some maps showed it normal, some grey. The buildings didn't appear *too* run down, though the occasional missing window and the general age of all the visible cars suggested this residential area held mostly poor people.

She flew in thirty feet off the ground, passing over a crowd of several hundred people that plugged an intersection where a four-lane road crossed a six-lane road. At a quick glance, she figured the group roughly eighty percent male. All wore the red-and-white colors of the Angels.

Four Division 6 A3Vs had been parked nose-to-tail, forming a barrier around the front of a residence tower covered in Angels graffiti up to the tenth story. Upward of thirty armored officers kept the gang members away, and by some miracle, violence hadn't broken out yet.

Stillness settled over the unruly crowd as she passed overhead and came in for a landing behind the giant armored personnel carriers. Angels often tangled with another gang, the Fei Len, who had numerous psionics (mostly kinetic adepts, people whose psionic abilities enhanced their bodies, making them stronger, faster, tougher, and so on.) When paired with extreme training in the fighting arts, encounters with them could verge quite far into the realm of the strange. Many rumors claimed the Fei Len also had 'other' more mystical abilities, though that part, she doubted. The Angels, however, didn't doubt as much. Having seen paranormal happenings, if only the psionic adepts, they knew exactly what an all-black police hovercar meant.

The whole crowd fell silent, watching.

She landed on the plastisteel sidewalk in front of the building.

Even before she opened the door, the pervasive sense of doom in the air made the hairs on the back of her neck stand up.

"This is different." Dorian looked around. "I think the abyssal may still be here."

All these people here... this could get ugly. "Hope not."

"Don't you want to catch this thing?"

She pushed the door up. "I do, but there's like 250 people in the street. No one wants a two-ton tap-dancing flea to rampage into a crowd."

Dorian dissipated into a silvery mist, blurred out of the car, and appeared standing beside her. "Do you think they all look like that?"

"Not sure. The one that took Konstantin's body didn't." She glanced past the gaps between A3Vs at the crowd of Angels. A few surface thought skims told her they knew of Herrera's death, wanted *someone* to pay for it, and didn't trust the cops would bother investigating. Much to her surprise, they'd turned out to protest police indifference. "Well, that's ironic."

"What is?" Dorian glanced at her.

"Members of an organized criminal street gang demonstrating to demand the police pay attention to them."

He laughed.

"Lieutenant?" asked a tall white-haired woman with a brush cut, clad in Division 6 armor except for a helmet, which she held under her left arm. A huge combat rifle hung on a strap across her shoulder. "Ahh, I was wondering why it got so quiet out here."

Kirsten started to raise her arm to salute, until she noticed the woman also wore 2LT rank insignia. She instead offered a handshake. "Oh, hi, lieutenant..."

"Müller," said the large woman. "Sofia."

"That name is far too delicate for her." Dorian chuckled. "She looks like she came straight out of that Monwyn game... the Vakken or something? Ice barbarians?"

She couldn't even fathom how he could fire off a quip given the overwhelming dark energy in the air. *Probably joking to keep himself sane. Yeah, she does kinda look like one of them. Damn, she's gotta be six-two. Makes me feel like I'm ten years old again.* "Kirsten… so what's going on here? Have you seen anything weird?"

"Oh, have I." Sofia gestured at the building. "Neighbor heard a scream. Almost everyone who lives in this building is either part of the Angels or friendly to them. Kinda impossible not to be for this area. Anyway, the first two guys to go check on the dead dude ran off screaming. They still haven't been seen. Someone finally called Div 1 in. They checked out the apartment and didn't make it two steps in the door before they got a bad case of 'fuck that.'"

"They saw something?" asked Kirsten.

"Not as far as I know." Sofia nodded toward the building. "Come on, maybe you'll have better luck. You're tiny, but the little ones always have the biggest balls."

Kirsten looked down at herself, little in the way of her shape hidden by the tight uniform. She almost made a joke about rather obviously lacking that particular body part, but the gloom in the air kept it from leaving her mouth. *I'm getting as bad as Dorian.* "The weird stuff doesn't bother me that much. So… Santiago Herrera is still in there?"

"Yep." Sofia shoved the door out of the way and headed to the elevator past two more Division 6 troops standing sentry in the lobby. "The forensics team is still on the roof. Refused to come down until a Zero cleared the scene. Oh, there's something even better."

"Better?" Kirsten followed her into an elevator.

"Witnesses reported every live dog and cat in the building went crazy all at the same time. A few even hurled themselves at windows, in a frenzy to leave the building."

She gasped in horror.

"None of them fell… but a few people had the shit clawed out of them trying to bring the animals outside safely."

The eeriness increased as the elevator climbed, far stronger than any previous site.

"It's still here," whispered Kirsten.

Sofia fidgeted. "Any idea what 'it' is?"

"A paranormal entity that's probably about as close to a demon as reality can get."

"Oh, so nothing major." Sofia let out a laugh that vibrated the air in Kirsten's lungs.

"Is there anyone in the apartment now?"

"Nope. Just a couple guys at the door."

Kirsten exhaled in relief. "Would you mind doing me a small favor?"

"As long as it doesn't involve jumper cables and wet sponges."

She blinked up at the big woman.

Sofia chuckled. "Wow, that look on your face. I was making a joke about military interrogation... not where you went with that. Guess you're not as innocent as you look."

"Umm." Kirsten blushed hard. "My other case is really twisted. I wish I'd never read that inquest."

"Oh, yeah, bad one?" Sofia stepped out into a hallway practically filled with gloom. "Whoa. Is it my eyes or is this hallway actually darker than it should be?"

"Seems dim, yeah. Like the lights are at half power." Kirsten slipped past her and walked toward a pair of Division 6 troopers flanking a door. Both of the large men trembled, but attempted to act as if they weren't scared shitless. "The favor I was going to ask is actually waiting outside. Last time I ran into an entity like this, it took control of several cops and tried to kill me with them."

Sofia whistled. "Crap. Yeah, no problem. I'll hang back if you want. EOD hasn't cleared the place yet, so there could be traps. Be careful."

"If she was the sort of person inclined to be careful, she wouldn't be walking *into* a place giving off energy like this." Dorian edged to the side, also seeming hesitant about entering the apartment.

"Lieutenant." One of the men, a sergeant, saluted them.

Sofia and Kirsten returned it.

"Zero's here." Sofia patted her on the back. "We wait outside unless she calls us in."

"No arguments here, LT." The other guy moved to the right, away from the door.

Kirsten went in, finding an apartment quite a bit more 'normal' than she'd expected for someone high up in a gang as big as the Angels. Other than it clearly being the home of a bachelor, it lacked the tacky display of wealth and power that always seemed to happen whenever a street thug had money.

The sense of darkness drew her across the living room to an alcove. Normality ended in the dining room, which appeared to serve as a mixture of chem lab and accounting office. Two cafeteria style tables held small machines she figured to be related to drug manufacture, at least on a small scale. Probably where they worked on 'improving' chems or making new ones before sending the formula elsewhere for large scale manufacture.

Santiago Herrera's bare foot stuck out from a doorway at the end of an impressively long hall for a century tower apartment. Forest green carpeting down its length appeared new, and a discoloration on the wall suggested the point where a wall formerly divided the space into two dwellings.

Constant, soft whispering emanated from the back bedroom, like a gathering of ghosts bickering in an indecipherable language.

"Sounds like a rather… spirited debate."

Kirsten stopped, turned, and glared at Dorian.

He gave her an innocent look of 'what?'

With a soft sigh, she faced the room again and concentrated on the Astral Lash. Her hand tingled from the energy tendril stretching out and gathering around her feet. Step by step, she crept toward the door, reaching out with her left hand. Long shadows stretched across the wall from the bright strand hovering around her.

Kirsten stopped the instant her fingertips touched the door. The dread in the air changed, becoming familiar in a way it hadn't before. Abyssal-tainted, yes, but thick with a sense of guilt that made it altogether weird. She peered down at the remains of a naked Hispanic man in his later thirties, his face permanently stuck in an expression of abject terror. A patch of snow white skin about the size of a serving platter on his chest surrounded the same jagged black 'claw' marks as she'd found on Modeus and Zack Rivera.

The door emitted a soft creak as she pushed it open.

A standing column of black vapor in the back corner grabbed her attention before she took in much of anything other than the sense of the area being a big bedroom. Two sparkling silver points near the ceiling shifted to stare at her.

"Oh…" Kirsten relaxed. "Just a Harbinger."

"*Just*, she says," muttered Dorian.

"Well, it's not an abyssal."

He raised a finger. "Technically…"

"Technicalities." She smirked. "Calling Harbingers 'abyssals' is like calling corrections officers prisoners."

"Corrections officers aren't generally made out of the literal fabric of suffering and pain." Dorian paused a second. "Unless you're talking about asteroid mines."

Kirsten stepped over the dead man and looked around. The bed had been turned down and ruffled up. A table lay askew, beer bottles littered on the floor. One set of women's clothes and two sets of men's clothes also decorated the carpet.

No one had mentioned anything about seeing a woman or second man leave the place. *Damn. I bet they saw what happened.*

The Harbinger, a hulking vaguely-human shaped apparition of shadows, slouched as if sad or disappointed. That, she'd never seen before.

Kirsten walked over to it, unable to fully hold back her trepidation. Something about these creatures unnerved her. Then again, many honest citizens became nervous around police. "Guess you missed him? Did you come here to collect this guy?"

It regarded her with as mournful a look as such a creature could manage, its sparkling silver eyes like tiny starbursts embedded in void. Despite lacking any semblance of human facial features, the Harbinger still somehow conveyed sorrow. As she neared, it tilted its head in evident confusion.

"Guess you guys don't talk much." She set her hands on her hips and looked back at the body. After sighing, she put a finger to her earbud. "Müller? This is Wren, are you on the channel."

"Yep," said Sofia.

"It's safe to come in. There is an entity in here, but it's no threat to the living. This particular type of being gives off fear, but they're not bad, just misunderstood."

Dorian shook his head.

"What?" Kirsten smirked at him. "They are. All big and scary and full of abyssal energy, but they're really only doing what needs to be done."

"Why is it hanging around? There's clearly no spirit here, other than me." Dorian glanced at the Harbinger. "If it got him, it wouldn't be here."

She took a knee beside Herrera's remains and rested a hand on his shoulder. *Why do I keep doing this? I'm no clairvoyant.* His body did give off paranormal residue, but offered no new information. Sofia tromped in the front door leading a reluctant pack of forensic techs.

"Hmm." Kirsten stood and approached the Harbinger. "Is something wrong?"

It fixated on her, staring for a few seconds before gliding closer. The slouched, despondent quality to its posture faded somewhat, though it lacked the usual foreboding ominousness she'd come to know from them. Having one of these entities hover so close still unsettled her, but it didn't give off any sense of malice beyond the substance of its existence.

"Still can't talk?"

The Harbinger stared down at her, seeming simultaneously terrifying and as lost as an orphan puppy.

Okay, this is beyond strange. I've never seen one of these guys act like this. Usually swoop in, grab soul, drag it down through the floor.

"Are you trying to tell me something? What should I be doing?"

"Kirsten?" asked Sofia, while stepping over Herrera. "Who are you talking to? Is there a ghost here?"

"Not exactly." She held up a 'wait a sec' finger to the Harbinger, then turned to face the tall woman. "Looks like this guy was in the middle of having sexy time when whatever happened, happened. Did anyone see where his guests went?"

Sofia glanced at the clothing on the ground. "Only heard that the first couple of people who came in here to check on him ran screaming into the night and still haven't turned up. No one mentioned anything about naked women running away."

"One was a guy." Kirsten pointed at the two pairs of men's underpants on the floor. "Assuming Herrera doesn't make a habit of wearing two pairs at once."

"Okay, rephrase. No one mentioned anything about naked *people* running away."

Kirsten poked her earbud. "Ops, can you send in some D1 backup? Need a bunch of bodies to go door to door."

"Copy that, Lieutenant," said a woman.

She sighed and looked up at Sofia. "They might be in another apartment here. Keep your fingers crossed."

The woman held up her hand and crossed her fingers.

"Damn, you're tall."

Sofia laughed and patted her on the head. "I'm only six-three. You're tiny. You sure you don't have any Girl Scout cookies in your trunk?"

Dorian snickered.

She let out a long sigh. "If I did, I'd be on my way out there to eat a whole box right about now. Oh, well. Might as well get on with it. I know it feels weird in here, but it's safe. I'm going to start on this hallway. When

Div 1 gets here, please have them go door to door in search of whoever these clothes belong to. They might've seen something I need to know about."

Sofia nodded. "No problem."

Kirsten headed out into the living room—the Harbinger following. She stopped and looked back at it. "Can I help you?"

It nodded once.

"What do you need?"

The Harbinger merely floated there in silence, its sparkling silver eyes twinkling.

"Ooo-kay. As soon as you figure out how to tell me what to do, I'll help." She regarded it for a moment, then kept walking.

It followed her out into the living room.

Dorian looked over as if he wanted to make a wiseass remark, but thought better of it.

Hah. Not smart to make fun of Harbingers when they can hear you. Kirsten whistled innocently to herself, trying not to laugh when the entire forensics crew froze like a pack of deer as she passed. For once, she didn't feel like the Mind Blast pariah.

It hadn't been her they reacted to.

20

SERIOUSLY BAD VIBES

Three hours later, having found no sign of the people she assumed had been with Herrera at the time of his attack, Kirsten trudged outside.

The Harbinger continued following her, as it had the whole time she went door-to-door. It flooded the entire back half of the car, becoming a cloud of darkness with eyes. She sighed to herself. On a few occasions, she'd communicated with them. The big one that had come to collect Albert Motte waited at her request and allowed her to talk to him for a moment. Another that had given Dorian the eye after the wraith tore him up may or may not have decided against claiming him because of her plea. She still hadn't quite figured out if Dorian had been on their radar or if the Harbinger had merely been confused and not known what to make of him.

She couldn't call her partner *dark*, but he had taken a strong sense of satisfaction for performing summary executions. Kirsten doubted he would have run around the city looking for anyone he could justifiably kill, but her opinion of what affected where a ghost wound up going didn't matter in the grand scheme of things. She didn't make that decision.

Kirsten could only try and stay as true to herself as possible, as in not simply gunning down those Harris cultists for nearly burning a child at the stake. The thought of that made her want to rush to the PAC and grab

Evan. He, too, had almost wound up suffering a similar fate... though the old man he described didn't sound malicious. They hadn't wanted to kill him, rather believed he'd already died.

Still, the thought of Evan laid out in a primitive crematory vessel got her crying.

"Frustrated, or random sad thought?" asked Dorian.

"Random sad thought." She wiped her cheeks. "And yes, I'm frustrated. I still haven't made the slightest bit of progress finding who killed Juan Miguel. I've got a twisted, sick son of a bitch running around the city doing unspeakable things to innocent women, and now there's some kind of abyssal killing people under the control of the Diablos—and I have no damned idea where to go from here."

He pursed his lips in thought. "What about the motel where they killed him?"

"Yeah. I need to check that out. And now I've got a Harbinger following me around. I've never seen one of them act like this. Two impossible cases and a beyond-bizarre situation. I'm almost at the point where I lock *myself* in a closet and try to forget the universe exists."

"Act like what?" asked Dorian.

She peered into the void in the back seat. "No offense, but... like a lost puppy."

Dorian snickered. "That is a powerful agent of the abyss, part of the inner-workings of the cosmos intended to drag the darkest of dark souls to an eternal prison. It's not a lost puppy."

The Harbinger seemed to inflate and deflate as if sighing.

"I wish they could speak."

"I'm quite sure he... or she does, too." Dorian glanced into the back.

Its eyes continued to sparkle with no discernible emotion.

Whatever.

She powered up the patrol craft and accessed the terminal. "Gonna go see what I can scrape off the walls at that motel."

"Literally or metaphorically." Dorian smiled.

"Ugh. Let's hope, metaphorically."

The old inquest record contained information about the motel where he'd been atomized by 20mm explosive rounds. She dreaded what had been a grey zone back in 2308 would be a full on black zone by now... but it surprisingly went the other way. NaturaLife Pharmaceuticals, Gravion Interstellar, and Manticore Investments had poured credits into the area,

SERIOUSLY BAD VIBES | 185

developing a corporate office complex surrounded by residential tower buildings. The ability to walk to work in ten minutes made rent steep, but they could only charge so much before the employees couldn't afford it. People who didn't work there wouldn't pay a premium for the living space.

"Shit. The motel's gone."

"That's... unfortunate."

Frustrated, and having no better ideas, plotted a course back to the PAC.

THE HARBINGER FLOATED OUT OF THE PATROL CRAFT AND FOLLOWED HER across the parking garage.

Kirsten paid it little mind, no different from having another cop walking along behind her. Its presence cast a dark shadow all the way around the overly white hallways in the Division 0 wing. Everyone she came near froze in place, staring at her. A few fainted. Some screamed and ran the other way. At two guys she knew not to be astrals noticing the darkness creeping along the walls, she blinked in awe.

Damn... this guy's potent.

Dozens of telepathic knocks hit her mind from people trying to understand why 'she' threw off such dread terror. Kirsten didn't bother blocking any of them out. Her head soon filled with voices asking her why she 'brought that thing' here.

It's following me. Not my idea.

She mentally repeated that phrase again and again until she reached her squad room. Dorian probably thought of a joke about getting in trouble for bringing a pet entity to work, but if he did, he kept it to himself.

Kurosawa and Montez froze at their desks, staring at her. Morelli sputtered coffee and wound up choking.

"Well," muttered Kirsten. "Now I know how Ashford feels."

"What?" Kurosawa looked past her at the dark patch of wall. "Are you doing that? What's making that enormous shadow?"

She plodded to her desk, the Harbinger hovering nearby. "Everyone stopped what they were doing to stare at me as soon as I walked in. That's what happens to Commander Ashford."

"To be fair, people don't usually scream and run from him." Dorian took a seat at his desk. "Don't let it get to you. They're not reacting to *you*."

Morelli coughed. "Wren, you're throwing off some seriously bad vibes today."

"Relax. I've got a friend. He's an exchange officer from another precinct that's pretty far away."

Captain Eze rushed out of his office, looking around warily.

"It's all right, Captain." Kirsten raised a hand. "I have a visitor. He's not dangerous."

"Not dangerous?" Eze blinked. "I can feel that dread and I'm nowhere near an astral. What the heck did you bring here?"

"He's following me for some reason. Umm… a Harbinger."

Everyone in the room skimmed her surface thoughts. Kirsten glanced at the Harbinger floating beside her so they all got a good look at him.

"Ooo! Shadow floof!" shouted Nicole, from the doorway. "He's cute!"

Even the Harbinger blinked in shock.

Kirsten pinched the bridge of her nose. *A manifestation of dread incarnate has been reduced to 'shadow floof.'* Of course, she had to admit, her usual feeling that making one wrong move around a Harbinger would be fatal didn't presently radiate from this one. The commanding epic-ness of its presence had vastly diminished.

Dorian whistled.

The redhead hurried over to Kirsten's desk. She trembled like a kid who'd just awoken from a nightmare, but smiled in a manic sort of way. "Oh, this is weird."

"Just a bit," said Kirsten. "Are you okay?"

"Yeah, I saw him in your head, but I'm all like 'aww cute' and I'm like totally terrified at the same time. It's so bizarre."

"Harbingers have—"

"Oh, the people who live downstairs from me are such idiots."

"—that effect on people." Kirsten smiled. "What did they—"

Nicole started crying while giggling. "Totally overreacted with noise complaints, and the guy got in my face last night. Oh, you want coffee?"

"Got in your face?"

"Crap. Why am I crying?" Nicole wiped her cheeks. "Wow, I'm like ready to piss myself I'm so scared. Look at me. My hands are shaking and I don't know why."

Kirsten glanced at the Harbinger, who continued to project glumness.

"You're more sensitive than most, I think, and his presence is—"

"The guy thought he could intimidate me into 'being quiet.' Didn't realize I was a cop."

"And you—"

"Strawberry mocha again?" asked Nicole, sniffling.

"That woman would be an amazing investigator if she could hold a topic for more than four seconds," said Dorian.

Kirsten bowed her head. "Yes on the strawberry mocha."

"Attention all Division 0 personnel," said the voice of Director Jane Carter via a PA system, "Whoever is radiating fear and guilt, you are to cease immediately."

"Someone's in trouble." Dorian grinned.

"Coffee!" Nicole ran off with her NetMini in hand. "Anyone else?"

Morelli passed, but Kurosawa and Montez put in requests, as did Captain Eze.

Kirsten stared blankly at her desk's holo-panels. None of them offered any useful information beyond still-churning searches. If anyone over the past hundred years had called in a report of molestation-by-ghost, it had either been laughed off or written up in such a way as to defy her search criteria. Anything prior to her activation probably would have wound up filed away in the 'whatever' column and ignored, a ghostly P10. Assuming, of course, it hadn't been trashed as a prank call.

She glanced over at the Harbinger. "I don't suppose you can help?"

It merely continued staring at her.

Oddly, Kirsten got the sense it liked being near her.

21

FOR THE TAKING

S trawberry-laced mocha coffee helped a little.

Since she didn't want to drag a Harbinger to the secure dorms, she sent an email to the staff and asked that someone pass along a message to Rafael Esparza that she was still working on the case. She also explained that she wanted to visit him, but had a 'dark manifestation' presently attached to her that she couldn't bring around troubled juvenile detainees—not that she'd want to bring it around any juvenile.

Another idea leaked into her consciousness.

Maybe the Harbinger is here to collect the abyssal that killed Herrera, and it can't do it alone. At the initial moment of death, dark spirits had no defense against being taken. She didn't know exactly how long it took for a new ghost to build up enough of a spectral presence that the Harbingers couldn't simply grab them.

Every spirit she'd ever encountered that they'd been interested in only became vulnerable to a Harbinger's claim after a few shots with Astral Lash weakened it. Maybe this one knew that and planned on following her around until she caught up to the thing the Diablos summoned. The theory seemed reasonable except for Harbingers' ability to materialize at will when she cornered a spirit worthy of their interest. It didn't make much sense for one to hang out with her and wait.

She leaned back in her chair pondering that, and other deep mysteries of the universe—like how boxes of herbal tea always seemed to contain an odd number of pouches. She always wound up having a single one left, which made it annoying for her using a giant mug and needing two sachets per cup.

Fate decided to be kind. It waited until she swallowed the last sip of her coffee.

No sooner had she set her cup down than an emergency dispatch appeared on her terminal, along with the face of a young woman in an Admin uniform.

"Lieutenant Wren, please proceed to Sector 5057, 204 City Road E99. 21-47 in progress."

Kirsten jumped up, 'grabbed' the woman's face out of the holo-panel and dragged it to her forearm guard. A plum-sized holographic head floated over her arm. She swiped her terminal locked and ran off down the corridor, Dorian and the Harbinger close behind.

"On the way. What am I walking into?"

The woman lowered her voice to a near whisper. "Caller indicated an unseen force touching them inappropriately."

Kirsten jumped into the elevator. "Why are you whispering?"

"There's a training class here today. Got a bunch of twelve-year-olds shadowing calls."

"Ahh." She glanced at the Harbinger's wispy, vaporous form packed into the corner of the elevator cab. "I'm being shadowed, too."

Dorian groaned. "That was horrible."

"I have to make myself laugh about *something* or I'm just going to give up."

"It's not in you to give up, K." Dorian patted her shoulder.

Kirsten sprinted down the hall to the garage, ignoring the stares, screams, and odd noises coming from other people. She jumped into her patrol craft, driving before the door finished closing. The instant she shot out from under the roof of the motor pool garage, she hit the lights and emergency transponder while simultaneously switching to hover mode. In a blur of brown and black, the holographic head leapt from floating above her arm to the middle of the car's console.

The Navcon picked up the address from the dispatch on its own, so she rammed the left stick forward, pinning herself against the seat with acceleration. A moment later, she leveled off at 600 feet doing 340 MPH.

Arms rigid, she held the sticks, staring out past an array of glowing lines and indicators on the windscreen. "Talk to me, dispatch. Who am I looking for?"

"Citizen's name is 'Freya.' No family name." A file image appeared in a small box on the windscreen, containing a youngish pale face with sky blue hair in a bob, glowing blue eyes, and a luminous pink raccoon band cybertattoo. Dark red painted lips managed a pouty sneer that tried to radiate 'don't mess with me' and 'why hello there' at the same time.

"Dammit... is that girl a minor?" asked Kirsten.

"Doesn't fit his MO." Dorian stuck his hand into the dashboard and another screen opened with the same portrait attached to a bunch of text. "She's like you... looks younger than she is. According to this, she's twenty-one. Has a bit of a record. She's no sweet innocent girl. Though it's a bunch of simple assault cases. She's augged."

"How much?"

"Umm..." Dorian read for a few seconds. "Both eyes, forearm blades, bunch of headware, and some low-grade speedware."

Kirsten cringed at the thought. Having wires implanted all throughout her body ranked right up there with jumping headfirst into that awful black gunk in the Beneath. "How does someone that age afford that shit?"

"Either a sponsor, or she's stealing credits. She's in a gang, Warp Spiders."

"Big? Dangerous?"

"Not really. Looks like a cyber-gang though, attracts people addicted to augmentation. Most of their criminal activity is in the GlobeNet. Poor girl's going to be mostly metal by the time she's forty."

"That's sad."

"Oh, they don't usually chop off healthy parts just to replace them... though some do. But, when one of your hobbies is dancing with vibro blades, shit happens." Dorian cringed.

Kirsten squeezed the control sticks. "Hate vibro claws."

The Harbinger, filling the back seat as a cloud of blackness, said nothing.

Two minutes and eighteen seconds after leaving the PAC, Kirsten set down on the roof of a low-end apartment building that reminded her of where she used to live. The roof had no spot for a hovercar—especially an oversized police model—to land properly. But, she'd had plenty of practice wedging that patrol craft on roofs where it didn't fit.

After balancing it on an air handler and a pipe loop, she jumped out and ran to the roof access door, which opened in response to her police override code. The air in the stairwell made her gag on a mixture of roasting chicken, urine, and sweaty foot. Ignoring the stink, she ran down from the 50th floor roof to the 34th floor, following the navigation aid to Freya's apartment.

Bottles and Cyberburger plastic clamshell cases rained down the steps around her. By the time she reached the 34th floor landing, the mess had become hip deep. She stepped on something soft and body-like when she approached the door out of the stairwell. A man's moan came from beneath the trash. She peered down at her boot on the back of someone sleeping face down under three-foot-deep clutter, too drunk or stoned to notice her standing on him.

Kirsten shoved the door open and kept going. Dorian and the Harbinger followed without a sound. She bee-lined to an open door that matched the dot on the minimap floating over her left arm. Despite responding to a paranormal event—the 21-47 code meant a manifestation attacking the living—she drew her E-90 and entered using standard police tactics.

Not only did this building sit right next to a grey zone, it probably served as a crash pad for a cybergang. The apartment turned out to be a single smallish room with a Comforgel pad that folded into a couch, autoshower tube in the corner beside the only window, and an epic amount of clothing randomly thrown about. A small table in front of the bed/couch held two net decks, a scattering of small electronic devices, and three silver holo-bars, but none were on.

"Shit," said Kirsten. "I'm too late."

Dorian stuck his head through the door of the only closet. "Not hiding in here."

"He's got her *right now*. I bet he's making her go somewhere this very moment... if she's not already being raped." Kirsten shivered with rage and frustration. She whirled on the Harbinger. "Malden Walker has been here, hasn't he?"

The Harbinger nodded once.

"Where is he?"

It stared at her, its silver eyes in a constant shifting state of sparkling. The creature's vaporous shoulders gave off an ever-so-slight sense of slouching in defeat.

"Dammit. You can't interfere, can you? Some of that Seraphim-Harbinger rule stupidity. Argh!" She kicked a small box across the apartment. "This is ten times worse, knowing it's happening *right now* and I can't do a damn thing."

Dorian looked around. "There's no NetMini in here. Maybe he didn't make her strip before leaving?"

Shaking with adrenaline, Kirsten swung her arm up and tried to control her fingers enough to pull up a device trace using Freya's PID. When it came up—moving—she screamed, "Yes!"

The Harbinger backed out of the door, making way for her.

Kirsten sprinted to the stairwell and hurried up to the roof, barely breathing by the time she arrived at the patrol craft. Running up sixteen stories of trash-filled stairs sucked, but it hadn't been the most grueling thing she'd ever done. If it made the difference for Freya, she'd do it ten more times. The bizarre circumstance of having a Harbinger in the back seat didn't even register as she lifted off again, angled the car toward the NetMini trace, and accelerated in a dive.

Ad-bots, private drones, and a handful of delivery bots scattered out of her way. Something she didn't see bounced off the car with a dull *clonk*, probably a personal bot with broken or deliberately-removed lights.

She leveled off at the third-story level, figuring Freya would likely be on foot, and drove as fast as she felt able to control the car in the tight confines of a plastisteel-and-glass canyon. The wide, heavy car threw trash and plasfilm scraps everywhere in its wake, tearing posters off walls, knocking a few pedestrians over, and in one case, smashing a window from the trailing air blast.

"I'd say you're not supposed to do 285 this low to the ground, but I'm sure Freya will appreciate it."

"Thanks," muttered Kirsten, too focused on driving to lend much thought to his remark.

The blinking yellow triangle on the Navcon display stopped moving one sector north in 5109, nearly at the border with 5161 above it.

"She's four and a half miles into the grey." Dorian drummed his fingers on his knee. "And not moving."

"I see that." *That girl's a minute away from the worst day of her life... if even that long.*

She slowed, mashing the button to extend the ground wheels, and set down hot, puffs of smoke chirping from the rubber rings wrapped around four e-motors. The ion thrusters shut down, and the louder whirr of the physical drive system kicked in. Intense azure snaps from the patrol craft's bar lights painted the faces of nearby buildings in a bright shade of eerie. She squealed around a corner driving as close as she could get to an alley from where the NetMini signal originated. Kirsten swerved to a stop and leapt out of the car, not even bothering to shut it down, then hauled ass for the alley mouth, between an abandoned pizza place and an old electronics store.

E-90 up, Kirsten ran into the alley and aimed at—nothing.

"Fuck!" shouted Kirsten.

"Isn't that what you're trying to prev—"

"Not now. Please," yelled Kirsten.

She stormed forward, searching around for signs of the NetMini. Thirty feet from the end of the alley, she found it on the ground behind a dumpster along with a skirt, top, sneakers, and underwear.

Kirsten hung her head. "Damn."

"Now that's odd." Dorian walked up beside her. "The last two victims we know about, he made them undress at home, then walked them outside. Why do you think he did this?"

Kirsten shook with anger and guilt. Her brain couldn't even figure out words at that moment, much less assemble a response to his question or consider the thought of it.

"Get off me!" shouted a woman. "Stop!"

The plea sounded almost rehearsed, like a not-terribly-skilled actress playing an assault victim.

"Go!" shouted Kirsten. She bolted into a run, unable to keep up with Dorian who didn't suffer the handicap of having a physical body to slow him down.

A man's scream came from deeper in the alley in time with a bluish shimmer of light in a rightward passage two buildings ahead. Someone let out a shriek like he'd had ice water poured over him.

Kirsten skidded around the turn into the side passage and stopped short, taking in the scene.

A skinny, pale woman with bright blue hair lay draped over a refrigerator-sized metal fan cabinet, naked, a pair of handcuffs securing her wrists around a pipe connecting the machine to the building. Scraps of wire bound one ankle to the bottom right corner of the machinery, another wire dangled from the hand of a stunned man making a face like a fish out of water. A few patches of translucent slime coated his arms and the front of his jacket.

Dorian, flat on his chest, picked himself up from the ground a few paces past the guy.

Ignoring the man for now, Kirsten stuffed her E-90 back in its holster. She charged at the woman, unfurling the Astral Lash into a swing. The shimmering tendril of light snagged on a squidgy presence inside her, like swinging a broadsword into a Comforgel pad. Amid a glowing blur, the figure of a pale thirtysomething man in a loose T-shirt and ripped cargo pants staggered into view.

"What the fuck?" whispered Freya. The soft clinking of handcuffs followed. "Oh, shit. Fuck! God dammit! What the fuck!" Soft clinking became thrashing and metallic banging. "Get these fucking shits the fuck off me. I'll rip your goddamn balls off."

She continued screaming curses mixed with threats and pleas.

Kirsten jumped at Malden, swinging the lash again. The ghost blurred out of the way, reappearing right next to her. Committed to her strike, she followed through on the motion to avoid landing on her ass. The ghost punched her in the head, his fist hitting her like a block of dense, icy foam. She flew off her feet, crashed into the wall, and slid to sit on the ground, the world around her spinning and full of flashing spots.

The Astral Lash unfurled over the alley like a giant glowing spaghetti noodle.

She stared up at the blurry form approaching her, barely aware of where she was until cold hands grabbed her by both cheeks. The pasty face of a man with stringy brown hair, a poor attempt at a goatee, and an expression somewhere between no-one-is-home and hunger hovered in front of her. He definitely didn't look quite right, the sort of person no one of sane mind would leave alone with children. He stared into her eyes. Kirsten sensed his consciousness starting to invade her mind; with every ounce of her psionic abilities, she slammed the door.

Malden stumbled away from her, bewildered.

"No damn way." Kirsten dragged herself upright. "This body's off limits to you."

"The fuck are you talking to?" shrieked Freya. "Get this motherfucker off me! The fuck is wrong with cops?"

Kirsten glanced sideways at the young woman. The man Dorian had stunned struggled to tie Freya's left leg to the machine frame's other corner, as though she, a cop, didn't stand ten feet away. Dorian tried grabbing him, but couldn't manage much of a grip. Still, she couldn't let Malden escape.

She swiped the lash in an upswing, scoring a phantasmal burn across his chest that knocked him reeling into the wall. Dorian gave up on the living fringer. He ran in and pounced on Malden, trying to wrestle him to the ground like a standard suspect.

Freya screamed.

"Hey, asshole!" shouted Kirsten.

The vagrant, crouched and wrapping wire around Freya's ankle, paused to look up.

"*Lie down,*" said Kirsten.

The man let go of the wire and fell over backward, lying flat on the ground.

Dorian sailed past Kirsten and disappeared into the wall. Malden recovered from throwing him and glared at her. She feigned a quick sideways strike, then spun, the lash coiled around her body, hidden until she brought it around in an overhead swing. Malden fell for the fake-out and leapt straight back, which didn't move him out of the way of the long energy whip coming down on top of him.

A burst of light accompanied the hit, which knocked him to the ground and set off a mild pulse of energy that sent phantasmal sparks crawling over glass surfaces nearby. Kirsten advanced, gathering the lash for another swing. Malden blurred, reorienting himself from flat on his back with his feet toward her to flying at her fists first.

Kirsten snapped the energy whip up in an attempt to block, but the spirit took the hit, flying into it while grabbing her around the throat in both hands. He lifted her off the ground and shoved her back until she crashed into the wall. He pinned her against the building by his grip on her neck, squeezing tighter while staring at her in a way that made her feel like a hunk of sushi he debated eating.

"What... are... you?" rasped Malden.

Freya, not far to her left, continued screaming curses and thrashing, trying to get her left leg out of the wires which currently held her in a most humiliatingly exposed position. The vagrant, still compelled to lie on the ground, stared lustfully up at her from behind.

Dorian jumped out of the wall and grabbed Malden, trying to drag him off Kirsten. The ghost removed his right hand from her neck long enough to punch Dorian in the head. The hit knocked him flying more than half a block away.

Shit... another Wharf Stalker... She struggled to breathe. *This bastard's strong.*

"Stop staring at me!" screamed Freya. "Hey, cop!" The blue-haired woman looked over at Kirsten—and froze, wide-eyed. "Whoa. How the fuck are you floating?"

Kirsten gurgled.

"Little help, please? Kinda in a bad position right now."

Kirsten gurgled louder.

Again, the sense of an invading entity brushed at her mind. Malden tried to possess her, but he may as well have been a living person trying to walk into a solid wall. Snarling, she let herself think about Konstantin, about being controlled, vulnerable, exposed, violated in the worst way by having her entire personality altered. This bastard of an entity in front of her did the same thing to any woman he felt like attacking.

Her fury sent a surge of intensity down the long energy cord. Pinned to the wall with little room to move, Kirsten made the tail end of the whip swipe up at Malden's back. The hit didn't feel all that strong, but Malden screamed in pain and let go of her throat. She dropped back to her feet, swung her arm up, and snapped the lash at him, dragging most of its length through his chest.

The Harbinger glided closer.

Malden emitted a belabored groan and fell to one knee. He shot a sideways glance at the approaching cloud of blackness before fixing Kirsten with an unsettling stare as if he found her simultaneously fascinating and deadly. The mere look on his face made her feel unclean. She roared and moved to strike again, but he dove into the ground barely a second before the energy whip would've hit him.

"What's going on?" yelled Freya. "I can't see anything bent over this fucking thing. Let me out. Oh, shit, this creep isn't taking pictures is he?"

Hit with sudden inspiration, the vagrant pulled out a NetMini. The second he raised it to snap an image of Freya's nether regions, Dorian grabbed the device. The screen flickered once and died.

"No!" shouted Kirsten, glaring at the ground. She swung the lash a few times, but the tendril met no resistance at all. Despondent and furious, she stood there fuming.

"Hey, cop chick," said Freya. "It's fuckin' October and I'm naked on top of a goddamned metal box. I'm freezing my tits off and I got sharp shit poking me everywhere."

Kirsten stared up at the Harbinger. She almost yelled at it, but held her tongue. "Not weak enough for you to take?"

It bowed its head.

She sighed.

The vagrant sat up. As if finally noticing a police officer standing there, he scrambled to his feet and took off.

Kirsten ran after him, jumping into a tackle that used her entire body weight to take him down and quite un-gently hammered his face into the plastisteel ground. She grabbed a fistful of his hair at the back of his neck, forcing him to make eye contact. "*Don't move.*"

He went limp.

She secured him in binders, then searched him for weapons, removing two small handguns and three knives.

Freya managed to get her left leg out of the wires and tried stepping on the cords binding her right ankle. A continuous stream of curses flowed from her lips.

Confident the man wouldn't be moving for at least four or five minutes, Kirsten trotted over to Freya. "Had to deal with that ghost. I'm really sorry for leaving you like this so long."

Freya stopped struggling. Her anger gave way to shaking and tears. "Shit, perfect timing. You got here at like the last damn second, too. What the fuck happened to me?"

"A ghost possessed you." Kirsten leaned over, peering into the narrow gap between the fan cabinet and the wall. A pair of non-electronic handcuffs looped under a two-inch-thick pipe kept the young woman bent over the machinery so far her feet couldn't reach the ground. "Damn. How the heck did he cuff you like that? There's no room in there."

Freya's cheeks reddened almost as much as the glowing pink raccoon band over her eyes. Other than emitting blue light, her cybernetic eyes appeared normal. "I cuffed myself here. But I didn't want to! Something was controlling me. Seriously, I'm not into this kinky shit. And even if I was, I wouldn't do it *outside.*"

Kirsten patted her on the shoulder. "Keys could be in the bag near the end of the alley."

"Doubt that bastard brought keys," muttered Dorian, still rubbing his chin. "He's got a hell of a right hook."

She pulled her Nano utility knife off her belt, ordinarily meant for cutting seat belts or wires. The dangerous synthetic diamond blade sat inside a housing that only allowed narrow items near the small cutting edge. It would work on the handcuff chain *if* she could reach it. She stooped and cut Freya's right leg free, then wound up bending over the fan cabinet right next to her to reach into the gap. With little room to move in there, and a horrible angle, she spent a few minutes trying to squeeze her arm down far enough to get the blade on the cuffs.

"Well, well, well," said a man. "Two perfectly-shaped asses in the air. What a treat."

Kirsten's cheeks burned with blush. She decided not to leave this girl helpless any longer, and risked the vulnerable position for a few more seconds to cut her free, but Freya pulled the binders against the pipe so tight, Kirsten couldn't get the chain into the uti knife.

"Oh, fuck!" shouted Freya. "Don't you even *think* about it!"

"Lean down, give it slack," whispered Kirsten. "Hurry."

Freya whimpered a few more curse words but scooted forward, stretching.

The uti knife made short work of the steel chain, cutting it as easily as a strip of pasta. Freya leapt up. Kirsten flung herself into a sideways roll off the top of the fan cabinet, landing on her feet beside it. Freya backed against the metal, covering herself as best she could with her hands and shivering.

A group about a dozen men, mostly scrawny and younger than twenty-five, surrounded them in an arc. The sight of Kirsten's uniform made a few lose some of their enthusiasm, but none of them went anywhere.

Kirsten drew her E-90. "Police. You should all just keep walking away before you do anything I'd have to arrest you for."

A man toward the left with spiked purple hair grinned. "You can't get us all before we're on you, sweet thing. Just be a good little girl and let's all have some fun."

The Harbinger emitted a low noise, like glass scraping over glass. Its vaporous body expanded, growing to about ten feet in height, arms held to either side, wispy claws of insubstantial darkness spread open.

Dorian simultaneously shimmered transparent, manifesting into the visible world and letting off a wave of radiant fear.

Only one of the punks noticed him. The others all stared at the Harbinger. One grabbed his chest and fell straight to the ground. Four fainted. Others screamed and darted off in random directions, many crashing straight into the wall, so desperate to get away they couldn't even see the building in their way. They bounced off, and ran again. A foul, fragrant testament to how frightened the punks had been soon filled the air.

Freya blinked. "Giant shadowy thing with eyes."

"Yeah." Kirsten looked at the Harbinger. "Thanks."

It bowed its head.

She examined the scrawny young woman, noting a few superficial cuts from the components on top of the fan cabinet as well as an impression of a rounded vent grille on her stomach. "Are you hurt?"

"I don't think so. Just freezing."

After walking Freya back to the spot where her clothing remained on the ground, Kirsten dragged the man who'd been about to assault her to the patrol craft. The young woman blurred like sped-up video, dressing herself in seconds. Expecting the Harbinger would occupy the back seat again, she stuffed the guy into the trunk. While she had it open, she took an evidence bag for the knives, ammo, chems, and handguns she confiscated from him.

Freya crept over. "Did that shit really happen?"

"I'm sorry, but it did. You called the police to report a ghost touching you?"

"Yeah. I was about to hop in the shower and felt this hand on my tit. Thought I might be having a flashback or something, but it didn't stop. I scrambled into my clothes as fast as I could move and ran out the door, calling you guys… but something happened to me once I got outside. Like cold hit me from behind and then I was just watching my body do stuff. Those handcuffs… it made me order them from a delivery bot."

"Wow, what an asshole," said Dorian. "Maybe the keys really are in her bag?"

Kirsten put an arm around her and led her over to the passenger seat. "C'mon. I'll explain everything."

"Where's that shithead who almost raped me?" Freya looked around inside the car.

"Trunk."

Freya laughed. "Seriously?"

"Yeah. Div 1 isn't gonna come out here to pick up one guy since I'm already here. And… putting him in the back seat isn't a good idea."

She glowered. "No shit. I'd smash his face in."

Soon after Kirsten got in, the Harbinger flooded the back seat

Dorian put a hand on the hood and seeped into the car, not appearing in the cabin.

"So, umm, what happened?" asked Freya.

Kirsten pulled into the air. As frustrating as it had been to watch Malden slip away, she at least felt a rush of relief at having shown up in time to stop the worst of it. "It may be a little difficult for you to believe, but you were attacked by a ghost."

"I saw that giant shadowy dude. Was that it?"

"No. He's…" Kirsten glanced back at the two eye spots in the gloom. "On our side."

22

LOST PUPPY

Confusion had thoroughly set in by the time Kirsten headed down to the school area to pick Evan up.

Though remarkable, being able to go home only two hours past the normal end of her shift didn't account for her bewilderment. The increasing sense that something vastly exceeding normal happened came from having a Harbinger follow her all the way to the school. It trailed after her like a giant black balloon with eyes, drifting silent and ominous.

Fortunately, at a little after 6 p.m., not many children remained at the school.

She found Evan waiting in the foyer by the main entrance, laughing and talking with the girl that had been with him in the Beneath. Maela looked over at Kirsten's approach and started to smile, but the Harbinger's presence made her blanch so white she could've passed for a Marsborn. Evan, on the other hand, simply raised an eyebrow. His eyes lit up with astral energy a second later.

He blinked, surprised, and seemed to disregard it as a non-threat. "It's okay. He won't hurt us."

Maela glanced at him, edging away. "Umm. Okay. If you say so. Guess you gotta go now. Thanks for hanging out."

"Yeah. See you tomorrow?"

"Sure." Her expression said 'as long as whatever's freaking me out isn't around.'

Evan waved at her and ran over into a hug. "Hey, Mom."

"Hey yourself." She squeezed him. "How'd it go today?"

"Pretty good. Specialist Vasquez spent most of the day on General Harlon E. Hewitt."

"Who's that?" asked Kirsten, while walking down the hall to the elevator.

Evan blinked. "You don't know General Hewitt?"

"Sounds kinda familiar."

He flailed his arms. "Mom! He basically started the UCF after this guy President Hornburrough got killed by the bad guys. He figured the old politicians weren't gonna do anything to win the Corporate War, just sit there bein' scared, so he took over. The Corporates did this thing they called 'Operation Winter Rain' and it was like a whole bunch of political assassinations. Because of General Hewitt, there's still a UCF and we're not all part of the stinky ACC."

"The normal people who live there aren't stinky." Kirsten patted him on the head.

"I know. They just have buttheads for leaders. We have a new girl in class today, name's Willow. She's sad 'cause her dad just died, but his ghost is here, too. She knows already that his ghost is here, but I helped them talk to each other at lunch. Someone did something really mean to her but she didn't want to say anything about it."

Wow. They put her into classes already? Guess she's handling things better than I did. Kirsten sighed to herself. "How did she seem?"

"Sad. But she's nice. Kept saying she couldn't believe how many kids there are with psionics, and she likes that 'cause she doesn't feel so alone now. She's a pyro."

On the walk to the patrol craft and most of the flight home, Kirsten explained that she'd met Willow already, and that some bad people hurt her dad and tried to hurt her.

"That's why you weren't in the office." He smiled. "I'm glad you helped her. Sorry for being scared when I couldn't find you."

"I still can't believe no one noticed you kids missing for hours." She grumbled.

"Mr. Short only wanted to play video games. He never watched us when we did cit point stuff. Miss Eisen ran the citizenship period today, and she even helped us clean stuff."

"That's nice."

Kirsten landed in the parking area of her apartment tower, still finding delight in the luxury of being able to set the car down in an actual marked space rather than wedge it between machines on the roof. The Harbinger exuded out of the car and followed her across the platform full of cars, down the hall, and all the way home.

Evan ran straight to the Yume Koujou system. It didn't seem right for a nine-year-old to put in almost a twelve-hour day between classes and after-school punishment, so she decided not to pester him about homework. They didn't exactly give the kids all that much at that age, and he'd probably already done it while waiting for her to pick him up.

She headed to the bedroom, changed out of her uniform to a far more comfortable outfit: a loose T-shirt and sweat pants. The Harbinger stood in the corner of the living room like an avant-garde statue from the fourth circle of hell. Since Evan didn't seem to mind it, she decided to leave it be. His clairvoyant talent evidently had the ability to sniff people—and even ghosts—out. He picked up a general sense of a being's intent, good or bad, so anyone he didn't like or seemed scared of, she would be wary of.

If not for the abyssal in that stupid bracelet, she'd have listened to his instinct about Konstantin.

Since he'd been so blasé about having a Harbinger trailing after them, his reaction must mean it wouldn't hurt them. Not that she really expected it to. For one thing, they couldn't harm the living. For another, she'd interacted with them a few times and they'd been polite, even pleasant. Well, as pleasant as a creature made of abyssal energy could be.

While throwing together some chicken-and-noodles for dinner, she debated if Harbingers came from once-human souls or, like They Who Always Were, predated humans. This, of course, set her off on a mental tangent trying to figure out why the universe would create such beings as Harbingers whose purpose appeared to be policing human souls. Did they go after 'dark' animals, too? Could animals have dark souls? It didn't seem plausible to think so.

How does one race of creature, humans, on this whole planet deserve Harbingers and Seraphim? Are there other races out there on other planets? Humanity can't be that cosmically significant. She shoved the pasta-chicken dish onto two plates when it finished, hoping she hadn't overdone it on the garlic, or whatever that green stuff was. Basil? It kinda smelled like it could work with chicken, so she used some.

"Ev," said Kirsten in a slightly raised voice. "Dinner."

"'Kay!"

She sat at the table, teasing a fork around the spiral noodles. Staring into the food, she drifted mentally back to being Evan's age, sitting on the floor of a locked closet, trying to figure out if Mother would give her a half-bowl of oatmeal on any given night. Whenever the ghosts pestered the apartment trying to get Kirsten's attention, Mother would sometimes refuse to feed her as punishment. Rather than sad and pitiful, the memory made her furious.

Evan rushed into the kitchen and leapt into his chair. "Ooh. Smells good!"

He proceeded to attack the food like he hadn't eaten all day. Morelli made a comment shortly after the adoption finalized that boys devour food like locust swarms. Kirsten had no idea what that even meant, but Evan certainly had no trouble inhaling food. He still looked too damn skinny, but the doctors called him healthy.

They talked about his day at school over dinner. Evan explained how he'd decided to be friends with Maela even if she was two grades ahead of him since she seemed so lonely. Hearing him so matter-of-factly discuss spending his lunch recess time trying to make her feel better choked her up. If not for having a table between them, she'd have squeezed him until he demanded air.

Once they finished eating, Kirsten tossed the dishes in the machine. Soon, she planted herself on the couch with Evan smushed against her side. Together, they put on senshelmets and entered the world of Monwyn.

Between a Harbinger lurking behind her and three active cases, she had a little trouble getting into the game, but eventually surrendered to the fun of running around the forest and firing arrows at orcs, goblins, and pyrodons. She rather disliked the fire elemental lizards. Bad enough having to fight a creature as big as a car that breathed flame, their armor made her arrows feel weak unless she kept running in circles to attack from behind and avoid their giant head plate.

Much sooner than she wanted, the timer went off. She snoozed it, allowing Evan an extra fifteen or so minutes until they completed a quest to collect twenty-five glowshrooms. Upon returning to the village, Monwyn the wizard pulled an enormous sack of luminous pumpkin-sized mushrooms out of his robe that should in no way have fit in there, and handed it over to a potbellied village alchemist.

Golden sparkles danced in the air along with a brief celebratory chime to go along with their experience point award. Alas, they both had quite a ways to go to make another level. Monwyn faced her.

"Guess it's bedtime. Goodnight, fair huntress." The tall, bearded Monwyn bowed, then faded away.

Kirsten thought the logout command. As soon as everything went black, she pulled the helmet off. "Night, brave wizard."

He leapt into a hug, then scrambled off to his room.

The Harbinger remained in the corner, staring impassively at her.

Wow. Guess those guys don't get bored.

She put the game system away, then headed down the hall to kiss Evan goodnight before going to her bedroom. It felt a bit weird to crawl into bed before 9:30, but she did wake up super early... and she'd had a rough day.

The Harbinger came through the wall and glided over to hang in the corner near her giant plush rune rabbit. Constant exposure to the pervasive dread that surrounded it had almost reached the point of numbness where she didn't notice it anymore. A sense that death snuck up behind her had ratcheted down a few notches to a feeling more like she did something wrong and didn't quite know if she got away with it or would wind up in Captain Eze's office for 'a talk.'

Of course, on top of her anxiety over having a spectral serial rapist and an abyssal loose in the city, a Harbinger hanging out in her bedroom barely rated.

If I can sleep with him in my room, I can sleep anywhere. And wow, he really is acting like a lost puppy that wants a home. What the hell is going on?

She laughed to herself. *Hell indeed.*

23

WEAPONIZED

The Harbinger followed Kirsten for the next two days, a silent presence always about twenty feet away.

Even the rest of Division 0 had more or less acclimated to it, except for an unfortunate panic attack in the shower area, the images of which would haunt several tactical officers for the rest of their careers. Nicole started joking about sponsoring an annual 'naked hall run' for charity, though no one thought it a good idea.

Malden hadn't attacked anyone else since she'd seen him, though that proved only that any potential victims didn't tell anyone. *Most of his victims probably kept quiet—or at least lied about the being possessed part, fearing they'd be called insane.*

Since the system couldn't offer any assistance tracking down a ghost or an abyssal, she spent some time looking for information about the Diablos. Even the Div 1 system contained little in the way of criminal record profiles for them. A meeting between Diablos and police went one of two ways depending on if the cops had armor on. Barring the occasional exception where the gang got a hold of weapons civilians shouldn't own, the standard issue Division 1 patrol armor rendered them impervious to most small arms fire. Leather jackets with 'trendy evil symbols' didn't do much against bullets.

Every so often, the Diablos would get their hands on Class 4 or larger combat rifles that could punch holes in police armor, but more often than not, exchanges went in favor of the police. Either way, few of them survived arrest. It didn't seem likely that upon seeing the cops, someone in Diablos colors would dive to the ground and scream out their surrender, so bullets often preceded words.

Kirsten felt reasonably certain that the Diablos had murdered Juan Miguel Esparza, though identifying the specific person among them who did it would be next to impossible without a literal hunting expedition and telepathy. It didn't strike her as likely Captain Eze would agree to let her run blindly into a black zone intending to hunt, mind-read, and kill Diablos. She didn't fancy the idea of that either. If she had any way to disengage from them without killing, she would've considered asking. But her getting even close enough to mind read a Diablo would end with someone dead, unless…

There's always Suggestion. 'Go away' works fairly well.

In order to settle her conscience about her promise to Rafael, she'd need to reach a point where she believed she had done everything possible to find his brother's killer and could do no more.

She also had a strong suspicion that Juan Miguel's death, as well as the other four murders arranged in a five-pointed star around the black zone at Sector 4196 had been part of a ritual that summoned the abyssal she had no luck finding. Worse, as with Charazu and Avarazel—both true demons or 'They Who Always Were' as Konstantin had called them—she would need to find out this one's name in order to have any hope of destroying it. And, the best way to do that would be to find the notes or materials used by whoever summoned it.

Of course, so far, the traces she'd picked up hadn't been that strong. With luck, she merely had to deal with an abyssal—a returned once-human—who escaped the 'bad place.' Only, this one felt even stronger than Seneschal, and not by a little bit.

At least no more paranormal killings had occurred since Santiago Herrera. She considered the possibility that the abyssal might've been summoned for specific, targeted assassinations and, having completed said murders, went back where it belonged.

However, that also meant that a street gang full of dangerously psychotic cretins who barely qualified as sentient beings managed to figure out mysticism to the degree that they could've done something like that.

"Hmm. Hey, Dorian?" She swung around in her chair to face his desk, behind hers.

He had his feet up, leaning back in his seat while looking at a datapad. Or at least a ghostly simulation thereof. He moved it aside so it no longer blocked his face. "Yes?"

"Assuming that those idiots managed to actually summon something, I'm starting to think they might've sent this abyssal after a handful of prominent enemies. We've gone two days and haven't had another body turn up with weird black lines. Maybe the abyssal went back."

The Harbinger, floating near the wall on the left, shook its head.

"Great." She sighed. "So I've been wasting time in here when I should've been out there looking for it."

Again, the Harbinger shook its head.

"What?" She peered at it.

It looked down, a vaporous apparition of black smoke somehow managing to convey sadness, and pointed at itself.

"You're here to help?"

It shook its head, then pointed at itself again before making a clawing motion.

"Perhaps you should read its mind instead of playing charades?" Dorian lowered his feet from the desk. The 'datapad' in his hand vanished into silvery fog.

"No surface thoughts to read. But he can understand me." She glanced at the holo-panel array over her desk showing case notes, then back at the Harbinger. Again it made a clawing gesture. She wound up staring at its wispy fingers. "Oh, shit."

"What?" asked Dorian.

"The answer's been right next to me for days and I haven't seen it. Abyssal energy, that weird sense of guilt, five claw marks... The Harbinger." She blinked at it. "Are you saying *you* killed those three people?"

It nodded.

Dorian about fell out of his chair.

Morelli eased himself up from his chair and walked out.

"I thought Harbingers couldn't harm the living." Kirsten swallowed.

It raised its arms in a gesture of frustration, then slouched in a defeated posture.

"Something the Diablos did gave you the ability to harm the living?" asked Kirsten.

The Harbinger tilted one vaporous hand side-to-side.

"Not exactly," muttered Kirsten. "Okay. You, err, Harbingers *can* hurt the living, but you usually don't?"

It gave a wispy thumbs-up.

"Usually don't or aren't allowed to?" asked Dorian.

It pointed at him.

"Not allowed?" Kirsten reached toward her terminal, tentatively adding some notes to the file.

The Harbinger glided closer, poking one finger into the word 'Diablos' on the screen.

"Normally, whatever laws of the universe there are state that Harbingers can't harm the living, but because of what they did, you can?"

It nodded, then bowed its head for a moment before wrapping its arms around her.

She stiffened at the beyond-cold embrace.

When it released her a second later, it again pointed at the word Diablos on the screen.

"I think he's trying to say you are somehow doing something to protect him from the forces controlling him. Fairly sure he didn't want to kill those people."

The Harbinger bowed at Dorian.

"Wait." Kirsten looked back and forth between them. "Are you seriously suggesting that Diablos, two chromosomes lower than cavemen, managed to summon a Harbinger, force it to stay in this plane, and somehow weaponized it?"

The Harbinger nodded.

Kirsten bowed her head. "Shit."

"I think this situation calls for something stronger than simply 'shit.'" Dorian chuckled. "But, at least you're doing something about it."

"Sitting here being frustrated?"

"No. Something about being near you is allowing the Harbinger to resist their control. He can't go home so he's doing the next best thing."

The Harbinger again gave a wispy thumbs-up.

"Okay, sorry for the random question. She, he, or it?"

It stared at her, tilting its head.

"Are you male?"

It shook its head.

"Female?"

It shook its head.

"You were never human, right?"

It nodded.

"Okay, it's a genderless elemental force of the universe."

"Sounds like this teacher I had in high school." Dorian snickered.

Two wispy thumbs up.

"It's kind of cute," said Dorian.

The cloud of inky blackness stared in Harbinger.

AN AWKWARD POSITION

K irsten leapt up and ran to Captain Eze's office.

He jumped as she barged in, almost spilling coffee down his chest. "Kirsten?"

"Captain, I've figured out what's going on." She didn't bother sitting, waving her arms around while explaining about the Harbinger. "The Diablos who did this have to be in Sector 4196. It's at the middle of the pentagram."

"Pentagram? What pentagram?"

She accessed her armband terminal, went to the inquest record, and flicked the image capture she'd taken of the Navcon screen toward his desk. It appeared on his screen. "The locations of the five murders from that P10 inquest correspond on the map to five points of a star. I'm sure the Diablos killed them as part of whatever ritual they used to either summon or entrap a Harbinger and bind it to service as an assassin."

Captain Eze steepled his fingers, staring at the screen. "And it's following you around because..."

"She's so sweet and innocent her mere presence neutralizes the evil magic affecting it," said Dorian.

Kirsten rolled her eyes and let out a heavy sigh.

"Who said what?" asked Captain Eze.

"Dorian has a rather twee theory on why I'm protecting the Harbinger.

In *my* opinion, it probably has more to do with the Seraphim choosing me as some kind of agent of theirs. Either way, as long as it's near me, it won't be forced to murder anyone else. But, I have to break whatever hold they have on it. Ideally, that also involves discovering how the Diablos managed to do this and taking steps to make sure they don't do it again."

"You know what you're asking…" Captain Eze raised both eyebrows.

"Yes, sir. I know. I'm asking for permission to go into a giant, ten-mile-wide black zone full of Diablos on a mission to arrest the ones responsible for this."

Dorian snickered.

She glared at him.

"Arrest. Cute."

Kirsten sighed. "I know how it's going to end, but I am not going in there with the intention of killing them."

"I'm worried for your safety, Kirsten." Captain Eze shifted his jaw around, then sighed.

She smiled. "I know. And I appreciate that. But, the NPF brass isn't going to want to touch this because 'only gang thugs' have been killed."

"Kirsten, the National Police Force has limited resources and needs to allocate those resources where they can do the most good for the most people."

Dorian leaned close to her and whispered, "That's manager speak for 'let the criminals kill each other. If someone rich dies, call us.'"

"Sir, if the Diablos are capable of weaponizing a Harbinger, they are not going to stop with street thugs. Exactly how would anyone stop a Harbinger from spree killing Senators? Or cops? Or whoever the heck they want to send it after?"

He shifted his eyes to her. "It is a bit of an awkward situation. Outside of Division 0, your mention of Harbingers would be disregarded as a product of insanity. They barely keep straight faces during discussions about ghosts. It would take someone prominent being found dead by unexplainable means for them to even agree to listen to any talk of these beings."

She opened her mouth to protest, but shut it at his raised hand.

"Give me a little while to see what I can manage."

Kirsten nodded. "Thank you, sir."

Head bowed, fists clenched, she trudged out of his office. Out of sheer randomness, she headed down the hall toward the cafeteria. The

Harbinger trailed along after her, having regained the usual imposingly regal posture she'd come to expect from them.

Whoa. Was it ashamed of me finding out what it did?

The crowd in the main foyer of the Police Administrative Center fell strangely quiet as she entered. Fortunately, the radiant dread of the Harbinger came from a point sufficiently behind her that only a handful of people (who knew she had a rating in Mind Blast) glared at her accusingly.

She walked by the corridors leading to the Division 1 and 2 areas, heading for the big hallway in the center of the wall opposite the main entrance that led to the food court. Division 0 (and 9) had their own private cafeterias, while Div 1, 2, 5, and 6 all shared a massive one. The food in the big cafeteria was *way* better, so she often went there on the rare occasion she didn't order something from an outside place. Delivery food beat both cafeterias, but here, active duty cops ate for free, just like the military.

The Harbinger hesitated near the middle of the atrium, gazing toward the Division 9 entrance.

She shivered. "Wouldn't surprise me if a few people in Nine interested you, but they're mostly okay."

The Harbinger tilted its hand back and forth.

"Wow, really? Some are that dark?" She sighed, and headed off to the cafeteria.

Perhaps due to the large number of people, reaction to a Harbinger gliding into the room took the subdued form of increased tension in conversations and people looking around in confusion. Naturally, some people associated the odd sensation with a Zero being around.

After claiming a moderately-decent-looking grilled chicken wrap sandwich and an iced green tea, she took a table off in the corner at the least-populated part of the room. The rigid metal stool bolted to the floor reminded her why she rarely ate here: uncomfortable, and cold through the thin material of her uniform. The Harbinger attempted to 'sit' opposite her at the table, floating above the stool.

She peered over her wrap at it, feeling altogether bizarre for sitting there having lunch with an immortal agent of the Universe Engine. "Sorry, I guess I should've asked if you wanted some food."

Its silvery eyes sparkled with a blank stare.

"Bad joke." She took a bite, thinking about her role in the grand scheme of things while chewing. "Do you know… did the Seraphim do something to give me my abilities or did they choose me because I already had them?"

The Harbinger held up two smoky fingers.

"Option two. Already had them."

It nodded.

Yay. I won the lottery of fate. She wondered about what happened to Mother. Ritchie, the ghost who'd convinced her to run away from home that night, started a rumor in the prison where Mother went after twelve-year-old Kirsten told the Division 0 people about what the woman had done to her since she'd been six. That rumor, whatever it had been, caused another inmate to murder her.

She ate a few more bites before finding the courage to ask.

"Did my mother go to the bad place?"

The Harbinger nodded.

"Guess you guys don't take an insanity defense."

It shook its head.

"That woman was clearly insane, what she did to me and why."

The Harbinger stared for a few seconds before wiggling its fingers and bouncing in a manner completely wrong for such a creature. Something that dark and ominous should not appear gleeful.

She raised an eyebrow. When the shock of seeing that wore off and she could think again, she got the hint. "She took pleasure in what she did to me."

The Harbinger nodded.

"Please," asked Dorian, from behind her. "Never do that again."

"What?" Kirsten glanced over at him.

"I was talking to our friend. That giddy gesture... Harbinger... no. That's a mental image I could've done without."

She smiled. "What about killing people?"

It made the 'so-so' gesture again.

"Intent, right? Someone forced to kill to protect themselves or another person isn't as bad as someone who kills for the heck of it, and even worse, someone who takes joy from causing pain and death."

The Harbinger gave a shadowy thumbs-up.

"Taking delight in killing more than the act itself." Dorian rubbed his chin.

Kirsten munched on grilled chicken, thinking. "Why did that one Harbinger look at Dorian so long?"

"Umm." Dorian flashed a cheesy smile. "I perhaps took an undue amount of satisfaction in one or two summary executions I performed."

The Harbinger raised one hand, making a pinching gesture.

"Oh, get dragged across spiritual planes and bound by dark forces, and everyone becomes a comedian." Dorian fake-rolled his eyes.

Kirsten laughed, almost choking on green tea.

25

MIDDLE GROUND

E xisting as a passive force that allowed a Harbinger to resist the Diablos' control made Kirsten feel at least somewhat useful.

When she returned to the squad room after eating, Captain Eze's window appeared dark, nearly opaque, the door closed. In the six years since she'd been activated at sixteen, she'd only seen him close the door and black out the window twice. Both times involved discussions of classified materials.

"Wow. Think he's trying to convince Command that a street gang might be a serious threat to the UCF?"

Dorian grinned. "I would love to be a fly on the wall in there."

She sat at her desk. "So why aren't you?"

"Because I'm not cleared to know whatever he's talking about."

"You're a ghost."

"I still consider myself active Division 0. It wouldn't be right to snoop on a captain."

She whistled. "Wow. Okay."

"Or are you asking me to snoop for you?"

"No."

"You answered that awfully fast."

She unlocked her terminal. "It just surprised me you aren't fully exploiting your ghostliness."

"I routinely exploit my ghostliness, but not when doing so is directly against regulations."

Kirsten almost laughed. "There is nothing in the regs about ghosts."

"Well, if I eavesdropped, it would eventually come out in conversation with you, and I don't want to put you in the position to know things you haven't been cleared to know and explain how it is you came to know them."

"You're so thoughtful." She winked.

Chin on her hand, she set about plotting the locations of wherever Malden Walker attacked women. She created dots for the victims' homes as well as the sites where the assaults occurred. Unfortunately, other than being mostly confined to the southern third of West City, no pattern emerged. It made sense that he stuck to the south during the later months, since areas too cold would reduce the odds some random piece of shit would attack the women he dangled as bait.

She sat there staring at the map, angry and guilty for not being able to do more to track Malden down. Freya had been a lucky break. Her neural accelerator had given her the time to call for help before he moved from spectral pawing to possession. Unless the next woman he targeted also had both speedware and a headware uplink to the GlobeNet, she'd be talking to another victim after the fact and no closer to finding him.

"I hate this part the most," said Kirsten, barely above a whisper.

Dorian peered over his datapad at her. "The waiting?"

"Not exactly. The sitting here knowing there's a dangerous ghost out there and having no damn way to find or stop him."

"Wren?" asked Captain Eze.

She sat up tall—relatively—and peered over the top of her holo-panel. The captain stood in the doorway to his office, beckoning her with a wave. Kirsten sprang out of her chair and rushed over, trembling with anxiety. She wanted him to say yes to her idea the way Evan wanted Monwyn stuff, but she also dreaded he *would* say yes... since that would mean an extremely dangerous trip into the black.

He closed the door after she entered.

"Uh oh. This is bad news, isn't it?"

Captain Eze shook his head. "I hope not. It's partially classified. What I'm about to discuss with you stays inside Division 0. It's not a good idea to discuss it with the younger cadets, but anyone activated is legally obligated to maintain confidentiality."

"I understand."

"This is going to be handled strictly inside Division 0. I approached the Command Council with your findings and theories. We've come up with a compromise that should work for everyone involved, except me."

"You?" Kirsten blinked.

"I'm going to be a nervous damn wreck until you're back here safe." He smiled.

"Thanks, Dad."

He chuckled. "All right. Here it is. There's a new officer in Tactical, a bit of a unique situation as her abilities are far into uncharted territory. Director Carter has agreed to the two of you going into Sector 4196 in search of the source of this Harbinger problem."

"Just *two* of us?" Kirsten swallowed. "Not like a whole unit?"

"Since when does the Command Council huff Icewhisper?" asked Dorian.

She nearly laughed.

"They are concerned about a similar situation as what happened in that 'church.' We're dealing with abyssals again. They also believe Officer Solomon is capable of handling the Diablos, and highly interested in seeing how this plays out. Deputy Director Burkhardt was quite keen on learning what she can do in there."

"I'll bet he was," muttered Dorian.

"Officer Solomon has already been approached with this mission, and she's agreed to help. Whenever you're ready to do this, head over to T-9 and talk to her."

"Who am I looking for?"

"Officer Kate Solomon. She stands out..." Captain Eze pulled at the corner of a holo-panel floating above his desk, turning the rectangle of light to face them. It showed the ID photo of a twentysomething woman with red hair, perfect skin, and the looks of a supermodel.

"Yeah, okay... she does stand out in a crowd."

"You are hereby ordered to wear armor, and a stim suit." Captain Eze smiled.

Kirsten nodded. "Oh, yeah. I was planning to. I was also planning to go in there with at least twelve people."

"Officer Solomon crossed the Badlands on foot. No weapons, not even clothing." Captain Eze fidgeted.

"Seriously? Naked? Is she insane? Why would she do that?" Kirsten gawked.

"I don't have those details. Maybe she'll explain when you meet her."

Kirsten checked over her belt. "Well, the sooner I deal with this, the sooner the Harbinger can go back where he belongs and the universe returns to normal." She caught herself shaking. "Umm, sir. Do you think it's really a good idea for just the two of us to go in?"

"There will be at least three of us." Dorian smiled.

"Not entirely, no. But… some of the things in her file defy explanation. I trust you to use your judgement. I'll have a strike team standing by around Sector 4090 or so with an A3HV, inside a one-minute response window. If you start getting in over your head, you call them in and get the hell out."

"Understood, sir." Kirsten saluted him.

She couldn't help but think about her disastrous raid on the cyberdoc that nearly resulted in Nila's death. That mistake, she would *not* make again. She would come home to Evan, even if the Diablos got away with murder—for now. Retreat from a bad situation didn't mean total loss. She'd merely have to find a new way to approach the problem.

But, she also had an unknown quantity to deal with.

Who is Kate Solomon and what on Earth makes the Council think she's worth an entire squad? And what kind of crazy person streaks the Badlands?

SQUAD ROOM T-9 SAT AT THE END OF A HALL ONE FLOOR DOWN AND ON the opposite side of the Division 0 wing.

Kirsten tried to be as unassuming as possible, but between a Harbinger following her and wearing lieutenant bars, walking down a corridor packed with enlisted psionics constituted a case study in the exact opposite of subtle.

A few tactical officers who didn't stand there staring, petrified by the radiant dread wafting off her shadowy friend managed to salute her. She returned it with only the requisite amount of enthusiasm required by decorum. Having people older than her acting like her inferiors made her feel all kinds of awkward.

I'm a kid with a rare power set. These people have been on the job for a long time. She clung to what Dorian had said a while back about how good officers heed the advice of experience over their pride. Kirsten wondered if constantly doubting herself and *still* feeling like a child in over her head meant she didn't *have* pride at all. Her promotion to second lieutenant didn't give her any sense of being better than anyone, merely validated her. As an agent, she'd always felt like a little kid prodigy allowed to hang with the adults.

The level of noise and activity in this part of the building—at least prior to the Harbinger's arrival—surprised her as well. Of course, Division 0 had something like twenty or so tactical personnel to every I-Ops officer. *This* hallway fit what she imagined a normal police station would be like.

Kirsten approached the plain white doors beside a silver panel with T-9 in black letters. With a soft *pssh,* the doors parted at her approach. The squad room beyond resembled hers in general aesthetic, only about three times the size. Rather than classroom-style rows, the desks in here stood in pinwheel clusters of four. Tons of plasfilm sheets hung from the walls bearing everything from suspect faces to humorous pictures to printouts from the Newsnet. It smelled like a locker room blended with sugary pastry and armpit. She also had the feeling the floor cleaning bots in here cried themselves to sleep each night.

Due to the size of the squad room, the captain's office at the far end seemed tiny, though it no doubt matched Captain Eze's. A man's shouting echoed from inside. Though the door was closed, the window remained clear, allowing a view of a tall man with Hispanic features, greying hair, and a muscular build looming over the desk, jabbing his finger at a pair of twentysomethings in tactical armor, bellowing about reckless jackassery. A pink-haired woman stood with a stoic expression while the guy next to her looked about ready to faint from dread.

About a third of the desks had people at them, the rest empty as their assigned officer would be out on patrol at this hour. Those nearer the door all turned to look at her. Based on their alarmed expressions, she figured they sensed the Harbinger's energy.

"Uh oh. Who's getting wiped?" whispered a man.

"No idea. Who is that? Feels stronger than Ashford."

"Don't be a dumbass," whispered a woman, "mind blasters don't throw off vibes like that."

Kirsten let it slide since they clearly had no idea who she was; they could only assume the ill feeling in the air came from her. Fair bet most of them, despite being in Division 0, wouldn't like being told about ghosts, or worse, Harbingers.

She homed in on a strikingly beautiful redhead the instant she stood from her desk and stuffed a few extra stimpaks into a belt case. The woman fist-bumped the guy at the desk to her right, then walked over to the door, her dark emerald eyes abruptly widening. Her uniform had an odd indigo tint as well as a metallic shimmer, though it hugged her every curve even more than the standard black fabric did. She looked like someone had sprayed her with liquid aluminum that formed a thin coating on her skin.

"You must be Lieutenant Wren." The woman offered a hand. "I'm Kate."

Dorian whistled. "Now it makes sense. The Diablos will take one look at her and all the blood in their body will go straight to their dicks. They won't even be able to think straight."

"Yeah. Hi." Kirsten accepted the handshake, ignoring her partner and peering up at the taller woman. "Don't mind the sense of infinite doom hanging over me. He won't hurt you."

Kate laughed. "You're a bit smaller than I expected. Are they seriously going to send a kid out to the black?"

Dorian snickered.

"I'm twenty-two. Just short. Still, how is it that they agreed to send just the two of us in?"

"C'mon. I'll explain on the way."

Kate slipped past her into the hall, eyeing the general vicinity of the Harbinger and walking around it. Once past the voluminous cloud of inky darkness, she took on a confident stride with a little sway. The woman didn't give off a sense of wanting to throw her sexuality around like a weapon, more that she felt absolutely confident without the slightest trace of worry.

The Harbinger remained close to Kirsten, though it drifted in front of her as if 'sniffing' the woman out. When they reached the elevator, it continued to hover nearby, its body language suggesting it didn't quite know what to make of her.

"So… how much did they tell you?" asked Kirsten.

"Only that they had someone who needed to go into a black zone to chase down people who did some shit I wouldn't believe, and they're probably Diablos. Also, that I'm cleared to do whatever I have to do to ensure we both go home."

"You don't seem too worried about going into a black zone."

Kate smiled. "I used to live in one, so I know the routine. Mine was in East City. Never been to 4196 before, so my reputation won't protect us. But that's okay. Diablos are simple to deal with. They don't listen to reason so there's no point talking."

"I don't even want to think about what they would do to you—or her if this goes bad." Dorian moved in front of Kirsten, staring into her eyes. "I know how you feel about killing, and it's what makes you who you are. However, if you're going to go in there, you need to think about Evan. Diablos no longer count as human beings. Consider them no different from those jackalwere things in Monwyn. Except, they won't kill and eat you. They make Malden Walker look like Bippy the Sunshine Rabbit."

Kirsten shivered—mostly because she remembered the irritatingly catchy theme song from that stupid show. The dorm nannies had it on all the time in the area with the youngest kids. "I know. But... don't forget I'm a suggestive. *If* we get captured, no one is going to lay a damned hand on me. Or Kate."

The redhead laughed again. "Captured... that's cute. Hon..." She threw an arm around Kirsten's shoulders. "We're not going to get captured."

When the elevator opened one level up, the Harbinger exited first, continuing to stare at Kate. Kirsten slipped past it and waited in the hall.

"There's something there, right?" asked Kate, one eyebrow up. "I feel a presence following us but don't see anything."

"Two entities actually. My partner, Dorian—a ghost, and I have a Harbinger tagging along as well. It seems... interested in you."

"Is that good or bad?" Kate edged out of the elevator, doing her best not to walk into the vaporous mass.

Kirsten worked her hair up into a twist that would fit in a helmet. "It's interested in you because you've done some bad shit, but it's confused I think because maybe you're trying to fix things. I'd say its reaction means you've managed to kinda get close to the middle."

"Yeah." Kate looked down as they walked. "I wasn't in a very good place for a while. Killing people was just something I had to do to survive. Guess I was pretty fucked up if it didn't mean anything to me."

"Nothing? You never enjoyed it?" Kirsten headed into the locker area near her squad room. "Not that I think you should; I mean it's darker if you take delight in it."

"Maybe one time." Kate folded her arms. "I used to have a thing against geneticists. Maybe I rather enjoyed killing one."

Kirsten removed her utility belt, boots, and armband, then stripped out of her Division 0 blacks, down to only panties. "You're not going to wear armor?"

"Nah. No point." Kate smiled at her. "No bra?"

"Not enough to put in one," muttered Kirsten.

"Aww, don't be so critical. They're cute."

"I'm not being critical." She grabbed a mesh stimsuit from the locker and stepped into it. "I'm making fun of some asshole I don't even remember his name. And, well... I hate bras. Not quite as much as I hate high heels. Portends of doom."

Kate grinned. "They're not that bad."

"Every single time I wear heels, I feel like a drunken ostrich on stilts... right up until I wind up barefoot and running for my life." Kirsten pulled her PSI armor leggings out of the locker and pulled them on.

"That sounds like an interesting story." Kate picked up the armor chest piece and helped her into it.

Kirsten glanced over at her. "Is it true you streaked naked across the Badlands?"

"Yeah."

"Umm..." She blinked, dumbfounded. "Why?"

"No choice. I had a little, umm, trouble with my pyro for a while. Anything I touched caught fire."

Dorian snickered. "Talk about a smoking hot body."

Kirsten sighed at him. "That's... wow. Never heard of anything like that happening before. So you're really going to skip armor and wear that into a black zone? What *is* it anyway?" She brushed her fingers down Kate's arm. "It's so thin. Is it metal?"

"Indirium threads, yeah. Heat resistant."

"What if you get shot?"

"As long as I see it coming, the bullets will melt."

Kirsten squeezed the two halves of her armored chest piece together until they clicked. "Melt? Are you serious?"

"Eze did say something about off the charts." Dorian raised an impressed eyebrow.

"Yeah. So..." Kate looked around. "Is toasting these Diablos going to, uhh, make me 'slide evil' or something?"

The Harbinger shook its head.

"Under normal circumstances, I'd say it would only be a problem if you took delight in killing them or if you kill one who surrenders... but these guys don't surrender."

Dorian pointed his thumb at the Harbinger. "And I think our friend is a little annoyed with them, so you get a pass."

26

BRING THE FIRE

An Advanced Armored Assault Hover Van trailed after Kirsten's patrol craft toward the black zone of Sector 4196.

Their escort broke off and hung motionless in midair at the five mile mark from the edge of the grey. The military had never attempted to take back this area, so the denizens here didn't have access to scavenged heavy weapons or rocket launchers left behind in the carnage.

Kirsten kept flying onward over blocks and blocks of high-rise towers that progressively appeared in worse states of decay. The term 'black zone' originated from how sectors too far gone to lawlessness and violence appeared as empty voids in the Navcon system. It didn't usually translate to the real world actually becoming black. However, in the case of Sector 4196 and its surroundings, the name proved more than metaphorical.

The wreckage of large industrial buildings hinted that the sector had once contained facilities for the manufacture of passenger shuttles or starships. Vast, cavernous pits like swimming pools for titans marked the landscape here and there, stained green from whatever chemicals they once held. No longer used for treating the hulls of enormous spacecraft, they'd become landfills, collecting mountains of scrap, debris, and trash— and likely hundreds of bodies. From the air, they didn't look *too* worrisome, though based on their size compared to nearby buildings, falling into one would entail at least a four-story drop before hitting junk.

Those pits have to go straight to the bottom of the plates...

"Whoa," whispered Kate. "Check that out."

Kirsten looked away from the old chemical baths, following the woman's pointing finger to a giant, glowing red pentagram. It hung suspended between two metal pipes, former chimneys of some kind, and appeared to be a physical object, not a hologram. She poked at the windscreen, zooming in on it. Strands of wires and LED lights created an inverted five-pointed-star within a circle about twenty feet high.

Plink.

"Looks like the natives have noticed us," said Kate. "That sounded like a bullet bouncing off the car."

Plink.

Kirsten shook her head at the ruin sprawled out below and rolled the patrol craft into a leftward dive. Handheld firearms didn't pose much threat to a patrol craft, unless they managed a lucky shot straight up into one of the ion thrusters, but hitting a three-inch target moving at 200 MPH with a handgun from 500 feet below may as well be impossible. That two bullets even hit the car at all probably meant a few dozen people had to be firing fully automatic at them. Or maybe one aug with targeting optics. She skimmed closer to the ground to guard the underside, heading for an intersection full of shot-up cars.

"You can't leave the pat-vee here," said Kate. "It'll be gone before we get back."

"Not planning to. Dorian can fly it to a safe distance after we're out."

"A ghost can fly the car?" Kate blinked.

"Yeah, he's real attached to it." Kirsten descended to a hover two feet off the ground, not bothering to deploy the wheels.

"Very funny," said Dorian.

"You got the stick." Kirsten opened her door.

Blue sparks crept randomly across the plastisteel ground from the ionic downblast, flashing within a blanket of dense Cryomil fog. As soon as Dorian vanished into the console, Kirsten jumped out, the plastic-like material of her PSI armor clicking and clattering on her sprint to cover behind the nearest ruined car.

Kate dropped to the ground and stood in place, hands on her hips, glancing around like a disappointed tourist. "Wow, this place is a real shithole. Gotta say, East City black zones are nicer. The locals don't usually knock whole buildings down back there."

The Harbinger exuded from the underside of the departing patrol craft and drifted over to her. Kirsten, hunkered down behind the wreck, sighed at her fastest way out of here leaving her behind. *Am I making a mistake?*

"Lieutenant Wren," said Captain Eze in her ear. "What's your status?"

"We're on the ground, about to go in."

"Copy. Be careful in there. The instant you feel like you're no longer in control of the situation, you call in Pemberley's team."

"On standby," said a bassy man's voice. The words 'E5 Pemberley, I' appeared at the corner of her visor as he spoke. "We're hovering 6.2 miles out, lieutenant. Oh, by the way, there's a static distortion six feet to your left."

"Yeah." Kirsten glanced at the Harbinger. "I'm aware. It's friendly."

"The disavowed area you've entered is large enough that you may lose signal near the center," said Captain Eze over comms. "I'm keeping an eye on this operation... as is the Command Council."

That means he's going to send Pemberley in if he thinks I'm in trouble. She exhaled, grateful he hadn't ordered her on an open channel to bail out if he pulled the plug. He probably thought it, but didn't want to undermine her authority.

Kate walked over and stood next to her, still casually looking around. "Any idea where they are?"

"Only that they're somewhere in this sector." Kirsten peeked up over the car. "Why are you just standing out in the open like that?"

"Because they're like wild animals. Showing fear will make them attack. And, I don't see anything yet. We're probably too far away from wherever they've made a nest."

Kirsten braced a hand on the car and stood, twisting side to side while panning her view around. The electronics in her helmet didn't show any amber 'ghosts' of people hiding behind objects or broken walls, so she relaxed—a little. "So, what did they mean by 'awakened?'"

"Ugh." Kate sighed. "It's a really long story. Your plan's basically walk around until we make contact with Diablos, then what?"

"Ask them who's using rituals to kill people."

"Yeah, that'll work."

Kirsten grinned. "I didn't expect them to answer, but as soon as I ask, they'll think it."

The Harbinger raised a large, shadowy arm, and pointed.

"That way?"

It nodded.

She hurried around the back end of the derelict car, waving for Kate to follow. "Come on. This isn't going to be as bad as I thought."

"Oh, I'm sure it will be." Dorian materialized in a silvery cloud beside her. "It just won't take as long to get bad."

"What do you mean?" asked Kate.

"The Harbinger can lead us right to the people who attacked it."

"Neat." Kate walked out ahead of her.

Kirsten moved up to a jog. "Unless you can follow the Harbinger, I should be out front. And, aren't you going to use your E-90?"

"Good point. It is less tiring that way." Kate pulled the laser pistol off her hip.

"You were going to take on Diablos with just your Pyrokinesis?"

"Usually, yeah. Not used to being able to touch a gun without melting it… and I think my pyro's more effective."

Dorian laughed. "She sounds like the exact reverse of you. You almost forget you even carry a sidearm half the time."

"Yeah, but laser weapons barely hurt spirits. They work fine on the living." Kirsten paused to let the Harbinger float into the lead.

For the next few minutes, they walked in single file. The total ruin of old factory buildings, massive elevated walkways reduced to naked steel beams, and the occasional scrap of starship hull jutting up from piles of rubble made it seem like they'd gone to another planet—or played a post-apocalyptic game on a high-end senshelmet. Only, she didn't have a 'health bar.' If she let a Diablo catch her off guard, there wouldn't be a saved game to restart from.

The Harbinger glided up to the crumbling remains of a twelve-story building. Its thin metal siding, riddled with bullet holes, peeled away from the plasticrete underneath. Spray painted symbols in a mix of red and black covered the lower two stories. Some of it reminded her of the pictograms involved in the summoning of Charazu, though she didn't study them enough to know if she looked at legit ritualism or idiots being infatuated with 'cool occult shit.'

Kirsten crept past a disintegrating doorway, her boots crunching on broken bits of wall and ceiling panels. Soft whimpering and the rattle of chains triggered a sick feeling in the pit of her stomach. Concern kicked her fear aside. She rushed toward the sound, following the corridor around a corner to the left where it opened into a former room. Ten stories of smashed floor overhead let daylight in, as well as trickles of water, making the area more of a courtyard with enormous walls than the ground level of a building.

Three men in black biker coats emblazoned with red pentagrams on the back sat around in dingy recliners at the center of the ruined space. Six cubbies the size of large closets lined the left side of the room under a section of intact second-story floor. The addition of chain link fencing turned the spaces into holding cells. A mix of nude women and men occupied the cells in varying degrees of restraint. Some had been chained to the wall like prisoners in a medieval dungeon, some curled up on the floor. Dirt and dried blood smeared all of them.

Kate eyed the prisoners. "I think I know why your captain asked me to help out here. These fuckers need to be purged from the Earth."

The three Diablos finally noticed them standing there and rose to their feet, grinning.

"We're not here to exterminate," said Kirsten.

Dorian walked toward the gangers. "They're Diablos. They will kill you on sight for being cops without any hesitation. You said yourself they don't surrender."

Kirsten pointed her E-90 at the gang thugs. "I know. That doesn't mean I have to like it." She raised her voice. "Who killed Juan Miguel Esparza, and who's playing around with ritual mysticism?"

"Yo, was that shit laced with zoom, or am I seeing cops *here*?" asked the guy in the middle, laughing.

"No, I see cops too," said the guy on the left.

"The fuck are cops doing here?" The man on the right made a rude hand motion at Kate, licking his fingers.

"Committin' suicide." The man on the left raised a large submachine gun in Kirsten's direction.

She started to skim their surface thoughts for any answers, but picked up only a mixture of 'cops, kill them' and the strong urge to rip Kate's uniform off her. The man on the right charged at the redhead with intent to grab. The middle guy drew two handguns.

Kirsten shot the man with the submachine gun dead center in the chest. His coat ignited front and back around the laser. A blue fireball the size of a grapefruit flew by on the right, striking the Diablo rushing at

Kate in the face. Skin vaporized; his eyes exploded in foamy sprays as a three-second burn cored a hollow out of his skull, leaving a charred bowl-shaped crater with exposed, scorched brain.

The ghastly sight stalled Kirsten in her tracks, staring dumbfounded at the corpse. Kate hurled another fireball into the center man simultaneously with him firing both pistols at Kirsten. Fortunately, his quick-draw routine killed his accuracy, and both shots hit the wall somewhere above and behind her. He grabbed at his chest where the flaming sphere hit, his scream of agony drawn in the air by the smoke coming from his lips. His ghost staggered backward away from the still-standing body, which fell two seconds later.

She blinked at Kate.

The Harbinger glided forward, raking its shadowy claws at three surprised ghosts, shredding them into strips of ethereal matter. Kirsten winced at the energy spike from three mild obliterations, not sure what to make of watching one of those beings *destroy* spirits rather than escort them to the Abyss.

It's either pissed or trapped here and can't *do its job.*

"Fuck yeah," shouted a woman with pink hair in a pixie cut from one of the cells, jumping to the end of a leash. "Kill them all."

Kirsten glanced at her long enough to realize the woman wore only a collar, handcuffs connected to said collar, and some random objects stuffed places they did *not* belong, then turned away, blushing, mortified, and furious. "Captain, are you seeing this?"

"Unfortunately…"

"Does Pemberley's A3HV have enough room for…" Kirsten forced herself to look at the cells again. "Nine people?"

Two young men and a woman about Kirsten's age remained on the floor in fetal positions, not reacting at all to what happened. Most of the prisoners bled from numerous minor injuries, small cuts, whip marks, and nails stabbed into their skin.

Kate grabbed a padlock securing one of the pens in her bare hand, the glowing steel melting as if she crushed raw dough between her fingers.

"Negative, lieutenant," said Pemberley in her earbud. "We're full up."

"Get them out of there and fall back to where you landed. Pemberley, move your team in to secure that area as an LZ. Another A3HV will be en route within two minutes for civilian transport."

"Copy, captain," said Pemberley.

Kirsten shot out a few padlocks, pulling the chain link gates open. She cringed at the overwhelming stink of feces and urine coating the floor as well as the captives. Her uti knife dealt with the cords and other restraints easily. The pink-haired woman hastily rid herself of unwanted objects, then ran out into the room and began kicking the dead Diablos over and over again. She grabbed a handgun off one and emptied the magazine into the corpses.

Those who retained enough sanity to process that they'd been rescued showered her with thanks, and an equal amount of disbelief that the police had bothered looking for them. Kirsten didn't mention they'd been discovered purely by accident, and helped escort them out to the intersection about a quarter mile from the building. One man, both his legs broken, screamed the entire way as two fellow captives carry-dragged him along, despite having four stimpaks pumped into him.

Twelve officers in PSI armor greeted them, standing in a defensive formation around an armored black hover van. Pemberley turned out to be a wiry man she thought too skinny for Tactical—or his deep voice—but he may well have been a kinetic. Size didn't necessarily correlate to strength for some psionics.

After getting all the abductees to relative safety, Kirsten followed the Harbinger back to the building where they had been beaten, tortured, starved, raped, and who knows what else for weeks.

"How can people be so cruel to other human beings… it's worse than anything true demons would do to us." She stared at the Diablo with the melted face.

The Harbinger tilted its wispy hand side-to-side.

"It's worse because they're human, too." Kirsten shook her head.

"That's debatable. That they're human, I mean." Kate shuddered, stepping around a few discarded bits of narrow pipe that had previously been inside people, and not only via natural body cavities.

Kirsten felt sick at the thought, but perhaps the members of this particular gang *did* deserve to be removed from existence. Though… she'd still wait for them to attempt to kill her first. On the off chance one of them *did* surrender, she'd hold her fire. But, she also wouldn't allow herself to feel much guilt over defending herself—especially from subhuman monsters like this.

The Harbinger drifted deeper into the building, down a hall past a crumbled cube farm. Nine bodies in various states of decay hung from hooks along the left wall, some still wearing jackets or shirts with logos from different gangs.

"It's a damn trophy room," muttered Kate.

I'm going to wind up on Dr. Loring's couch after this is over. Kirsten swallowed bile. "Yeah."

At the far end of the room, the Harbinger squeezed its billowy form through a doorway into a short hallway that ended where the outer wall of the building on that side—all ten stories of it—had collapsed into a field of rubble and giant plasticrete chunks. An improvised ramp of metal grating led from the edge of the concrete slab floor to the ground.

Kirsten hurried down, taking cover behind the nearest mound. The Harbinger drifted in a straight line, ignoring the physical barriers while she ran from spot to spot, pausing each time to look around for threats before dashing to the next hiding place.

They covered a little more than a city block's distance before the Harbinger stopped and sank low, merely eye level with her. It pointed past a tall slab of broken thermacrete standing vertically. Metal housings dangling from the facing side suggested it had once been a piece of roof before falling with enough force to stick into the metal ground like a giant, square shuriken.

The din of numerous voices came from the other side. Her helmet attempted to create amber ghosts on the electronic display to show the position of people, but it couldn't quite manage it, either due to signal interference or too many targets too close together.

Sensing the Harbinger's reluctance to go any farther, Kirsten nodded. "The people who did the ritual are there?"

It held up one finger.

"One person?"

"You know..." Kate looked around. "It's kind of disturbing to hear you carrying on conversations with thin air... and getting answers."

"Look into my head if you want to see what I'm seeing." She turned back to the Harbinger. "Which one is it?"

"Oh, I think you'll know." Dorian pulled his head back out from the slab. "He's kind of obvious."

"What's out there?" asked Kirsten. Kate started to lean around the wall to peek, but she grabbed her shoulder. "I'm talking to Dorian. He can look without being seen."

"Around thirty gang members. The area's set up like an open air auditorium. Bench seats all facing a throne. There are a handful more kidnap victims, one right by the throne."

Kirsten relayed the description.

"Damn. So much for going nova," whispered Kate.

"What?" asked Kirsten. "Nova?"

Kate shrugged. "Forget it. I can't exactly do that when I want to anyway."

"Looks like everyone is armed except for the guy in the funny hat." Dorian stuck his head into the wall again. "If he's got a weapon, he's sitting on it."

Funny hat? Kirsten crept to the edge of the wall and leaned enough so the camera dots on the right side of the helmet could see past it. A thick layer of pulverized concrete made the landscape beyond the wall appear more like the surface of the Moon. The Diablos had set up a sort of amphitheater at the base of a shallow crater roughly a hundred meters on each side. Unless the city plate had been dented down, the rubble forming the bowl-shaped depression had to be quite deep.

As Dorian described, nine rows of long bench seats made of rubble formed a semicircle around a dais of concrete slab. Crude rebar candlesticks held up black candles, six per side of the throne, though none were lit. Men and women in Diablos colors lounged around. Some occupied themselves with NetMinis, others cleaned guns or sharpened blades, one or two molested captives. She counted five innocents: two women and two men among the 'congregation' and one woman by the throne. It wouldn't be difficult to identify the civilians in the midst of a firefight as none had any clothes.

A man in black robes occupied the throne, his face painted white and black to resemble a skull. He wore a tall black and white hat somewhat shaped like a spearhead as well as a long stole of dark red fabric around his neck, covered in black pictogram writing. Kirsten had seen a similar hat years ago in a picture Mother had on the wall, only red and gold. She remembered the awful woman saying something about him being named Bishop, and he worked for another guy named Pope. It angered Mother that most of the people in the UCF didn't believe in her fairy tale, and she routinely threatened to pick up and move to Italy where belief still held strong. Of course, no one in their right mind would ever move *to* the ACC. But... Mother had definitely not been in her right mind.

This 'black bishop' certainly seemed to be trying to parody that whole look though.

Kirsten narrowed her eyes. That Pope guy her mother so adored condoned abusing a small girl for having psionic gifts the woman didn't understand. Ghosts seeking help, trying to send warnings to protect their living families couldn't have been the work of any sort of devil. If this robe-wearing Diablo wanted to be the reverse of that Pope guy, he should've been a nice, sweet man.

However, after meeting Father Villera, Kirsten had to wonder if Mother had simply been thoroughly insane. Perhaps Pope was completely different from what she'd thought. That priest had been horrified to hear what her mother had done to her. Maybe Pope would, too? Not that she ever cared to ask him—she'd *never* go to the ACC. They shot psionics on sight there. Another reason Mother probably wanted to go. Of course, the Allied Corporate Council didn't hate psionics over theoretical supreme beings—they feared people they couldn't keep secrets from.

Motion beside the throne drew Kirsten's attention to a slim dark-haired woman with light brown skin and hollow, empty eye sockets. Trails of dried blood ran like tears down her cheeks. She knelt beside the black bishop, her only clothing a spiked black collar and thick chain connected to the ground between her knees not long enough to allow her to stand, or even fully sit up. Except for her missing eyes, she didn't have other visible injuries. Kirsten cringed in sympathetic pain, certain the Diablos hadn't been gentle when they did that to her.

The woman's surface thoughts contained a simple repetition of 'please kill me.'

Kirsten fought hard not to throw up. She shifted her attention to the bishop, who seemed rather angry. His thoughts centered mostly on confused as to why several people hadn't yet died while he feverishly read over pages of incomprehensible scribblings trying to understand where his ritual went wrong. He believed the demon he'd summoned refused to obey commands or return due to an error he'd made. She poked deeper into his consciousness. The man didn't appear to have any real understanding of the differences between Harbingers, abyssals, and They Who Always Were, lumping them all together into 'demon.'

He had no visible weapons, though the rest of the Diablos carried a veritable arsenal of small arms, up to and including swords, axes, and a cybernetic limb or two.

Kirsten moved away from the edge, rolling to put her back to the wall. "Okay, this is going to be a pain in the ass."

"Nah," said Kate. "I got it. Just keep an eye out for someone trying to get me from a blind angle."

Before Kirsten could say another word, Kate stepped out into view, brazen as anything.

"Police," called Kate. "You're all under arrest for... umm." She scratched her head. "Illegal demon summoning."

Dorian cracked up.

Kirsten gasped and spun to aim her E-90 around the end of the wall.

Mostly, the Diablos laughed. The Black Bishop quirked an eyebrow, his face a mask of utter disbelief.

The laughter continued for a few seconds until the *crack* of a gunshot rang out.

A splash of molten lead sprayed off Kate's left shoulder, her body rocking back as if she'd been punched.

"Oh, that wasn't very nice." Her mood darkened, and she stepped forward. "You boys have a fetish for hell?" Dark red flames erupted from thin air, shrouding Kate in a column of burning before drifting upward into the general shape of wings. A head-sized blue fireball appeared in each of her outstretched hands. "Well... I brought the fire."

Both fireballs zipped forward, each striking a different Diablo. One's head vaporized entirely to a smoldering neck stump. The other caught it in the chest and fell without even screaming.

The Black Bishop jumped to his feet, pointing at Kate and shouting in a weird language as if giving her commands.

She didn't seem impressed, and hurled a somewhat smaller blue fireball at him.

He screamed, diving off the dais. The flaming projectile missed him by inches, striking the back of the metal chair and covering it with burn.

All the Diablos opened fire. A fusillade of bullets kicked dust and debris into the air, clanking off stone and whistling by close to Kirsten's head. Every so often, a fleshy *thump* came from Kate's direction, but she didn't make any noise other than angry grunts. Dorian ran into the fray, taking up a position a short distance in front of Kirsten. He drew power from one weapon after another, focusing his attention mostly on the ones pointed her way.

Kirsten opened a psionic link to her armor, energizing its force field. The pale grey trim on her arms and legs lit up with a soft violet glow. She fired as fast as her E-90 could cycle, taking kill shots purely out of trained reaction. Amid the sudden explosion of chaos, the scene in front of her became another training sim with person-shaped targets. Only the occasional spray of concrete fragments across the helmet or a bullet glancing off her armor proved otherwise. Any Diablo with a raised weapon that she noticed ate a laser blast. Once or twice, the gang thug she aimed at went up in a conflagration of fire before she could click the trigger.

With a loud plastic *clack,* pain lanced through her right arm and knocked her back around the wall. A bullet had tunneled completely through her bicep, leaving two holes in her armor seeping blood. The stimsuit activated with a soft *hiss,* automatically injecting her with the equivalent of a single stimpak dose of synthetic adrenaline and medical nanobots. The path the bullet carved in her flesh erupted in a mass of cold itching.

Kirsten frowned at the perfect hole in the armor plate, as if it had been laser drilled. *Ugh. Someone's got a rifle.*

She screamed past gritted teeth, spraying her visor with spittle. Moving amber light appeared to the left, her helmet electronics highlighting a Diablo climbing over a chunk of building behind Kate. Kirsten tried to raise her arm, but it wouldn't respond. She grabbed her right wrist with her left hand to lift the stunned limb, and managed to fire at the guy before he could spray Kate with bullets.

Alas, the blue streak of her laser missed him by a few feet, but the shot warned Kate enough to spot the guy. She dove into a somersault as he opened up with full automatic from a submachine gun, chasing her across the dusty ground. Kirsten adjusted her aim and fired again, putting a beam into the man's chest. His gun kept spitting bullets for another half second as he fell over, stopping only after the magazine ran out.

Feeling returned to her right arm behind a wave of pins and needles.

A female voice behind her screamed in sheer terror.

Kirsten spun to her right, aiming at a muscular woman with a shaved head in a Diablos' jacket. She had a six-foot-long sword poised high, likely to bury it in Kirsten's head, but had frozen still, staring at the Harbinger hovering beside her. Though it appeared no different to her, it had to have manifested.

She started to turn away, regarding the large woman as no longer a threat, but the Diablo's scream mutated into manic laughter—and she lunged. Kirsten flung herself to the ground, narrowly avoiding the enormous blade, which sank several inches deep in the thermacrete wall.

Flat on her back, she raised the E-90 and fired four times into the crazy woman's chest.

The body fell away from a bewildered spirit.

Agonized screams, manic laughter, and the soft flutter of fireballs continued on the other side of the wall. The ghost turned toward Kirsten and swung her huge sword. It bounced away from the energized field of psionic energy radiating from her armor, barely even registering as an impact. A spirit not even a minute old barely had enough power to make a candle flame flutter.

Kirsten saw no point to lashing a harmless ghost, even if the woman might become a problem in forty years. At least, she had more important matters at the moment, like living Diablos. She scrambled to her feet and ran out from behind the wall, heading down the crater to the nearest chunk of broken building. She slid to a stop on her knees, aiming over the top of the crude barricade, and took out another Diablo lobbing bullets at Kate.

Blue fireballs shot back and forth like something out of a Monwyn game. Kate, disregarding the occasional bullet hitting her as little more than a spitball annoyance, walked in a slow, deliberate gait toward the dais, tossing flames at any Diablo who dared show themselves. She looked like the Princess of Hell retaking her palace.

The Black Bishop, hiding behind his throne, kept shouting at her like he tried to take control of a demon, but whatever he said did nothing but make him look insane.

"Stop or I'll kill this bitch!" yelled a man.

Kirsten swiveled her gaze—and E-90—toward a guy in a Diablo jacket using a nude young woman with a vacant, lifeless stare as a shield. He tried to back up, but the leash tethering her to a massive hunk of thermacrete and rebar kept him from going too far. The woman didn't react to the giant handgun pressed to the side of her head, hanging limp like a broken doll.

Kate stopped, staring at him.

"Don't do it, bitch!" shouted the man at Kate.

Dorian rushed over to him and raised his arm at the handgun. The ammo counter went dark a second later.

"His gun's dead," shouted Kirsten, trying to aim for a shot past the woman's head at the man's face.

"Don't try me, bitches!" shouted the Diablo.

Kate stared at him. He twitched, then grimaced.

"Back the fuck off or I'll shoot this meat hole," roared the Diablo.

Malice in Kate's stare intensified.

He shuddered. The woman in his grip slipped loose, collapsing to the ground. He dropped the gun, staggering backward while grabbing at his chest. A cry of pain started, drowning under a blast of bloody spray erupting from his mouth. His jacket inflated for two seconds before a muted, splattery *pop* preceded a gush of steaming gore running down his legs to the ground. Had he not been wearing such a heavy jacket, he would've sprayed a large area. The body fell to the side, exposing a twitching ghost with an expression of pure agony. A smell like overcooked steak mixed with boiled shit rolled by.

Kirsten gagged.

Dorian muttered something in Arabic.

"I hate being called a bitch," said Kate.

The thin woman on the dais tried to stand, but her leash kept her kneeling with a slight bow. She waved her arms in an effort to get attention. "Someone shoot me!"

Kirsten looked around. All the Diablos lay dead, except for the Black Bishop, who still hid behind the throne.

A tingle of a surface thought read swept over her mind. She locked stares with the man in the silly hat.

The Black Bishop stepped out from behind the throne, hands out to either side. "I am unarmed. I can see in your heart that you won't kill someone who isn't a threat."

He's psionic. She pointed her E-90 at him. "Move away from that woman. Keep your hands where I can see them."

Kate walked up to stand next to her, fists on her hips. She breathed somewhat rapidly, a trickle of sweat on her face.

"You didn't use your E-90," whispered Kirsten.

"Meh. Forgot. Still not used to being able to hold a gun. Besides. I wanted to be showy to mess with their little brains." She laughed. "Jackass there thought I was a demon."

The Black Bishop stepped down off the dais, approaching the first row of benches. His gaze focused to the left, at the Harbinger hovering at the edge of the crater. Though he made no sound she could hear, his lips moved in a continuous whisper.

He's trying to control it. "Stop doing whatever you're doing."

"I do nothing but follow your instructions," said the man in a soothing used-hovercar-salesman voice.

The Harbinger floated down the crater and stopped at Kirsten's left, almost hiding behind her.

Kate glanced over at her. "Is melting this guy's face off too 'evil?'"

"Umm..." Kirsten shifted her eyes toward the vaporous entity next to her, keeping her aim on the Black Bishop.

The Harbinger clasped its hands behind its back and turned away, as if appraising the beautiful scenery of the area... *not* looking at Kate or the Black Bishop.

Holy shit. It's giving us permission to kill him. Kirsten stared through the blue ring-dot sight of her E-90 at the man's chest. *I... can't just murder a guy.*

She didn't notice the telepathic connection until Kate dropped it. "My new friend here might be innocent... but I'm not." Kate summoned a fist-sized fireball.

The Black Bishop's scream cut off under the burning orb hitting him in the face. Since it didn't core out his skull—likely due to her being tired —Kate threw a second one into his chest, and his body erupted in a conflagration that burst into a raging bonfire far too fast. She gestured at him a bit like a wizard, the fire building in time with the man's screams.

Cringing, Kirsten shot him in the chest to spare him the agony.

At the instant the laser pierced him, a shadowy flash erupted from the body and raced over to the Harbinger. The Black Bishop collapsed in a burning heap.

The Harbinger leaned back, stretching its arms wide, body inflating as if it took a great breath. Its hesitant demeanor evaporated, and it glared down at the writhing ghost dragging himself out of the Black Bishop's smoldering remains.

Kirsten had always regarded the agents of the abyss with a strong degree of respect and fear. In that moment, the one she'd almost come to think of as 'friendly' radiated such intense power she couldn't even bring herself to look at it out of dread it would be angry with her. For an instant, she felt like she did the first time she'd ever seen one of them— after the Wharf Stalker.

With a great, scraping hiss, the Harbinger hurled itself forward and pounced on the spirit of the Black Bishop, dragging it down into the earth. A great wall of shadow rose at the lip of the crater seconds later. Dozens of sparkling silver eyes appeared in the murk. Ghostly Diablos scrambled in all directions, futilely attempting to flee from the legion of Harbingers pouring into the crater as a wall of jet-black fog. The woman with the huge sword ran *at* one, but her blade had no visible effect on it. She screamed, rage becoming horror as the creature engulfed her and dove into the ground, dragging her out of sight.

Kate rushed over to Kirsten and grabbed her from behind, peering over her shoulder. "Okay. What's going on? It just got *way* extra here. I don't think I've *ever* felt this randomly afraid before. Come to think of it, I don't think I've ever been this scared before at all."

"Don't worry." Kirsten rubbed her arm where she'd been shot—not that it helped much with armor in the way. "They didn't come here for us."

"What didn't come here for us?"

"Look if you dare."

Her mind tingled briefly.

"Whoa..." whispered Kate.

Kirsten held her ground, nodding respectfully to the shadow forms gliding around her, collecting the wretched souls of the former Diablos. Spectral screams rose into the air one by one from ghosts engulfed in darkness. Kate clung to Kirsten until the last of the Harbingers disappeared into the ground.

The black zone hung in silence, except for the delicate clinking of chain by the throne and moaning emanating from one of the male prisoners. The Black Bishop's favorite 'pet' still tried to stand. Kirsten hurried over to her. Hearing the crunch of boots approach, the woman stilled, then leaned back, exposing her chest, crisscrossed with faint whip marks.

"I'm not going to kill you," said Kirsten. "I'm going to get you out of here."

"W-who... are you?" The woman reached out, obviously blind, grabbing at the air.

Kirsten grasped her hands. "My name is Kirsten. I'm a cop. Division 0. You're safe now. What's your name?"

"I... don't have a name anymore. I'm just talking meat."

"No. Listen to me. The bastards who kidnapped you are all dead. I'm going to get you out of here. You are a person with a name. Remember who you are."

"I'm talking meat. I don't have a name."

Kirsten narrowed her eyes. "*You are a person.* Whatever those bastards told you, *ignore them.*"

Despite the woman's lack of eyeballs, the suggestion appeared to work.

"A..." She flinched, raising her arms to shield her face. "Ali..."

"They're dead. All of them."

"Alicia..." The woman erupted in sobs; unable to jump at Kirsten, she tried to pull her close and clamped on. "You're psionic, aren't you? Please... please make me forget. I don't want to remember what they did to me. I don't want to remember anything." She shivered. "If you can't do that, please just kill me."

"I'm not talented enough to erase a memory like that. And I won't kill you. All killing you will do is make you a ghost that still has all those memories to deal with."

Kate roamed around the area, melting the other captives free.

The woman's jaw dropped. "No... I can't take this anymore. I don't want..."

"If you really do want to forget everything, when you get to the medical center, ask for Lieutenant Commander Ashford. He'll help. I'll send him a message so he's aware of your request."

"Really? He can do that? Make it so I don't remember anything?" The woman again tried to stand, but the leash jerked her to a stop. "They did things to me... I don't want to remember. I can't."

"Let go of me a sec so I can get you out of that, okay?"

Alicia only clung tighter.

Kirsten shifted her around enough to get a hand on the padlock securing the collar and snipped it with her uti knife. The instant the metal ring fell away from her neck, Alicia leapt into Kirsten's arms.

"The other four are pretty much catatonic, and I am *not* going into their minds to see what happened to them." Kate walked up behind her. "What a damn mess."

"Pemberley, you still there?" Kirsten blinked in disbelief, watching Kate flick bits of lead off her chest and legs. "How..."

"Many times did I get shot? Not sure. Lost count. I'm pretty damn tired so probably a lot." She administered two stimpaks to herself. "And I feel like I fell down twenty flights of stairs. I'm a huge bruise."

"No... I mean how the f—heck did bullets melt so damn fast?"

Kate laughed. "Remember that 'awakened' thing? Yeah. It's complicated."

"Go ahead, Lieutenant," said Pemberley. "We're still here. You need help?"

"Yeah, but only because we can't carry five people. The site is secure. Can you pick up a few more kidnap victims? I need a minute or ten to check over the 'demonic altar' back here."

"I do not want to know." Pemberley chuckled. "Right. We'll be at your position in a minute. Sit tight."

"Well, one good thing…" Dorian looked around. "Everything else is so damn scared of Diablos, this black zone is probably the safest place in the city at the moment. Nothing here but us and bugs."

Alicia continued clinging to Kirsten, muttering random whispers, begging no one in particular not to punish her for daring to stand up straight or speaking.

Dorian stared at her. "I have no idea what's down there in the Abyss, but whatever it is… it's too damn nice for these fuckers."

"Yeah. It means a lot when a Harbinger says 'go ahead and just kill them.'" Kirsten looked over the bodies, then at Kate. "Thanks for the help."

"No problem." She kicked a hunk of blackened thermacrete into the air. "Some infestations can only be purged with fire."

The whirr of ion thrusters glided in overhead. The A3HV kicked up a massive amount of silt as it settled in for a landing between the auditorium benches and the dais. Kirsten carried Alicia over and tried to coax her into letting go. The woman started screaming when one of the other tactical officers tried to wrap a blanket around her, believing she'd be punished severely for covering up.

"*Calm* down," said Kirsten.

Alicia relaxed her grip, tolerated being wrapped in a blanket, and offered no protest when Officer Tina Estevez helped her into the back of the hover van. While the rest of the team collected the four catatonic victims, Kirsten returned to the dais to catalog and confiscate the Black Bishop's various books, datapads and ritual implements.

"Be right back," said Dorian. "Gonna go get the car."

Kirsten nodded at him, then piled the stuff together for collection. The lack of perpetual gloom radiating from a nearby Harbinger made even this place seem cheery. Much to Kirsten's surprise, another A3HV landed beside Pemberley's team. Four men in Admin uniforms and blue gloves hopped out and hastily collected the remains of the Diablos, loading them into the back like cargo.

Huh. That's odd.

Alicia resumed screaming from inside the A3HV… at least until someone gave her a tranquilizer. Or maybe one of the tactical officers also had Suggestion. Kirsten accessed her holo-terminal, and started typing an email to Lieutenant Commander Ashford.

That woman really doesn't need to remember any of this. In fact, I hope he wipes all the victims' minds. The mere thought of being kept prisoner and abused like that made her want to crawl under her bed and not come back out. But… no one could ever do that to her. Not with Suggestion to defend herself. No matter how badly Mother hurt her for her 'evil' psionic abilities, Kirsten hugged herself, beyond grateful for being who she was.

PARADISE

Consciousness pulled Kirsten out of a bizarre, but happy dream.

In the body of Asara the Huntress from the Monwyn game, she'd been streaking through the woods, bare as a wood nymph, playfully running away from a satyr version of Samuel Chang. Colorful animals followed along singing some nonsensical tune. She'd jumped past a thick hedgerow and emerged on the other side dressed in Asara's armor to find a pint-sized Monwyn the Wizard waiting for her.

As soon as she scooped him up into a hug, she woke up, clinging to Evan.

Sometimes, she'd sleep in on the weekend when neither of them had to go anywhere. He usually got out of bed first and flopped beside her until she woke up. She peered over his shoulder at the portable video game system where a cartoony knight navigated a forest. The retro-style game using a physical screen looked cute.

"Case make you sad?" asked Evan, still playing.

"A bit, yeah. But I'm actually in a rather good mood now." After a week with a Harbinger around, its mere absence made her feel happy enough to bounce around and sing. Being safe at home with Evan in her arms set off an explosion of bliss.

He gurgled. "Air. Mom. Need air."

Kirsten relaxed her hug, kissed him on the side of the head—which made him squirm—and sat up.

"Can we still go today or do you have to work?" asked Evan.

"One case down. Maybe two." She bit her lip. *The Diablos killed Rafael's brother as part of the ritual to bind that Harbinger. I still don't know which one of them specifically did it, but there's no way to find out now. Does it matter?* "Go on and get ready."

"Cool!" He shut off the game, rolled into a hug, then ran off.

Halfway down the hall, he flung off his pajama pants, threw them into his bedroom, and went the other way into the bathroom. The *clonk* of the autoshower tube closing followed a moment later. Kirsten crawled out of bed, pulled her night shirt off, and climbed into the autoshower in the attached bathroom.

The warm, soapy spray rolled down her body, as awesome as if it leeched away all the horrible memories of the raid. Reading case files about the depravity of what Diablos did to their kidnap victims didn't compare to seeing people who'd been tortured to the point where they'd gone permanently catatonic. She hated to admit it to herself, but perhaps in some cases, summary execution was justified. Even the Harbinger had no problem with killing them.

Lieutenant Commander Ashford had replied with two emails. A simple 'acknowledged' in the first, the second a somewhat more verbose, 'Miss Alicia Rios is fine.' Though a non-psionic person abducted by a street gang didn't fall under Kirsten's jurisdiction, she peeked into the Division 2 inquest. Alicia Rios had been missing for two months, having disappeared during an onsite appointment with her job as a maintenance technician for home/apartment management systems. At least her health plan covered cybernetic eye replacements. Ashford had altered her memories such that she believed she had experienced an unidentified illness that left her comatose for two months and destroyed her eyes.

It felt so wonderful to have played a part in getting those people out of such an unimaginably awful situation, she nearly melted into a metaphorical puddle in the autoshower from relief. No dangerous abyssal ran around the city killing people; the man responsible for it was no longer a threat; and she could probably assure a ten-year-old boy that his brother's killer had been brought to justice.

Even if her elevated mood came from some kind of rebound effect of no longer having a strong source of constant paranormal dread nearby, she'd take it. After the first twelve years of her life, Fate owed her a little happy.

"You okay, Mom?" asked Evan from the doorway.

Kirsten froze, still in the tube. *The boy has personal space issues.* She'd finally more or less acclimated to commingled showers at the PAC, but having her son see her in the shower brought a full on blush. Of course, he'd grown accustomed to that horrible excuse of a birth mother going naked all the time—mostly because she'd sold off her clothes to buy drugs. *Hopefully, when he gets a little older, he'll grow out of this.*

"Yeah, fine. Why?"

"You don't usually shower that long." He grinned. "Gonna go 'sem coffee, okay?"

"Go ahead. I'll be right there."

He dashed off.

Kirsten ran her hands through her hair to check dryness. Satisfied, she hopped out of the tube and scrambled into her clothes: leggings, skirt, fuzzy socks, and a plush top with a chibi Asara the Huntress graphic.

Sam Chang arrived soon after breakfast. They went down from the 41st to the 39th floor to pick Shani up so her mother, Nila, could relax for a few hours. The kids laughed and chattered the whole way to the parking deck on the 50th floor, at the midpoint of the building.

They spent the morning exploring a life science exhibit, roaming around an indoor forest filled with synthetic animals. According to the holographic tour guide, some places on Earth still had growth like this, and even a few living animals.

After a stop for lunch, they headed to a Funzone. Though Evan did seem to enjoy the educational exhibit visits, he adored the interactive games. Augmented reality made for more physical activity while still having all the coolness of video games. Older gamers preferred plugging in to total virtual reality in the comfort of their homes, so places like this tended to have mostly the under-eighteen crowd who couldn't legally have cybernetics installed. The predominance of kids kept the games reasonably tame... though the place did run some ads for adults-only events, mostly horror/scary stuff too intense for children.

Despite hours of exploring 'forest' before noon and hours of playing AR games after, neither Evan nor Shani showed any sign of slowing down. Kirsten almost wanted to crawl back into bed by six that afternoon. They gathered the reluctant kids from a dizziness-inducing game where they navigated narrow neon-blue walkways 'inside a computer.' Each player had a 'laser sword' that they used to defend themselves from various 'hostile programs' trying to fly at them. What appeared to be a long fall into nothingness turned out to be simple paint on the floor, though the game would end if a player stepped off the narrow pathway.

At 6:28 p.m., Kirsten and Sam dropped the kids off at Nila's.

She reached for the button to her floor so she could change to go out for dinner, but Sam caught her hand and directed her finger to the 50th floor button.

"Huh?"

"Dinner?"

She smiled. "Yeah. I was going to put something nicer on."

"You look beautiful already."

Kirsten laughed and glanced down at the cartoon elf with an oversized head. "I'm dressed like a kid."

"Nah. You're dressed like a Monwyn fan with a mild addiction to cute."

She leaned against him, deciding to see where things went. "Okay."

He held her hand on the walk to his personal vehicle, a silver *Inazuma* hovercar, made by Matsushita Corporation. It looked about half the size of a patrol craft, and didn't have armor plating. Then again, civilian vehicles didn't, at least not without some executive customization options. It had a sporty appearance, but one well within the price range of normal people.

She found it cozy, and oddly barren. Without all the police equipment, the dashboard felt empty. He did, however, have a small model spaceship on a post in the middle of the console.

Sam hopped in. "It's really good to see you so happy."

"A lot of it is genuine. Some of it is from no longer having a Harbinger following me around."

He lifted off, surprising her unintentionally with the zippiness of the car. A patrol craft could hit much higher top speeds than most civilian vehicles, but all that armor had an effect on acceleration.

Over the course of a brief ride, she told him about the shadowy friend following her around for about a week. To protect her mood, and not ruin the evening, she glazed over any details about the Diablos' encampment, leaving it at 'they got the bastard' and the Harbinger went home.

Sam followed a transition lane to ground level, a virtual 'off ramp' that connected the hover lane at the 50th story level to ground traffic. This car's wheels made barely any noticeable sound when they extended. Kirsten asked him about his past few days—she'd spent so much time thinking (rather worrying) about active cases, she hadn't spoken with him longer than a few minutes in a while.

He regaled her with tales of epic boredom, mostly financial forensics stuff in computer systems.

Eventually, he parked in a nice commercial district solidly in the realm of middle class. Samuel Chang would never randomly detour to buy her a ₡10,000 dress, but she considered that a bonus.

They walked a few blocks under Halloween decorations, most of which made her laugh—though one hologram ghost did manage to startle a yelp out of her. Sam stopped in front of a Cyberburger pretending to be a real restaurant with a large dining area done up in black-and-silver trim.

Kirsten broke into laughter and hugged him. "It's perfect."

Despite its appearance as a nicer establishment, it remained a Cyberburger, thus it had no servers. After a brief wait in line, they reached the counter. She went for a Galaxy Chicken, spicy, while Sam got the Double Orbital combo.

"Would you like to Ultra that?" asked a doll made to resemble a fifteen-ish girl with bright red hair and overeager smile.

"Sure." Sam leaned close to Kirsten. "I hear the Ultra is actually fairly good."

"What's that mean?" asked Kirsten.

The fake teen behind the counter smiled. "I can explain—"

"No!" shouted about eleven customers at the same time.

"Better machines, better OmniSoy, better food," said Sam.

Kirsten shrugged. "Sure."

Less than a minute later, their food came out on a small conveyor belt. Still grinning, the ersatz teen girl transferred it to a tray, which she handed to Sam. On the way to their table, Kirsten smiled at the overwhelmingly ordinary surroundings. This place felt right. No one trying to act more important than anyone, no requirement to wear overly expensive clothing, no condescension toward anyone not of the 'proper social standing.' No people pretending to clap for someone else's accomplishment while seething with jealousy. No car-sized ice swans, no pretentiousness.

No bullshit.

Just her, Sam, and some basic food.

The Ultra chicken sandwich did taste shockingly close to vat-grown. Supposedly, the higher grade OmniSoy coupled with newer technology in the machinery prevented it from degenerating back into flavorless beige slime if not eaten within twenty minutes. She didn't have any plans to test that out. Wrangling two kids for most of the morning plus a lot of walking left her hungry.

She told Sam about the weird dream she had, making him blush.

"I think you'd look pretty good as a satyr."

"Do you?" He grinned. "You know I dabble a bit in sim coding. I might be able to tweak a VR routine."

She held a fry up. "How does that work, exactly? Doing *things* in VR. I heard somewhere they don't have bodily functions in games because it makes accidents happen for real."

"Umm. It can get messy sometimes."

"I prefer my Sam in reality." She glanced at the fry. "Ultra Sam even."

He laughed.

"VR Sam couldn't keep up."

A middle-aged, slightly chubby guy in a frumpy white polo shirt with an Imperial Hotel logo walked by carrying a tray. She glanced at him in passing. He sat at a table two spots away, arranged several cartons, a drink, and a container of fries with meticulous care, then opened a burger carton.

"Back to the routine then huh?" asked Sam. "Cases cleared? Hopefully, you'll get a break for a while."

She sighed. "Not yet. I still have one outstanding case. And it's a bad one."

"Do you want to talk about it?"

"Not sure I should right now. It could ruin the night."

"It's already on your mind. I'm here to listen if you need."

She reached over and took his hand. "Maybe. It's a real mess."

"I don't know why I only get forty-five minutes for lunch. I'm the senior systems administrator," muttered the guy in the polo shirt. "All the mid-level managers get a full hour. I'm laterally equivalent to that. So what if I don't have any employees under me. And I'm working on Saturday. That should count for something. I don't know why they ask *me* to work on Saturday. They never ask any of the other managers to work on Saturday. I really should send an email to HR and complain."

Sam and Kirsten glanced at the guy as he continued to mutter to himself.

She looked away after a moment, shaking her head. "Anyway... I'm trying to track down the ghost of a man who, umm... Oh, hell. We're both adults. He's a hundred-year-old serial rapist, and he's attacking women again."

"Oof." Sam cringed. "That sounds bad."

"Yeah... I'm going in circles with no real way to find him." She told him about her brief encounter with him by chance. "Only thing I have to go on is the place he died in. But they demolished it years ago, so it might not even be anything. Going to go to the area Monday and look around just in case, but I'm sure it's going to be a waste of time."

Sam nodded.

"Hey... do you think something like that is part of a person from the start, or does it take mental trauma to create a monster like that?"

"I'm hardly a psychologist." Sam took a bite of his burger, thinking while chewing. "It's probably a combination of both. Someone would need to be born with some flaw in their brain that allowed them to not feel remorse, and then bad shit happened to them to twist them that way. If you're worried about Evan, I don't think you need to be."

"Yeah." Kirsten sighed. "What he went through before I found him... it's almost like he's totally forgotten it." Her happy mood returned and she smiled at him. "You're a good influence on him."

Sam grinned. "We could always spend the night at your place and stay up late playing Monwyn?"

"Tempting... but he's having fun at Shani's. Maybe tomorrow? Tonight's for us... assuming that damn ghost doesn't interrupt." She stared down at her plate of crumbs. "Part of me doesn't feel right having a good time with you while that guy is still out there."

"You're doing everything you can. There's no reason you should stop having a life because other people do bad things. It's not like you know where the guy is and just haven't bothered to go after him."

She squeezed his hand. It seemed doubtful she'd find herself in the mood to get romantic after what she saw at the Diablos' camp. She could tell herself over and over again that what those monsters did to innocent people had nothing to do with sex and everything to do with cruelty and humiliation... and it wouldn't purge those images from her mind.

"You're right. I think I just need some Sam time."

28

CLIMBING FISH

S unday died as a sacrifice on the altar of Monwyn.

Sam had spent the night while Evan slept over at Nila's. Sufficient cuddling had eventually led her and Sam to the bedroom once her need to erase the Diablos' camp from her mind grew strong enough. He'd been gentle and so loving she had to work not to break down crying afterward at being with someone who both cared for her and wanted her to be part of his life.

And, all day Sunday with Evan and Sam there, she felt like someone playing a holo-sim of a normal family.

The emotional high of the weekend helped her cope with the pain of a too-early alarm clock and the distasteful realization of still having to stop a spectral monster. Coffee in hand, she flopped into her chair. With any luck, she could accomplish something before Captain Eze summoned her to go back and forth over the raid.

Another horror—tons of reports and digital paperwork—waited for her, but that, she'd gladly deal with if she could only stop Malden Walker. Of course, the motel where he died no longer existed, but maybe he'd taken up residence somewhere in that area. It didn't offer *much* promise, but she could at least go there and look around.

"The motel's gone… but maybe he's still haunting the physical area where he died."

Dorian's chair creaked. "This guy is truly disconnected from any location, remains, or object. That makes him difficult to locate, but also means he should take a long time to recover from the beating you gave him. Even the car isn't wonderful for that. Sometimes I do go for a nap in the old urn."

She rubbed her temples as a headache rolled over her brain. "Ugh. I think I spent too much time in a senshelmet yesterday."

"How long?"

Kirsten drank a few mouthfuls of mocha latte and leaned back, eyes closed. "Probably around twelve hours with breaks for food and bathroom. The boy is unstoppable. I don't regret it."

"You're not an old lady yet. Don't make yourself old before your time. Playing games for such long stretches takes getting used to. Though it's easier with the neural interface jack. Some people stay in the GlobeNet for days at a time."

"What the heck do they do for food or other needs?"

"They have gel tanks specifically designed for long net sessions. And people who can't afford those literally sit on the toilet and plug in."

"Ugh. That's taking it way too far."

Dorian laughed.

"The Coffee Fairy is here!" yelled Nicole.

The redhead floated into the room wearing a set of cheap pink costume fairy wings and carrying a plastiboard tray of cups. With a look of intense concentration, she levitated one coffee at a time from the tray to the desks of everyone in the room, then landed on her feet.

"Whew."

"Nice." Morelli clapped. "Working on your finesse?"

"Yeah. Holding myself up and moving coffee around at the same time is *hard*."

Kirsten took another sip of her mocha. "I suppose today is going to be a two-coffee Monday."

A little more than an hour—and both lattes—later, Kirsten hadn't found any useful information in the system. She'd hunted for records connected to anyone involved with the original inquest, starting with the Division 5 man who shot Malden a century ago. As far as had been documented, no unexplained paranormal events happened to him, the daughter, her kids or anyone else related to his various victims before his death.

Kirsten's terminal flashed. A window opened with the portrait of a man in an Admin uniform with dreadlocks. "Lieutenant Wren?"

"Either you're hallucinating me, or you've got her." Kirsten smiled.

The man appeared confused for a second. "Umm. Your presence is needed in interview room C2. There's a young woman, Emma Mero, here with claims of being attacked by a spiritual entity." A link popped up to a PID and citizen record.

"Hmm. What happened to Cadet Peña?" asked Dorian.

"Crap." Kirsten bowed her head. "On my way." She got up and looked at him. "It's not even ten in the morning yet. The girl's eleven. She's in school."

Dorian's eyebrows rose. "Wow. Yeah. That kid acts so much like a small tactical officer I forgot she's so young."

"This is going to be 'the one' for me, I have a feeling." Kirsten hurried out of the room.

Dorian caught up to her in the elevator. "The one?"

"The case that drives me nuts, turns me into a police cliché."

"Every case that takes more than a week feels like that to every detective right up until they figure it out."

She smirked. "Except the one that finally breaks their last scrap of sanity."

"I'd argue that what the Diablos did to the people they kidnapped is worse."

"You can't rate sex crimes by degree, Dorian. It doesn't work like that. Awful is awful."

He held his hands up. "I'm not trying to. Just pointing out that none of Malden's victims have gone permanently catatonic."

"That does not make me feel better."

He followed her out into the corridor when the elevator stopped. "Sorry. I suppose permanent catatonia could also be induced by watching too many hours of Senate hearings. Or what's that kid's show with the annoying talking baby?"

She sighed. "I appreciate you trying to cheer me up, but I'm about to walk into a room with a woman who's quite likely just been assaulted in the worst possible way by a spirit plus a living person. This isn't the time for cheer."

"K…" He grasped her shoulder. "I'm hoping to give you a cushion of sanity so you can tolerate this case. You really shouldn't doubt yourself as much as you do. Would you consider a fish to be a failure because it can't climb the side of a building?"

"That doesn't make any sense?" She badged her way past a security door into the interview area.

"Fish can't climb buildings."

"No shit." Kirsten stormed down the hall.

He sighed. "Stop a sec. Breathe."

She halted in the middle of the corridor and fixed him with a stare.

"You're upset, angry, hurt, and feeling guilty because you are a fish who can't climb a building. You're so wound up that you can't even process my metaphor."

"But it doesn't make any sense. A fish isn't capable of climbing a building. Why would it be a failure at fish-dom for that?" She blinked. "Oh. You're trying to tell me I *can't* do anything and I shouldn't be kicking myself for not stopping this guy?"

"Do you have the ability to magically know where a ghost is at any given moment?"

"No." She scowled at the wall.

"Do you have any *solid* information about where Malden Walker's remains might be or where he 'sleeps'?"

"Okay. Okay." She took a few deep breaths. "Thanks."

He patted her back, his touch a series of cool pulses.

Kirsten steeled herself and opened the door.

The smell of mildew laced with garbage hung in the small room. A young woman with fair skin and bright green hair down to her elbows sat at the edge of one of the bland cushioned chairs, both hands gripping her knees. Her long-sleeved top had a large neck that bared one shoulder, the faded pink fabric liberally stained with dirt. Neon green lip gloss covered half her mouth, the rest smeared up onto her cheek. The girl's black skirt clung to her thighs like polished onyx glass, her legs bare, grimy and bruised. Black boots that looked a little too big for her had so many scuffs and scratches they had to have been scavenged from the trash.

She looked as scrawny as Kirsten ten years ago when the police found her, only older.

"Emma?" asked Kirsten.

The girl lifted her head just enough to peer out from under her bangs. Slate grey-blue eyes ringed with red widened. "I need to talk to a psionic cop, not a kid."

"I understand you were attacked by a ghost?"

Emma trembled harder. "Yes. I'm kinda surprised no one's called me crazy yet."

"Because you're not." She sat in the nearest chair. "I'm Kirsten. Have you ever heard of an astral sensitive?"

The girl shook her head.

"I can see, talk to, and in some cases, destroy ghosts. I'm also not a kid. Just short."

Emma pulled her hair off her face. "Okay. The other cops didn't take me seriously. Thought I was lying for attention."

"I believe you."

"How? I didn't even say anything yet."

"A ghost touched you inappropriately, right?"

Emma sniffled and looked down. "Yeah."

"Did this ghost take over your body?"

"Yeah," mumbled Emma at her lap. "I was raped."

Dorian glared at the wall.

"I'm trying to find this ghost so I can destroy it, but he doesn't have an anchor point like most spirits do. He's free to roam the whole city and every piece of information I get helps me find him. Please, tell me as much as you're comfortable with."

Emma fussed at her oversized shirt, then spent a moment picking at her flaking purple nail polish. "Umm. I was at home. Felt like someone stuck their hand under my clothes. I woke up screaming, but there wasn't anyone there. Like, someone held me down and kept touching me for a while, then I blacked out. I woke up on a bed with some old dude on top of me." She curled forward, shaking.

"It's okay. Take your time. I understand if it's too much so soon."

"No, I'm good." Emma sat up straight and let out a long breath. "Gotta say it now, so you don't think I'm forgettin' stuff, right? It's just so damn scary."

Kirsten nodded.

"I'm... so I blacked out. Woke up on a bed. I'm naked, my hands are chained to the top of the bed. This old guy with greasy hair's on top of me. I'm begging him to let me go and stuff, but it's not me. I'm not tryin' to say a damn thing but I'm still talkin'. He whips it out, then puts a goddamn gun in my face. Says some creepy ass shit about how it's like the ultimate thing to 'shoot a bitch' right when he gets off."

"We're going after whoever this guy is," said Dorian. "He needs to be taken off the street... preferably hurled into the Abyss."

Kirsten somehow managed to keep from cringing or crying.

"So, like I can't move, and not just 'cause my hands are tied. Like my whole body just won't listen to me. Soon as this bastard pulls out a gun, feels like someone dumped a bucket of ice all over me. Dude flies off me, lands on the floor, and like starts kicking his own ass." Emma pantomimed holding a gun and smashing it into her face.

"That had to be the ghost. Is it okay if I look into your memory?" Kirsten leaned closer.

Emma shrugged. "Sure, knock yourself out."

The interview room faded away. Kirsten's point of view—Emma's memory—stared over a glowing orange Comforgel pad at a fortysomething man in torn fringer clothes, grey jacket, dark pants, sprawled face down on the rug of a cheap motel room decorated with framed pornographic images. The man flew up as though an invisible bouncer grabbed him by the back of the coat. He spun around and smashed into the wall. The invisible man beat the guy back and forth around the room for a few minutes before leaving him in a bloody heap on the floor. Emma looked up at her wrists, secured with handcuffs through the headboard. She struggled for a few seconds before swinging her legs up and bracing her feet against the bed. Her hands turned purple as she strained to pull them loose.

Bang.

She screamed, but refused to look to her left, continuing to squirm and twist her hands around. After an agonizing few minutes, her malnourishment and delicate build paid off—her right hand popped loose. Emma jumped off the bed, vaguely aware of the man sitting in the corner with his brains blown out all over the wall. She hurriedly gathered her clothing from the rug, dressed, and ran outside, cuffs still dangling from her left wrist.

Kirsten released the telepathic link.

"So, maybe I lied a little," whispered Emma.

"About?" Kirsten raised an eyebrow.

"The guy didn't like stick me, so I guess it wasn't really rape."

Kirsten rested her hand on top of Emma's, still on her knee. "Oh, I think what you experienced still counts. I'm glad he didn't get a chance to start."

"Yeah." Emma fidgeted. "That was a ghost, right?"

"Pretty sure it was." *Malden let go of the possession as soon as that guy made it clear he intended to kill her. That's weird. The original inquest mentioned he tried not to hurt his victims, delicate flowers or some twisted crap like that.* "This is getting strange."

"Getting?" asked Emma. "Being felt up by a ghost and nearly murdered is kinda beyond strange."

"Sorry. I meant this whole investigation." Kirsten accessed her armband terminal, pulling up the case record, and Emma's PID information. The girl turned eighteen four months ago. She had a handful of juvenile arrests for shoplifting, but nothing since her birthday. No information appeared in the address field. "Hmm. Your address is blank. Where do you live?"

"Plastiboard box in Sector 8094." Emma looked off to the side. "My father died a couple months ago. Construction... fell off the seventieth story."

Dorian cringed.

"I'm sorry. No mother? Other family?"

"Nah. Dad was lonely so he got me from FamilyPerfect."

Kirsten bit her lip. "Never heard of that."

"It's for people who don't wanna relationship but want a kid. They took his DNA and combined it with some synthesized DNA and... here I am. I'm basically a Cyberburger, half of me is like OmniSoy. My father designed me on their computer. No, my hair's not really green. It's dye."

"That's... interesting."

Emma shrugged.

"No other remaining relatives?"

"Nah. Just an asshole boyfriend who left me as soon as I told him I was on the street."

Kirsten sent a text message ‹Can you make her eligible for adoption?› to Sam along with Emma's PID. "Well, since you're four months away from turning eighteen and still legally a minor, you can still get in the door of colony adoption."

"I don't wanna go to no other planet." Emma folded her arms. "And I'm four months *past* eighteen."

Kirsten smiled at the screen when the girl's birthdate changed and *minor* appeared at the top of the record. *Thanks, Sam.* "Is a colony worse than a plastiboard box? And..." She held her arm out to the side so the girl could see the screen. "Your age is just a number in a computer."

"Holy shit... did you hack the system?" Emma blinked.

"*I* did not alter anything." Kirsten winked. "Off world colonies aren't worse than living in an alley. In fact, they're quite a bit better. You could pass yourself off as sixteen if you wanted to."

"I'm on this new celebrity diet." Emma held her hands up, spreading them apart as if revealing a glimmering marquee. "It's the 'no money, no damn food' diet. With a 'run like hell or die' fitness package."

"I can see why you'd rather stay on Earth." Kirsten smiled.

"Come on. I'm not a kid anymore. I'll just go up there and be handed to someone as a wife. The colonies just want baby factories."

"That's a common misconception put out by disinformation groups. From what I understand, the only thing they'll really force on you is training for whatever job is in demand at the time that you're an aptitude match for."

Emma stared down at herself, picking at her filthy clothes. "Ghosts can't go to other planets, can they?"

"Usually not. Though I've seen them go to the Moon, but they had to possess someone to get away from Earth. But... this particular ghost who attacked you chooses his victims at random and has never attacked the same woman twice. I honestly don't think you're at risk from him even if you stay on Earth."

"Okay, fine." She reached down, scratching at the side of her leg. "Do I have to wait in line or something? How long before someone picks me up at home? Can I have a shower?"

"Do you have a NetMini?"

"Yeah." Emma patted her small handbag.

Kirsten spent a moment checking the trace logs for Emma's NetMini. A line led out from the PAC to a grey zone thirty miles from Sector 8094. The system showed the device remaining in a static location for forty-six minutes. Also, an online order was placed from the account to a sex toy shop for one pair of handcuffs, delivered to that location. *That has to be the cheap hotel.* "Okay. I can't think of any other information you can provide that would help me more than what you've already said. Is there anything at ho—that plastiboard box you want to keep?"

"Not really. Landlord Fatass stole all my shit when he locked me out of my real home. My old life is gone." Emma scratched at random itches. "Sorry if I give you fleas."

"Come on. I'll walk you over to Div 1. They'll get you set up with the adoption program, shower, new clothes, food, and a bunk until the paperwork's finished."

"Wow. It's really that easy?" Emma stood.

"It is when a minor's involved. Once past eighteen, it's not quite as easy."

"There's always joining the military," said Dorian.

"Oh. Cool. Umm. Thanks for that. Guess I gotta memorize a new hatch date."

"Hatch date?" Kirsten blinked.

"Single dad… the uterus I came out of was plastic. I started callin' it my hatch date. Dad didn't think it was funny."

Kirsten guided her to the door. *This world gets stranger and stranger.*

29

THE BIG GUNS

Phantom itches sent Kirsten to the shower area once she returned from the Division 1 wing.

It didn't matter if the girl actually *had* fleas, the mere suggestion of it made her send the cloth parts of her uniform down for a quick wash while she hopped in an autoshower tube. Standing around naked for a few minutes in the locker room waiting for her stuff to come back up from being cleaned was well worth the peace of mind.

When the tube steamed a little, she spotted the word 'help' smeared on the plastic as if by a finger. A look around revealed only two other officers showering and no spirits.

Someone's being a wiseass.

She disregarded the smeared plea and concentrated on making sure she had no fleas in her hair. She exited the autoshower once it finished and tried to act casual while sitting on a bench waiting for her uniform and underwear to come back up from the automatic laundry.

Once back in the squad room, she paced circles around her desk, furious and despondent over being unable to find Malden Walker. She wondered if he realized the girl he'd grabbed had been so young. The creep targeted women in their young twenties, which put Emma outside the usual profile. Of course, the girl slept in a box in an alley, so would've been alone and vulnerable. Perhaps a target of opportunity.

Without remains or a 'home' to go to, she considered the possibility that he recovered his energy from people. Perhaps he'd possessed her before she noticed him, 'sleeping' inside her body. And the prolonged blackout didn't fit the pattern either. He appeared to like having his victims aware of being controlled and helpless to stop what he planned to do to them.

Maybe she fainted?

She fell heavily into her chair and glared at the holo-panels over her desk.

That Malden had saved her life and killed the man who almost shot her didn't change how she felt about him much. After all, Emma would not have been in that situation to begin with unless he'd attacked her.

Kirsten hammered the keyboard, going over the inquest files and the maps again. All the victims had been chosen at random. Nothing connected any of them together. The attacks had happened without pattern or predictability. Only that they had all occurred in the southern third of West City made for any sort of commonality among victims.

"Grr. They don't even all have cybernetic implants."

Dorian rested his hand on her shoulder. "That doesn't matter to him now. He can get into their heads without it."

"And he made that poor girl spend the last of her credits on the damn handcuffs." She eyed the terminal. "Hang on a sec…" Kirsten ran a search for purchases of cuffs by women between the ages of twenty and thirty over the past two months.

The search came back with 118,740 hits.

Kirsten blinked. "What the hell is wrong with people?"

"Now *that* is a question no one should ever ask," said Dorian.

"I've got another effing Wharf Stalker on my hands, only that guy had a home."

Dorian pursed his lips. "A cargo box half buried under a pier is hardly a home."

"To a ghost? It's where his remains were. He had a limited range based on his attachment. Like the way you couldn't go more than 200 meters away from the car."

"I'm over that."

She crumpled over the desk, groaning. "I'm never going to find this bastard. And even if I do, he'll just dive into the ground again."

"Now that I know he's a bit on the strong side, I'll focus more on holding him down than trying to beat the energy out of him."

"Dorian, he threw you a block away in a single punch."

"Well, he has been a ghost for over a century." Dorian folded his arms. "Maybe it's time you called in the big guns? Theodore?"

"I... I can't keep asking him for help for everything. *The Kind* will get sick of seeing me. If I overdo it, they might not want to help me when I really need it."

Dorian raised an eyebrow. "Fish climbing the building. This bastard is all over the city. You can't go through walls. Asking Theodore and his friends for help might just be the only way you'll ever find this guy. I don't think this is wasting their time for something you could do on your own. You're not being lazy."

"Okay..." She hung her head. "Fine. You're right. Wow. I sound like Emma being talked into a colony adoption."

"Well, you *do* look like a kid. Sam could tweak the records and they'd take you."

"Die," said Kirsten, laughing.

"Too late. Already did." He grinned, and gave her shoulder a chilly squeeze. "Come on. At least talk to them. Start off asking them if they know of a way you could find him instead of asking them to go do it for you. I'll mention how strong he was and that he dove into the ground to get away from you, and they'll hopefully offer to help. You've spent years assisting spirits without ever asking anything in return for it. They know this. It's okay to ask for help sometimes."

Kirsten infused her body with energy so it became solid to astral beings and hugged him. "Okay. I'll talk to him tonight... assuming they show up. Might as well go check where that hotel used to be."

EVAN SPRAWLED ON THE LIVING ROOM FLOOR, ABSORBED IN HOMEWORK.

He divided his attention between two holo-panels projected from his datapad, one with the textbook page, the other with homework questions. Kirsten couldn't read it from the couch, but animated pictures of various animals made her assume it science classwork.

As expected, she found no sign of Malden's presence anywhere around the location where he'd been vaporized. It confirmed her worst fear, that she had to find a genuinely untethered spirit. Perhaps that's why she'd been holding off on going there. Deep down, she knew it would be useless and worse, eliminate the last of her hope she could track the guy.

Speaking of classwork, she felt far too much like she'd gotten in trouble at school and had to go talk to the principal. Not that she dreaded speaking to Theodore or *The Kind*. She worried—rather irrationally—that they'd refuse to help her and leave her unable to do anything about Malden. In all honesty, those ancient ghosts had been happy to help with Senator Winchester. Her owing them a favor didn't matter much because she'd always help a spirit in need. Unless, of course, they asked her to do something malicious.

Upon noticing the sun had gone down, she got up and went to her room. Evan walked in a moment after she finished putting her uniform back on.

"Mom?"

She waved him over and hugged him. "I'm just going to go talk to Theodore. I need help on a case. You can stay with Nila for a little while until I get back. Shouldn't be long at all."

"Can I go? Theo's funny."

"Umm." She shifted her jaw back and forth. No way did she want Evan anywhere near Malden when she confronted him… *if* she caught up to him again. But she also didn't expect Theodore or any of the other ancient ghosts to find him right away tonight. "I suppose you could—"

A strong sense of dread came out of nowhere.

Evan looked around, stepping closer to her. "Careful."

"I feel it, too."

"No. I mean, I'm barefoot and you got your boots on."

If not for the pervasive, supernatural gloom, she would have laughed. "Feels like a Harbinger's nearby."

"Yeah. That's weird, right?"

"They usually don't visit living people…" Kirsten looked up and down. "Unless one of our neighbors just died and they had some dark secrets, I'm not sure what's going on."

A black spot appeared on the wall beyond the foot of the bed, the stain racing outward until it covered the entire surface. Shadowy vapors welled up from the midpoint until they coalesced into the shape of an emerging Harbinger. It drifted forward, peeling the gloom from the wall into itself as it floated silently closer.

Kirsten faced it and offered a nod of greeting.

"Hi." Evan waved at it.

Other than variances in size, every Harbinger she'd ever run into had appeared identical. Despite that, she suspected she'd met this one before. Something indefinable about it gave off a sense of familiarity.

"Hello," said Kirsten. "Is... something wrong?"

The Harbinger half turned away, beckoning her as if to follow. It pointed at Evan, then the floor.

"He should get down?" asked Kirsten.

"I think he wants me to go to Nila's."

It nodded.

"Be careful, Mom." He hugged her. "Must be important if one of these guys wants your help."

Kirsten walked him to the elevator and down to the 39th floor. The Harbinger followed, watching from enough distance that its dread aura didn't reach into Nila's apartment. Dorian's former duty partner answered the door with a confused eyebrow lift.

"Something came up. I probably won't be long, but would you mind watching Ev for a bit?"

"Oh, sure."

"Yay!" shouted Shani from the living room.

Evan ran inside and jumped onto the giant sectional.

"Thanks. Be back as fast as I can."

"Don't be reckless." Nila grinned. "And say hi to Dorian for me."

"Will do."

Kirsten hurried down the hall to where the Harbinger floated. "Okay. Lead on."

THE FUNDAMENTAL FABRIC OF THE UNIVERSE

Two sparkling silver eyes hovered amid a cloud of darkness that flooded the back half of the patrol craft.

Dorian kept looking over at her, clearly unnerved by the presence sharing the car with them. He didn't say anything, though she couldn't help but think of his demeanor as someone with a half million credits of stolen merchandise hidden on their person trying to have a casual conversation with a cop. Not that she blamed him. Free of the Black Bishop's control, the Harbinger radiated an air of dire trepidation that left her muscles taut and whitened her knuckles on the control sticks. While she considered it an ally, being close to such primal energy always made her wary of committing the tiniest error of decorum.

She'd climbed to 2,000 feet, high enough to avoid almost every building in West City, and had been flying in a straight line ever since the Harbinger's vaporous arm pointed her in a specific direction. It made no further motions, so she kept on heading that way: mostly north with a slightly eastward drift.

"How'd it go with Theodore?" asked Dorian after about twenty minutes of silence.

"Haven't spoken to him yet. I was just about to leave when the Harbinger showed up."

"Ahh." Dorian nodded. "That's a good reason to wait." He paused. "Any idea what it wants?"

Kirsten eyed the Navcon, watching the top-down view of buildings on the minimap scroll by. "Not entirely. They're not big on conversation. But... I trust it's important so, here we are."

"What does it need help with?" asked Dorian.

"Harbingers don't need help from mortals."

Dorian tilted his head. "Except in cases where they're trapped by ritual magic."

She sighed. "Okay. Fair point."

"I've been wondering something... dark spirits who have established a foothold in the normal world are, for whatever reason, not susceptible to Harbingers simply grabbing them."

"Yeah. Seems that way." She nodded.

"Prior to your birth, how exactly did Harbingers do their jobs? Did they exist before you?"

She rolled her eyes. "Of course they did."

He waved his hand about. "Then how did they do their job without you to 'soften up' the bad ones for them?"

Kirsten glanced sideways at him. "I still haven't quite worked out that whole omniscient thing. I have no idea. But... I guess there had to be someone like me. Heck, Father Villera seemed to know quite a bit about this stuff. Maybe they did it."

"Priests?" He quirked an eyebrow.

"No. Spiritual people. Funny clothes and titles prove membership in an organization, not spiritualism."

Silence lingered in the car for another thirty minutes.

The Harbinger extended its arm, pointing down.

"Guess we're here." Kirsten slowed from 350 to 200 and pitched the car into a dive.

She reduced speed to seventy once they neared the ground. The shadowy arm extended again and pointed left. She leveled off at thirty feet and followed its directions until it indicated she should land. Kirsten set the patrol craft down in the nearest opening among a long line of shot-up husks that used to be passenger cars parked at the side of the road. One or two looked like they might still even drive. Mostly-ruined high-rises lined both sides of the street, aglow in green and pink holograms from three bars and a Chinese food place, the only operating businesses in sight. They'd wound up in a rough neighborhood only ninety meters from a grey zone. Light pedestrian traffic flowed in two directions, oblivious or unconcerned with a police patrol craft.

The Harbinger drifted out of the car, causing a dark spot where the restaurant's signage failed. Kirsten shut down the drive system and got out. The area didn't look *too* bad, certainly not so dangerous that she worried someone would steal or damage the patrol craft. She rounded the nose end and walked after the departing Harbinger.

Holographic signs, streetlights, NetMinis, NanoLED tattoos, and any other electronic device emitting a glow darkened in a modest radius around the Harbinger, making the creature appear to give off negative light.

People turned to watch the spot of nothingness drifting by. No one reacted to Kirsten's uniform—perhaps between the late hour and slow-gliding blackout, they didn't recognize it. Black fabric in a poorly lit section of the city blended in well. She followed the Harbinger to the end of the block. It took the corner around a bar, momentarily shutting down every light inside and causing a mild panic.

Like a robot with a singular purpose, it advanced at a steady speed, not looking back, not hesitating. At the next block, it crossed the street, oblivious to a car that drove through it and conked out. Kirsten ignored the man screaming about his piece of shit. When the Harbinger moved out of range, the e-motors in all four wheels kicked back on, right at the speed they'd been spinning before shutting down, hurtling the car into a wild spin-out. The driver barely managed to avoid slamming into a building, recovering at the last minute. The car wound up on the sidewalk, sideways between a vendomat and a PubTran kiosk.

The Harbinger entered an alley and continued going for a few blocks. Kirsten looked up at the high-rises, certain they'd crossed over into a grey zone. Synthbeer canisters, a waft of chems in the air, and a prickling psionic sense made her think that people had been here recently.

They probably felt us coming and ran for cover.

Even non-psionics could pick up on the direness of a Harbinger in the area. A sudden, intense feeling of danger or that something was quite wrong usually made people go away. Kirsten didn't mind. Fewer people made for fewer problems, especially in grey zones.

Upon reaching a decrepit eighty-story building still bearing metal lettering that identified it as 'The Grand Providence Hotel,' the Harbinger swerved to the left and entered via a huge crack in the wall. The building looked as though a large truck or similar vehicle had crashed into it. Fragments of rubble still littered the ground, both inside and out, though the damage appeared decades' old. The interior consisted of bare thermacrete walls coated in graffiti, many with such large holes exposing rebar.

She gawked at the holes. *Holy shit. Do the locals have missile launchers?*

The Harbinger stopped in the middle of the space.

Kirsten wandered in a circle, gazing around at the destruction. "Are we where you wanted me to go?"

It nodded.

Old autoinjectors, drug derms, tons of Cyberburger plastic clamshell cases, and other scraps littered the floor near the walls, along with a handful of improvised sleeping mats. The place stank with a mixture of wet dog and rotting Chinese food. Fortunately, none of the residents appeared to be home at the moment. It appeared as though at least a dozen people had set up defined areas of 'personal space.'

"There's nothing here."

The Harbinger raised a shadowy hand.

"Wait?" asked Kirsten.

It nodded.

Kirsten stood there for a little while feeling nervous and confused. This level of interaction with a Harbinger both terrified and fascinated her. Eventually, she calmed enough to take out her NetMini, but found it dark. She side-eyed the Harbinger, and edged away from it until the device powered back up. Once it came online, she sent a text message to Evan. ‹This is going to take longer than I thought. You'll be in bed before I'm back. Do you want to sleep at Nila's, or should I carry you home when I'm done?›

A chirp came from the device a moment later.

‹I can sleep here but if you're squeezy, come get me. Love you.›

She choked up a little, and slid the NetMini back into its holder on her belt.

They stood in relative silence for about eleven minutes, at which point, the distant scuff of footsteps became noticeable, growing louder. The Harbinger pointed at the wall. Kirsten crept over to the breach she'd entered from and peered out.

A woman, younger twenties, wearing an expensive skirt suit and high heels, strolled by with a slow, meandering gait that swished her long, violet hair side to side and made her appear intoxicated. Kirsten stepped out onto the sidewalk behind the woman, not entirely sure what she'd been brought here to see.

The woman approached a fallen vendomat beside a light pole at the corner. She sidled up to the boxy machine, pulled her skirt up to expose herself below the waist, then removed a pair of handcuffs from her purse before locking one end around her left wrist.

Shit! It's Malden!

Kirsten sprinted at her, channeling mental energy into the lash. Shadows crawled over the buildings from the scintillating blue-white light, tiny bits of trash stretched to gargantuan proportion. The woman bent over the vendomat, stretching to get her arms around the light pole.

She swiped the lash down into the woman's back.

In a burst of dim white-grey light, Malden Walker went flying out of her, landing on his chest in a slide that spun to a halt in the middle of an abandoned intersection. A startled scream came from the woman.

Kirsten jumped the vendomat, boots crunching on fragments of smashed plastic, coiling the lash for another swipe.

"Crap!" not-quite-yelled the woman. "Where the hell am I?"

Kirsten whipped the lash at Malden before he finished getting to his feet. A blast of light erupted from the contact point, the energy tendril tearing a gash in his insubstantial body. He careened over, rolling.

The soft clatter of dangling handcuffs accompanied the rapid clicks of nice shoes and the rustle of deep trash.

Malden's prone form blurred into an energy blob that stretched vertical before focusing back to his normal appearance, standing. He made to run—but the Harbinger popped up out of the street in front of him. The ghost stopped short and whirled around to go the other way.

"Hi!" Kirsten swung the lash in a sideways slice, aiming for his chest.

Growling, Malden dissipated into mist that flowed around her whip, re-solidifying in mid punch. His fist connected with Kirsten's chest like a block of gelatin fired out of a cannon. She flipped over fully in midair before landing on her front and sliding backward, unable to breathe.

Dorian leapt in, wrapping himself around Malden for barely two seconds before the man elbowed him in the gut and launched him ass-first through the wall of a building at the corner of the intersection. Malden started to dive into the ground, but the Harbinger welled up beneath him, forcing him back. Kirsten, still seeing spots, dragged herself upright.

"Problem?" She coughed. Despite the ghostly punch lacking solidity, it felt as if she'd broken a rib.

"What's that glowy thing?" asked the trash pile in the woman's voice.

"Need a minute, miss," said Kirsten. "Dealing with an issue at the moment."

"Obviously you have issues if you're talking to nothing."

Malden tried to run into the building where he'd thrown Dorian, but the Harbinger swooshed around to block him. Kirsten dashed in swinging low, and scored another hit across his back that let off a muted *boom*. She gritted her teeth from the wash of loose paranormal energy creating an electric prickle across her front. Screaming in anger and pain, Malden swooned to his knees. Dorian charged out of the wall into a right hook that connected with the ghost's chin. Malden rocked back, but drove an uppercut into Dorian's stomach that crumpled him over on top of him. He refused to let go, attempting to drag Malden to the ground in a judo hold.

Unable to get a clear shot with the lash, Kirsten shot a brief look at the shivering pile of plastic cartons and cups beside an overfull dumpster. "Something possessed you and made you walk out here, right?"

A hand lifted a carton out of the way; the violet-haired woman stared blank-faced at her.

"I'll be with you in a moment. Dealing with the bastard that attacked you."

"Oh, okay. That's a good idea. I'll, umm, wait here." The woman lowered the carton back down, hiding.

Dorian let out a loud *oof* and went sailing down the street. Malden swerved away from Kirsten, but the Harbinger flowed up like a wall of infinity, blocking him. Kirsten, not too worried about accidentally nicking the Harbinger with the lash, ran in and took a swing.

"Damn, it. Go away!" shouted Malden, after diving under the glowing cord and launching himself at her.

Kirsten focused on his presence, trying to 'block' his approach the way she'd held back the crazy doctor at the Saguaro Asylum. Latching onto a sense of his existence at the back of her mind, she wrapped her psionic energy around it and pushed. Malden's leap slowed to a near standstill in midair. He sank to the ground, forcing himself closer, step by step as if in slow motion.

"Bitch!" Malden roared and surged at her. The crash of his energy into her psionic will knocked her on her back. He ran right over her, intending to flee.

She rolled onto her stomach and changed her focus from pushing him away to pulling him back. For a few seconds, Malden appeared to be attempting to walk into a hurricane, barely inching forward. Kirsten grunted with the exertion of fighting such a powerful spirit, drawing strength from her desperation not to let him attack any more innocent women.

Two pulses of white energy hit Malden in the back, having come from Dorian's direction. He 'fired' again, striking the ghost in the back of the head. The shots hit with little more effect than hard punches, barely disrupting Malden's essence. Though Dorian's weapon looked like an E-90, he only projected a spectral attack no more powerful than him punching someone. The dark spirit grunted, fighting Kirsten's control enough to twist toward Dorian and raise an empty hand as if holding a pistol. A giant gun appeared in his grip and went off several times, each shot a streak of whitish energy.

With Malden distracted shooting at Dorian, Kirsten jumped to her feet. Malden saw her coming and tried to flee, but everywhere he turned, the Harbinger hemmed him in. He spun back toward Kirsten, and cocked his fist.

Screaming in a mixture of rage and frustration, Kirsten grabbed the lash in both hands, plowing it straight down on top of Malden, hoping to hit him before she went flying again. The energy whip burrowed into his body, meeting squidgy resistance and becoming stuck, more than half its length dangling out the other side of his body. She twisted to the right and leaned backward, his giant fist passing over her left shoulder. With a grunt, she whirled away, ripping the psionic whip loose.

Malden emitted an agonized groan and stumbled down to one knee.

She continued the spin, following through with another crossing slash to his chest.

At the moment of contact, a rippling pulse of white energy burst out of him, expanding in a ring. It blasted him flat on his back and washed over her like a rain of freezing needles; she screamed in pain, involuntarily cringing into a ball. The shattering of hundreds of windows exploding filled the silence in the wake of the spectral blast.

Shaking from being simultaneously frozen and shredded, Kirsten struggled back to her feet.

Malden rolled onto his side and dragged himself along the road by one hand, his right arm and both legs evidently no longer working.

The Harbinger drifted over to hover in front of him, head tilted back, arms held to either side, its silver eyes sparkling with an imperious stare. Malden cringed, shielding his face with his left arm, and screamed as the great cloud of inky blackness fell upon him. Vaporous claws tore into the spectral man's body, setting loose scraps of ethereal light adrift on the breeze.

Ghost and Harbinger seeped into the ground in a combined mass, Malden's shrieks fading gradually to silence.

Kirsten looked down at herself. No blood. No cuts, though a handful of tiny white lightning bolts still crawled randomly over her body. *Shit. That was almost the same way the Wharf Stalker went.* She stared at the spot of ground where Malden had been in silence.

Groaning, Dorian limped over to stand beside her, favoring his left side.

"Thank you."

He managed a faint bow, wincing. "It's what I'm here for."

She looked away from the road to him. "Gah. Are you okay?"

"Moderate to severe ass kicking. I'll be okay after a couple days of rest."

"Thank you, too. First one was for the Harbinger... leading me to Malden."

Dorian smiled. "They're not supposed to do that."

She sighed into a chuckle, her teeth chattering from the lingering chill. "I guess either I'm changing the fundamental fabric of the universe... or he wanted to thank me for freeing him from that ritual."

"Six of one..." said Dorian.

"Right. I don't really care how it happened. We got him."

"So what now?"

Kirsten let the Astral Lash recede back into her hand. "A long, hot soak."

CARING

K irsten glanced over at the woman, who stared out from a small gap in the trash pile at the spot where Malden had been taken. "Aww, crap. She saw it."

"Saw what?"

"The claiming… or whatever you want to call it when someone gets a one way ticket to the bad place." Kirsten headed over to the woman, rubbing her shoulder. "Miss? Are you okay?"

"No. Not really."

Kirsten reached a hand toward the trash pile. "It's over. You're okay. C'mon out of there. The ghost that assaulted you is gone for good."

After staring in shock for a little over a minute, the woman stood, causing an avalanche of empty plastic cartons. The handcuffs still dangled from her left wrist, other side open. "What happened? I think someone slipped something in my drink and I had a wild trip."

"Should I let her keep thinking it was a hallucination?" Kirsten glanced at Dorian. "Or do I make some therapist wealthy?"

Dorian rubbed his side. "Well, if you're now part of the universal fabric, maybe you shouldn't get involved."

"Ha. Ha." She poked the button on her armband to summon the patrol craft. Assuming the ghost had made her order the cuffs, she fetched the woman's handbag, which remained on the ground by the vendomat. Sure enough, it contained the keys still in the packaging. "Okay, start at the beginning, Miss...?"

"Luna Ortiz. There was a company party tonight. I think Alfred dropped something in my drink. I felt light headed and then had these weird hallucinations that someone was groping me under my clothes."

Kirsten sighed internally while unlocking the cuff. *I can't lie to her.* "You were attacked by a paranormal entity. I destroyed it. No one tampered with your drink. We can run a chem screen to make sure."

"Okay."

The patrol craft cruised in to land in the middle of the street nearby.

"C'mon, Miss Ortiz." Kirsten put an arm around her shoulders and guided her over to the car. *This is going to be a long night... but I'll take it.* She smiled at the blank spot of road. *Bastard's where he belongs.*

As part of Kirsten's bargain with the universe, she didn't procrastinate on filling out reports the next day.

Much.

A few extra minutes when dropping Evan off at the school wing, and a few more minutes going to pick up coffee orders from the delivery bot at the garage exit didn't really count as simple procrastination. Both had been necessary tasks.

One double espresso mostly took away the fatigue of staying up too late, but the long, hot soak had been worth it, even if she did have to sit neck-deep like a mediating monk in a cramped autoshower tube. Maybe someday she'd have an actual bathtub installed. Only high-end luxury apartments still even included those anymore, even though they didn't cost all that much. She sipped a large standard coffee while working on the reports. With both of her inquests completed, as well as the P10 being basically solved, she expected to burn the entire day writing documentation and filling out forms.

Of course, the one major upside to being a Division 0 investigator was that her cases rarely ever landed in front of a judge. As soon as she submitted the inquest as complete and it went to Captain Eze for review, she'd more or less finished with it. No worrying about testimony, witnesses flaking out and disappearing, a slick lawyer exploiting a flaw in the process, or overcrowded prisons cutting a spirit loose early 'for good behavior.'

Three hours into going over the medical reports of the people they recovered from the Diablo camp, Kirsten briefly considered having an M3 port and NIU installed so she could 'type' at the speed of thought, but cringed as if someone had covered her in that horrible slime from the Beneath.

No thanks... no wiring in this brain.

She shuddered again and continued working. All of the Diablos had been killed on site and no criminal trial would ensue; however, she had to do a full crosslinking with the medical reports for the inevitable war that would erupt between lawyers and the abductees' insurance companies over how much to not cover. No doubt, care for a person tortured to a state of catatonia would be expensive... and she assumed the insurance providers would do as much as they could to dodge or minimize their liability. She didn't want to make any errors that could wind up making the difference between an innocent victim recovering or spending the rest of their life as a shell of a person.

Kirsten finished that part a little before lunch, and decided to take a quick look at the intake reports for the deceased Diablos. Apparently, with them having managed to successfully do 'something mystical,' Command wanted their remains brought in for further analysis, including psychometry.

"Oh, that's not going to end well."

"Hmm?" asked Dorian from his desk.

"They want a clairvoyant to read the Diablos' remains."

Dorian laughed. "I hope they reconsider that before some poor slob winds up needing a reset button."

"What?"

"Ashford," said Dorian.

"Oh..." *Sometimes, I'm glad I'm not a clairvoyant.*

A few pages down the list, she scrolled over yet another image taken of all items removed from one of the bodies. The report had been a nearly endless parade of autopsy photos, various personal effects, and weapons. Though, in the section for suspect eight, she spotted a large combat knife with pictograms and strange symbols scratched onto the blade.

Kirsten zoomed in on it, then tapped the screen to extract a separate holographic representation of the weapon. She pinched the ends of the floating image, stretching it larger for a better look. The markings made no literal sense to her in terms of any written language, but it came close enough to resembling the sort of scribblings that Konstantin had used in the circle for summoning Charazu.

After bringing up the autopsy files of the five murdered young men, she shrank the holographic knife to actual size and superimposed it over the 3D image of Juan Miguel Esparza's remains. The blade slid into the wound channel, visually a match. 'Looks right' wouldn't stand up in a criminal trial, but her near-certainty that the Diablos had killed those five people plus finding such a close match of a knife on one of them made for too much of a coincidence.

For added certainty, she ran an analysis routine to compare the knife to the fatal wounds on the five individuals the Diablos had dumped in the pentagram formation. While that processed, she made a quick trip to the cafeteria for lunch. By the time she returned to her desk, the forensic AI had concluded a ninety-two percent chance that the knife created those wounds, as close as it could get based on 3D scan data.

She didn't exactly need to pin it down any further with traces of metal in the wound or biological matter on the blade since none of this would ever go to trial, only give her the confidence to reassure a small boy in a scary situation that the thug who killed his brother had answered for it.

Kirsten locked her terminal and made her way down the hall to the elevator, then up three floors to the secure dorms. Even as an adult, active-duty commissioned officer in Division 0, going there still came with a mild sense of dread. Not that she had ever felt the slightest inclination to break rules enough to be considered delinquent, but the mere thought of being locked in a room tapped into her fear of Mother's closet. Fortunately, none of the other kids around her back then had made fun of her for being such a rule follower.

Though, she had to laugh at herself a little now. She'd let Adrienne slide for using Technokinesis to pump up the balance of a credstick to pay for her Reinventions procedure. It didn't bother her that much because the money hadn't been taken away from someone else, merely generated from thin air. She'd also bent the rules with Emma Mero, asking Sam to alter the records to make her eight months younger so she could slip into the adoption program as a minor. However, Division 1 did that all the time when they thought a recently-eighteen street kid had a good enough attitude to be worth saving. That hadn't been breaking the rules as much as a rule made to be bent.

"What are you going to tell him if he asks about his brother's ghost?" asked Dorian.

Kirsten sighed. "Do you think he transcended?"

"I suppose it's possible. More likely, his essence was consumed in the ritual that forced the Harbinger into the mortal world."

She folded her arms. "But... the souls Konstantin collected didn't obliterate. They got away... even if they were stuck with some serious latent self image issues."

"You interrupted him before he completed the ritual. Those souls— and me—*would* have been devoured in the process. I don't think Juan Miguel was that lucky. But... I could be wrong. Who knows what that dark bishop actually accomplished?"

"So..." She exhaled, lips fluttering. "Better off avoiding talking about his ghost altogether."

"That is one way not to lie, yes."

"Is it a lie saying I don't know but I hope?" She fidgeted. "Okay, fine. I won't bring it up if he doesn't."

Dorian nodded.

The elevator doors parted to a painfully white room reeking of disinfectant. Two men and a woman in Division 0 blacks staffed a security station on the left, the remainder of the foyer empty except for plain black bench seats on the right by the wall. One large corridor stretched deeper into the building from the center of the area.

She hooked a left out of the elevator and approached the desk. The nearest man, later twenties with dark brown skin and hair almost the same exact shade, smiled at her. Burgundy eyes, no doubt a bit of custom work, startled her in their oddity to the point she forgot what she intended to say.

"Can I help you, lieutenant?" asked the man, Specialist Troyer, M. (Admin) according to his nameplate.

"Yes. I need to see one of the kids you've got here. Rafael Esparza."

He shifted his gaze to the holo-screen in front of him, the computer reacting on its own. Since he didn't have any wires plugged into his head, she assumed him a Technokinetic. "Oh, I'm sorry, lieutenant. The boy is a suggestive. We'll need to get clearance to approve a visit."

"Yes, I'm aware he's a suggestive. I am, too. I'm the one who brought him in. Even if he tried to use it on me, I can block him. But... I know he won't. I'm bringing good news."

Troyer, M. glanced at his screen again. Light on his face shifted color. "Oh. Right. Yes, that appears to be the case." He smiled at her. "It's nice to see not everyone with that power winds up on the wrong side of a locked door."

"Having Suggestion doesn't make someone a criminal," said Kirsten. "Lacking respect for others and a sense of right and wrong does."

Dorian put an arm around her shoulders. "Isn't she adorable?"

None of the security team reacted to him.

"You can go on back. He's in room 116." Troyer pointed at the hallway.

"Not in class at this hour?" asked Kirsten. "It's not even one yet."

"He isn't in an education program yet. Still undergoing psych evaluation and threat level assessment."

Kirsten suppressed a cringe of guilt. "Please tell me you're not keeping him locked in his room twenty-four hours a day?"

"No, he's out routinely for meetings with medics, counselors, and meals… whenever Hans is available to escort him."

"One specific guard?" asked Kirsten.

"Hans is our only suggestive on staff."

"Right. Well that's two of us on the right side of locked doors." Kirsten nodded and headed down the hall.

Dorian chuckled.

"What?"

"Oh, just thinking about ancient history."

She gave him a 'do I really want to ask' look.

"Nothing bad. Before they put fingerprint locks on firearms, even cops had to turn in their weapons before going into a detention area, afraid prisoners might grab for one."

"Oh. Why would anyone make a firearm *without* a fingerprint trigger safety?"

He blinked at her. "Why would anyone make a car that couldn't fly?"

"Umm." She shook her head. "Right. Dumb question."

"This habit of yours not to think when you're worried is becoming worse."

She walked on, muttering, "Yeah… yeah. I've got too much in my head to care about what year they invented electronic triggers."

Room after room passed on both sides, plain white doors marked with numbers. Most were open, the rooms evidently not in use. The secure dorms took in psionic juveniles who had misused their powers in ways that couldn't be brushed aside or excused to bad circumstances. Homeless kids using their abilities to force people to give them food wouldn't put them here. The young offenders who landed in secure detention varied from the recklessly dangerous, to kids who used their abilities without care, feeling superior to normals and doing whatever they could get away with, to the truly criminal-minded.

As psionics made up something like six percent of the population, the fraction of a percent of juveniles among them with true criminal tendencies made for a small number of detainees. She didn't think Rafael belonged among kids who burglarized stores, attacked people for fun, and in a few cases, thought nothing of murdering anyone who annoyed them. She put him in with the 'desperate circumstances' group, but compelling two Division 1 officers to point their weapons at each other crossed a line. Suggestives put everyone on edge to begin with, and using psionic abilities on cops... Had he done the same exact thing with civilians—made two people threaten to shoot each other if the police didn't investigate his brother's death—Division 0 probably would've looked the other way and sent him to the standard dorms as long as no one had died.

Maybe there's a chance once it settles... Being in this place is going to traumatize him more. He's not a bad kid. She decided to go talk to the two officers involved, Gage and Kepler. If she could convince them to send in official requests not to prosecute, that might do the trick. Of course, she'd need to bring a witness along—maybe Captain Eze—so no one accused her of compelling the cops to ask for leniency.

Kirsten stopped at the door of room 116 and waited. A few seconds later, it chirped. Security people at the front could watch every inch of this place on screens. The plain white door slid sideways, allowing her into a square room she found large for a cell but small for a bedroom. Two sets of cabinet doors on the right, flush with the wall, likely held an assortment of bright pink 'juvenile detainee' jumpsuits and plastic shoes.

Rafael sat on a Comforgel pad, arms wrapped around his legs, head down. His jumpsuit looked too big on him, and a shiny silver band locked around his left ankle made her feel like an ogre for her part in his being here. The electronic bracelet mostly served as a tracker in case a detainee tried to run, but they could also deliver a stunning shock.

The boy appeared even thinner than the last time she'd seen him, but no longer smelled like street. The barrenness of the room—no toys, no color, no electronics—worsened her sense of guilt.

She stiffened when the door closed behind her. *I'm not locked in. They'll let me out when I try to leave.*

The boy lifted his head off his knees, his large brown eyes wet with tears. "Oh. Hi."

Kirsten crossed the room in three steps and sat on the end of the bed. "Hey."

"I'm sorry for making those cops do that."

"I know you are." She smiled. "That's why I wanted to help you. I can tell you're a good kid in a bad situation."

He fussed at the anklet. "It's not that bad in here. I'm scared of this thing. The guy told me if I didn't behave, it would shock me so bad I'd pee myself. They put it on my leg 'cause my hand is too small. It kept falling off."

Kirsten scowled off in a random direction. "They'd only use that shock if someone became actively violent, about to hurt someone... they're not going to shock you for staying up too late or being a smartass."

He almost smiled. "I know he said that just to scare me. He thought I looked like a girly little wimp, but he was afraid of me. It's not breaking the rules to *read* emotions. And I know you're sad."

She reached out and took his hand. "Rafael, I found the man who killed Juan Miguel. He's dead. The people who helped him do it are also dead."

The boy stared at her for a long moment, then broke down in sobs. She moved to sit beside him and put an arm around him. He leaned against her, crying for a while before managing to say, "Thank you."

She mulled over what to do while he sniffled and wiped at his face.

"How long am I gonna be in jail? They won't tell me."

"I'm not exactly sure. You did use Suggestion on cops and threaten to kill them." She sighed. "There is a good chance you'll be here until you turn eighteen. It's better than being on the street."

He shivered.

"But... I don't believe you really would've hurt them. You were scared, alone, and didn't think you had any voice in the world. You don't seem like the sort of kid who belongs locked up."

Rafael lifted his head to peer at her, eyes widening.

"Don't get too hopeful, yet." She sighed. "I'm going to try talking to those two cops, see if I can get them to believe you wouldn't have hurt them."

"I wouldn't. I don't hate cops, just wanted them to care about Juan Miguel."

"It's not me who needs to be convinced of that. Trust me when I say that as a suggestive, you need to be extra careful. They watch us. Most of the time, someone with that ability who goes bad doesn't make it to jail."

Rafael stared down at the bed. "I'm really sorry. I didn't know what else to do. Juan Miguel was dead and no one cared. I wanted to die, too. I thought the cops would kill me."

Overcome at hearing a boy his age say that, she lost the war against tears and let a few slip free.

"I don't wanna die anymore. Thought I was gonna die anyway on the street without my brother. I swear I won't do anything like that again. I got too sad when Juan Miguel died an' the cops didn't care about us."

Kirsten squeezed his shoulder. "Maybe once they trust you won't abuse your powers, you'll be transferred to the standard dorms, but that's out of my control."

"What's going to happen?"

"Oh, lots of meetings with psychologists and a telepath or two to see what's going on in your head, make sure you're not lying."

"I'm not. So I don't care if they look in my head." He hugged her. "I know I'm just a street kid, but thank you for caring."

She choked up, unable to speak.

"You helped Juan Miguel... and me. I'm not mad at you for arresting me. It's your job. Cops should do their job. Don't be sad. No one's gonna try an' hurt me in here."

They shouldn't keep a ten-year-old in freakin' solitary confinement, even if it is a 'bedroom.' She bristled at the paranoia around suggestives. Granted, in most cases, it made sense. "I'll check up on you, okay?"

He nodded, smiling.

Kirsten spent another twenty or so minutes with him talking about his brother. They'd lived on the street ever since the parents died, his brother earning enough to buy food from working at a restaurant. Rafael had liked school and missed it, despite admitting to not having the best grades.

Eventually, she dragged herself away with promises to visit again soon, and trudged down the corridor.

Dorian materialized at her side. "You've won me over. That kid's a victim of policy."

"How can those Div 1 guys get so damn jaded they can laugh off a murder because the victim belonged to a gang?"

"K, if you're drowning in a swimming pool full of oatmeal, and someone goes to hand you a bowl of oatmeal..."

Kirsten sighed. "I hope I never reach that point of just... giving up on society."

"Oh, you won't." Dorian grinned. "You're much too sweet."

She nodded to the three people at the security desk on her way by and walked into the elevator. As soon as the doors shut, she stuck her tongue out at him.

"Well, the storm's over. With any luck, you'll have a nice quiet rest of the month."

"Not exactly." She poked the button for her squad room's floor. "Evan's invited his friends over Saturday."

"Walter and Shawn?"

"I should be so lucky. No, I'll be responsible for *four* additional kids. That older girl he fell down the elevator with and Willow. It's like he has this sixth sense to find and make friends with the lonely ones who really need it." She pointed at him. "Don't say it."

"Didn't plan to." Dorian chuckled. "Five kids under twelve for an entire Saturday? That's more harrowing than sending the giant flea back to the Abyss. You should probably call in reinforcements."

"Ha. Ha." Kirsten raised an eyebrow, thinking of Sam. "You know, calling in some backup might not be a bad idea."

fin

ACKNOWLEDGMENTS

Thank you for reading Division Zero: Harbinger!

I'd like to thank the readers who have emailed, chatted, and commented asking for (and reminding me to write) another Division Zero book.
Thanks to Lee Sheridan for editing.
Dianne Webb and Daniel Cox (no relation) for beta reading.
Additional thanks to Alexandria Thompson for the cover art!

ABOUT THE AUTHOR

Originally from South Amboy NJ, Matthew has been creating science fiction and fantasy worlds for most of his reasoning life. Since 1996, he has developed the "Divergent Fates" world, in which *Division Zero, Virtual Immortality, The Awakened Series, The Harmony Paradox, and the Daughter of Mars series* take place. Along with being an editor at Curiosity Quills press, he has worked in IT and technical support.

Matthew is an avid gamer, a recovered WoW addict, Gamemaster for two custom RPG systems, and a fan of anime, British humour, and intellectual science fiction that questions the nature of reality, life, and what happens after it.

He is also fond of cats.

Visit me online at:
    Facebook: https://www.facebook.com/MatthewSCoxAuthor
    Amazon: https://www.amazon.com/author/mscox
    Pinterest: https://www.pinterest.com/matthewcox10420/
    Goodreads: https://www.goodreads.com/author/show/
7712730.Matthew_S_Cox
    Email: mcox2112@gmail.com

OTHER BOOKS BY MATTHEW S. COX

Divergent Fates Universe Novels

Division Zero series

- Division Zero
- Lex De Mortuis
- Thrall
- Guardian

The Awakened series

- Prophet of the Badlands
- Archon's Queen
- Grey Ronin
- Daughter of Ash
- Zero Rogue
- Angel Descended

Daughter of Mars series

- The Hand of Raziel
- Araphel
- Ghost Black

Virtual Immortality series

- Virtual Immortality
- The Harmony Paradox

Divergent Fates Anthology

(Fiction Novels - Adult)

The Roadhouse Chronicles Series

- One More Run
- The Redeemed
- Dead Man's Number

Faded Skies series

- Heir Ascendant
- Ascendant Unrest
- Ascendant Revolution

Temporal Armistice Series

- Nascent Shadow
- The Shadow Collector
- The Gate to Oblivion

Vampire Innocent series

- A Nighttime of Forever
- A Beginner's Guide to Fangs
- The Artist of Ruin
- The Last Family Road Trip

Standalones

- Wayfarer: AV494
- Axillon99
- Chiaroscuro: The Mouse and the Candle
- The Far Side of Promise anthology
- Operation: Chimera (with Tony Healey)
- The Dysfunctional Conspiracy (with Christopher Veltmann)

Winter Solstice series (with J.R. Rain)

- Convergence
- Containment
- Catalyst

Alexis Silver series (with J.R. Rain)

- Silver Light
- Deep Silver

Samantha Moon Origins series (with J.R. Rain)

- New Moon Rising
- Moon Mourning

Maddy Wimsey series (with J.R. Rain)

- The Devil's Eye
- The Drifting Gloom

Samantha Moon Case Files series (with J.R. Rain)

- Blood Moon
- Dead Moon

Young Adult Novels

- Caller 107
- The Summer the World Ended
- Nine Candles of Deepest Black
- The Eldritch Heart
- The Forest Beyond the Earth
- Out of Sight

Middle Grade Novels

Tales of Widowswood series

- Emma and the Banderwigh
- Emma and the Silk Thieves
- Emma and the Silverbell Faeries
- Emma and the Elixir of Madness
- Emma and the Weeping Spirit

Standalones

- Citadel: The Concordant Sequence
- The Cursed Codex
- The Menagerie of Jenkins Bailey
- Sophie's Light